The shining splendor of [illegible] ver of this book reflects the [illegible] de. Look for the Zebra Lovegram whenever you buy a historical romance. It's a trademark that guarantees the very best in quality and reading entertainment.

SWEET TEMPTATION

Slowly, Randall took the final step that brought him within inches of touching her.

Emily swallowed hard then spoke in a firm voice. "If you'd be kind enough to step out of my way, I'll leave immediately."

Randall studied the high color of her cheeks and the determined thrust of her chin for a long moment. Suddenly he did not feel quite so adamant about forcing her to leave, at least not right away. . . .

"I think not," he finally answered, placing his hands against the wall, and trapping her between his arms. Emily was certainly the most beautiful woman he'd ever known. Slowly, he brought his gaze down to her parted lips and watched her pink tongue dark across the surface in anticipation of a kiss. The implication was too tempting to resist. . . .

SURRENDER TO THE PASSION

LOVE'S SWEET BOUNTY (3313, $4.50)
by Colleen Faulkner

Jessica Landon swore revenge of the masked bandits who robbed the train and stole all the money she had in the world. She set out after the thieves without consulting the handsome railroad detective, Adam Stern. When he finally caught up with her, she admitted she needed his assistance. She never imagined that she would also begin to need his scorching kisses and tender caresses.

WILD WESTERN BRIDE (3140, $4.50)
by Rosalyn Alsobrook

Anna Thomas loved riding the Orphan Train and finding loving homes for her young charges. But when a judge tried to separate two brothers, the dedicated beauty went beyond the call of duty. She proposed to the handsome, blue-eyed Mark Gates, planning to adopt the boys herself! Of course the marriage would be in name only, but yet as time went on, Anna found herself dreaming of being a loving wife in every sense of the word . . .

QUICKSILVER PASSION (3117, $4.50)
by Georgina Gentry

Beautiful Silver Jones had been called every name in the book, and now that she owned her own tavern in Buckskin Joe, Colorado, the independent didn't care what the townsfolk thought of her. She never let a man touch her and she earned her money fair and square. Then one night handsome Cherokee Evans swaggered up to her bar and destroyed the peace she'd made with herself. For the irresistible miner made her yearn for the melting kisses and satin caresses she had sworn she could live without!

MISSISSIPPI MISTRESS (3118, $4.50)
by Gina Robins

Cori Pierce was outraged at her father's murder and the loss of her inheritance. She swore revenge and vowed to get her independence back, even if it meant singing as an entertainer on a Mississippi steamboat. But she hadn't reckoned on the swarthy giant in tight buckskins who turned out to be her boss. Jacob Wolf was, after all, the giant of the man Cori vowed to destroy. Though she swore not to forget her mission for even a moment, she was powerfully tempted to submit to Jake's fiery caresses and have one night of passion in his irresistible embrace.

Available wherever paperbacks are sold, or order direct from the Publisher. Send cover price plus 50¢ per copy for mailing and handling to Zebra Books, Dept. 3412, 475 Park Avenue South, New York, N.Y. 10016. Residents of New York, New Jersey and Pennsylvania must include sales tax. DO NOT SEND CASH.

ZEBRA BOOKS
KENSINGTON PUBLISHING CORP.

ZEBRA BOOKS

are published by

Kensington Publishing Corp.
475 Park Avenue South
New York, NY 10016

First printing: June, 1991

Printed in the United States of America

To Mom, for always being there when we need her the most.

Spring, 1878

"Will you please stand a little straighter this time?" Emily Felcher muttered through tightly compressed lips, not wanting to lose the half dozen straight pins she held in her mouth. "I really don't want to have to do this again, Carole Jeanne." After all, it was her *third* attempt to pin an even hemline on the excessively wide skirts of her best friend's graduation dress.

"I'm standing as straight as I know how," Carole protested with a heavy sigh. She crossed her arms and shifted her weight to one leg in a very unladylike stance, which was what she always did whenever she was either annoyed or bored. Today, she was both.

Emily closed her brown eyes briefly in an attempt to hold on to the last of her rapidly waning patience. Carole Jeanne might be her best friend in all the world, but she could certainly be trying at times. "Will you please balance your weight on both feet like I told you so I can finish this? That's all I ask."

She then sat back on her heels and waited for her friend to comply. When Carole failed to redistribute her weight evenly, Emily's shoulders sagged. Carefully, she removed the pins from her mouth then pursed her lips into a weary pout. She was tired of kneeling on the hardwood floor with nothing to cushion her knees but a flimsy bed pillow. Sighing heavily, she lifted her hand to push an errant brown curl away from her face then tilted her head to a slight angle while she stared up into her friend's frowning face. "Please, Carole Jeanne. I don't have all day for this. Neither do you. Graduation is only two days away and I still have several finishing touches to make on my own dress."

"What more can you do to your dress? It's already perfect. Mine looks like something a March wind blew in," Carole responded in her most pitiful Louisiana drawl, then she turned her attention to the tall oval mirror across the room, still frowning while she surveyed her latest futile attempt at sewing. "I don't know why we can't just go out and buy our graduation dresses. It would certainly make my life a lot simpler."

Emily's pout lifted into an understanding smile while she watched the continued disappointment in her friend's expression. It was clear to both of them that sewing would never be one of Carole's stronger talents, but then it wouldn't need to be. Because of their economic positions, neither girl would ever have to worry about sewing her own clothing. They could easily hire professional seamstresses to do that, which made them wonder why they had to bother with learning to sew or embroider at all. Still those had been two basic skills their head mistress had felt every young lady needed to know; therefore, for one hour each day, they practiced the mundane task. And for the past three weeks, all the girls had been hard at work creating their own graduation dresses, the direct result of yet another of their head mistress's directives.

"Come on, Carole Jeanne. I told you that as soon

as I have finished with my dress, I will help with the alterations to improve yours. All it really needs are a few extra tucks at the waistline and it will look just fine." Emily's golden eyes narrowed with clear warning when she lifted the skirt hem high enough to thump Carole playfully on the ankle. "Now stand straight and hold still."

Carole's expression lifted immediately. She knew Emily had a special aptitude with a needle and thread and was the type of person to keep her promise and repair the dress. Smiling, once again reassured, she reached for the bulky material at her narrow waistline and pinched it together as Emily had done earlier. Yes, the tucks Emily had in mind would improve the sagging lines of the dress immensely. All was not hopeless.

"I guess you're right," she finally admitted then shifted her weight evenly. But not wanting to give Emily an opportunity to gloat, she quickly added, "*This* time."

Laughing, Emily bent forward, glad that Carole had chosen to cooperate at last. "I thought I was always right."

Carole snorted at the cockiness in Emily's voice and shook her strawberry blonde curls in response. "Shall I remind you of a certain pale blue tunic skirt that had to be taken apart so many times that it wore out not one but *two* seam rippers?"

"That was years ago," Emily protested, grimacing at the memory. Why couldn't Carole just forget about that? "I was just learning how to sew."

"Learning? You call that a learning experience?" Carole teased. Her blue eyes sparkled with amusement. "Yes, I guess that's an appropriate term. I'll have to admit I learned a whole new vocabulary the day you had to take the waistband off and rip those side seams apart for the fourth time."

Before Emily could come back with a redeeming retort, there came a sharp knock at their bedroom door. Instantly forgetting their playful banter, both girls gave the small room they shared a quick glance to make certain nothing lay about that shouldn't. Once assured that everything was in order, they called out harmoniously. "Come in."

When the door swung open and Mrs. Tucker of all people stepped inside, Emily rose immediately from the floor and quickly brushed her skirts with her hands.

The teachers at Miss Boswell's School For Young Women did not often visit the students' private rooms. Emily exchanged a questioning glance with Carole before turning back to face their grammar teacher. "May we help you with something, Mrs. Tucker?"

A curious frown creased Milbra Tucker's usually smiling face. "Yes. Miss Boswell would like a word with you in private, Emily. She's waiting in her office."

Carole's eyes widened with instant concern for her friend. "What's Emily done wrong?"

"It's nothing to worry yourself with, I'm sure," Mrs. Tucker answered briskly, but then forced a smile that did not quite reach the hazel depths of her eyes. "All she said to me about the matter is that she wants to speak with Emily alone for a few minutes. She did not go into any details."

But it was obvious by Mrs. Tucker's odd behavior that something made her believe trouble was afoot.

Normally, Emily would not find an unexpected summons to the headmistress's office very disturbing. With graduation only two days away, such last minute calls were to be expected, especially when Miss Boswell had selected her to give one of the opening speeches during the ceremony. But the awkwardness in Mrs. Tucker's usually warm smile alarmed her.

What *had* she done? Were they just now discovering the paper novel she had tossed up under the dormitory two years ago, the afternoon she'd almost gotten caught reading it in the garden? If so, how could they know it belonged to her—unless one of the other girls had told them. But who?

A cold, foreboding chill swept over her when she headed for the open door. That must be what happened. They had found the novel and read some of the more risqué passages near the end. She closed her eyes at the thought. After five years of a perfectly clean record and only two days away from graduation, she was about to be expelled. What would her father say to that?

Her stomach knotted as she reopened her eyes and walked on through the door. When she passed Mrs. Tucker, who had stepped back out into the hallway to give her room, she paused and glanced worriedly at the young teacher. Was she really unaware of what Miss Boswell wanted with her? Or was she merely trying to stay out of it.

"Miss Boswell is waiting for you," Mrs. Tucker said, not giving Emily the opportunity to ask any questions. "You'd better hurry."

"Aren't you coming too?" She would certainly feel better if Mrs. Tucker was there to remind Miss Boswell of her otherwise untainted record.

"I'll be down as soon as I've delivered the rest of these letters to the proper girls."

"The mail's come?" Carole asked, forgetting her concern for Emily and hurrying forward to see if she had a letter. It had been three days since the school had sent into town for the last batch of mail. "Is there a letter for me?"

"I think there might be," Mrs. Tucker said and

her smile turned genuine while she flipped through the handful of envelopes to find the one addressed from New Orleans.

"Do I also have a letter?" Emily asked, staring eagerly at the envelopes in Mrs. Tucker's hand. For now, Miss Boswell would have to wait. It had been far too long since the last letter from her father and she was very eager to hear if he still planned to come to her graduation—that is *if* she would be allowed to graduate after Miss Boswell finished with her. Her heart thumped hard at such a thought.

"I'm sorry, but I don't have one for you," Mrs. Tucker admitted. Her smile faded as she quickly tucked the remaining letters under her arm and waved her hand. "You'd better go on. You don't want to keep Miss Boswell waiting very long."

"Yes, ma'am." Emily's shoulders slumped. She was disappointed not to have received a letter from home—not even a postal card. Nodding sharply in response to Mrs. Tucker's implied warning, she turned immediately for the stairs and hurried away.

Tears stung her eyes while she counted back the days. It had been well over three weeks since the last letter from her father. That was not like him. Until recently he had always written at least twice a week so she could have a letter almost every time the school sent into town for the mail.

Was he suddenly too busy with his latest business venture to find time to write? Or perhaps he was off traveling again and had simply forgotten to tell her. Was he still planning to come to her graduation like he had promised? Surely he was. He had said he was looking forward to the day. But, then, perhaps Cynthia had managed to change his mind about that, too. The woman had a real talent for changing her father's priorities.

Anger welled up inside of Emily when she

thought of her interfering stepmother. *She* was probably the reason why her father had not taken the time to write. No doubt Cynthia kept him busy with *other* matters, too busy to jot a quick note to his only daughter. Or perhaps the woman had intercepted her letters before her father ever saw them and had destroyed them so he would not feel obligated to answer any of them, much less attend her graduation ceremony.

That was certainly a possibility worth considering. Emily had known all along that Cynthia cared very little for her. During Emily's last few holiday visits home her dear stepmother had rarely acted cordial toward her—and the few times she had pretended to be nice had been only when her father was present. It wasn't until he left the house that Cynthia dropped all pretenses and ignored her completely.

Clearly, Cynthia saw her stepdaughter's holiday visits as nuisances to be barely tolerated. Emily now wondered how the woman viewed the prospect of her permanent return. With graduation only days away, she would soon return home to stay. She would probably leave with her father shortly after the farewell picnic.

Emily suspected part of the reason Cynthia treated her like she did was because she resembled her mother so much. Cynthia had to know how deeply her father had loved his first wife and how devastated he had been by her death. Because of that, Emily realized she would have to make a special effort to earn her stepmother's tolerance. There would never be peace in the Felcher household unless Emily did something to bring it about.

For her father's sake, she would do what she could to become friends with her father's second wife. After all, the woman couldn't be all bad. Her father had to have seen *something* in Cynthia besides a pretty face and a youthful smile. Then, remembering the way Cynthia filled out a ball gown, Emily understood better. She glanced down at her own young breasts and wondered if she would ever be endowed in such a lavish way. At age eighteen, she had already filled out the more feminine lines of her own dresses, but not with quite the same aplomb as Cynthia.

Pausing in the hallway outside the heavy oak door, she glanced at the tall gold-plated letters. On the opposite side lay the elegantly furnished office of their headmistress. Before lifting her hand to knock, she took a deep reassuring breath, then rapped lightly on the door frame. Secretly, she hoped she would not be heard from within. She could then return to her room knowing she'd tried. But she also realized it would only delay the inevitable. When she heard no immediate response, she knocked a second time, much louder.

"Come in," said the high-pitched voice from inside.

Swallowing hard, Emily reached for the brass handle and bravely opened the door. As expected, the older woman sat behind her desk, her wire-rimmed glasses perched high on her nose while she waited for Emily to speak.

"Mrs. Tucker said you wanted to see me."

"Yes, do come in and sit down," Miss Boswell said, lifting a heavily veined hand to pat an imagined unruly curl back into place. She then stood and indicated the small tufted sofa near her desk.

Emily knew by the severe expression on Miss Boswell's face that the next few minutes were not to serve her well. She quickly took the seat offered and glanced toward the desk to see if the paper novel lay in sight. When she did not notice it among the carefully arranged clutter, she returned her gaze to the stern expression on Miss Boswell's aging face.

"Emily, I'm afraid I have some tragic news for you," she began. She reached for a handkerchief that lay on her desk then crossed the room to join Emily on the sofa.

Tiny bite-like stings prickled along the sensitive skin at the back of Emily's neck. Miss Boswell's expression revealed her concern. Suddenly, Emily knew this summons had nothing to do with the paper novel she had discarded. It had to do with her father and the reason he had not written. Something was wrong, terribly wrong.

When Emily spoke, her voice was so strained, so choked with emotion, it sounded foreign even to her, "It's Father, isn't it?"

Tears filled the old woman's eyes when she leaned forward and gathered Emily to her. "Yes, dear, I'm afraid it is."

Emily's heart slammed hard against her chest. "How ill is he?"

There was a long, heavy silence before Miss Boswell spoke again. "I'm a-afraid he's dead, dear. Killed in a train accident of some sort. The telegram arrived a few minutes ago. I sent Mrs. Tucker to get you immediately."

The pain was so overwhelming that for a moment Emily could not breathe. Certain that Miss Boswell had misinterpreted the telegram, she refused to believe what she'd been told. "No. You are wrong. My father is still alive. He was merely injured."

"Oh, dear child, how I wish that could be true. But the telegram read quite clear. He was killed in a train accident. You are to go home right away."

"May I see this telegram?" Emily asked, calmly extending her hand, ready to prove the headmistress wrong. Her father could not be dead. Not now. Not *ever.* He was too important a man.

"Yes, of course." Miss Boswell then rose on quaking legs and walked the short distance to her desk. When she turned back, she offered the telegram and her handkerchief. Emily accepted both.

During the time it took to read the short message that reaffirmed what Miss Boswell had told her, the room grew terribly cold. With trembling hands, Emily set the telegram aside and glanced toward the window, allowing the reality to soak in at last. Her father was dead. He'd been the only person left in her life worth loving and the only person to return that love, and now he was gone.

Caught between a wild rush of anger and fear, and bound to the sofa by the weight of her confusion, she stared at the flowering apple trees off in the distance, not really seeing them yet strangely aware of their beauty.

"My father is dead, Miss Boswell," she said, as if suddenly unaware that the woman already knew. She fought the tears that threatened her eyes. "He's been killed."

Miss Boswell rested a wrinkled hand on Emily's trembling shoulder. "I'm so sorry, child. I am so very, very sorry. I know how much he meant to you."

Suddenly the pain that lashed out at Emily was so severe, she could not help but respond. Turning a hardened gaze on the elderly woman, she brushed the hand aside, not yet ready for anyone's comfort. "What do you mean you know how much he *meant* to me. He still means everything to me—everything in the world." She stood up and held her arms stiffly at her sides while her chest filled with senseless anger. "Just because he is gone doesn't mean he is any less important to me!"

"That's not at all what I meant to imply," Miss Boswell said, her face contorted with compassion. She tried again to rest a comforting hand on Emily's shoulder. "I know how very much you love him and how very difficult it must be to learn of his death."

That sounded better to Emily. Still fighting the tears, she thrust her chin forward and spoke in a much calmer voice. "I must go home. I must be there for the funeral."

"Of course, I would expect nothing less," Miss Boswell assured her. "I do so regret that you will miss your graduation, especially under such tragic circumstances; but I will find someone else to give your speech and I will mail your diploma to you the moment it has been delivered." She put her arm around Emily's shoulder. "I will go with you to your room and explain to Carole. Under the circumstances, I feel certain she will want to help you pack your things."

When Carole learned about what had happened, she was too dumbstruck to say anything at first. Instead, she merely nodded, her eyes wide and her face ashen, when Miss Boswell asked her to help Emily pack.

Before leaving the girls' room, Miss Boswell took Emily into her arms one last time. "As soon as you and Carole have your things packed, I want you to try to get some sleep. I will arrange passage on the early morning train to New York and will wire your stepmother when to expect you. You should be home by late afternoon."

Having somehow gone this long without a childish burst of tears, Emily refused to speak, afraid the strained sound of her own voice would break the emotional dam inside her. When Miss Boswell finally released her, she merely nodded she'd understood and would try to get some rest, though she doubted sleep would be possible.

"I'll take care of her," Carole promised, her voice barely above a raspy whisper. "I'll see that she's packed in plenty of time to get some sleep."

"Thank you." Miss Boswell turned her face to the door for fear the girls would see how affected she had been by all this. "I'd better go make the arrangements for the train."

After Miss Boswell left, it was several minutes before either Emily or Carole moved. Both stood right where they'd been when she left, staring vacantly at the hardwood floor, each lost in her own thoughts. Finally, Carole walked to the door and gently closed it.

"Oh, Emily, I am so sorry," is all she could think to say before slowly heading toward her best friend, wishing she knew what she might do to comfort her.

"This cannot be happening," Emily said through tight lips, again refusing to accept her father's fate. "It can't be real."

"I know," Carole said softly, then opened her arms wide.

Seeing the open arms and at last ready for comfort, Emily flew into her friend's embrace. "I must be having a bad dream, Carole. None of this can possibly be real."

But the arms that came around her were real. The tears that finally filled her eyes and spilled down her face were real, and the scream that swelled inside her throat until it had to come out was very, *very* real.

"That's good," Carole said in a soothing voice, her heart aching right along with Emily's. "Let it out. Let it all out. Scream and cry with all your might—until you can scream and cry no more."

And she did. She screamed out in anger. She

cried aloud with hopelessness. Stamping her feet with all her might, she cried out for her father again and again, all the while knowing there would be no response. No answer to her pain. Carole's voice rose above her cries of anguish, encouraging her to scream louder, to kick and stamp all she wanted. To cry until the tears became a balm to soothe her pain.

But nothing could ever soothe Emily's pain. She was now alone in the world. Alone with no family to love, no family to love her. All that remained were her memories. Memories she would cling to and cherish for the rest of her life. Memories of her father and of all the wonderful stories he had told her about her mother.

The following morning passed in a blur for Emily. She remembered giving Carole her graduation dress, since they were the same size and she no longer had the time to help her repair her own dress. And she remembered everyone gathering on the front steps to tell her good-bye, but for the life of her she could not remember the carriage ride to the train station. Nor did she recall boarding the passenger car that would carry her to New York. From that point until she arrived in New York and found no one waiting for her, she barely remembered anything.

Suspecting that Cynthia had refused to send a carriage for her, but not really caring about such discourtesy at the moment, Emily wasted little time hailing a hansom cab and asked to be delivered to number six Branson Street.

By the time she arrived in front of the three-story brownstone, evening shadows had fallen across the front steps, cloaking the door with a gloomy darkness. Emily tried not to dwell on previous visits to that house, when her father had greeted her at the door with a hug and a kiss; because, today, he would not be there to greet her. Never again, would he be there to greet her.

Fighting a new rush of tears, amazed she still had any left to shed, Emily paid the coach driver his six cents. She left her things at the curbside and slowly climbed the mason steps to the front door and pulled on the bell cord.

When the heavy door swung open and she saw the surprised expression on Samuel Evans's face, her brave attempt not to cry collapsed. Needing to be hugged by someone, though she knew it was highly improper to expect it from her father's personal butler, she flew immediately into his arms.

Samuel's brown eyes widened with alarm while he quickly pulled her inside, away from the street; but then, sensing her need, he gently wrapped his thin, black arms around her and held her close. "There, there, Emmie. You mustn't carry on so." He spoke in a soft, soothing voice, stretching his wrinkled face and blinking hard in an effort to stop his own tears. "Your father wouldn't want you grievin' so on his account."

But Emily could not help it. Pressing her cheek against the rich material of Samuel's dark red uniform, she sobbed aloud her misery to the longtime family employee and her personal friend. "I'm sorry, Samuel. I can't help it. I simply can't help it."

"I know. I know. I've done shed a tear or two myself," he admitted, then sniffed loudly. " 'Specially yesterday, when I finally got my courage up and went to pay a visit to his grave."

Emily brought her head off Samuel's narrow chest with a start. "His grave? Father's already buried? But that can't be. I only received the telegram yesterday."

Samuel's thin face hardened with ill-repressed

anger. "I know. Your stepmother felt it be best not to notify you right away. I tried to change her mind, knowin' you'd want to be there when they laid him down for his final rest, but she'd hear no part of anything I had to say." Unable to look down into Emily's tear-filled eyes any longer, he lifted his chin and stared up at the intricate design stenciled over the doorway. "She's a cruel woman, that one. A cruel woman indeed."

"Why? What has she done now?" she asked, curious to know what had happened to make this generous-hearted man speak so ill of someone. It was not at all like Samuel to say anything disparaging about anyone, even Cynthia.

Samuel slowly brought his gaze back down to hers. "Awh, missy, I don't want to be the one to tell you, but that woman's done got worse since your father's death. She's done already had your things packed up and has 'em waitin' on you at the back of the house."

"Packed my things! But why?" Emily asked, though the prickly feeling along the nape of her neck told her why.

"She says she don't want you livin' here with her. Fact is, that woman is so mean in spirit, she don't intend to even let you stay in your own father's house. She plans to send you away again."

"Can she do that?" Emily asked, unable to believe her father would allow that to be her fate. Surely he had provided for her in his will.

"I don't rightly know if she can or if she can't, but *she* seems to think she can," Samuel said, shaking his head sadly while he thought more about it.

"And indeed I can," came a shrill response from somewhere overhead, startling both of them. Quickly Samuel pushed Emily away and dropped his arms to his sides, his eyes round with alarm.

Emily turned immediately toward the sound and discovered her stepmother standing at the top of the massive staircase, scowling angrily at the pair.

"But how?" she asked, her voice so charged with emotion, she could hardly speak. "And why?"

Cynthia's blue eyes narrowed for a moment before she finally curved her delicate lips into a menacing smile. "I think you know why. As for how, come with me." She then lifted her silken skirts and descended the stairs with catlike grace. Without turning to look at Emily again, she headed toward the back of the house. With her chin jutted at a haughty angle, she called back to them over her shoulder. "Samuel, you might as well bring her things inside. Since it is so late, I will allow her to stay the night. I certainly don't want you telling people behind my back how mean-spirited I was in sending her away at night. Besides, the neighbors might see her leave so soon after her arrival and ask questions I don't care to answer. But she must be out of this house first thing in the morning. She can sleep in your room. *You* can sleep on the floor in the kitchen. But for now, see that the trunk she brought with her is taken to the back. I'll not have it in my way. Now move!"

The thought of Samuel forced to lie on a hard kitchen floor made Emily's blood boil, but until she had seen whatever Cynthia wanted to show her, she felt it wise to keep any opinions she had to herself. It would serve no real purpose to lambast the woman with her anger, at least not yet. Still, she had no intention of allowing Samuel to sleep on a cold, damp floor. Samuel was far too old for such as that. If anyone had to sleep on a floor, it would be her. She wondered then why she could not simply sleep in her own room.

"Where are you taking me?" she asked, wondering why all the secrecy.

"Into Joshua's study. I have something I think you should read," Cynthia answered. Her voice revealed nothing.

When they entered the large, book-lined room so familiar to Emily, Cynthia headed directly for her late husband's desk and reached for a small packet of papers that rested in the center. Turning to smile triumphantly at Emily, she slipped the papers out of their jacket and immediately thrust them into her hands. "Here read this."

"What is it?" Emily asked, staring curiously at the folded pages. A hollow pain settled in the pit of her stomach.

"Your father's will. And, as you will see, it clearly states that upon his death, I, his *beloved* wife, am to inherit his entire estate. You, on the other hand, are to inherit nothing." She crossed her arms defiantly. Her eyes were illuminated with an eerie light. "Other than your personal belongings, my dear child, you have no legal claim to anything in this house."

Unable to believe her father would allow such a thing, Emily quickly unfolded the document and read the first two pages then scanned the third and fourth. It was true. In this will, dated barely two months earlier, her father had indeed left everything he owned to Cynthia, but in it he had also claimed to be confident his beloved wife would then see to the complete loving care of his only daughter, Emily.

"But it says here you are to take care of me," Emily pointed out, glancing up from the page to meet Cynthia's gaze straight on.

"Ah, but it says only that he was *confident* I would. There is no actual demand I do so."

"But that's what he meant. He clearly intended for you to take care of me."

An evil smile lifted the outer corners of Cynthia's lips. "That very well may be, but the document doesn't actually demand it—my lawyer made certain of that. You can take me to court if you like, but you'll only find that the will is binding just as it is. I am his only heir."

Shuffling quickly to the last page, Emily found her father's signature above that of an attorney she didn't recognize, along with two witnesses, both close friends of the family. The will was indeed valid. She had clearly been left to her stepmother's mercy, of which there obviously would be none. She was too stunned by the realization to speak aloud the anger that filled her heart. She merely stared at the evil woman, dumbfounded.

"As Samuel has already told you, I have all your personal belongings packed and ready for you. You'll find a trunk and a small valise in the pantry near the back door. If you feel the servants may have overlooked anything, you have my permission to go up to your old rooms and look around for anything they may have missed. Otherwise, I'd prefer that you keep to Samuel's room for the rest of the evening. If you are hungry you may dine with the servants at eight. In the morning, I'll have a carriage waiting for you shortly after breakfast. It will take you anywhere you wish, as long as it is within the city."

"But I have nowhere to go."

"That is not my problem," Cynthia said with no trace of compassion in either her expression or her voice while she quickly took the papers from Emily's weak grasp. "I have put up with you for five long years. And now that your father is dead and I have officially inherited everything, I don't intend to put up with you a minute longer."

With that, she spun about and marched haughtily out of the room, leaving Emily all alone in her father's study—with no one to turn to and nothing to fill her heart but anger and despair.

Chapter Two

Overcome by the sheer weight of her own anger and confusion, Emily sank into one of the pale gold rococo chairs that faced her father's desk while she tried to reason through everything that had happened.

How could her father have been duped so easily? What had made him agree to sign such an ambiguous will? Had he really believed Cynthia would willingly see to anyone's personal care other than her own? Had he misjudged the woman's character so completely?

Apparently so. He had definitely signed the papers that now gave Cynthia legal right to everything. Emily knew her father's signature as well as she knew her own. But why? And where did such a will leave her, his only daughter?

Out on the street with no place to turn, nor anyone to turn to.

Where could she go? What would she possibly do to support herself—work as a seamstress in one of New York's crowded clothing factories? Or maybe she would become a desk clerk in some dark, dingy office, or possibly a rich woman's laundress, or a housemaid.

She closed her eyes against the fresh onrush of tears and pressed trembling hands against her hot cheeks while she tried her best to make sense of what had happened. Other than her personal belongings, which Cynthia would have no use for anyway, Emily now had no legal claim to anything that had ever been her father's. All she had, other than whatever items her stepmother had ordered packed from her room, was the clothing she'd already had with her at Miss Boswell's School for Young Ladies, which were mostly uniforms. That and what money her father had sent to her through the years.

Fortunately, she had spent very little of the money, since the school provided so many of her needs. But would the money be enough to help establish herself somewhere?

She doubted it, but then she really did not know how much she had saved because, until now, the money had never been very important to her. The accompanying letters had been worth far more to her than any weekly allowance—so much so, she'd kept every letter he had ever written and had read each one several times. Yet, she had never bothered to tally her money. Instead, she had merely tossed it into the small pewter canister, thinking one day she would buy something truly grand for her father as a means of repaying him in some small way for his many kindnesses.

In addition to whatever money she'd saved, Emily also had her mother's jewelry. But because so much of the jewelry had been bought before her father had made his fortune in the stock market, it was neither elaborate nor expensive. Still she adored every piece and would never part with any of it willingly. Especially not the beautiful antique necklace and matching dinner ring which were both made from crescent-shaped, faceted rubies, surrounded by a tiny scattering of diamonds, and set in polished gold.

Because her maternal grandmother had given both the necklace and the ring to her mother on her mother's sixteenth birthday, and her father had in turn passed the heirlooms on to Emily on her own sixteenth birthday, she had kept the jewelry at school with her, mainly because she'd found such comfort in touching it.

She had also found comfort in touching the lace handkerchief he had given her that same day. It, too, had been her mother's and may have also been her grandmother's. It bore an elaborately detailed monogram *E,* which was the first letter in all their names.

With Emily's thoughts momentarily on her mother and what life might have been like had she not died so very young, Emily decided the time had come to do something she had always dreamed of doing—find her maternal grandmother.

Although Emily had never met her, she had heard so many wondrous stories about her through the years that she'd always yearned to meet her one day. With nowhere else to go, and no other family to turn to, Emily decided the time had come to search for the woman her mother had spoken about with such sad fondness.

She would find her grandmother.

But how? All she really knew about the woman was that her name had been Elmira Townsend the day her mother had chosen to leave Texas and run away to New York. But after becoming a widow approximately ten years ago, her grandmother could very well have remarried and taken on a new last name. Still, how large could Galveston be? Surely she could find someone there who either knew her grandmother or knew of her—someone who would direct her to her grandmother's door.

Emily's next thought concerned what her grandmother might say or do when a granddaughter she'd never known appeared unexpectedly on her doorstep. Would she welcome her with open arms, or scorn her and send her away? Because of the heartbreaking circumstances behind her mother's sudden decision to leave, Emily was not sure how the woman might receive her runaway daughter's only child. Surely the years must have mellowed some of the anger. Besides, it had been her mother who had been ordered never to set foot in the family home, not her.

If only Emily could be certain the woman would not send her away. But, then again, what difference would it make? She would be no more or no less homeless than now, and there was certainly nothing binding her to New York. Nothing to keep her from traveling to Texas in search of her mother's family. Even if it turned out her grandmother did not want her, or had died, she still had an aunt out there somewhere. Surely her mother's only sister would not turn her away.

With the decision finally made, Emily felt better. She had a new purpose in her life and hurried to formulate her plans. First she needed to count her money, to see if she had enough to make the trip to Texas. Then she planned to catch Cynthia alone and tell her exactly what she thought of her, in no uncertain terms. But, for now, she wanted to visit her father's grave and explain her decision to him.

Two days later, Emily Felcher had booked passage on a small passenger ship headed for New Orleans, where she hoped to spend a night or two with Carole Jeanne before boarding a second ship to take her on to Galveston. After having discovered how much less it cost to travel by ship than by train, Emily had put aside her eagerness to start her actual search in favor of the slower mode of travel.

Even though she had been pleasantly surprised by how much money she had accumulated during the five years she'd been enrolled at Miss Boswell's, and could have easily afforded to make the trip to Texas by train in far shorter time, she was not at all certain of what she might find after she reached the coastal city of Galveston.

Having always been the practical sort, she decided to make her money stretch as far as possible. There was no way for her to know what it would cost or how long it would take to locate her mother's family.

With her mission set firmly in her heart, Emily boarded the ship, determined to find the part of her family she had never known. During those first few days of travel, she tried to focus on what her mother's family might be like and not dwell on her father's untimely death, nor the fact he'd unwittingly left her homeless and alone. Samuel had been right. Her father would not want her to dwell on such sad thoughts. He would want her to put the pain behind her and go on with her life, as hard as that might be.

Even so, Emily was given to long moments of melancholy in those first few days, and it was during just such a moment, while she stood at the ship's railing gazing out upon the vastness of the water around her, that she met Josephine Bradley.

"Why such a sad face?" Josephine had said as a way of introduction, catching Emily quite off guard. "You look as if you have lost your best friend."

Having turned to face the elegantly dressed

woman, Emily was instantly touched by such deep concern. "In a way I have. I recently lost my father."

"Oh, I see," came a compassionate response. Detecting Emily's discomfort, she then glanced out over the water, in the same direction Emily had earlier focused her own attention. "And I guess you've decided to take a long trip to help you over your grief."

Emily found comfort in the woman's soft, lilting accent that indicated she'd come from somewhere in the South. "Not exactly. I'm on my way to Galveston to find my mother's family."

"Oh, then your mother is traveling with you?" She looked back at Emily with a questioning lift of a perfectly arched brow.

"No, my mother died years ago." For some reason there was a renewed pain linked to her mother's death, though it had happened over fourteen years ago. She gripped the railing to keep this new flood of anguish from overwhelming her.

"Oh, I am sorry. I always find the wrong thing to say." She pressed her gloved hand over Emily's to comfort her. "Here I wanted to cheer you a little and all I've done is make you sadder still."

Emily glanced down at the hand resting lightly over her own and smiled. "No, you haven't. To tell you the truth, it is nice to have someone to talk with. Even though I'm having to share a room with five other women, I'm afraid I've purposely cut myself off from the rest of the passengers and that's not what Father would have wanted me to do."

She lifted her gaze to Josephine's jade green eyes and wondered for the first time how old the woman might be. Although she appeared to be in her early thirties, her exact age was hard to guess because of all the face color she wore—everything from a delicate tracing of kohl that she used to line her almond-shaped eyelids, to a blending of different rouges to highlight her high cheeks. With her dark, ebony hair piled into a thick array of rich curls high atop her head, she was a beautiful woman—a woman of both elegance and wealth. Her clothing alone told that.

Josephine returned Emily's smile. "Well, then, let me officially introduce myself. My name is Josephine, Josephine Bradley. Perhaps you would agree to have supper with me this evening. I do so detest dining by myself."

"Oh, then you are traveling alone, too," Emily surmised, wondering why a woman as beautiful and as splendidly dressed as Josephine would be traveling anywhere alone.

Josephine's eyes widened with even more concern while she pressed her hand against an emerald studded throat. "Too? Do you mean to tell me that a girl your age is traveling without a companion? Why you can't be more than seventeen years old. A girl that young should never attempt to travel anywhere alone. It is far too dangerous."

"I'm eighteen," Emily quickly corrected, thinking that might make all the difference.

"Still, eighteen is far too young to be traveling alone. Have you no maid?"

Emily's smile widened. Undoubtedly, the woman was accustomed to the many luxuries wealth afforded, and until her father's death, Emily would have had her choice of personal maids to accompany her. There had always been at least four or more in his employ. But those same women were now in her stepmother's care and no longer available to her. "No, I am quite alone."

"Not anymore," Josephine said with a determined shake of her head. "That is a situation I intend to remedy right away. A girl your age needs a companion watching over her at all times. Either I, or my own personal maid, Constance, will be your companion from now on."

"That's not necessary," Emily assured her, although it felt good to have someone act so concerned about her, especially after Cynthia's cruel treatment.

"It most certainly is necessary," Josephine shot back, determined to have her way. "And, as it happens, I live right in Galveston, which is where I'm also headed, so I should be able to watch over you for the remainder of your trip. You will not have to be alone anymore." She smiled brightly. "And neither will I."

Josephine proved true to her word. From that afternoon forward, Emily did not have to spend another moment alone. If she wanted company, for whatever reason, all she had to do was knock at Josephine's door and either Josephine or Constance joined her in a leisurely stroll along the deck or a friendly game of hearts in the main saloon.

By the time they reached New Orleans, Josephine had begun a slow transformation in Emily. She had brought her out of her melancholic mood bit by bit, until once again Emily's voice was edged with laughter and her eyes were bright with hope.

Having decided the young girl's wardrobe—which consisted mainly of drab-colored school uniforms—was sorely lacking, Josephine convinced Emily to forego any surprise visit with her young school friend and instead accompany her on a shopping spree in some of the more elite dress shops of New Orleans. Because they were both scheduled to board the same ship to transport them on to Galveston early the following morning, she also convinced Emily to stay with her that night at the elegant Orleans Hotel, adamant that it all be her treat.

Thinking she had taken advantage of the older woman too long, Emily tried to decline the invitation, but Josephine would have no part of it. In the end, Emily agreed to give up her plans to visit Carole Jeanne and spend the day with her new friend.

"I realize you are still in mourning for your father," Josephine stated only moments after the three women had settled into a hired carriage. "But, I do think you have worn those dark colors long enough. It is springtime. Time to wear bright colors. And, as you have undoubtedly discovered, down here in the South, wool is not at all a good choice for clothing. We must find you dresses made of much lighter material."

"But I have no money for new clothing," Emily protested, still wanting to save her money for more important things. "My wool dresses will have to do for now."

Josephine shook her head, unable to believe the girl's innocence. "I do not intend for you to spend any of your own money. I want to buy the dresses for you—as a way of thanking you for making this trip such a pleasant one."

"I can't let you do that," Emily spoke adamantly, though warmed by the thought anyone would want to do such a thing.

Josephine smiled and waved it off as unimportant. "I'm afraid you can't stop me. My mind is made up. Just as it is made up that you will have a private cabin near mine once we board that ship to Galveston."

"But I can't . . ."

"Oh, but you can."

Constance grinned, forming long dimples in her thin, brown cheeks while she slowly shook her head. "I think you're 'bout to discover that once Miss Josephine has gone and made up her mind the way she has, there ain't no changin' it. If I was you, I wouldn't even try. 'Sides, you do look a might warm in that dress you got on."

Emily had to admit the heavy material of her dark grey skirt and waistcoat were not at all comfortable in such a stifling climate. It trapped her own body's heat against her skin, making the humidity that much more unbearable. She shrugged and accepted defeat gracefully. "Well, if I can't change her mind, then I guess all that's left for me to do is thank her."

Constance nodded, indicating she had made the best choice. "I sure hope you can find room in your two trunks for all she plans to buy you. I can tell by that twinkle in those green eyes of hers, that we're in for a full day of shoppin'."

And Constance was right. By the time the trio arrived at the Orleans Hotel that evening, the rented carriage was so full of packages, there was hardly room for the three of them to sit. Although many of Josephine's selections had been questionable, the styles far more daring than Emily usually wore, Emily was grateful for each new dress and undergarment.

All together she had seven new outfits, complete with gloves and slippers, and all were extremely low in cut. At first, she had hesitated to make such purchases, but had been reassured by both Josephine and Constance as well as several of the various sales ladies that the dresses were the very latest in fashion. They would in no way be considered risqué.

Of all the garments they had purchased, Emily favored the white linen. She liked the way it was tucked at the waistline, ruffled in layers several inches above the hemline, and trimmed with touches of pink lace embedded with tiny pink pearls. Though the deep neckline revealed ample amounts of feminine flesh, the dress was the epitome of womanhood and a far cry from the dull-colored jumpers and straight-lined tunics she'd worn at Miss Boswell's School for Young Ladies.

That night, for dining with Josephine in the Orleans Hotel restaurant, Emily chose to wear the white linen with a pair of pale pink elbow-length gloves and a delicate pair of pink and white slippers, also gifts from Josephine.

Before leaving her room for the restaurant downstairs, Constance took Emily's long hair down out of its usual double twist at the back of her head, then brushed and curled it with a crimping iron until it shaped into a massive array of shimmering brown curls that hung down her back and draped across her ivory shoulders. Never had Emily felt so beautiful, and never had she turned so many heads.

All through dinner, she noticed both men and women turning to glance at her with open admiration while others looked her way with clear jealousy hardening their expressions. It was a whole new experience for Emily. Still, she tried not to be affected by all the special notice. She tried to concentrate on her meal.

"I do believe you have an admirer," Josephine said matter-of-factly while she lifted her fork to her mouth and nibbled at the last of her cherry cake. Though she spoke to Emily, her gaze roamed idly about the room. "There's a young man sitting near the far wall who can't keep his eyes off you. In fact, there are several such young men, but I do believe this one will be the first to find the courage to come and speak with you."

"Me? Oh, come now," Emily said, aware of the blush climbing her cheeks. "I'm sure that you are mistaken. If these men are truly taken by anyone, it is you. You are exquisite in your new emerald gown."

Josephine smiled appreciatively as she glanced down at the low cut of Emily's ivory gown. "I won't argue that. But I'm experienced enough in such matters to know in which direction a young man's eyes have wandered. And in this case, with this particular young man, his eyes have wandered to you—and have rarely found another place to light upon all evening. In fact, I do believe he has finally worked up the courage to come speak to you. He has placed his napkin aside and is headed this way."

Emily's brown eyes widened with alarm. "Oh, no. What do I say to him?"

Josephine reached out to pat Emily's hand reassuringly. "That will all depend on what he says first. Relax and be yourself. As pretty and as sweet as you are, I have no doubt that you will charm him into oblivion with whatever you say."

"Good evening, ladies," came the male voice from just behind Emily's left shoulder. The young man came to a grand halt beside the table. "Are you enjoying your supper?"

Emily glanced up at the man, not expecting to find him so handsome, though in a boyish sort of way. And, it was obvious by his arrogant stance that he was already quite aware of his good looks. Finding herself at an uncharacteristic loss for words, her cheeks paled. She immediately looked to Josephine for help.

"Yes, we are enjoying the meal immensely," Josephine responded with a friendly smile, boldly meeting the man's gaze. "And you? Did you find your meal to be pleasant?"

"Only because two such beautiful ladies as yourselves were in the room," he said gallantly, then stepped closer to the table so Emily could better gaze upon his smiling face. "Do you two live here in New Orleans? Or are you visiting? Oh, by the way, I hope you don't find my behavior too forward, but my name's Phillip—Phillip Vicke—and I was so enthralled by your beauty that I could not possibly stay away."

"Please join us, Mr. Vicke," Josephine said, waving toward a vacant chair. She watched while Emily's face grew paler and more rigid by the moment. "No, I'm afraid we do not live in New Orleans. We are only here for the night. We leave for Galveston first thing in the morning."

Disappointment fell across the young man's handsome face. "Oh, I had hoped I'd have a little more time to get to know you."

Josephine smiled sweetly then lifted her hand to touch the feminine swell of her ample bosom, just inches above the bulging neckline of her snugly fitted bodice. "Well, perhaps you have occasion to travel to Galveston from time to time."

Emily felt as if the room had grown stifling hot. She couldn't believe how easily Josephine could converse with a total stranger when she herself could hardly summon the courage to look the young man in the eye.

"Yes, I do travel to Galveston every now and then. But I don't even know who I should ask for the next time I visit that fair port. Or where I should ask," he added in a strained voice while he openly admired Emily.

Josephine hesitated, then answered in a soft, sultry tone. "My name is Miss Josephine Bradley and my young companion is Miss Emily Felcher. I can be found on Second Street. Ask anyone in that neighborhood and you should be given accurate directions."

"And what about you, Miss Felcher? Do you also live on Second Street?"

Emily realized the time had come to meet the

man's eyes, and she slowly lifted her gaze from her dessert. But for the life of her, she could not think of a worthwhile response. Her mind was in such a whirl she was not at all sure of the question.

Josephine hurried to intervene. "Not just yet, but I'm hoping to convince her to come live with me, at least for a little while, until she can find the grandmother that she's traveled all the way from New York to locate."

Emily looked at Josephine with surprise. Suddenly, the young man was forgotten. "You have already done enough for me. I can't possibly impose further."

"It will be no imposition, I assure you," Josephine responded quickly. "I've already told you what a large house I have, and money is certainly no problem for me. Besides, where else can you go? Until you've located your grandmother, my house is the perfect place for you to stay."

Not too pleased to be left out of the conversation, Phillip Vicke cleared his throat and shifted in his seat. "Besides, it will make it far easier for me to find you when I visit."

"I don't know," Emily said, for the first time addressing the young man. "She's already done so much for me. I don't know how I can possibly repay her for all her kindnesses."

Josephine bubbled a deep, throaty laugh. "If that's all that is stopping you, quit worrying. I'm certain I can find a way for you to repay me. Just promise me you will stay with me until you find your grandmother. I'll see that one day you repay any debts you think you owe."

Emily studied Josephine for a long moment, then smiled with open gratitude. "You are so kind. Okay, I'll stay. But only until I find my grandmother, and only if you promise to accept some form of payment for my room and board. I am not totally destitute. I do have some money."

"I really don't want your money, but if it'll make you feel better, I promise," Josephine said, her eyes bright with the prospect of a new house guest. "I will accept *some* form of payment from you."

Phillip Vicke soon excused himself and left the restaurant, looking very rejected. As soon as he was gone, Josephine commented on Emily's obvious lack of experience with men. "You really must do something about that. A girl your age should be able to converse freely with a man. She should also know how to use her eyes and her smile to entrance and entrap. We must work on that. Starting tonight, I will show you the finer aspects of flirting. By the time we reach Galveston, you will have every man aboard the ship doting on you hand and foot."

Emily shook her head. She felt the color rise in her cheeks. "I doubt that."

"Don't doubt it. Believe in it. You are a very pretty girl. The sort who naturally captures a man's eye. All you need are a few lessons in how to entice a man once he's noticed you. We'll begin immediately."

Chapter Three

At first, Emily considered many of the gestures Josephine wanted her to imitate whenever she was around any attractive young men to be silly if not downright embarrassing. But when she later experimented with the different hand motions and facial expressions on a real, live, unsuspecting male, she discovered how very well they worked. Suddenly, she was quite willing to rehearse the coy little flirtations in front of a mirror until finally she could mimic Josephine's actions perfectly. By the time their ship had left the port of New Orleans, headed at last for Galveston Bay, she sensed a very real power in what she had just learned.

At first, it had been hard to imagine a grown man being made to behave like a foolish schoolboy simply because of the way a woman looked at him, or because of the way she held her fan or sipped her wine. Why a man could be driven to total distraction by merely lifting one's hand and resting it lightly on the swell of a rising bosom. It seemed insane, this art of flirting, but it certainly produced results. There was no denying that. Still, it would take some getting used to. Often she had to be reminded to put her newly acquired skills into use whenever a handsome young man looked her way. It was just not part of her nature.

"You are not glancing about," Josephine scolded softly after she'd discovered Emily's attention on her food and not on the many male passengers about them. She frowned as if truly annoyed. "You have to let a few of these men catch you glancing up at them. Unless you do, you won't hold their interest long enough to matter. Remember: the best way to capture a man's heart is to feed his precious ego. And what man wouldn't want to be noticed by a beautiful young lady such as yourself?"

"But I'm not interested in any of these men," Emily protested, already having surveyed the men seated about the room. "They are either too old or too pompous-looking. I'm not interested in talking with a man twice my age or with some strutting rooster who thinks he can woo a woman simply by the way he fills out an expensive dinner jacket."

Josephine chuckled at such a keen perception while she again met someone's eye. She let her gaze linger only a moment, then lowered her lashes to stare shyly into her plate. "A man is never too old, especially if he has money; and all men are pompous to some extent."

"Still, my mind is too preoccupied with thoughts of finding my grandmother right now. I'm really not interested in flirting with any of these men. It takes far too much concentration."

Josephine hesitated, as though Emily had said something she hadn't expected, before offering a response. "Not after it's become second nature to you. But, I do understand. You are worried about finding your grandmother and afraid of how that first meeting might turn out. I can't say I blame you for that. Not after hearing the sad circumstances behind your mother's decision to leave home, or how angry your grandmother became after she'd left."

"Angry enough to tell Mother never to come back," Emily reminded her. She fought a sudden hollow feeling in the pit of her stomach—it was that same anger that Emily now feared—yet not enough to deter her from her mission.

Josephine shook her head while she thought more about the situation. "It is hard to imagine anyone being so deeply in love that she'd be willing to break all ties with her family forever. But then, I'm not a real believer in true, everlasting love, never have been. Still, some people do put quite a lot of stock in the emotion. Obviously your mother was one of those people. But look what it cost her—and you. Then again, a lot of time has passed since she ran away. Your grandmother has had a lot of time to get over the hurt and the anger. I honestly think you are worrying for nothing. I believe you will be pleasantly surprised by the outcome of that first meeting."

"Why is that?" Emily set her fork down and leaned forward, eager to hear Josephine's opinion.

Smiling, Josephine reached for her wine glass. Her tone of voice was reassuring. "Because as soon as this grandmother of yours discovers what a true gem you are, she will be quite taken by you. She'll be so taken that she will welcome you into her home with open arms."

"Oh, I hope so." Emily's brown eyes sparkled with hope, though her expression remained grim. If only she could know that for sure.

Josephine lifted the small-stemmed glass to her lips. She sipped the dark red liquid ever so delicately while she allowed her gaze to again wander about the room. "Don't worry so. It'll form tiny, unattractive lines at the outer corners of your eyes. Besides, even if your grandmother turns out to be a total idiot and refuses to take you in because of something someone else did years ago, you'll still have me. No matter what the outcome of your meeting with your family, you are welcome to live with me for as long as you like. You've become very much like a younger sister to me. I hope you know that."

Tears of gratitude filled Emily's eyes, causing her to blink. It felt wonderful to know someone still cared about her. "Thank you."

"I didn't say that for . . ." Josephine started to say, but lost her train of thought when she glanced over Emily's shoulder and noticed something that interested her greatly. Her hand froze, holding the wine glass just inches from her parted lips while her eyes widened noticeably.

Emily watched with mounting curiosity while Josephine quickly recovered, hurriedly setting the glass down at the same time she straightened in her chair, then lowered her dark lashes to a more demure height. Tilting her head to a flirtatious angle, she continued to stare intently at whoever had come up the isle behind Emily.

Clearly, someone had captured Josephine's eye, making Emily want to turn around and see who it might be. But at the same time she knew she would embarrass Josephine if she actually did so. Instead, she waited for that person to enter her line of vision.

"Well hello, Josie."

The deep, vibrant male voice came from just behind Emily's left shoulder, so rich in tone, it sent a tiny wave of prickly shivers splashing through her body. Again, she fought the urge to turn around and see what sort of man had caused such odd reactions in them both. Meanwhile, the voice continued, "I wasn't aware you were aboard."

Josephine quickly cut her gaze to Emily then bristled at such bold familiarity. "Please, sir, the name is and always has been Josephine Bradley. *Miss Bradley* to you," she announced, her chin jutted at an insulted angle. Her gaze bore into his.

"Oh, is it now?" The man sounded both surprised and amused.

Emily could stand it no longer. She had to see his face. With careful deliberation, she brushed her napkin out of her lap and watched it flutter onto the floor. She never considered that the man might attempt to pick it up for her. Instead she immediately bent to retrieve it, using the opportunity to glance back at the same time, only to discover he had taken a quick step forward and now stood only two feet away with his hand outstretched, staring curiously at her.

Not having expected him to be so close, she produced a soft gasping noise when her breath rushed suddenly past the painful constriction that had formed in her throat.

No wonder Josephine had behaved so strangely. Though he looked to be several years younger than she thought Josephine to be—probably somewhere in his late twenties—the man was without a doubt the most startlingly handsome human being Emily had ever seen. It might be a term not usually associated with men, but this man was absolutely *gorgeous*—from the top of his thick, wavy brown hair, all the way down to the curved tips of his shiny black dress boots—he was magnificent. Just looking at him left Emily breathless and sent her pulse racing at a dangerous speed.

Astounded that a complete stranger could cause such an alarming response inside her, Emily quickly righted herself and mentally tried to force her heart to stop its rapid pounding. She wondered what about this man made her react so differently from how she ever had before.

While making a grand show of smoothing the napkin across her lap, she positioned herself in the small dining chair and rested her shoulder against the back. That way she still faced the table yet could continue to glance back over her shoulder at the man himself. For some reason she did not want to have to pull her gaze off his handsome face for long. Besides, she felt it awkward to know he was standing behind her the way he was, aware that her overly rounded backside was not at all her most appealing attribute. And, although she was not sure why, she definitely wanted to appeal to this man.

When she glanced back at him, the young man did look at her momentarily, and with apparent interest, just as she'd hoped. But, to her dismay, he immediately returned his attention to Josephine, who had just spoken to him. At least it allowed her the opportunity to study his features without his notice. How could any man be so perfect? His nose, the shape of his eyes, his strong, solid chin. All perfect.

Emily's heart fluttered like a newly captured bird trying to break free while she watched his dark brown eyebrows arch high above a pair of the bluest eyes imaginable. He then shrugged his broad shoulders and responded to Josephine with a slow, agreeable nod. "Very well—*Miss Bradley.* I meant no harm. I assure you."

Josephine immediately relaxed and a genuine smile replaced the resentful pout. "No irreparable harm was done, I suppose." Then with a light wave of her hand she indicated the vacant chair to her right. "Would you care to join us, Mr. Gipson? Surely you have enough time to visit with us."

The man lifted a wide, sturdy hand to his chin and

stroked the solid lines of his freshly shaven jaw while he contemplated Josephine's invitation. His eyebrows remained arched with amused interest.

"*Mr. Gipson,* is it?" he asked, as though the name were foreign to him. "Very well, Miss Bradley, although I personally would prefer to be called Randall. But, as it just so happens, I do have a moment or two." In one flowing movement, he pulled out the chair and sat down. Then he promptly turned his attention to Emily, obviously intrigued by her beauty and not opposed to showing his interest. "May I ask the name of your lovely companion? I don't believe we've ever met."

Smiling proudly, Josephine laced her hands together and rested them at the edge of the table. "No, you two have never met and, yes, of course you may ask her name. This is Miss Emily Felcher. A very, *very* dear friend of mine."

The man's silvery gaze dipped boldly to take in the fashionable cut of Emily's blue silk dinner gown for several lingering seconds before slowly returning to meet her startled expression. Although he continued to stare at Emily in a manner that she found most alarming, his next words were directed to Josephine. "Oh? And what might I do to make Miss Emily Felcher a very, *very* dear friend of mine?" he asked, his diction perfect, but his tone of voice mocking.

A suggestive smile played at the outside corners of his strong, virile mouth until finally his lips parted to reveal the tips of his white teeth. Again, he deliberately lowered his gaze and quietly assessed Emily's most feminine of charms, which, to Emily's growing dismay, were left partially revealed to him by the daring neckline.

Aware of Emily's immediate discomfort, Josephine rushed to intervene. Obviously, she hoped to avoid a verbal confrontation between the two.

"Randall Gipson, you are incorrigible," she scolded playfully, unlacing her hands and leaning forward in an effort to draw his attention away from Emily's firm, young breasts by exposing a view of her own ample bosom. "Either you promise to behave yourself or I shall have to insist you be on your way." Then, tilting more toward Emily, she shook her head as if not knowing what to do with him. "You'll have to forgive Mr. Gipson, my dear. He sometimes forgets his manners."

Embarrassed and angered by the man's continued bold perusal, but not yet ready to cause a scene that would embarrass them all, Emily swallowed hard then reached for her water glass, as if unconcerned with anything Randall Gipson had to say or do. "Oh, I see. Well, if that's the case, I suppose we'll just have to do what we can to remind him of such things from time to time."

"Exactly," Josephine laughed nervously before returning her gaze to their visitor. She was eager to change the topic of conversation to something less volatile. "I must say, I am delighted to see you again, Mr. Gipson. It has been far too long since our last encounter."

Another slow smile spread across Randall's face, forming long, curving indentations in the lean muscles of his cheeks. Finally, he pulled his gaze away from Emily then looked knowingly at Josephine. It was as if the two exchanged private thoughts.

When he turned to face Josephine, the candlelight from the chandeliers that swayed overhead caught the shimmering highlights of his thick, brown hair. It took all the willpower Emily possessed to look away and not gape at the man.

"I've been very busy," he explained, his tone casual as he divided his attention between the two women. "Fact is, I'm presently returning from my third business trip to New Orleans this month. And as soon as I have collected the information I need to close a special deal my cousin and I have been working on for nearly a year now, I'll be headed back to New Orleans yet again."

"My, that sounds exciting," Josephine responded. Her eyes widened with practiced interest while she carefully rested her hand on the swell of her bosom. Then, when she chanced a quick glance at Emily, only to discover the girl's attention again riveted to her plate, she nudged her young friend under the table with the toe of her slippers. "Doesn't that sound exciting to you, Emily?"

"Oh, yes, of course," she responded immediately. Knowing why Josephine had nudged her, she then braved another quick glance at the handsome, but overbearing young man.

Heat stained her pale cheeks when she discovered him again studying her with his roving gaze. Although she was fairly used to men admiring her by now, she was used to having them gaze upon her face like Phillip Vicke had. But this man was admiring her in an entirely different way. She felt very much like a tiny little field mouse in the company of an extremely cunning and tremendously hungry farmer's cat. She immediately returned her attention to her plate and fervently wished he'd go away.

Josephine nudged her again, harder, but continued to smile as if nothing concerned her. She lowered her dark lashes a second time then tilted her head to a slight angle and spoke in her most beguiling voice. "You do sound extremely busy with this new business venture. But are you so busy that you cannot take enough time to pay a little call on us before you go rushing back to New Orleans?"

"I doubt I could ever be that busy," he answered then leaned back in the chair, carelessly at ease in his three-piece dinner suit. "I can always find an hour or two for personal leisure. That is if Emily—I mean, Miss Felcher—has no objections."

Upon hearing her name, Emily forced her gaze away from her plate again. She found it far less disturbing to discover his attention was now focused on her lips. Obviously, he awaited her response. But, while she hurriedly tried to decide just what she should say, he again allowed his gaze to drift slowly downward. Quietly, he assessed every curve and contour.

Emily took a deep breath and held it. His continued bold behavior was as annoying as it was unnerving. Just who did he think he was anyway?

"Only an hour or two?" she said finally, smiling sweetly as she repeated his words back to him. She hoped he had not noticed how long it had taken her to produce a rational response. "I suppose I have no objection to that. I am certain we can tolerate your company for *that* long."

Josephine's hand flew first to her gaping mouth and then to Randall's elbow. Her voice burst forward in a stammering rush. "Well, then, it's all set. Come by the first opportunity you have. I—I assure you, we will do our best to make you feel welcome." She then looked at Emily with silent warning.

"As only you can," he responded, appearing quite amused and not at all insulted. Undaunted, he slowly ran the base of his tongue over his lower lip while he dropped his gaze to the fitted lines of Emily's dress one last time. "I look forward to it."

Visibly shaken by such a sensual look, Emily started to tell him just what she thought of such brazen behavior, but the pleading expression on Josephine's face stopped her before the words quite reached her lips. Instead, she heaved out an exasperated sigh then glared at him with an odd mixture of undeniable outrage and unexplainable pleasure.

Though deeply shocked by such inexcusable behavior, she was nonetheless inwardly pleased that a man as handsome and as worldly as this one had indicated a very real interest in her. He had the same as promised to pay a personal call after their arrival in Galveston.

Her insides twisted wildly at the thought. She had never had a gentleman pay a formal call on her. After all, that sort of thing was not allowed at Miss Boswell's. But then again, it was not exactly a *gentleman* who'd be paying a call on her now. She wondered if he would even bother to give advance notice of his intended visit so she might look her best. If so, what should she wear? She glanced down at the low neckline that seemed to fascinate him so. Obviously, something with a very high collar and loose fitting seams.

"But for now, I'm afraid I must take my leave of your beautiful company," he said, interrupting her straying thoughts. His gaze never left hers. "I've guests waiting at my table."

"Of course, we understand," Josephine told him, though unable to completely hide her disappointment. "Perhaps we will run into each other again before we dock in Galveston on Friday."

"I'll make a point of it," he assured them then pushed himself out of the chair in one easy motion. While he stood towering over their table, he gave Emily one last lingering look. "I'm so pleased to have met you, Miss Felcher. And I do so look forward to becoming better acquainted."

Casually, he tapped the side of his finger against the curve of his forehead in a cocky salute, then resumed his slow journey across the crowded dining room, pausing twice to speak to people he passed. A majority of the women in the room stared after him in silent awe—including Emily.

"He certainly thinks highly of himself," Emily muttered, after finally finding her voice again. Not wanting to reveal how deeply the man had affected her, she immediately reached for her fork and proceeded to pierce a tiny piece of glazed carrot.

"He has every reason to," Josephine said and nodded agreeably while she, too, returned her gaze to her plate. "Not only is he attractive in every sense of the word, he's one of the wealthiest, most sought-after bachelors in all of Galveston. Fact is, he and his cousin own this very ship—and dozens more like it."

Emily's eyes widened. "He's a sea captain?" Although he was sturdy enough in build and his skin was richly tanned, he had not looked like he'd spent many relentless hours toiling outdoors in the harsh, salty sea air. "One would never have guessed."

"No, he's not a sea captain, though I believe he used to be." She paused to think. "As far as I know, what he does now is manage the shipping company. Or at least he's in charge of the Galveston branch."

"The Galveston branch? How large is the company?"

"Large enough to have offices and warehouses in both Galveston and New Orleans and no telling where else. The way I understand it, his cousin, Terrence Gipson, attends to whatever shipping concerns they hold in New Orleans while Randall takes care of the offices and warehouses in Galveston. Because Southwind Shipping was started by their grandfather and eventually taken over by their own fathers, who now are all dead, the two Gipson cousins work together as equal partners. And both live equally as well. You should see the house where

Randall lives. It's magnificent." She waved her hands in the air for emphasis.

"How do you know so much about him?"

Josephine smiled then clasped her hands together. "Anyone who reads a Galveston newspaper knows plenty about the Gipson cousins, Randall in particular. His name appears in either the financial or social columns at least once a week."

"What else do you know about him?" she asked, her curiosity overpowering her desire to seem disinterested.

"You mean besides the fact that he's incredibly handsome and disgustingly wealthy?" She laughed. "What else is there to know? According to *The Galveston Daily News,* he enjoys the finest European wines, dines at the most expensive restaurants, attends all the right social functions, and enjoys many of the local concerts and plays. Oh, and evidently he *loves* swimming in the ocean at night." Her smile widened.

"How do you know that?" Emily asked, knowing that was exactly what Josephine wanted her to do.

Josephine leaned forward so she could speak without anyone else overhearing. "I learned that once, about a year ago, he was caught swimming in the gulf during the wee hours of the morning—as naked as the day he was born."

Her eyes widened with whatever images that must have presented her while she continued, "Mind you, it is not illegal to swim *au naturel* after 10 P.M., that is, as long as the swimmer chooses to do so along certain beaches at the far west end of Galveston, but the scandalous part about Randall's decision to go into the ocean without the aid of any beachwear was the fact he wasn't at the west end beach, and he was *not alone.*"

Emily looked away, too embarrassed by her own

imaginings to meet Josephine's gaze. "Who was he with?"

"I can't say for absolute certain, but I heard it was Anne Wray, the terribly promiscuous and quite voluptuous daughter of one of Galveston's most prominent attorneys. But, because he *is* such a prominent attorney, the story never actually appeared in any of the newspapers. Still, the gossips were busy for several weeks after."

"I can imagine," Emily muttered, though in truth she was trying her best *not* to imagine. But the images refused to go away. Even though she was not exactly sure what a man's body looked like fully unclothed, she had enough of an idea to paint a vivid scene in her mind. Heat climbed to her cheeks, forcing her to reach for her fan.

"But then Randall is always giving the gossips something to wag their tongues about," Josephine admitted with a wry chuckle as she, too, reached for her fan. "He's quite a gadabout, that one."

Emily's eyebrows knitted. "How can you speak of him with what almost sounds like admiration? He's undoubtedly an unscrupulous rogue and a womanizer, the sort of man a proper lady would be wise to avoid."

"Yes, I guess he is a bit of a rogue." She fought to keep from grinning as she rested her closed fan lightly on her breast. "But his uncanny looks and all that money make up for any little indiscretions he may have committed through the years."

Emily was surprised by such a statement, especially coming from a woman of Josephine's stature. "Surely you don't mean that."

Josephine stared at her a long moment, then smiled and reached forward to rest a bejeweled hand on Emily's slender wrist. "It's not as if he's an out-in-out troublemaker. He's just a little impulsive is all. And, my dear, as you grow older, you'll soon discover that men are often allowed that luxury."

Still, Emily was not at all sure she wanted a man like that calling on her, no matter how attractive or wealthy. She had more than enough complications in her life already. But then, again, he had never actually said that he intended to pay his call on her personally. In all truth, he had indicated he would call on *both* of them. Perhaps she had misread the situation and Randall Gipson meant to do nothing more than pay a friendly little visit to them both.

Yet, for some reason, that realization left Emily far more disappointed than relieved.

Chapter Four

Despite Emily's firm resolve to remain unaffected by Randall Gipson's sophisticated charm and good looks, she was unable to stop herself from becoming slowly attracted to him. Despite the boldness in his nature, which sometimes frightened her, there was just something about Randall she could not resist, no matter how hard she tried.

Maybe it was his quick wit. Perhaps it was nothing more than his startlingly attractive smile. But there was definitely something endearing about him that drew her to him like a moth to a flame. But, then again, she didn't have to be *drawn* to him in any real sense of the word because the man had a real talent for finding her whenever she was off somewhere alone, and whenever he did discover her alone somewhere, he descended out of nowhere and flirted with her and teased her shamelessly.

Though she was not always pleased and certainly never comfortable with the audacious, self-assured manner in which he came on to her, she was very flattered by his relentless pursuit nonetheless. Soon—after having come to the conclusion that such bold behavior must be considered quite normal for the more noted of Southern society—she caught herself actually flirting back, encouraged by Josephine and Constance, who had both decided Emily and Randall would make a delightful couple.

"You know you should count yourself quite lucky to be invited to have dinner with someone as prestigious as Randall Gipson," Josephine said, excited to hear about the private invitation Emily had received. She frowned then folded her arms across her ample bosom and leaned against Emily's cabin door. "I don't understand why you appear so concerned. You should be thrilled."

"But he wants me to dine with him in his own quarters," Emily reiterated, then bit the tender pulp that lined the inner curve of her lower lip in an attempt to steady her rapidly thudding heart. Just the thought of being alone with Randall in his room put her in such a state of turmoil she could hardly swallow. She had a hard enough time keeping her senses about her when they were out among the other passengers; she could imagine what she would be like all alone with him. "It would be different if his invitation had been to dine in the main dining room, but it wasn't. He wants me to come to his *private* quarters." She stressed the word private, not yet sure Josephine understood the significance.

"You aren't thinking of turning him down are you?" Josephine's eyebrows vaulted skyward to form narrow points above her pale green eyes, as if she could not imagine such tomfoolery.

"Shouldn't I?" Emily looked to Josephine with a perplexed expression. After all, dining alone with an unmarried man in his *private* quarters went against everything she'd been taught about propriety at Miss Boswell's School for Young Women.

"All I can tell you is what I'd do," Josephine said with a slight shrug of her silk-clad shoulders as she leaned toward a mirror to better examine the shape of her kohl-painted eyes. She then glanced at Emily's eyes as if annoyed that the younger girl did not need to add color to her lashes to bring out their beauty.

"And what is that?" Emily asked, eager to know. She trusted Josephine's judgement.

"I'd go and enjoy myself to the fullest. After all, how many opportunities does a young woman have to share an evening alone with a man like Randall Gipson?"

"But what will the other passengers think?"

Again Josephine shrugged. "Most of them will probably think what a lucky girl you are to have interested such an attractive man. Besides, what do you care what those people think? They are all strangers to you. Tomorrow, after we've docked in Galveston, you will probably never see any of them ever again. Galveston is a large city, the largest in all of Texas. What few passengers don't head inland on the next train north will be lost in the multitude."

"I suppose that's true. Still, gossip has a way of spreading. I really do have my reputation to consider." In the back of her mind, she could see Miss Boswell's condescending frown. The headmistress would not approve of Josephine's views at all.

Still studying her reflection in the mirror, Josephine picked a fleck of black out of the corner of her eye, then tilted her head to examine herself from a different angle. Finally, she stopped her close scrutiny and turned to look directly at Emily. "Would it make you feel better if I gave up my dinner plans and joined the two of you instead?"

"Would you? Do you think Mr. Gipson would mind?" Emily asked, unable to force herself to call him by his given name the way he wanted.

"Yes, probably. But I'm sure, if I explain the situation carefully, he'll understand. I'll go have a word with him right away."

"You will?" Emily was so relieved, she sighed aloud. Though dining alone with a man might be considered acceptable in the South, the thought of having to spend an entire evening alone with anyone as handsome and as desirable as Randall Gipson made her stomach knot. Besides, what would she ever think to say to him in all that time. "I'd be forever grateful."

Josephine smiled indulgently then headed immediately for the door. "Prepare to don your prettiest dress. I'll be right back."

As soon as Josephine had left the room, Emily turned to the small wardrobe chest fastened to the narrow wall opposite her bunk and examined the dresses hanging there. How would she ever decide which was her *prettiest* dress? They were all so lovely.

While she carefully weighed the advantages and disadvantages of each garment, an eternity slowly passed. Finally, Josephine returned, bearing a wide, satisfied smile. She did not speak until she had stepped inside and closed the door.

"It's all set, my dear. After I explained your misgivings to him, I was promptly invited to share dinner with the two of you. You won't have to worry about any gossip now, because I will be there the entire time. But, I did promise to make myself scarce later, when the time comes for him to escort you back to your cabin."

Emily's eyes widened with alarm. "But why?"

"Oh, come now. *Why* do you think?" Josephine's eyes rolled heavenward as if unable to believe anyone could be so naive. "The man wants to be alone with you. Although I'm not too sure what the proper rules are up North, let me assure you that in the South there's nothing wrong with sharing a little stroll in the moonlight while on board a passenger ship."

"Alone?" she repeated breathlessly. She felt momentarily weakened under the onslaught of a floundering pulse beat. "Just the two of us? Together? In the *moonlight?*"

Though they had shared several moments alone over the past few days, never had those meetings been intentional, at least not on her part. And never had these accidental moments alone occurred at night—much less out in the moonlight.

"Oh, I seriously doubt that you'll be completely alone," Josephine hurried to assure her. "On a ship this size there are almost always other people around. And if it's conversation you're worried about, don't be. Just keep him talking about himself and you'll do fine. You'll discover that most men love any opportunity to brag about themselves or their work."

That sounded like good advice. Keep him talking. "Then you think I should agree to have dinner with him."

"You already have. I told him we'd be there promptly at seven," Josephine announced with an offhanded toss of her shoulders while she returned her grip to the door latch. "I'll be by for you a few minutes before. But I'll send Constance over earlier to help you look your best." Then, before Emily could find another reason to protest, she opened the door and was gone.

Emily spent the rest of the afternoon preparing for their dinner engagement. While she soaked in the scented bubble bath Josephine had ordered for her, Constance carefully crimped and curled her hair a small strand at a time until it lay in a thick mass of tiny ringlets that fell to the middle of her back.

Although she had several colorful outfits from which to choose, each bringing out a different aspect of her own natural coloring, she eventually selected the white linen with pink trim—mainly because it had a higher neckline than some of the others. Her theory was that by covering as much of her charms as possible, she might finally manage to divert his gaze to more respectable areas of her body. And with that same objective in mind, she also chose not to wear her mother's ruby necklace or the elegant choker Josephine had wanted to loan her. The less she wore to draw his attention to any area below her chin, the better.

At precisely eight minutes before seven, Josephine knocked at Emily's cabin door. The sound startled Emily far more than it should, bringing her out of her chair with a jump.

Because Emily had finished dressing twenty minutes too early, she'd had plenty of time to consider the frightening prospect of later being alone with Randall in the moonlight. And the more she'd thought about it, the more apprehensive she'd become. If it had not been for Josephine's calm, reassuring manner, she might have called the whole engagement off, even before it began. Never had she felt so utterly terrified—and she wasn't even sure what it was about him that frightened her so. Yet it was with profound courage that she accompanied Josephine up to the main deck, across to the front of the ship, then down a second flight of narrow steps that led to Randall's rooms.

"Good evening, ladies," Randall stated as soon as he'd opened the small door leading into his quarters. He then offered a gallant bow and stepped back to allow them entrance. "My, don't you both look lovely."

Upon entering the small sitting room, Emily's attention became equally divided between the elegance of their surroundings and the elegance of the man himself. As was Randall's custom in the early evenings, he wore a dark blue fashionable cutaway tailored to fit his broad shoulders comfortably. Beneath it he wore a shirt so white it made his startling blue eyes and his suntanned skin all the more noticeable by contrast.

"Good evening to you, Mr. Gipson," Josephine said when she realized Emily was not prepared to respond to his complimentary greeting. "I hope we aren't late. I do so loathe people who are habitually late."

Randall glanced at the tall Jeffrey clock bolted to the corner of a small writing desk near the back of the room, then smiled. "Right on time."

He then gestured to a small dining table that had been placed in the center of the room. The table, though small compared to the ones in the main dining salon, left very little walking room between the couch or the two armchairs that had been pushed back against opposite walls to make room for the evening's festivities. The table was draped with white linen and set with the finest silver and imported china. The glasses appeared to be crystal.

"Our meal will arrive shortly," he said. "Why don't you ladies make yourselves comfortable." He gestured toward the table.

Starting with Josephine, he quickly pulled out one of the three high-backed chairs and seated her. Next he turned to Emily and offered a most satisfied smile. He took in her appearance a second time while politely leaning over to provide her seating as well. His sultry expression let her know he definitely approved of what he saw.

"I hope you are both hungry," he stated, never taking his gaze off Emily while he slowly lowered his lithe frame into the chair nearest hers. "I've told Sam to bring plenty of everything." He then reached for a small gold cord that hung along one of the inner walls. The cord was securely fastened at the ceiling and disappeared into a small hole in the floor. "Personally, I am as hungry as a lion just setting out on a long night's prowl."

He and Josephine exchanged quick glances, then looked away.

Emily shifted uncomfortably in her chair. "What are we having?"

"Lamb." He then cocked his head to one side and met her gaze straight on before expounding. He sounded almost like a waiter in a fancy restaurant. "Lamb, braised to perfection with a sizable portion of almond rice and buttered green beans."

Why Emily thought of the Sacrificial Lamb at that moment, she was not sure, but it sent icy shivers skittering through her body. Again she shifted her weight in the chair and forcibly turned her attention to Josephine. "I guess after missing lunch the way you did, you are pretty hungry, too." Although she was curious as to why Josephine had not appeared in the main dining area during the noontime meal, she did not bother to ask about her absence. Josephine had a right to her privacy.

"Yes, I am a bit hungry," came a ready response. Josephine wet her lips with the tip of her tongue while a tentative smile played at the outer corners of her mouth. "But I am also exhausted. I'm afraid that as soon as we have eaten, I must deprive myself of your fine company and retire to my room."

Emily's pulse jumped with an alarming force. She'd hoped Josephine would forget her promise to make herself scarce after the meal. "But you don't look tired."

"You are far too kind. The truth is I've been feeling tired all day. I guess I didn't get enough sleep last night."

"But you went to bed at such an early hour," Emily protested. She rested her hand on top of Josephine's, eager to convince her to stay longer. "You retired hours before Constance and I."

Another tiny smile played at the outer corners of Josephine's mouth, as if she were amused by some private thought. "I know, but I just couldn't fall asleep for some reason. And I do want to be fully refreshed when we dock in Galveston tomorrow. I have a bit of shopping I want to do over on Market Street before going on to the house. I'll need lots of energy for that. Market Street is a busy place, especially near the end of the week."

She lifted an eyebrow when she looked at Emily. "You *do* understand why I need my rest, don't you? Tomorrow will be a long and tiring day."

Aware that Josephine fully intended to keep her promise to Randall, Emily closed her eyes briefly. There was little point trying to change her mind. Josephine planned to leave her at this man's mercy. Frustrated, she returned her hands to her lap and clasped them firmly together to keep them from wringing back and forth.

"Yes, of course, I understand," she finally said, forcing a smile. Then, under her breath so that only Josephine might hear, she added, "Only too well."

Josephine pursed her lips out to keep from smiling, clearly amused by the situation.

Admitting defeat, Emily let out a heavy sigh. There would be no getting away from an evening stroll with Randall. Too many people favored it. She was clearly outnumbered.

Knowing that she would indeed have to spend time alone with Randall in such a romantic setting made her bones feel as if they had turned to cold, watery soup. The thought of what might happen during their short stroll caused her heart to flounder.

Again, she could not decide why she was so terribly afraid of being alone in the moonlight with him. He was just one man for heaven's sake. Surely, she could handle one man should he attempt to get out of line with her in some way. And even if she could not handle him herself, she could always scream for help. On a ship as large and as crowded as this one, surely she could convince someone to come to her aid.

With that reassuring thought to calm her, Emily decided to do what she could to push aside all her worries and simply enjoy the delicious meal. It came to them a course at a time, on gleaming silver trays brought in by a burly man dressed all in white. Though Sam moved about with the agility of a much smaller man, his appearance was not what one expected from a waiter and Emily found his odd appearance helped distract her.

But all too soon, the final course was served and as soon as they had finished, Josephine rose from her chair in preparation to leave.

"I'll have Sam escort you back to your cabin," Randall offered, also rising as he reached for the gold cord yet again. "I'd hate for any harm to come to you."

Seconds later the burly servant, whom Emily had come to suspect was a seaman of some sort substituting as a personal waiter, reappeared in the doorway. Josephine quickly offered her hand to Randall for a gentle farewell squeeze. "It was a lovely dinner, Mr. Gipson. I enjoyed it thoroughly."

"The pleasure was all mine," he said, then looked at Emily with a knowing smile. "Or at least it soon will be."

Emily's eyes widened as panic filled her body, setting her heart once again into rapid motion. What had he meant by that remark?

"Don't forget your promise to stop by for a visit before returning to New Orleans," Josephine said then turned toward the door. "We can settle things then."

"I'll see to everything," he promised. That wide, knowing smile of his twitched at the outer corners, as if he'd considered pulling it in but somehow couldn't. "But then a lot of what I do will depend on how long it takes to gather all the information I'll need to carry back with me. Even so, I'll try to come by long enough to settle."

Emily thought that a strange conversation and looked at him quizzically. It sounded like they had made a business arrangement of some sort. She waited to see if they'd discuss it further, but Josephine was ready to leave.

"I'll see you then," Josephine said, dismissing the topic entirely. Then, all too soon, she and Sam left the room, carefully closing the door behind them.

Emily stood beside Randall, still facing the door. All alone. With nothing clever to say to break the sudden silence. She felt as awkward as she did apprehensive. "I—I really should be getting back to my cabin, too. Josephine was right. Tomorrow will be a long and tiring day, especially if she plans to go shopping again."

"Not so tiring for someone as young and vivacious as you," he commented. He turned to face her squarely. When he looked at her then, there was something in his expression that caused Emily to take a tiny step back. He countered with a small step forward. "Why not stay for a glass of wine—or perhaps you'd prefer something a little more spirited to drink."

Emily bristled at the insinuation that he thought she might be the sort to drink liquor. A glass of a light dinner wine was one thing, though she herself hated the taste; but only women of the lowest morals drank strong liquor. Is that what he thought of her? How dare he!

"I don't think I'd care for any," she said.

Though the words themselves had been polite enough, they'd been spoken through tightly clenched teeth in a voice so rigid that it sent chills cascading along the nape of Randall's neck, making him wonder for a brief moment if he'd misjudged her. But then he remembered the company she kept and the seductive way she dressed. Quickly he pushed any doubts aside. "Not even a small glass of brandy?"

Emily paused to take in a long, shuddering breath in an attempt to remain civil. "No. And I'd really prefer to go to my own room."

Thinking that just as suitable an arrangement as any, he quickly agreed. "Of course. Just let me snuff the candles and turn out the table lamps so we can be on our way."

Soon the room was cloaked in utter darkness. Afraid Randall might try to take unfair advantage of that darkness, especially if he thought her the sort of woman who would partake of hard liquor, Emily immediately felt for the door latch and quickly jerked the door open. Snatching up her voluminous skirts in the same instance that the door swung back and bumped against the metal stop, she stepped over the raised doorway and well into the narrow corridor. She did not turn back to face him until she was certain of her safety.

"Are you ready?" she asked, her voice indicating none of the alarm that had propelled her from the room with such haste.

"And willing," he responded, looking perplexed as he glanced back into the darkened room to see what might have frightened her. He'd thought she would at least have allowed him a quick sample of what was to come before heading over to her cabin, if for no other reason than to keep him interested. Perhaps she was more eager for them to reach her room than she had first let on. He smiled at the thought and glanced once again at her tempting curves. "Shall we?"

When he then extended his arm to her, Emily hesitated but eventually accepted. She steeled herself for the onslaught of fluttery sensations she knew would follow while she quietly slipped her arm around his and allowed him to escort her toward the small stairway that led to the main deck.

Again apprehension filled her heart, making it difficult to keep an even pulse beat. Though she did not quite understand her own body's reactions to something so simple as two arms touching, she could not deny that she had suddenly been overcome by a variety of unfamiliar sensations. She was not too sure how to handle all the different emotions that had suddenly burst to life inside her. Nor did she have an idea of what she might do to lessen the danger she felt. Then she remembered Josephine's advice. Keep him talking.

Nervously, she wet her lips and considered what she might say to launch a lengthy conversation. "I understand you are a part owner of Southwind Shipping. My, but that must keep you very busy."

Thinking that a clever choice of topics, she prepared to hear all about the many duties and about the important responsibilities that went along with being the owner of such a large shipping company.

"Pretty much," he answered simply and let it go at that.

Emily frowned when he turned out to be not quite as eager to talk about his work as most men. She'd have to think of something else. Next, she decided to center the conversation around himself and his family. Anything that might preoccupy his mind during their short stroll to her room.

"Josephine also mentioned that you live right there in Galveston, yet judging by your accent you can't possibly be a true native of the South. Where did you live before coming to Texas?"

"In New Orleans for a while. But I suppose the reason I don't have a very strong Southern accent is because I spent so much of my youth in New Hampshire. You don't run into many Southerners in New Hampshire."

Emily gave an inward sigh of relief. She'd evidently found something he was willing to discuss. "You're originally from the North then. What made you want to move to New Orleans?"

"I didn't. My father did. It was a couple of years before the war finally broke out and long before the railroad had taken any real foothold in the South. My paternal grandfather had started a small shipping company in Louisiana that prospered a lot faster than anyone could have anticipated, which meant Grandfather soon needed his two sons to move to New Orleans and help him run it. And being barely thirteen at the time, I had no choice but to follow," he told her. "I later moved to Galveston as a favor to my grandmother."

At that moment they reached the narrow staircase that rose to the main deck, but rather than release Emily's arm and allow her to ascend first, as she'd expected, he pressed closer so they could climb the narrow stairs together. They were so close her skirts brushed against his pant leg everytime she took a step up.

He waited until they were on deck before he resumed their conversation. "What made you decide to come to Galveston?"

Not eager to discuss her personal problems with a man who was little more than a stranger to her, she answered with what seemed like a plausible answer. "I've come looking for work." Which she decided was true enough because she'd have to find a way to support herself until she finally located her grandmother.

Randall nodded as if he understood. "Well, you should find plenty of that in Galveston. The opportunities for a girl like you are endless."

Emily glanced at him curiously. She wasn't so sure she liked the way he'd said that, but decided she was being overly sensitive. Probably because all her emotions seemed oddly intensified whenever he was around.

"I certainly hope that proves true," she commented, aware that the only opportunity she truly cared anything about was the one that would finally allow her to be united with her missing family. "I've come a long way."

Feeling suddenly melancholy, worried what the future might bring, she paused near the railing and stared out across the moonlit ocean. A light breeze tugged at her hair while her thoughts drifted beyond the gently rolling sea to frightful images of what might happen to her if she was unable to locate her grandmother.

Unaware of the reason Emily had chosen to stop, yet fully aware that there were no other people milling about on deck at such a late hour, he decided the opportunity perfect and reached out to cup her chin with his long fingers. Gently, he turned her face toward him.

Afraid he might read her thoughts and know her

worst fears, which would make her feel even more vulnerable than she already felt whenever she was around him, Emily lowered her lashes to prevent him from seeing into her eyes. She did not know he might misread the action as an unspoken invitation to take a kiss.

For a brief moment Randall merely studied her upturned face in the moonlight, wondering about the strange allure she held for him. Everything about this young woman attracted him. She was absolutely breathtaking—from her thick mane of shimmering brown hair to her full, sensuous lips. Lips that parted and beckoned. Unable to resist the temptation a moment longer, he bent forward to sample the tantalizing sweetness he knew he'd find there.

Emily's eyes flew open the instant she realized what had happened. At first she was too stunned by the hungry pressure to pull away and by the time the thought of escape finally occurred to her, she had already started to enjoy the unfamiliar feelings that had burst to life within her. She was no longer sure escape was exactly what she wanted. Everything was happening too quickly for her to have time to sort through her emotions. The unexpected kiss had created a strange, warm, beckoning sensation somewhere beneath her breast. The feeling had quickly spread to every part of her body, and was now attempting to take possession of all her senses. Immediately aware of the danger, her heart sounded an alarm, but the warning went unheeded. All the resulting rush of blood did was to leave her light-headed and short of breath.

She had never before experienced anything like the tingling warmth that had so quickly overtaken her and the sheer intensity of it frightened her. It continued to grow even stronger. Yet she did not find the resulting sensations altogether displeasing. If the truth be known, Randall's was the most pleasurable kiss she'd ever experienced, limited though her experience might be.

Still she knew she should pull away and she lifted her hands to his shoulders with every intention of pushing the two of them apart. But when she pressed her hands against the hard plain of his chest, he moaned from somewhere deep within his throat and moved closer still, leaving but a scant inch between their bodies.

Not at all the result she'd expected.

In an effort to make her intentions more clearly known, Emily flattened her hands against the rounded muscle and pressed harder. But instead of letting go as she'd presumed he would, he continued to hold her chin imprisoned within the strong curves of his fingers. He quickly slid his other arm around her waist and drew her body into hard, direct contact with his. The resulting jolt to Emily's already muddled senses left her feeling unexpectedly weak around the knees, so weak she had to lean against him to steady herself—which only made matters worse.

Aware that her breasts were pressed firmly against his chest in a most intimate manner, her blood raged throughout her body, leaving her frantic for some sort of release. Desperate to save herself from the onslaught, she tried to collect her thoughts. She needed to reason through all that was happening to her, but her thoughts only scattered more. The feelings Randall had so abruptly aroused within her were far stronger than any she'd ever experienced. Frighteningly so.

Then, when the hands she had placed on his chest to aid in her escape suddenly relaxed of their own volition and eased upward to explore the taut muscles along his strong, corded neck, she knew she was in serious trouble.

Slowly, the strange, tumbling warmth collected inside the more intimate recesses of her body, and an unfamiliar hunger grew forth. It was an emotional awakening so strong, so completely overwhelming, that it rendered Emily momentarily helpless—it made her *want* to be helpless. That in itself was terrifying, but there was nothing she could do about it. The beckoning sensation that had so quickly invaded her soul already held her well within its power—urging her to surrender to her newly awakened needs. Any desire she may have had to escape had weakened until all that remained was an unexplainable need to explore these alien sensations further.

Although her strongly moralistic upbringing dictated that she make another attempt to free herself from this madness—before it was too late—her body refused to obey. Even when his hand left her chin to trail lightly across her shoulder then down her back until his palm came to rest on the soft curve of her hips, she was unable to push him away.

His mouth was far too maddeningly sweet, too alarmingly hungry; and as the kiss slowly deepened, she became so lost in his wondrous magic that she hardly noticed his hand moving away from the curve of her hip and slowly working its way up her rib cage.

Still, a small part of her continued to sense the impending danger. Yet she remained helpless to do anything about it. Even though they stood out on the main deck near the railing in plain sight of anyone who might happen by, she was beyond all hopes of fighting him, whatever his intentions. She no longer had the inner strength, and was too unfamiliar with the passions that had so suddenly overcome her to know *how* to fight them—and, too, she'd become less and less sure they *should* be fought.

It was not until Randall's hand moved to cover her breast and his thumb came into contact with the sensitive peak straining beneath the soft material of her dress that Emily's sanity finally broke surface. The feel of his hand touching such an intimate part of her, coupled with the rising sound of voices off somewhere in the distance, made her realize just how far she had allowed Randall to carry his seduction.

The reality of all that had just happened came crashing down around her, and she pushed against him with all her might, finally breaking his hold.

"Randall, don't Someone's coming!"

Gasping for air, just as stunned by the overwhelming affect of the kiss as she, Randall turned toward the rising sound of footsteps, his expression somewhat dazed. "Well then, I suggest we go somewhere a little more private. Somewhere where we won't be so easily interrupted."

"No," she gasped, outraged as much by her own behavior as his. "I am not as free with my kisses as you seem to think."

Enthralled by the fiery impact of that kiss, and eager to know what other pleasures lay in store, Randall nodded that he understood and fully agreed. A kiss like that deserved a fair price. While drawing in several more needed gulps of air, he reached into his coat pocket and felt for his wallet, but just as his fingers came into contact with the leather binding, he heard someone call his name. Immediately, he recognized Sam's voice and brought his hand back out of his pocket.

"Mr. Gipson, come quick. There's trouble brewin' in the gamin' room and we can't find the Capt'n nowhere. I think there's fixin' to be a bad brawl. Bones are sure to get busted if someone don't do somethin' to stop it quick."

Heaving out a curse beneath his breath, Randall scanned the darkened deck until he located Sam's broad frame standing near one of the narrow doorways in the main area below.

"I'll be right there," he muttered, then turned and looked apologetically at Emily. "I'd better get in there and see if I can smooth over some ruffled feathers. I'll try to hurry."

"Please, don't put yourself out on my account," she told him, eager for any opportunity to get away from him. "I'm going on to bed anyway. I'll see you in the morning after we've docked."

"In the morning?" he repeated, perplexed when she then turned and walked quickly away. It was obvious he'd been dismissed for the rest of the evening.

After a kiss like that?

Frowning, he wondered what he'd done wrong, but he had no time to worry about it at the moment. He'd have to see to the trouble in the gaming room first.

Chapter Five

Bewildered and mortified by what had just happened, Emily quickly slammed the heavy security bolt into place then pressed her back against the cold surface of the cabin door. Although the room was pitch black and she could not make out as much as the shape of her own nose in front of her, her eyes were stretched to their limits. Her breath came in short, raspy gasps. Having lived such a sheltered life, Emily was both baffled and terrified by the unexpected yet undeniable response she had felt to Randall Gipson's kiss.

Never in her wildest imaginings had she believed a mere touching of lips could hold such mesmerizing power. Suddenly, those silly romantic novels she and Carole Jeanne had read on the sly did not seem so silly. Aware now that those stories had been based on true life—true emotions—the heroines in those novels no longer seemed to be such mindless ninnies. How astonishing to discover that those powerful emotions not only existed, but had hidden away inside her very own breast all these years.

It staggered the mind and weakened the knees. She desperately needed to sit down and think. Or perhaps it might be better to put the incident out of her mind entirely. Maybe she should simply go on to sleep and pretend none of it had ever happened. But that would be asking the impossible. Her heart pounded with far too much force to consider sleep. No, it would be better to face the problem straight on—and find out why Randall Gipson had triggered such a wild response inside her.

If she wanted to prevent such a thing from ever happening again, she had to understand how it had happened to begin with. But what had happened was still too confusing, too new, too overwhelming, to allow her to think clearly. It amazed her she could think at all.

Why was it that whenver Randall Gipson was around she immediately regressed to the level of a mindless idiot? What about him made it so difficult for her to think properly? It was obvious he possessed some strange, forbidden magic that had prevented her from pushing him away sooner, but how did one fight against such powerful magic?

So many questions. So much she didn't understand. Where could she find the answers? Maybe Josephine knew. That was the solution. It had to be. She'd ask Josephine.

Emily quietly reopened the door and peered cautiously into the narrow corridor. She wanted to be certain Randall had not changed his mind and followed her. Once assured the corridor was empty, she lifted her slippered foot high over the raised doorway, then hurried to Josephine's door. When she raised her hand to knock, she heard a girlish giggle come from within and was relieved to know her friend was still awake.

Glancing in both directions, relieved to discover she was still alone, Emily tapped on the wooden door just loud enough to be heard inside. There was no response. She knocked again, this time calling softly through the door, "Josephine, it's me. Are you awake?"

When there still came no response, Emily decided she must not have heard a giggle after all. She must have imagined the playful sound. Rather than try Constance's door, knowing how dearly the young maid loved her sleep, Emily decided her questions could wait until morning. Eventually she returned to her room, doubting her sanity all the more while she prepared for bed.

Although she managed to drift in and out of sleep through the remainder of the night, by the time Constance knocked on her door early the following morning, Emily felt physically exhausted and had early indications of a headache. While she hurried to dress, careful to choose a demure pale blue traveling outfit, a man tramped through the corridor, knocking loudly at every door, calling out again and again that the ship would dock within the hour.

Worried she might encounter Randall again if she left her cabin too early, Emily decided to skip breakfast, though it was to be the final meal of their trip and possibly the last meal she'd be offered until evening. Her excuse to Constance and Josephine when they stopped for her was that she still had some last minute packing to finish.

When she finally did emerge from her room an hour later, she did so with conflicting emotions. A tiny part of her actually wanted to cross paths with Randall again before departing the ship, if for no other reason than to have another glimpse of his handsome face. Yet a much stronger part of her was still too mortified by what she'd allowed to happen the evening before. It was that part of her that prayed she would be spared the humiliation she would surely suffer if she had to face him again. It was that same fear of humiliation that prevented her from discussing the matter with Josephine after all. Emily decided the dilemma was something she would have to work out on her own.

Because Josephine and Constance had done most of their packing the evening before, they returned from breakfast with three stewards ready to carry their trunks up to the deck. The ship had finally docked and Josephine was as eager as Emily to be on her way. But to Emily's dismay, when they stepped out onto the deck, they discovered most of the other passengers were just as eager to leave the ship as they.

Because there were so many passengers demanding to have their belongings brought out on deck, their trunks were not carried off the ship and set on the docks as Emily had hoped. Instead, they were piled into a heap in the middle of the sun-washed deck and immediately abandoned.

Before heading back down for another passenger's baggage, one of the stewards assured them someone would see that their trunks were carried ashore as soon as possible. Yet it was hours before that someone appeared. By then, Emily's headache had grown to mammoth proportions and her nerves were frazzled from the worry that Randall would discover her hidden in among all the other passengers. She feared he might make some brash comment about what had passed between them the night before, and Josephine would know her shame. Yet, probably because of the large number of people milling about, waiting impatiently for their baggage to be transported off the ship, she was spared the humiliation. He never found her.

By the time their trunks had finally been carried ashore and deposited in another disorderly pile on a wharf near the offices of Southwind Shipping, Emily was in no mood to do any shopping. She was hot, her head pounded with each throbbing beat of her heart, and she started to feel nauseated from the dank smell that clung to the wharves. All she wanted was to go on to Josephine's and collapse in a tub filled with cool water and scented bath salts.

But Josephine proved as eager as ever to stop by some of her favorite shops along Market Street and see what merchandise had come in while she had been gone. She told Emily and Constance to wait with their trunks while she disappeared into the busy crowd and headed toward the street.

Emily watched until all but the top bauble of her jade green parasol had been swallowed from sight. Then, fearing her skull would burst wide open if she didn't find a place to rest, she sank down on top of Josephine's largest steamer trunk, facing the ship at an angle. Knowing she suffered from too little sleep and too much sun, she pulled off her wide-brimmed hat and used it as a fan. The gentle ocean breeze she had felt when they'd first stepped out onto the deck, and later when they'd come down the gangplank, could no longer be felt. Too many people crowded the wharf, effectively blocking the wind's path.

Thinking the heat the most miserable she had ever endured, Emily looked skyward. She hoped to spot an approaching cloud, anything to offer a moment's respite, but was further disappointed. There was hardly a patch of white to be seen in the pale blue expanse overhead. Sighing wearily, she lowered her gaze, letting it rest first on the ship's flag, then on the upper railing of the ship. She felt an alarming leap of her senses when she noticed Randall standing near the edge, scanning the crowded docks below.

Worried he might see her and decide to come ashore and embarrass her, she immediately threw her hat up to cover her face then turned her back to him. Her heart hammered wildly when, seconds later, she gathered the courage to peek back over her shoulder to see if he was on his way. She felt oddly disappointed yet also greatly relieved when she noticed that instead of heading for the nearest gangplank, he had returned to the main part of the ship with Sam at his side.

He had not noticed her after all. Perhaps he had not been looking for her. Perhaps it was merely the activity that had drawn his attention to the docks below.

Even so, it was several minutes before Emily regained a smattering of control over her scattered senses. Her rapid pulse finally slowed to a more normal rate but with as much force as ever. She closed her eyes against the resulting pain near the back of her head as she plopped her hat back in place and slowly massaged her temples with her fingers.

Eventually, Josephine returned with a tall, stocky man at her side. Emily pushed herself away from the trunk and stood to the side. Josephine pointed out which trunks were theirs and crossed her arms impatiently while he bent to pick up the closest of the lot.

"You wouldn't believe how hard it was to find a cab that hadn't already been taken," Josephine grumbled while she waited for the man to heave the trunk high over his shoulder. "Seems two other passenger ships docked at almost the same time ours did, which means all the cabs are suddenly in great demand and are being taken by the highest bidders."

"How much did you have to pay?" Emily asked, though it was really none of her business. She lifted her hand to her temple and pressed lightly against the pain.

"Two dollars!" Josephine responded in a loud voice, as if she wanted to make certain the cabbie heard her. "Outrageous."

The cabbie hefted a second trunk onto his strong back, turned, and headed immediately toward the street. Josephine huffed loudly, then indicated Emily should follow. "I want you stay with the trunks that get left in the cab while Constance watches over the ones still on the wharf. You just never know what sort of riffraff is waiting to pick your belongings clean."

Glad to have a reason to be further away from the ship since Randall would have a harder time seeing her should he return to the railing, Emily followed willingly. As they moved away from the crowded docks, past the shipping offices, and headed toward the street, she felt wisps of air brush past her heated skin. Soon, she stood beside the odd-looking carriage, which was half surrey, half dray, while the man hoisted the two trunks into place.

Emily climbed onto one of the tattered passenger seats and leaned back into the cool shade provided by a sagging canopy. While waiting for the cabbie and Josephine to return with more baggage, her attention was slowly drawn to the bustling activity around her.

Galveston was certainly a busy place.

Although the center of activity lay along the main wharves where cargo was constantly being loaded and unloaded with the use of stout, overhead cranes, the nearby streets teamed with a constant flow of traffic. Freight wagons, carriages, coaches, streetcars, drays, as well as men, and even women, riding horseback all moved along the street at a frantic pace. Nearby, along the raised brick sidewalks, barkers noisily hawked their wares while children and stray dogs darted in and out of the steadily moving throng of pedestrians. Meanwhile, sour-looking cabbies covered with dust and sweat hurried to load their carriages, eager to be on their way. Everywhere Emily glanced, large white seagulls swooped down in small groups of five or six to steal scraps of food which had been tossed out onto the street, or to capture unsuspecting insects, filling the air with their raucous laughter.

Galveston was different from any seaport Emily had ever visited, though she wasn't sure exactly what it was that made it seem so different. Perhaps it was the high level of activity along the docks even during the midday heat, or possibly it was the heavy feel of the gulf breeze against her skin, or it might even be something as simple as the fact that the land did not rise sharply from the gulf, but instead lay flat for as far as she could see. But whatever the difference between this port and any others she'd visited, Emily clearly sensed it.

"You ready?" Josephine asked, breaking into her roving thoughts.

Emily turned to her, startled. She had not noticed her return.

Although Josephine had spoken to Emily, her attention remained centered on the cabbie who busily loaded the last of their belongings into the back of the odd-looking vehicle. As soon as Josephine was certain their trunks were secure, she snapped her parasol closed, tied the sash around it, and quickly climbed up onto the seat beside Emily. That left Constance no choice but to take the seat beside the cabbie, which obviously did not please the cabbie one bit. He scowled with obvious disgust when he realized the black woman intended to sit in the front seat beside him, but said nothing since the baggage area of his rig was already filled beyond normal capacity.

Emily shook her head at the show of such prejudice, but she knew the man had a right to his own opinion—no matter how foolish. Then she wondered what Constance thought of having to sit beside such a foul-smelling man. She hoped that the ride to Market Street would prove to be a short one, for both their sakes.

When the cab stopped only a few minutes later in front of the ornately painted dress shop Josephine and Constance had raved so about, Josephine reached for her parasol and politely nudged Emily with her elbow. "You'll simply love Dorothy's shop. She specializes in all the latest European and New York fashions."

Aware the time had come to disembark, though no more eager to spend the next few hours shopping than before, Emily gathered up her handbag and stepped down, automatically stretching her arm out for balance. Though they had been ashore for almost two hours, she still felt the gentle pitch of the ocean beneath her feet.

"How long do you think we'll be here?" she asked then turned to watch while Josephine stepped from the cab, adjusting her skirts just so, and hooked the loop of her parasol over her wrist.

"I'm not sure how long it'll take. Sometimes there's so much to see that I am here for hours," she commented as she waved the cab on, with Constance still perched on the front seat. "And right next door is another shop owned by Shelly Sanford. I'll want to stop in there before we head back. She always has the daintiest underthings. Perfect for these hot summer afternoons."

Emily wasn't that interested in purchasing any more dainty undergarments. She was curious to know why Constance had not come with them. Watching while the cab disappeared into the main flow of traffic, she commented, "I thought Constance would be coming with us."

"Not this time," Josephine answered with a sulky expression. "That stubborn cabbie flat refused to wait while we shopped. Too many high-priced fares to be made on a busy day like today. So, I asked Constance to ride along with him to be sure he delivers our trunks to the correct address. Besides, I want her to see to it I have a bath waiting and that everything is all set for the party tonight."

"Party? What party?" Emily's shoulders felt weighted by the sheer thought of having to endure a party. All she wanted was to take a long, cool bath and go straight to bed.

"Didn't I tell you?" Josephine asked, glancing at her questioningly before she headed toward the shaded entrance. "I always have a big party whenever I come back from a long trip. I'm always so eager to see all my friends again that throwing a party whenever I return seems the perfect solution. But tonight I have a special reason to look forward to such a party. Tonight I'll get to introduce you, my new best friend, to all my other dear friends. I can hardly wait for everyone to meet you." She smiled then reached out and patted Emily's arm reassuringly. "They'll love you."

Emily felt all warm inside as she followed Josephine into the lavishly decorated dress shop. Her friend's words made her feel wanted again, something she desperately needed after the cold rejection she'd suffered at the hands of her cruel stepmother. She was grateful to Josephine for everything she'd done for her, and if Josephine wanted her to attend a party that evening and meet some of her friends, then she would do just that.

She could tolerate her throbbing head a while longer—if it meant repaying Josephine for the many kindnesses she'd shown her during the past few weeks.

Upon entering the shop, Josephine headed straight for the back where the ready-made dresses hung in a wide assortment of colors along a tall, metal rack that ran the entire width of the store. Two women standing near the front glanced up after they had entered and to Emily's surprise promptly turned up their noses, laid aside the merchandise they had held in their hands, then hurriedly marched out of the shop.

Emily had watched them go with such a perplexed expression that Josephine felt it necessary to offer an explanation. "That was the Widow Murphy and one of her closest friends. They don't like me." But she offered no reason why. Instead, she turned to greet the proprietress—a tall, willowy woman who was all too pleased to see her.

"Miss Bradley, I've been hoping you would come in," Dorothy said, already thumbing through the many dresses hanging from the rack. "I've just recently received a new shipment of gowns from New York that I think you are going to love."

Not at all interested in purchasing anything for herself, Emily noticed a pair of silver and pink upholstered chairs nearby and quietly eased herself into one. Leaning her head against the padded back, she watched while Dorothy pulled dress after dress off the hangers and handed them to Josephine, who held them high into the air to study them.

"Oh, look Emily," Josephine exclaimed, clearly delighted by what she saw. "This one would be perfect for you. It's just your color!"

Emily eyed the bright red dress doubtfully. "I

hope you don't plan to buy anything else for me. You have already done far more than you should."

"Oh, please, let me buy this dress for you." She set aside the other dresses so she could take the red one over for Emily to have a closer look. "Consider it a favor to me."

"Perhaps she would like to try it on," Dorothy put in, clasping her hands together, clearly eager to make the sale. "I'm sure that once she sees how it fits, how beautifully the boning in the dress lifts the bustline into a most fetching profile, she'll be pleading with you to buy it for her."

"Yes, try it on," Josephine agreed, still hoping to persuade her. "If it fits, you must have it." Then, even though Emily had yet to agree, she turned back to Dorothy. "Show her where the dressing rooms are. While she's trying on this gown, I want to try the emerald one."

Rolling her eyes skyward in a gesture of defeat, Emily pressed against the arms of the chair, pushing herself up with a low, guttural moan. She then followed Dorothy into a small corridor at the very back of the building. Along one side of the hallway stood three doors. Each led into a small dressing room furnished with a wooden chair and two floor length mirrors.

Emily stepped inside the first room and waited for Dorothy to finish undoing the many buttons along the back of the shimmering red gown before asking that she be left alone to dress. Dorothy appeared rather startled by her modesty, but gladly complied. "I'll wait right outside. Call if you want help with the buttons."

Before Emily could quite squirm her rounded curves into the tight-fitting gown, Josephine popped into the room unannounced, a red velvet choker draped across her open palm.

"I think this will look perfect with that dress," she commented, then proceeded to slip the choker around Emily's slender throat and tied it in place. When she noticed Emily had not finished with the buttons, she shook her head and immediately took over, giving the material sharp tugs to bring it together in back. "Here let me help you."

The dress had already felt tight, but by the time Josephine finished with the last button, Emily could barely breathe.

"That dress looks as if it had been made for you," Josephine commented then stepped back to have a better look. "You will be the envy of every woman at the party tonight."

Emily arched a disbelieving eyebrow and ran her hands over the tight fit of the bodice. "Don't you think it is a little too small for me?"

"Small?" Josephine asked, clearly perplexed by such a suggestion. "Why I've never seen a better fit."

Emily glanced into the mirror, her expression doubtful. "But I can barely breathe." Her eyes widened when her gaze fell on the low neckline. Whether it was the upward push of the boning along the front of the bodice or the fact that there was simply not room inside the gown for all that flesh, the dress definitely uplifted the bustline—uplifted it right out of the dress. Emily feared there was more of her spilling out of the garment than remaining in it.

"Oh, you'll learn to take smaller breaths," Josephine insisted, then smiled proudly as she grasped her by her shoulders. "You look so beautiful in that dress. You must wear it tonight."

"I don't think I'd feel very comfortable wearing this dress in front of all your friends," she answered, running her hand nervously over the exposed flesh.

"You'll feel a lot more comfortable once you've learned to take those shorter breaths I mentioned," Josephine assured her, misunderstanding what Emily had meant by uncomfortable. She then called out to Dorothy, who still waited patiently in the hall. "Come take a look. This dress is perfect. You won't have to make any alterations at all."

Emily turned toward the door, hoping Dorothy would explain to Josephine that the dress was far too tight. But instead, Dorothy pressed her hands against her cheeks and nodded enthusiastically. "Yes, yes, that dress was made for her. Look at how the color highlights her cheeks."

"You don't think it is a little too—daring?" Emily asked, bewildered by their insistence that the dress was perfect.

"Oh but that's the latest style," Josephine quickly assured her, then turned to Dorothy for verification. "Isn't it?"

"Oh, yes, the very latest," the eager proprietress responded, bobbing her head.

Rather than argue further, when it was clear that Josephine's mind was already set, Emily sighed with resignation and agreed to let her friend purchase the dress. Though she truly hated the garment, for it was too flashy and exposed far more of her breasts and ankles than she cared to have exposed, she would wear it to the party—for Josephine's sake. After everything Josephine had done for her since they'd met, Emily decided she could suffer the embarrassment of wearing the gawdy dress for a few hours. Besides, she could always wrap herself in a lightweight summer shawl. And there was one other consolation—Randall Gipson wouldn't be at the party to gawk at her. Or would he? She shuddered to think what his already low opinion of her would become if he happened to see her in such an outrageous outfit.

Her cheeks stained a high color at the thought. Quickly she tried to rid herself of the images that had come to mind, images of what Randall's expression would be were he allowed to see her in that dress—or see how much of her was *not* in that dress. No, it was definitely something she did not want to think about.

The rest of the afternoon passed at a snail's pace. It was nearly four o'clock by the time Josephine had selected her own gown for the evening and purchased a vast assortment of lacy undergarments for both of them at Shelly's next door. By the time they had finally hailed a cab and were headed toward Josephine's house, Emily noticed it was well after four.

Glad to be on their way at last, Emily said very little during the bumpy ride across town. Instead, she leaned back against the padded seat and turned her attention to the unique designs of the houses they passed.

Each house was built off the ground, some as high as ten feet off the ground, which put them at what Emily thought an awkward level. The stairways that led to a majority of the front verandas included anywhere from twelve to sixteen steps. Most of the windows were braced with brightly painted storm shutters. Though the houses looked a bit odd, perched on stilts the way they were, with open space below the main floor, Emily decided they still looked quite charming. They gave Galveston a special charm all its own.

"I gather by the manner these houses have been built, high off the ground like that, and with storm shutters placed on almost every window, that Galveston is often plagued by heavy storms," she commented aloud when she noticed that even the carriage houses had shutters.

"Yes, every few years a bad storm tends to blow through." Josephine nodded. "And when they do, these houses through here usually get a lot of flood water."

"And do you have a lot of flooding in your neighborhood?" she asked, wondering if Josephine's house stood on pedestals, too.

"No, not as much. Oh, I've had my cellar filled once or twice, but nothing like what they get here. That's why these houses don't even bother with cellars and their main parlors are almost always on the second floor."

"Then your house sits closer to the ground?"

"Oh, yes, much closer, which you shall soon see. The higher the elevation of the land, the closer to the ground you'll find the houses. In fact, over on Broadway, where Randall Gipson lives, there's hardly any reason to raise the houses at all. The floodwaters rarely do much damage in that area. And it's a good thing they don't get much flooding. As large and as expensively built as those homes are, it is better that they sit closer to the ground."

Emily felt her senses leap at the mere mention of Randall's name. All the giddiness and confusion she'd been trying to put behind her returned with sudden force. What was it about that man that made her react so? She closed her eyes and tried to calm the disturbance inside her but was instead met with vivid images of his devilish smile. Was there no getting away from him?

Apparently not.

At that moment, while Emily tried again to free her mind of any thoughts of Randall Gibson, the cab turned sharply to the right and jolted Emily's attention back to her immediate surroundings. When they rounded the corner, they entered into an entirely different style neighborhood.

The housing on this street was more like what Emily considered normal, though the street itself looked a little odd. At some point after having left the wharf area where most of the streets had been laid of durable brick or flat stone, the makeup of the streets had changed drastically. Here the street consisted of small wooden blocks pressed close together and held in place with black tar. Curious to discover more about her unusual surroundings, she was finally able to push all unwanted thoughts of Randall to the back of her mind.

"Which house is yours?" she asked, pleased to find that the further inland they rode, the more prominent the houses and the larger the yards. She'd begun to worry that Josephine might not have room for her after all.

"Next block," Josephine said, nodding in that direction. Mine's the yard with the tall oleander hedge there, near the end of the street.

Emily turned her attention to the narrow carriage drive that entered the hedge row off to one side. She was eager to get her first glimpse of Josephine's house.

"I imagine the first thing you'll want to do is have a long, soaking bath," Josephine commented then reached for the parasol she'd placed on the seat beside her. "Your baggage should already be in your room, waiting for you. Meanwhile, I'll have your new purchases sent on up, although I don't think you should try to unpack everything right away. You'd probably rather rest a little while before dinner. We've put in a pretty long day."

Emily never took her gaze from the driveway that parted the tall hedge while she waited for the cab to turn onto the oyster shell drive that spilled out onto the road. She wondered if the house would prove to be as elegant and as stately as the woman herself.

"Tomorrow will be soon enough for you to start putting your things away," Josephine continued, unaware that she held only a part of Emily's attention. She lifted a hand to repair any errant curls. "For the next few hours I expect you to do nothing more than bathe, eat a good meal, then get dressed for the party. Though I personally will want to be downstairs by eight clock to greet any early arrivals, I won't look for you to be downstairs until around nine."

Emily cut her gaze to Josephine when the first part of what she'd said finally penetrated her straying thoughts. She decided the woman's suggestion that she eat first bordered on the absurd. If she dared put away any food at all before the party, it would be impossible to fit back into that dress. "If you don't mind, I'll wait until after the party to have something to eat."

"Certainly," Josephine said and nodded with understanding. "That will give you more time to rest and then dress. I'll probably wait and eat afterward myself." Then, leaning forward, she clasped her hands together and peered in the direction of her house, her green eyes wide with expectation. "I can hardly wait for you to meet the girls. You are going to love them."

Girls? Emily wondered, startled to learn Josephine had daughters, yet at the same time eager to meet them. Looking toward the drive with increased interest, she sat a little straighter on the leather seat, eager to make the very best first impression possible.

Chapter Six

When Josephine's house finally came into view, Emily was not disappointed. Although the house was not quite as grandiose as her parent's home, where she'd spent most of her youth, it was far nicer and much larger than many of the other homes they had passed since leaving the docks—and far more secluded.

It was obvious Josephine preferred privacy. Not only had the front lawn been concealed from the street by a tall hedgerow of thick, green oleander bushes in front, the backyard had been made just as secluded by the many tall, drooping trees and the lavish, brick-walled gardens that seemed to go on forever.

What impressed Emily most about the garden area was its size. Josephine's property covered nearly an entire block. Back in New York City, where land brought a premium price, only the very wealthy could afford the luxury of a flower garden, much less a tropical garden of such magnitude. She supposed land was as hard to come by here in Galveston, since both cities were built on islands where there was little room for expansion.

She wondered just how wealthy Josephine really

was. And upon remembering how impressed Josephine had been with Randall Gipson's home, she tried to imagine what it must be like. The thought of Randall Gipson sent her stomach into momentary turmoil, but she quickly overcame the strange, fluttery sensation and forced her attention back to her surroundings. A man like Randall Gibson did not deserve even a moment of her thoughts. She had decided he was far too forward and judgmental for her to give him a second thought.

Rather than think about someone so annoying, she studied the beauty of the secluded gardens a moment longer, then turned to look at the house itself, which could best be described as stately. The sprawling wooden structure had two floors, both designed to form a large, four-column pavilion with enormous wings branching off to either side. Each wing looked to house six to eight rooms and sported three more of the tall mason columns that supported the main roof.

The numerous windows and doors stood floor-to-ceiling, flanked by the ever present storm shutters, and all had been painted a rich, deep, cinnamon red. The red offered a colorful contrast to the rest of the house, which had been painted a brilliant white. There were a wide veranda and a deep, second-floor balcony running the width of the house, in both front and back, giving the many rooms of the house the greatest possible ventilation.

Off to one side, set back into a tall grove of trees, was a large carriage house and stable, designed and painted to match the main structure, as were most of the other outbuildings. Nestled in the plush garden area near the back of the property, nearly hidden from view, Emily noticed what appeared to be a large guest house, again painted white with cinnamon red accents.

Emily wondered if that was where she'd stay during the next few days, but she did not have time to worry about it for long because, within seconds of having pulled to a stop near the back of the house, a short, well-rounded young woman appeared from the nearest door and bounded across the lawn to greet them.

"Ah, Patricia, dearest," Josephine said with a warm smile, then stepped down to offer the young woman a quick hug. "I've missed you. How is everyone?"

"We're all doing fine," the young woman answered, her dark eyes bright with excitement, obviously very happy to see Josephine again. Emily noticed a heavy accent of some sort, but could not determine the nationality. "Tina got rid of her problem, thanks to Shirley's tender skills, but had to stay in the bed for three days because of the bleeding. But she's fine now, already back at work, good as ever."

"Glad to hear that." Josephine glanced toward the house briefly then turned her attention to the packages that had been piled haphazardly on the floor of the cab.

"Did you bring me back something pretty?" Patricia asked, wetting her lips while she eyed the many colorful boxes. She looked very much like a small child anticipating Christmas.

Emily studied the young woman with growing curiosity. Though Patricia appeared to be about her own age, maybe a little older, she stood barely five foot tall and looked to be either Mexican or Indian. Judging by her amply rounded figure and her wide, almost homely facial features, the girl was no blood relation to Josephine—yet they obviously cared for each other a great deal. Emily then decided this Patricia was one of Josephine's longtime servants; but then again, the girl did not dress like a housemaid or a cook.

Far from it.

Although it was still afternoon and there were several daylight hours left, the young woman wore a black and yellow silk dressing robe and dainty black satin slippers. Her long brown hair was for the most part uncombed and allowed to hang loose around her shoulders.

Emily lifted an eyebrow while she tried to decide just what Patricia's place in Josephine's household might be. She waited for the two to finish talking so she could be introduced.

"Don't I always bring you something?" Josephine answered with an indulgent smile before she turned to glare impatiently at the cab driver, who had not bothered to climb down from his perch.

When it became apparent that the cabbie intended to offer no help whatever, obviously not expecting much of a tip, Josephine let out an annoyed huff and started to hand several of the larger packages to Patricia. "You know that whenever I take a long trip, I always bring back gifts for everyone. But the gifts I brought this time are packed away inside the trunks I had delivered to my rooms earlier. You'll have to wait until later to see what I've brought you."

While the girl dutifully held out her arms for the packages, she glanced up into the cab and noticed Emily. Her dark brown eyes widened with interest, but she waited until Josephine was finished explaining about the gifts before asking, "Is this the girl Connie has been telling us so much about? The one you befriended on the ship?"

Josephine glanced curiously at the Mexican girl,

then at Emily with sudden realization. "Oh, I'm sorry. Yes, this is Emily. She's come all the way from New York and will be staying here with us for a little while. But then I guess Constance told you that, too."

"*Sí.* She told us to put her in DeAnne's old room." Patricia nodded while she continued to give Emily a quick once-over. "We've already carried her things there and set them inside the door."

"Thank you." Josephine then turned to Emily and finished the introduction. "This, as you have probably guessed, is Patricia. She has the room right next to yours."

"Pleased to meet you," Emily responded with a friendly nod. While she climbed down from the cab and held out her arms, eager to help carry in some of the packages, she wondered more about the other people in Josephine's household. Shirley? Tina? DeAnne? Patricia? How many people lived there? She also wondered why Josephine had not mentioned them earlier.

"Oh, no, I can't have you carrying in anything. You are a guest here," Josephine protested with a decisive shake of her head. "Patricia, where are the other girls?"

"Some are sleeping. Some are already getting ready for tonight," Patricia explained, arching her neck in an effort to peer over the growing bundle of boxes. Her eyebrows dipped questioningly when she then looked at Emily, who remained empty-handed at her side. "But I think Joe Boy is around somewhere. I can call him to help carry in the packages if you want."

"That won't be necessary. There are only a few more. I can carry them myself."

"No, please, you must let me carry something," Emily insisted, feeling awkward to have nothing in her hands but her own handbag while the other girl was loaded down to the point she could hardly see in front of her. "I am certainly not helpless."

Josephine studied the four packages left. "If you insist, here, you may carry the new dress I bought for you to wear to the party tonight."

Patricia's gaze cut to the huge box Josephine held out to Emily, but she offered no comment. Instead she waited to be told what to do with the packages she'd been handed.

"That looks like everything," Josephine commented aloud, shifting the boxes she carried to her left arm while she gave the cab floor a last look. Confident she had everything, she slipped her free hand into her skirt pocket and came out with a coin to pay the cabbie. "Patricia, take those packages inside, then hurry back. I'll want you to show Emily to her room."

"*Sí,*" Patricia commented then hurried off to do as she'd been told.

Emily waited while Josephine paid the cabbie, then turned to walk with her toward the house. "What a lovely home you have. How many people live here with you?" she asked, hoping that sounded far less nosy than if she'd asked how many rooms it had, or who the other girls were, or why an unmarried woman needed such a grand house in the first place.

"Several," Josephine answered. "You'll meet most of them later tonight at the party. Right now, they have too much to do."

Before Emily had time to ask any more questions about the house or the unseen people who lived there, Patricia hurried back out, her unbound bosom bouncing as she ran. Emily wondered what the others who lived there thought of the Mexican girl's scanty attire and decided they had probably learned to live with it.

"After you've shown Emily to her room," Josephine said, breaking into Emily's thoughts, "show her where she can take a long, soaking bath."

"But Ruby is in there right now," Patricia protested as she fell in step with the other two.

"Well, ask her to hurry. Emily hasn't had the luxury of relaxing in a full-sized bathtub in weeks. I'd let her use my tub, but I also plan to take a long, leisurely bath."

"Anything more?" Patricia asked, sounding somewhat perturbed.

"Not at the moment. Just see that Emily is shown where the bath salts and towels are stored. And make sure no one disturbs her while she's bathing. She likes her privacy."

"I'll put a sign on the door," Patricia promised, twisting her mouth to one side. Her eyes narrowed and she fell into an annoyed silence, making Emily feel awkward.

"Oh, and after Emily is all settled in, you might ask Shirley to take her a cup of my special herbal tea. I'll want one, too. It'll help me relax after a very trying day, and it might help ease Emily's headache."

Emily blinked with surprise. She had been so curious about what was going on around her, she had forgotten all about her headache. But now reminded of her pain, she again felt the dull throbbing at the back of her head. She hoped they would hurry with the herbal tea if there was any chance that it would help ease the discomfort.

After they entered the house, which proved to be every bit as elegant on the inside as it had been on the outside, Josephine paused.

"My rooms are here on the lower floor," she explained, gesturing in the direction of the tiled hallway behind her. "Which is where I'm headed right now. Constance should have my bath ready by now. Patricia will show you to your room, which is just up those stairs. I imagine I'll be too busy to check on your welfare before the party begins, but if you need anything, anything at all, just mention it to Patricia or one of the other girls. They'll help you in any way they can."

Sighing tiredly, she then walked off into the wide hallway that led into the east wing.

"Miss Josie," Patricia called out in an urgent voice then followed Josephine a few steps into the hall. She waited until she had turned around. "Before you go, I think I need to mention that I am almost out of sponges. I'll have barely enough for tonight."

Emily's eyebrows rose questioningly. So Patricia *was* a housemaid. But how odd that she would do her cleaning at night. Was that because of the stifling afternoon heat? Was that why everyone was still asleep? Because they did all their work at night, when it was cooler? But, then again, why would a housemaid stay in one of the bedrooms upstairs instead of in servants' quarters at the back of the house? They certainly did things differently in the South.

"I have plenty more sponges," Josephine assured her, glancing uncomfortably at Emily. "As soon as you've shown my new guest to her room and where the upstairs bathroom is, come back down and I'll give you another box."

Emily tilted her head to one side. She thought it a little unhandy that Josephine chose to keep the cleaning supplies in her bedroom of all places, but at the same time she knew it was none of her business how Josephine chose to run her household. It just could be that cleaning supplies had a way of disappearing and Josephine hoped to prevent any further thievery by keeping the supplies under surveillance.

With her sponge problem solved, Patricia hurried back to escort Emily upstairs.

"This is to be your room," she told Emily as soon as she'd entered a large bedroom near the top of the stairs. The room had been decorated all in pink and white and had an unusual number of mirrors.

"As you can see, your belongings are over there," she continued without giving Emily a chance to speak. She waved her hand abruptly toward Emily's trunk and valises. "If you want the trunk moved to somewhere else, just say so. I'll have Joe Boy come upstairs and move it for you."

Emily frowned as she set the dress box on a table near the door. Although Patricia was not exactly hostile toward her, she was not outwardly friendly either. Emily decided to remedy that by making an effort to be extra nice. "Thank you. You are very helpful."

"The bathroom is across the hall," Patricia continued, obviously unaffected by the compliment. Without bothering to look back to make sure Emily had followed, she crossed the hall to a large door and hammered loudly. "Ruby, you had better hurry up in there. Miss Josie's new guest she has arrived and is wanting to take a bath. *Pronto!*"

"I'm hurryin'. I'm hurryin'," came a mumbled response from within.

While waiting for the door to open, Patricia leaned heavily against the frame and crossed her arms over her bosom impatiently. "You'll have to let the water run for a minute or two before you start getting any hot. It has to come from a sun-warmed cistern outside. You'll find the bath salts, soap, towels, and several different kinds of perfumed talcum in the cabinets. If you need anything more, you are to just say so."

When the door opened, Patricia stepped back and out came a young woman with her long brown hair tied into a loose knot at the top of her head and dressed solely in her lacy underwear. Emily tried not to seem startled by the obvious lack of attire. True, it was hot enough to make anyone want to shuck all her heavier clothing; but with men around—and she remembered there was at least one male named Joe Boy—she would think these two would want to wear something more appropriate.

"Well, if you don't need anything more, I'll be on my way," Patricia said as soon as Ruby had toddled off toward a door at the far end of the hall. "I'll see that Shirley brings you the tea Miss Josie wanted you to have."

Within seconds, Emily was alone and feeling decidedly out of place. Things were certainly done differently in the South.

Eager to have that bath and aware she had only a few hours until Josephine's party, Emily returned to her room to find her own dressing robe and slippers, having decided that if the other girls were not bothered by wearing such garments in the hall, she should not be either.

While gathering the necessary things, she noticed how thick the mattress on her bed looked and laid down across it to see if it felt anywhere as comfortable as it appeared. It did. The downy soft pillows, of which there were many, felt wondrous beneath her aching head. Thinking she'd lie there for just a few seconds before treking across the hall to take that bath, she closed her eyes. Next thing she knew, she was startled awake by a sharp knock at her open door.

"May I come in?"

Confused by the fact she'd fallen asleep when she hadn't meant to, Emily sat up and blinked, then glanced at her unexpected visitor. "Yes, of course."

Assured of permission, a tiny black woman with springy white hair and a wide, inviting smile entered. In her hands, she carried a small serving tray that held a steaming cup of tea.

"Where do you want this?"

"On the table beside the bed will be fine," she said, still trying to clear her sleep-muddled brain while she watched the woman set the tray nearby. Though she thought it was a bit too warm to be drinking tea quite that hot, she felt it was indeed a good idea to put something into her empty stomach. She had started to feel weak.

"Miss Josie said I was to stay right here 'side you till you drank that there tea all the way down," the black woman said when Emily did not reach for the cup right away. "She's worried because you ain't had nothin' to eat or drink since yesterday. She's also worried because you had the headache all day. It's not that time of the month for you, is it? Because if it is, I got something' I can put in that tea that slow down the monthlies and help ease the pain."

Pleased that Josephine was so concerned but a little embarrassed by the direction the woman's conversation had taken, Emily assured her she felt fine. Then to oblige her, she scooted across the bed, closer to the table, and lifted the cup into her hands. Even though the tea proved to be more bitter than she'd expected, she quickly drank it down.

"You can tell Josephine that I finished it all," she said with a smile when she set the empty cup back onto the tray. "And be sure to thank her for me."

"Will do," she answered with a brisk nod and quickly removed the tray. "By the way, my name's Shirley. I do all the cookin' around here as well as a little of the doctorin' because I knows a little somethin' about medicine. Miss Josie already told me how you and her won't be eaten' until after the party. So, if there's anythin' special you want me to fix up, just let me know. I can cook just about anythin' that can be th'owed together."

Glad that there was at least one friendly person in this place, Emily laughed. "I'll eat whatever you prepare. As hungry as I am, you'll get no complaints out of me."

"How about curried shrimp with rice? Miss Josie just loves my curried shrimp." She beamed with pride.

Though she'd never had curried shrimp, Emily nodded agreeably. "That will be fine."

By the time Shirley left, the pain in her head had already started to subside, and by the time she'd had her bath, she was so relaxed she wanted to do nothing more than put on a cool cotton gown and go right back to sleep. But she'd promised Josephine she would be downstairs by nine o'clock and did not want to disappoint her. She hurried to put on her new red gown and her black sequin-toed slippers.

After tucking as much of herself into the gown as was humanly possible, she turned her attention to her hair and was still putting the finishing touches to the delicate curls she'd shaped about her face when Patricia entered the room without first knocking. Though a little annoyed by the inconsideration, Emily decided she'd failed to knock because she'd brought another tray. This one held a small porcelain pot and a fresh cup.

"Miss Josie thought you might like another cup

of tea," Patricia explained while she looked around for a place to set the tray. "She's worried about you. Says you haven't had nothing to eat all day."

Pleased by Josephine's continued concern, and only slightly startled by the black lace ball gown Patricia wore, Emily accepted the second cup with a gracious smile. Again, the tea was far more bitter than she liked, but it coated her stomach with warmth and that made her feel better.

Patricia tapped her foot impatiently while she watched Emily drink her tea, making Emily wonder if she'd also been ordered to wait in the room until she had drunk it all. Aware Patricia must have other duties pressing for her time, and not wanting to be a hindrance to anyone, she drank the tea in large gulps then quickly returned the cup to the tray.

As soon as she had set the cup down, Patricia glanced inside to make sure it was empty then nodded toward the clock. "Miss Josie said I should remember to remind you of the time before I leave. Several people downstairs are already wanting to meet you."

Emily glanced once more into one of the many mirrors in the room and decided she'd already accomplished all she could hope to accomplish, as tired as she felt. "I guess I'm ready. Just let me find my shawl and I'll go back down with you."

"Your shawl?" Patricia asked then looked at her as if she'd suddenly grown a second head. "On a night like this? Here I am burning up and you want to wear a shawl?"

Emily lifted her hand self-consciously to the daringly low neckline of her dress, then responded hesitantly, "No, I guess I don't need my shawl after all. I don't know what I was thinking."

She glanced longingly toward her open trunk, but followed Patricia to the stairs without anything to cover her bared flesh. Though Patricia's dress was just as revealing as hers, perhaps more so—because she had more to reveal—Emily still felt extremely uncomfortable. Then, when she gazed down into the crowded room below, she suddenly felt far more than uncomfortable. She felt downright lightheaded, enough so that she had to grip the top post of the bannister to steady herself.

"What's the matter?" Patricia asked, setting the tray on a nearby table.

"Nothing," Emily said, shaking her head to clear the dizziness. "It's just that I'm a little more tired than I realized. Give me a second to catch my breath. I'll be okay."

"Maybe you should have something to eat," Patricia suggested, staring at her with a troubled expression. "Miss Josie will take the skin off of my back if I let you get sick. There's a whole table of refreshments against the far wall. Maybe you should make your way over and eat a sandwich or something."

It was the first evidence of concern Patricia had shown toward her and Emily decided she was finally making headway with her. That alone made her feel better. "Thank you, Patricia, I will. Just as soon as I've met Josephine's friends," she promised. It was then she realized that although she felt a little woozy, her headache was completely gone. The herbal tea had worked. "I'm sure I'll be just fine after I've eaten something."

Taking a deep breath and discovering that helped, she let go of the gleaming post and proceeded slowly down the stairs with Patricia right behind her. She again felt self-conscious about her dress, or lack of it, when she noticed how many heads had turned to watch her descend. She had hoped to enter the room unnoticed.

"Emily!" She heard Josephine before she actually spotted her standing with a small group of men near a wide, open door that led to the outside. It was then Emily realized that the men in the room outnumbered the women at least two, and perhaps three, to one. She wondered if such an odd turnout had made Josephine feel awkward.

By the time she reached the bottom of the stairs and had entered into what appeared to be an elaborately decorated ballroom of some sort, Josephine had left her small group of friends and hurried through the crowd to greet her.

"I was starting to worry about you," she exclaimed when she'd come close enough to be heard over the loud din.

"There was no need for—," Emily started to respond but her words were cut short.

"Come with me," Josephine said, her voice bubbling with exuberance. She still did not allow Emily enough time to respond. Instead, she took her hand and led her toward the group of men she'd just left. "I have so many friends who want to meet you."

Emily glanced back to see what had happened to Patricia, but was unable to locate her in the crowded room. When she turned her head back around to look where they were going, she had another sudden dizzy spell and stumbled slightly. She felt a little like she had that time she and Carole Jeanne had shared that bottle of imported wine Carole's father had sent for her sixteenth birthday. Yet it wasn't quite the same. Still she had trouble judging where to place her feet and stumbled more than once.

"You simply must meet Edward and John Peterson," Josephine insisted, obviously unaware of Emily's predicament while she continued to lead her through to the group of men who stood waiting. "They are very dear friends of mine, especially Edward. I just know you will adore him as much as I do. He's such a special friend."

Emily bumped into a man whose back was turned and her vision blurred temporarily as a result, but when it refocused, she caught a glimpse of the refreshment table, and dearly yearned to go there instead. She was certain a bit of food would help recapture some of her strength, but at the same time knew her duty was to meet Josephine's friends first.

"Here she is," Josephine said in a singsong voice when she and Emily came to a dizzying halt near the four men. "This is Emily."

Although she could not seem to focus on any one face at first, Emily smiled and curtsied politely while Josephine rattled off the names of the men who surrounded her. Aware that the long trip and all the emotional strain she'd suffered during the past few weeks had finally taken its toll, Emily hoped Josephine would not expect her to visit with these men for very long. It took all the concentration she had just to remain standing, and because of that she had a hard time understanding exactly what the men said to her. She saw their mouths move and was aware their gazes were upon her, but the words came to her in a meaningless jumble.

"Would you care for some punch?" one of the men asked, leaning close to her, obviously believing her lack of response was due to the noise around them.

That Emily had understood. "Yes, please. And perhaps a little something to nibble on."

The man immediately disappeared and returned within minutes with two cups of ruby red punch and a small plate filled with tiny sandwiches and cakes. To Emily it looked to be a feast. Eagerly she accepted one of the cups and had to force herself to sip the sweetness instead of gulp it down. Smiling, she tried to seem only politely interested in the food just before she snatched up the largest of the sandwiches and quickly nibbled it away.

The men looked at each other with raised eyebrows, but said nothing while they watched her clear the plate of food.

"Would you care for more?" the same man asked, glancing curiously at the empty plate.

Aware that at some point Josephine had left her alone with these men, Emily wished she could remember what the man's name was so she could thank him properly. But for the life of her she could not. She was too near exhaustion for that.

"No, thank you," she finally responded after she noticed that he stood waiting for her to speak. "I've had plenty." Or at least enough to regain some of her strength. Feeling much better, she found she could finally concentrate on what was going on around her, though she still felt a little light-headed at times.

At least she was again able to remember names when she was later introduced to the others milling about the room. And she was able to keep straight in her mind which of them did what for a living, and that helped to keep the conversation alive. Although she had originally come to the party to make Josephine happy, she was soon having too enjoyable a time to want to leave. She met a lot of fascinating people, so many she had not noticed when Josephine left the room all together.

It was not until Edward Peterson, an older man who reminded her a little of her father, had asked her to take a walk with him out in the gardens so he could get a little fresh air, that she realized she was one of very few women left in the room, and that the number of men had also diminished considerably. Josephine's party was playing out rather quickly.

Also, having noticed that the other ladies present had seen nothing wrong with casual strolls out into the dimly lit gardens, and thinking a breath of fresh air would help her too, she nodded agreeably. "Yes, a stroll out in the garden would be nice. It is awfully hot in here." When he offered his arm to her, she gladly accepted, knowing it would help steady her. She was only vaguely aware of the disappointed expressions of the other men when she turned and allowed Edward to guide her toward the door.

"I imagine you are used to a much cooler climate," Edward commented, glancing back at the other men only briefly before he escorted her through the open door into the backyard.

To Emily, it felt like stepping into utopia.

"Now isn't it far more pleasant out here?" he continued, as if determined to keep their conversation alive.

"Yes, it is," she agreed and tilted her head back so the cool, gulf breeze could soothe her neck. When she glanced back at Edward and noticed how the torchlight highlighted the silver in his hair, she smiled. He so reminded her of her father.

"You are a nice man," she said, and meant it. In fact, he was the only man in that entire room who had not gazed openly at the daring cut of her dress, though she had to admit the dress did invite such brazen behavior. Suddenly she was reminded of the disturbing way Randall Gipson had looked at her the night he'd stolen that kiss aboard ship. Tiny chill bumps scattered across her heated skin.

"I always try to be nice," Edward commented with a pleased smile, then nodded toward the torch-lit gardens. "This way."

While breathing deeply the sweet scent of oleander and honeysuckle, Emily allowed Edward to lead her further into the garden. They walked along the curving walkway in amiable silence for several minutes before Edward glanced skyward and commented, "I wish it weren't so cloudy tonight. I so love to see the stars. Don't you?"

Emily glanced up and noticed that he was right. A thin covering of clouds blocked out the night sky, obliterating both the moon and stars. When she looked back down, she experienced another sharp wave of dizziness and closed her eyes briefly. When she eventually reopened them to see if her head had cleared, she was startled to find that Edward had moved closer, close enough she could feel his moist breath on her cheek.

Feeling awkward about his sudden preoccupation with her lips, she hurriedly took a step back, wishing now that he did not have a hold of her arm.

"Th-the gardens certainly are lovely at night," she said, hoping to distract his thoughts away from her mouth. She glanced around, trying to find something else to comment about, and noticed they stood only a few feet away from the guest house. She was relieved to see light glowing from two of the windows. The light meant someone was close enough to help should she need it.

"Not as lovely as you," he commented quickly, then wet his lips with the tip of his tongue while he continued to stare at hers.

"Mr. Peterson, please," she said, glancing toward the lighted window, wondering if she would be forced to make a scene.

Without speaking another word and without letting go of her arm, Edward leaned to one side, brushing his shoulder against hers as he opened the door closest to them, then in the next instant, pulled her inside and slammed it closed behind them. To her relief, he released her arm, although it made it harder to detect his exact whereabouts in the dark room.

"What do you think you are doing?" she cried, her voice strained with alarm while she turned around and felt for the door handle. Her head spun crazily while she struggled to find a way out. Although she was not sure of his intentions, she was not about to stay and find out.

"Come here, my sweet," Edward murmured then grasped her by the shoulders and twirled her around. Instantly, his mouth covered hers with a hot, damp kiss, making it impossible for her to cry out for help.

Confused and angered by this sudden change in his behavior, she tried to shove him away, but his grip was too tight. Then, when one hand moved to capture her breast, panic set in. Even as muddled as her mind had been that evening, she fully understood that this man was set on raping her.

Twisting her head to one side and fighting the resulting dizziness, she was able to free her mouth long enough to scream for help. She continued to struggle against him, outraged that he would dare do something like that to her, all the while waiting for help to arrive.

"If you don't stop this right now, you'll leave me no choice but to tell Josephine," she threatened, hoping to bring him to his senses.

"And if you don't cooperate like you are supposed to, I'll be the one forced to tell Josie," he said, grunting while he fought to bring her under control.

When help did not come, and the man managed to work his hand into her dress to cup her bare flesh with his trembling fingers, she tried again to shove him away. This time, she thought to kick him in the leg at the same time.

Caught off balance by how quickly he then let go of her, she fell against a nearby table, knocking over a porcelain pitcher in the process, but not breaking it.

When the man grabbed her from behind again, cooing something about the pleasures that lay ahead, she did not stop to think about the consequences. She curled her fingers around the top of the pitcher until she had a tight hold, then swung it with all her might against the side of his head. She immediately felt his grip loosen on her shoulder and watched with a combination of relief and horror while his shadowed form slipped to the ground. Aware that she may have done nothing more than stun him, and not about to wait around long enough to find out the extent of his injury, Emily ran to the door and fled for her life.

Confused and in a wild state of panic, Emily pushed her way through a nearby hedgerow, the branches pulled her hair until it broke free of its pins and fell about her shoulders in wild disarray.

On the other side of the hedgerow she was relieved to discover a narrow alley, lined with oleander bushes on either side. At both ends of the dark alley lay a street. Turning to the left, for no other reason than that the light was brighter there, she continued to run as fast as the confining cut of her gown would allow. Her only goal at that moment was to put as much distance as possible between herself and Josephine's guest house.

When she finally neared the street, she glanced back to make sure the man had not followed her, never slowing her steps. She did not see anyone in the dark shadows that lined the narrow alley. Nor did she see any movement near the bushes. But she also did not see the iron gaslight in front of her—until it was too late.

She hit the wrought iron pole with such force it knocked her to the ground and left her temporarily dazed.

Blinking, she watched with stunned disbelief while the dim light swirled crazily overhead. Aware she had not yet put a safe enough distance between Josephine's guest house and herself, she tried to stand but discovered her legs no longer wanted to hold her weight. Again panic set in.

At that moment, while she tried her best to keep from crying aloud her frustration, a gleaming black carriage pulled to a jangling stop only a few feet away. A man leaped out onto the sidewalk. Within seconds he was at her side, offering his assistance.

"What happened?" an all-too familiar voice asked, clearly concerned with her welfare.

"I didn't see the gaslight," Emily offered feebly as her gaze slowly came to focus on Randall's handsome face. She felt a strong rush of both relief and embarrassment. Why did it have to be him of all people? Why did *he* have to be the one to see her sprawled out on the sidewalk like that?

"Obviously not," he commented, battling an urge to grin yet losing profusely when he reached into his dress coat and brought out a clean handkerchief. Gently he dabbed away a trickle of blood that had trailed down the side of her face, all the while allowing himself an ample view of the womanly flesh the bright red dress so aptly displayed. "Here let me help you."

When he slipped his hands beneath her arms to help her to her feet, his thumbs pressed into the sides of her breasts and Emily's relief turned to alarm. Suddenly she realized she might not be any better off in this man's company than she had been in Edward's. After all, Randall had as much as tried the very same thing. True, he had not used force on her the way Edward had, but his intentions had been almost identical.

Emily's heart raced with a furious force when she remembered what had happened that night aboard his ship and the strange, hypnotic power he'd had over her. Although she'd been able to fight off Edward's unwanted advances, she might not be as successful against Randall. Besides being much stronger and far younger than Edward, he had an odd way of reducing her resistance to nothing.

"Come on." He spoke in a low soothing voice as soon as she regained her footing. "I think you need to sleep this one off. I'll take you back to Josie's."

Frightened at the thought of being forced back into Mr. Peterson's company, afraid of what he might do to her in retaliation, Emily shrieked with alarm and shoved him with all her remaining strength. "No! I won't go back there. You can't make me."

Having been caught off guard, Randall stumbled backward and almost fell. He expression darkened from confusion to instant anger.

Emily's heart pounded painfully against her chest as she spun about to continue her flight. She would not go back to Josephine's. Now now. Not ever!

Frightened beyond reason, she lifted her torn skirts and headed for the street, where there would be no more gaslights with which to contend. But in her haste to escape, she did not see the small crevice that caught her foot at an angle and sent her tumbling forward. She watched as much with annoyance as disbelief when the ground suddenly rose up to meet her. The pain that followed when her chin struck the hard, uneven surface of the wooden street was the last thing she felt before the blissful darkness fell over her.

Chapter Seven

It must have been the combination of the raw pain pulsating at the back of her head and the slanting rays of sunlight across her face that awoke Emily. There were no noises other than a pair of seagulls squawking in the distance, nor was there anyone stirring about in the unfamiliar room. Just her.

Blinking with momentary confusion, Emily rolled her head to one side and studied the elegantly furnished room. For several seconds, she could not remember what had happened to land her in this unknown place nor did she understand the dull, ceaseless pain that throbbed along the left side and back of her head. It was not until she lifted her hand to touch her chin and found it was bandaged that she suddenly remembered—remembered *everything.*

Panic filled her when she realized Randall must have taken her back to Josephine's after all, but the panic was short-lived.

It was obvious that Josephine had not allowed any further harm to befall her.

Instead, she had been tucked safely away inside a bedroom, though it was clearly not the same bedroom she had before. This room was more tastefully decorated in mute shades of ivory and pale blue with only one mirror. This room was also twice the size of the other bedroom and had the unusual luxury of two ceiling fans. She must have been taken to Josephine's bedroom for safety's sake. And someone had been kind enough to exchange a soft, comfortable cotton gown for the tattered red dress she'd worn. Such consideration was heartwarming.

Wanting to get a better look at her lovely surroundings, she attempted to sit up, but was met with such a jolting pain at the back of her head, her vision blurred. Closing her eyes against the onslaught, she lowered her head back into the soft pillows. The view she had of the room around her suddenly seemed quite sufficient.

Groaning softly, she pressed the flat of her palm against her forehead, hoping to ease the discomfort with the gentle pressure. There she discovered yet another bandage. While exploring the shape of the second bandage with her fingertips, she remembered having struck the gaslight and felt a momentary wave of embarrassment. She also remembered that Randall had witnessed the entire incident. Of all people. She pressed her lips into a flat grimace and glanced toward the open door. Someone was coming, probably Josephine.

Eager to thank her friend for having seen to her injuries, she waited for her to appear in the doorway. But instead of Josephine's smiling face, she was met with that of a large, scowling black woman who was too busy muttering to herself to have yet noticed her.

"Who are you?" Emily asked, frowning when she did not immediately recognize the face. But, with her thoughts still so fuzzy, it was hard to concentrate on much more than the pain at the back of her head. Still, she could find nothing familiar about the woman. Nothing at all.

Having heard Emily's voice, the woman stopped suddenly and spun about to face her. Her eyebrows arched with startled surprise and her hand flew to the vicinity of her breastbone. "You're awake."

"Yes, I am," Emily agreed, still wondering who the woman might be. "I woke up a few minutes ago."

A pleased smile spread across her round face when she stepped closer to the bed. Without actually touching Emily, she bent forward at her nonexistent waist and gave the bandages a closer look. "Surely am glad to find you awake. Child, I was worried sick about you. You took a nasty fall. The doctor had to take a stitch in the side of your head in order to close that cut you got. I've had to change those bandages at least six times since then because a cut like that can get the 'flammation right easy. 'Specially this time of the year."

"I'm sorry if I've been any trouble, and I don't want to appear rude when I should offer nothing but my gratitude, but do I know you?" The woman behaved so friendly toward her, Emily wondered again if they'd already met.

"Not that I know nothing' about," came a ready response, yet she did not bother to introduce herself. "So, how you feelin'?"

"Terrible," she admitted, then realized if she wanted any of her questions answered, she would have to speak with Josephine. "Is Josephine around?"

"Who?" The woman looked truly confused.

"Josephine. Josephine Bradley. Is she around?"

"No, but the missus is here. And I think she'll want to know you finally come awake." Then without further explanation, the large black woman spun about and hurried from the room, her wide green skirts swishing with lively animation.

Emily's frown deepened, causing the injury at the side of her face to hurt. Lifting her hand to gingerly touch the bandage, she wondered who "the missus" might be. And where *was* Josephine? Perhaps out offering her dear friend, Mr. Peterson, a large piece of her mind. But then again, something Mr. Peterson had said during their struggle kept coming back to haunt Emily. "If you don't cooperate like you are supposed to, I'll be the one forced to tell Josie."

He had meant that as a threat. But why would he think telling Josephine about his horrible deed could possibly be a threat to her? Unless—unless Josephine had had something to do with his assault upon her. Could she have actually helped set up such a terrible thing? Had she known beforehand what sort of man Mr. Peterson really was? Surely not. But then again—Josephine had not given a second thought to leaving her alone with all those men. Instead, she had seemed very pleased by it all.

Emily closed her eyes tightly. She did not want to believe it. But the more she thought about that night, the better it all fit together. The dress Josephine had chosen, the way she'd encouraged her to be bolder around men, as if she had *wanted* her to make them believe they could take liberties with her. But why?

What had she ever done to Josephine to make the woman want to do such a cruel thing to her? Tears pushed past the outer rims of her eyes. Never had she felt so betrayed. Not even when Cynthia had sent her away penniless, because she had come to expect evil from someone like Cynthia, but she had trusted Josephine—had truly believed she was her friend.

"I thought she was supposed to be awake," a soft,

friendly voice said from a short distance away, luring Emily's eyes back open.

Quickly blinking the moisture away, hoping the stranger would not notice her tears, Emily turned toward an older woman whose wrinkled face revealed genuine concerned. Emily guessed her to be in her late fifties or early sixties. She was frail in build, with stark white hair and the bluest eyes she had ever seen—with one exception. Immediately, she tried to push the unwanted image of Randall Gipson aside. She had enough to worry about at the moment without adding more.

"Oh, you *are* awake. I'm so glad. You had us very worried when you didn't respond to the ammonia Dr. Weathers waved under your nose." She shook her head, causing her white hair to bounce softly around her thin face, then clasped her vein-streaked hands in front of her. She rested them just below her tiny waist. "We thought your injuries might be worse than they first appeared to be."

"How long have I been unconscious?"

"At least nineteen hours. Let's see. It was already past eleven when Randall brought you here last night, and it is almost six o'clock now."

The mention of Randall's name made Emily's heart jump.

"In the afternoon?" she asked, surprised so much time had passed since she had blacked out. "Where am I?"

"Nora didn't tell you?"

"Is Nora the woman who was just here?"

"Yes'm, that's me," came a deeper voice from somewhere near the door. Emily turned toward the sound and found that the other woman had returned but had not yet advanced into the room. "And, no missus, I hain't told her nothin'. But then, she didn't ask me nothin', cept'n to find out if some woman named Josephine was around."

"Well, then, let me begin by introducing myself," the older woman stated as she pulled a small, straight-backed chair closer to the bed. "My name is Bernice Gipson. I am Randall's grandmother."

Smiling, she sat primly on the edge of the chair with her hands folded in her lap, then turned to look back across the room. "And that is Nora, my housekeeper and best friend." She cut her gaze back to Emily, her blue eyes wide, while she spoke in hushed tones. "Now, I know it isn't considered proper for someone like me to claim a Negress to be my best friend, but it's a fact, pure and simple. There's nothing Nora wouldn't do for me, nor I for her. And there are very few other people I can say the same for."

"Oh, missus, you've got yourself plenty of friends," Nora commented, as if trying to pass her words off as nonsense, yet a wide smile stretched across her plump face, revealing how pleased she was with what Bernice had said. "Just ask Mr. Randall. He'll surely tell you."

"And where is Mr. Randall?" Emily asked, using the same terminology Nora had used, not wanting them to believe she was too familiar with him. She glanced toward the door, thinking he might appear at any moment. Fear of having to confront him yet again created a painful tightening at the base of her throat.

"Randall?" Bernice interrupted. She frowned with annoyance. "Why that boy's already on his way back to New Orleans. I don't know what I'm ever going to do with that one. Always headed somewhere and can never seem to get there fast enough." She clicked her tongue. "Always has his mind on business."

Not always, Emily thought, but offered no comment while she listened to his grandmother explain about his sudden decision to cut his stay short so he could return to New Orleans and take care of some urgent business he and his cousin had underway.

"Sometimes I wonder what I'm going to do with those two. At times I think they are just a little too dedicated to their work. A lot more than is healthy. And Terrence has a family to worry about. I tell you one thing, if I was that wife of his I'd have packed up my belongings and left him years ago. How can they ever expect to have any more children if he's never home? Do you also know Terrence?"

"No," Emily admitted. "I hardly know Randall. I met him while traveling on one of his ships on my way from New Orleans to Galveston."

"And you two were out together last night?" Bernice probed. She leaned forward with interest, but did not give Emily enough time to answer before asking her next question. "How'd the accident happen? Randall wouldn't tell me anything about it. He's always so closemouthed about everything."

"I wasn't with Randall at the time of the accident. He just happened to be passing by and saw it." She felt a sickening weight in the pit of her stomach while she tried to decide how much of the story she should relate to his grandmother, and how much she should keep to herself. "When he realized I was hurt, he stopped to help."

"I see. And who is Josephine Bradley?" Bernice asked, curious to know more and not opposed to asking. "Randall said something about returning you to a Miss Josephine Bradley's house just as soon as you were well enough to travel."

"No! Don't take me back there." Emily gasped, truly frightened. "Please!"

Bernice glanced back at Nora with surprise, then reached out a reassuring hand and rested it on Emily's cotton-clad shoulder. "I won't if you don't want me to, but why are you so afraid of going back there? Did this Bradley woman have something to do with your accident?"

"In a way, yes," Emily admitted, then decided to tell her the entire story. She started with the day she first met Josephine and ended with having awakened in the strange bedroom. The only part of the story that she purposely omitted was the night when Randall had stolen that kiss from her and had rendered her momentarily helpless—that and the names of some of the people who had been involved in the events that led up to her accident. She didn't feel naming names would benefit anyone. She also felt that whatever feelings she harbored for Randall had little or nothing to do with the outcome of the story. And she certainly did not care to admit to his grandmother that a mere kiss had left such an overall impression on her that she now thought about him constantly.

"Oh, my, what a terrible experience," Bernice said, her blue eyes wide with concern. "No, of course I won't take you back there. You may stay here as long as you like, or at least until you've gotten your things back from that vile woman." She tapped a fingertip restlessly against the outer corner of her mouth for a moment while she mulled over the situation. "I wish Randall were here. He'd know what to do. But we certainly can't wait until he returns before doing something about this. It'll be days before he comes back and you'll need your clothes long before then. You certainly don't want to put that horrible red dress back on. Besides, I've already thrown it away. It was so torn and tattered that, before he left, Randall ordered me to toss it out. He then told me to find a nightgown that would fit you. I hope it's not too small. It's the largest one I had."

"No, it feels fine," she assured her, though it did feel a bit snug in the shoulders. She then fell silent for a few moments while she tried to figure out why she suddenly felt so depressed. At first, she thought the bleak feeling had something to do with the embarrassment she felt knowing that Randall had seen her in such a gaudy outfit. But soon she realized the sad feeling was because she was oddly disappointed—disappointed to discover he was so very far away. It in no way made sense, especially when she knew what a continued threat he was to her. But, threat or no threat, that was how she felt—disappointed beyond belief.

"How long till he returns?"

"At least a week, probably two. But we can't wait that long. We need to act on this now." Bernice's eyes brightened as a new thought occurred to her. "I know. I'll send a note to my attorney. I'll ask him to come over and talk with us. He'll know what to do. He'll know how to go about getting your things back. He may even know how to find that grandmother of yours. He's a pretty smart man, that one," she muttered to herself while she thought more about it. "Yes, that's just what I'll do. I send for my lawyer."

Having stated her intentions, she rose from her chair and headed for the door. She paused just inside the opening and offered a warm, reassuring smile. "Don't you fret about anything, my dear. I'll see to it that your things are returned. You just stay in that bed and try to get some of your strength back. I'll have Nora bring a glass of iced chocolate. The milk will do you good and the chocolate will help restore some of your energy."

Aware of how hungry she felt, Emily didn't decline the offer. She sipped down the tall glass of iced chocolate and nibbled away on a fat, buttered biscuit Nora had included on the tray. Then Nora changed her bandages and gave her a mild pain powder. Emily fell back asleep and she slept until late the following morning.

Bernice had already left for church services when Emily awoke, but Nora was still there, waiting to prepare a hearty breakfast of eggs, ham, and chopped fruit, which Emily ate gratefully.

Shortly after noon, Bernice returned and went directly to Emily's room, eager to tell her about the conversation she'd had with her attorney. "We didn't have a chance to talk very long because he was feeling a bit poorly due to some sort of fall he'd taken yesterday and he wanted to get on home, but he told me that he had received the note I sent over and had already made arrangements to stop here sometime tomorrow morning, probably on the way to his office."

"And does he think he'll be able to get my things back?" Emily asked, wondering just how the man would go about accomplishing that—and if her belongings would still be there when he did. Josephine might have been so angry with her for having bashed her friend over the head with the water pitcher that she may have tossed her belongings right out into the street in retaliation.

"I didn't get a chance to go into detail with him. All I really told him was that I had a young woman staying with me who desperately needed his legal assistance. But that was enough to make him agree to stop by. He's a very conscientious person. I guess that's why he's one of the most prominent lawyers in all of Galveston. And, too, he and his brother have been here long enough to know a lot of people. There's a very real possibility that one of them will know your grandmother."

Emily's heart filled with hope. "Do you really think so?"

"If they don't, they'll know who to ask. And they'll help you locate her. I haven't lived here long enough to know too many people, but they've lived here nearly all of their lives. If your grandmother is still living in this area, they will find her."

"But I don't have any money to pay him right now," Emily reminded her. "I spent most of my money just getting here. And I left what little money I had at Josephine's."

"That's not a problem. I have lots of money. I'll be glad to take care of the lawyer's fee for you."

"I can't let you do that. You don't even know me."

"I know enough about you to know I want to help," Bernice insisted. "But if it'll make you feel better, you can repay me whenever you get better situated."

"It would indeed make me feel better," Emily said, then bit her lower lip to contain her excitement. The thought of finding her grandmother thrilled her.

Emily awoke early the following morning and, despite Bernice's sharp protests, got out of bed so she could be there when the lawyer arrived. Although she had nothing to wear other than the cotton gown and dressing robe Bernice had provided her, she had taken the time to brush her hair and gathered it into a simple twist at the back of her head. She felt a little ridiculous in the gown and robe, as much because of the short length as the fact that it was clothing she would not normally wear to a meeting with a lawyer. But at the moment, she had little choice. Until Nora returned from town with the dresses she'd been sent to buy, Emily had no clothing of her own. But then that was the reason they wanted to speak to the lawyer in the first place, to see what they should do about getting her belongings back.

Feeling much better after a second night's sleep, Emily went downstairs to have breakfast before the meeting. By the time Bernice announced the lawyer's arrival, she'd finished her meal and felt a lot like her old self.

"He's in the front parlor," Bernice told her, already headed for the door. "I told Nora to tell him we'd be right there."

Because Emily had not explored the front part of the house and feared becoming lost in a house so large, she hurried to follow. "Does he know about me yet?"

"No, but he soon will," she said in a lilting voice. "He's right in there waiting for us." She indicated a pair of doors that had been left partially open. She then stepped back to allow Emily to enter first.

Again wishing that she were more appropriately dressed, but not about to let that stop her from meeting with the only man who could offer her hope, Emily stepped into the large room. Eagerly, she scanned the area until her gaze rested on the sole occupant. Her eyes widened with alarm as her hand flew to cover her mouth while she took a protective step backward. "You!"

Bernice entered in time to see the lawyer's startled expression and Emily's frightened reaction. "What's at odds here? Do you two know each other?"

Emily took another frightened step back. "He's the one. He's the one I told you about. The one who tried to attack me."

"Edward?" Bernice turned to look at him with shocked disbelief.

"Yes, Edward, Edward Peterson." Emily said, remembering the name.

"I—I," he tried to explain only to discover the words failed to materialize.

"Edward, is this true? Did you try to molest this child?" Bernice took a protective step forward, her frown as perplexed as it was annoyed.

Edward finally found his tongue. "This *child,* as you so ridiculously put it, happens to work in one of the most exclusive brothels in all of Galveston."

"I most certainly do not!" Emily's arms stiffened at the sides.

"Then what were you doing there? And why were you dressed like you were?" he demanded, eager to prove her guilt.

"I was attending a party, nothing more. And I was dressed the way I was because that's the way Josephine wanted me to dress. I only wore that outfit to please her."

"And why would you care if you pleased the madam of a brothel unless you worked there?"

"Madam? *Josephine?*" Suddenly it all made perfect sense. As shocking as it was to learn that Josephine operated a brothel, it explained why she had seemed so eager to have her learn to flirt with men. And it explained why she had been so willing to buy her all those clothes. It also explained why the other girls had kept disappearing all that night.

"Josie's House of Delights," Edward stated, his way of verifying what he had told her. "Where men like me—," he hesitated when he noticed Bernice's shocked expression. "Ah, where men who have lost their beloved wives, and men whose wives refuse their marital advances can purchase a few moments of needed affection."

"You mean a whorehouse?" Bernice clarified, startling them both with her directness. "You patronize common whorehouses?"

Edward cleared his throat and tucked his finger inside his collar. "Josie's place is not a common whorehouse. It accomodates a very elite clientele. Besides I only go there on occasion. Ever since Emma died, I've—well, I've—had certain needs."

Bernice shook her head with disgust. "And does meeting these needs of yours often include attacking innocent young girls?"

"How was I to know she was innocent? How do I know even now that she is innocent?"

"Because I'm telling you that she is." Her blue eyes narrowed with intent.

Emily felt grateful that the woman had not allowed Edward Peterson to cast any doubts in her mind. "Mr. Peterson, I assure you, I had no idea I was inside a brothel."

Bernice interrupted by muttering, "A whorehouse. You were inside a whorehouse. Call it what it is."

Emily fought the urge to grin. Such words coming out of Bernice's mouth seemed downright comical, but she managed to hold a straight face while she continued with her explanation. "Josephine Bradley and I became acquainted during our trip to Texas and, while pretending to be my friend, she offered me a place to stay for a few days. As far as I knew, I was there as a temporary guest. I had no idea she had other plans for me."

"Well, she had other plans for you all right. She was asking thirty dollars for a—," he hesitated again, then reached up to touch a jagged cut that started near his eyebrow and disappeared into his hairline. "For a few hours alone in your company. She promised you'd be a real spitfire—well worth two weeks wages. But I had no idea how much of a spitfire you'd turn out to be."

He paused to think more about what had happened. "I do want to apologize. Had I known you were not one of Josie's regular girls, I never would have—." He grinned sheepishly before finding the words to finish the statement. "Had I known, I never would have gotten knocked over the head. Goodness, girl, you sure pack a wallop. What can I ever do to make it up to you?"

"Get her things back," Bernice put in, still eager to find solutions to Emily's problems. "And help her locate her grandmother."

Ready to make amends, the attorney sat down and immediately began questioning them and taking notes. After Emily finished relating her story, with frequent interruptions from Bernice who wanted to make sure everything was told, he promised to do all that was humanly possible to get her things back.

"What about finding my grandmother?" Emily wanted to know. She felt that was the more important issue.

"I'll start looking for her right away. I don't recognize the name offhand, but that doesn't mean much. There are tens of thousands of people living in and around Galveston. I can't possibly know all of them. But I do know where to start searching and I promise not to stop until I've found her."

"That's what we'll be paying you for," Bernice commented, nodding her approval.

"Not this time," Edward said, holding up his palm. "I feel I owe this child something for what I tried to do to her. I won't be asking a fee for any of this."

Emily glanced back at Bernice, expecting an argument of some sort and was surprised to see her shrug. "Good. Then she won't have to worry about repaying either one of us. Besides, you always charge way more than you are worth anyway."

Edward chuckled, then asked Emily. "Where can I reach you?"

"Right here," Bernice interrupted yet again. "I've already told her she's staying right here at least until you've gotten her belongings back—and right here is where she's going to stay."

"But what about Randall?" Emily asked. "I thought he wanted me out of here just as soon as I was well enough to travel. And I'm certainly well enough for that."

"You let me worry about Randall," she responded, her blue eyes sparkling with mischief. "You are not leaving here until Edward has your things back. How long can that take anyway? You'll probably have all your trunks back and be safe in the loving arms of your grandmother long before he ever returns."

"But that could take several weeks," Edward cautioned, thinking only to help.

"Hush up, Edward. Haven't you done enough?" she snapped. "Emily's staying here until you've gotten her things back, and that's all there is to it." Then before either of them could offer another argument, she turned and left the room.

Chapter Eight

"What you plan to do with all her things?" Patricia asked with a lazy yawn, plopping belly-down across the rumpled four-poster bed to watch with drooping, red-veined eyes while Josephine searched through Emily's belongings. Although it was only a little after noon and Patricia was usually still asleep at that hour, she had been too curious to find out what would become of the previous night's incident to remain in bed a moment longer.

"I'm not sure yet," Josephine answered, then grunted through tightly clenched teeth when she pushed down on the curved end of the heavy iron crowbar she'd had Joe Boy bring upstairs. She was determined to pry open the traveling trunk Emily had failed to unlock. "It all depends on if I can find what I'm looking for."

"And what is that?" Patricia queried, propping her chin on top of her crossed arms then tilting her head to one side as if she did not have enough energy to hold it erect. Her uncombed dark brown hair fell in a tangled mass across her plump shoulders.

"Her mother's jewelry."

Patricia's head came upright again with a jerk.

Her dark brown eyes rounded with sudden interest when she turned her attention to the stubborn trunk. "Is this jewelry expensive?"

"I doubt it," Josephine admitted, grimacing while she tried again to force the lock. "But if it is still here, and I have every reason to believe it is, I do think it will eventually bring a very pretty price."

Patricia frowned at the same time she worked her stubby round fingers into the wide gap between her dangling breasts and scratched in a most indelicate manner. "I no understand. If it is not expensive jewelry, how can it bring a pretty price?"

At that moment, the lock gave way and the trunk lid popped up several inches. Josephine smiled with triumph as she dropped the heavy iron bar, then she tossed the lid back and peered at the clothing inside. Although she had not wanted Joe Boy to know what she was up to, Patricia offered no threat to her plans. Patricia did not have enough sense to use whatever information was given her to her own advantage, so Josephine told her the truth. The poor girl was part Mexican and part Indian, but neither part of her saw past the flat little nose on her face. "Blackmail, my dear. Blackmail in its purest and simplest form."

Patricia's thick eyebrows rose high beneath tufts of tousled brown hair while she considered Josephine's answer. She continued to absently scratch the gap between her breasts while she gave Josephine's words more thought. "So you think Emily herself will pay a high price to get the jewelry back. Will it be enough to get the three dollars back that you had to return to Mr. Peterson?"

Josephine shrugged, not about to tell Patricia the truth, that the man had been willing to pay ten times that amount for a quick romp in bed with a true beauty like Emily. It had been *thirty* dollars she'd had to return to the man after Emily had failed to cooperate. But Josephine knew it would serve no purpose for Patricia to discover that some of her girls brought in more money than others since they were all paid the same in the end. Besides, she was after far more than even the thirty dollars she'd been forced to return to Peterson. Far more. "I doubt I'll even mention the jewelry to Emily. She has no money. But her grandmother does and I think that same grandmother will pay a very dear price to get Emily back."

"But I still no understand. You don't have Emily no more." She shook her head. "Despite all that opium you put in her tea, she still managed to run away—her maidenhood still intact. And I don't think she wishes ever to come back here again. No, she's gone for good."

"I know that. And you know that," Josephine said with a coy lift of her delicate brow. "But Emily's grandmother has no way of knowing that."

"Ohhh, now I start to understand. This grandmother, just how much money does she have?"

"If she's who I think she is, she has more than she knows what to do with." Josephine pushed her pale green silk sleeves up past her elbows before she started tossing Emily's clothing out of the trunk a garment at a time.

"I see," Patricia said. Her smile widened to reveal the tips of her crooked white teeth. "And you—being the kind-hearted *gringo* that you are—plan to provide this grandmother with a whole new reason to spend part of all her money."

"Something like that," Josephine said, never glancing up during her search for the jewelry. She was determined to find some way to cash in on all the time and effort she'd spent on Emily. "I'm not exactly sure how I plan to word the letter that will accompany a piece of the jewelry, but it will say something to the effect that if the old woman ever wants to see her granddaughter alive, she'd better come up with at least a hundred thousand dollars."

Patricia responded to the large amount by letting out a long, low whistle. "Has she *that* much money?"

"If she's who I think she is, she has that much and plenty more. And all I need to get my hands on a big part of that money, is to find Emily's jewelry and decide just how to word the blackmail letter."

Late Thursday afternoon, Edward Peterson stopped by the Gipson home with the first information he'd gathered concerning Emily's grandmother. He was so delighted with all he had managed to find out in so short of time, his words came out in an excited rush while he waved a rumpled sheet of yellow paper in the air in front of the two women.

"I am almost certain that this is the same woman," he said, waving the paper all the harder. "It has to be. Her name is Elmira Townsend. She's a widow. Her husband's name was Douglas. After losing two sons in separate stillbirths about thirty-five years ago, the woman finally succeeded in giving birth to the first of two daughters. The older girl was given the name Eleanor and the younger one was named Elizabeth."

Aware that all the information fit, Emily sank down into a nearby armchair, so stunned her knees felt suddenly too weak to hold her. Swallowing hard, she gripped the wooden arms with both hands while gathering the courage to ask, "And where is she now?"

"She lives alone, except for a few servants and several field workers, on a large plantation somewhere on the mainland, several miles northwest of here. She is reported to be very ill."

Fear clutched Emily's very soul with a painful grip, causing instant tears to fill her golden brown eyes. "How ill?"

"I'm not really sure. The man I had researching all this could not find out the exact nature of her illness, nor could he find out who her doctor is. But in an attempt to find out more about it, I've sent a letter to her youngest daughter, Elizabeth, whom we've learned lives right here on Galveston Island."

"My aunt lives on the island?" Her eyes widened at the thought. Her mother's younger sister. So very close by. Her heart filled with excitement while she wondered if her aunt looked anything like her mother. "Right here on the island?"

Edward nodded, then again indicated the scribbling that covered one side of the yellow paper. "Your aunt has a nice house only a few blocks away from here."

Emily's pulses fluttered with so much hope and excitement, she could hardly breathe. Her mother's very own sister, living within walking distance. "Well, what are we waiting for? Let's go talk to her. Let's find out what exactly is wrong with my grandmother and if there's anything I can do to help her get well."

"You mustn't be in such a hurry," he commented with a knowing chuckle while he folded the rumpled piece of paper into his inside coat pocket. "I understand the reason for your impatience, I really do, but I think it would be better for everyone concerned if you would wait until your aunt responds to my letter. Give her time to digest the fact that you are here, in Galveston, wanting to see her. In the letter I not only told her who you are, I also explained that your only desire is to meet her and your grandmother—and that you do not intend to cause either of them any harm. I ended the letter by requesting her to contact me as soon as possible so I can set up a meeting between you."

"And when do you expect to hear from her?" Yesterday could not be soon enough as far as Emily was concerned.

Edward stroked his chin for a moment. "Hard to say. There's a chance I'll hear as early as tomorrow afternoon, or there's always the possibility I won't hear for days after. It really depends on whether or not your aunt wants to discuss the matter with your grandmother first."

Emily was gravely disappointed, yet at the same time extremely excited. Her disappointment had stemmed from discovering she'd have to wait until they had received a formal response from her aunt, which could obviously take days. Yet at the same time she was excited to know she was that close to finally meeting her mother's family, especially her grandmother. Then, as quickly as the excitement had filled her, she felt a cold new stirring of apprehension. She met Edward's gaze with wide fearful eyes. "But what if they don't like me?"

"What's not to like?" Bernice interrupted, having kept quiet until now. She rose from the chair she had taken near Emily and shook her head. "Why would you worry about something like that?"

"I don't know. I can't seem to help it. What if she dislikes me simply because I'm my mother's daughter. She did so hate my mother."

"Hate is a pretty strong word," Bernice cautioned, then to allay any of Emily's fears, she continued. "I suspect your grandmother was very disappointed by your mother's brash actions, but I doubt she ever truly hated her. I know I could never have truly hated any of my children, no matter what terrible thing they did. Even if your grandmother does still resent your mother for leaving the way she did, there's no reason for her to resent you, too. You had nothing to do with what happened. You weren't even born yet."

"Still, I worry," Emily admitted. "I worry that she and my aunt will refuse to accept me, that they will turn me away before ever letting me get to know them. I don't think I could stand that."

Bernice continued to shake her head. "Will you at least wait until you have heard from this unknown aunt of yours before you start all this unnecessary worrying? For now, all you really need to worry about is getting your clothing returned from that evil woman who tried to set you up as one of her prostitutes. You can't continue wearing the same three dresses over and over," she said, referring to the clothes she'd had Nora go over to Market Street and purchase for their unexpected guest. She then turned to Edward and lifted an eyebrow expectantly, wanting to hear what he had to say about the matter.

Aware that all eyes had turned in his direction, Edward tugged at his collar while noisily clearing his throat. "I—ah—I'm afraid Josie Bradley has not yet responded to any of my letters. I guess I'll have to make a special trip over there so I can talk with her face-to-face."

"And no doubt you'll want to question a few of her *girls* while you are at it," Bernice said, arching her eyebrow higher.

Edward swallowed hard then suddenly became interested in the elaborate design woven into Bernice's expensive carpets. "No, I'll stop by there sometime over the weekend and talk with Josie herself about the matter." He then glanced at Emily.

"I hope to have your trunks back to you sometime Monday morning."

"See that you do," Bernice said. She tapped her slippered foot impatiently. "After all it has been three days since we first told you about all this."

"And I'll take care of it," he promised, nodding with renewed conviction. "I should be by here first thing Monday morning with all her things, and I should also have more news about her grandmother by then."

"Unless, of course, you hear from my aunt sooner than that," Emily inserted. She did not want him to wait until Monday if he heard something beforehand.

He smiled, then to reassure her that he understood, he repeated, "If I don't hear from her sooner."

Turning then to Bernice, he spoke with even more conviction. "When you see me next, I'll not only have Emily's trunks for her, I should also be the bearer of good news. I'm certain I will have heard from her aunt by then."

But when he returned late Monday morning with a sheepish expression, Emily knew he bore none of the good news he'd hoped to bear. Judging by his expression, which appeared to be neither glum nor particularly happy, she suspected he had no news at all.

Within minutes she discovered that she had predicted correctly. Josephine had been conveniently away from her house all weekend, which made it impossible for Mr. Peterson to collect Emily's things. In addition to that, Emily's aunt had not wanted to set up an appointment to meet with Emily after all. Instead, she had written a scathing response to Edward's letter that had called him an out and out schemer and a blackhearted liar.

"What it really boils down to is the surprising fact that your aunt does not believe you exist. She claims that her only sister is dead, has been for several years, and never bore any children. Therefore, she has refused to meet with either of us and even went as far as to threaten to call the authorities if we tried to pursue the matter."

"You mean they don't even know Mother had a child—me?" Emily felt a severe pain near the base of her heart. "But I thought they had been told. I thought Mother had written letters about me."

"Well, if she did write any letters to them about you, they apparently never reached Galveston. Did you happen to bring any proof of your identity?"

Emily thought about that. She hadn't bothered to bring a birth certificate. She hadn't thought she'd need one. Nor did she stay in New York long enough to receive her diploma from Miss Boswell's. She didn't even have a picture of herself with her mother. Cynthia had destroyed all such pictures shortly after her father's death. "No, I really don't. I guess I should have brought something with me, but I didn't."

"You have absolutely nothing that will prove you are who you say you are?" he asked, encouraging her to think harder.

Suddenly Emily remembered her mother's jewelry. It had at one time been her *grandmother's* jewelry. Perhaps her grandmother would recognize it. "If you could ever get my things back from Josephine, I just might have something that would help."

"What's that?"

"My grandmother's jewelry. It has an unusual design. It is very possible she might recognize it. That is if we can find a way to get it to her."

"How unusual?"

"It has odd shaped rubies surrounded by tiny diamonds set in backgrounds of gold, each piece is in the shape of a crescent moon. If turned one way, the diamonds look like they are smiling at you, yet if turned the opposite way, they look like they are frowning. Surely she would remember such a unique design. I think my grandfather had the jewelry made up especially for her because she was so fond of a quarter moon. My mother told me it had something to do with the night my grandfather proposed to her."

"Then perhaps she will remember it, but first we'll have to get the jewelry back from Josephine. One of her housekeepers mentioned something about Josie having said she would probably return later this week. She promised to send word to my office just as soon as Josie has arrived."

"And what makes you so sure this housekeeper will fulfill such a promise?" Bernice asked, clearly doubtful. "She may decide that sending word to you about Josie's return is not quite worth the effort. Or she could conveniently forget all about everything when the time comes."

"I handed her a two-dollar gold piece to help her with her memory. And to make certain it would be worth the trouble, I promised to give her another two-dollar gold piece just as soon as she's sent word. I also promised not to tell Josie anything about it, so her job would not be in any sort of jeopardy."

"I don't understand why you can't just go in there and take her things," Bernice complained. "Why should we have to wait for that harlot to finally return?"

"Because I happen to be an attorney with a reputation to uphold. I must abide by the law, and to go in there and take Emily's belongings without permission would be viewed the same as stealing."

"Even though they belong to me?" Emily asked, frowning because she saw no logic in that.

"Even though they belong to you. Unless someone willingly lets me into that house and then gives me either verbal or written permission to take those trunks out of there, it would be viewed in the courts as theft."

"Well get someone to let you in," Bernice quipped. She folded her arms, evidence that she was annoyed by all the senseless delay.

"I've tried. All her employees would allow me to do is enter the lower floor, and then only as a . . . customer." He avoided Bernice's probing gaze. "Without Josie there to give her permission, they refuse even to let me upstairs, and that is where the trunks are obviously being kept. Therefore, I have little choice but to wait until Josie returns from wherever it is she's gone."

"Which gives Emily little choice but to stay here and wait until you have finally recovered her things," Bernice commented with a slight shrug, displaying far less disappointment than Emily.

Fighting hot tears of frustration, knowing she was much closer to finding her grandmother than she'd ever been, yet still had so very, very far to go, Emily nodded sadly. There really was little else she could do other than stay there and wait. But for how long?

For the next two days Bernice did all she could to help Emily keep her mind occupied with other matters. They took long walks on the beach in the early mornings, talked or napped in the afternoons, and played croquet or spiffet in the early evenings, after the hottest part of the day had passed. But even so, Emily's thoughts were never far from the frustration that stemmed from her dilemma. Knowing that she had no way to prove her identity until Mr. Peterson got her belongings back from Josephine, and knowing that he couldn't get anything back until Josephine returned home infuriated her.

There was nothing Emily could do to remedy her situation but wait and hope for the best—and pray that Randall Gipson did not return before everything was settled. He had left his grandmother with specific orders concerning her. He did not want her staying there and would not understand why she had not left immediately.

Emily was better, much better. The only real pain she still suffered as a result of her accident were the headaches she occasionally had, and they had never been severe enough to prevent her from leaving. Randall would be furious with them both if he ever learned the truth. But surely she would be out of there by then.

But by Wednesday, Emily doubted she would ever leave. Twelve days after her ill-fated arrival in Galveston she was still there, barely able to tolerate the endless hours of waiting. Angry, frustrated, and restless, she'd begun to conjure up various schemes to get her things back, none of which seemed feasible. She'd even considered sneaking into Josephine's house during the morning hours while many of the girls slept, and stealing her own jewelry and whatever else she could carry off of her belongings. Take it by force if necessary.

It was the principle of the matter.

After all, those were *her* possessions—all except for a few dresses and undergarments Josephine had bought her. She deserved to have everything that belonged to her back. But was she willing to risk jail in order to get them? Jail was a very real possibility, one she knew she had better take into consideration. Would getting her things back be worth going to jail?

She would not be able to continue the search for her grandmother from jail. And even if Mr. Peterson did finally convince her aunt of her identity and get her to agree to meet with her, she would not want that first meeting to be on opposite sides of iron bars. No, stealing her belongings back was far too risky. She had too much to lose. She had to think of something else, something more practical. But what?

Having chosen to stay behind while Bernice and Nora rode over to the docks to purchase a pail of fresh shrimp for supper, Emily had the house to herself, which gave her plenty of time to try to come up with a less chancy idea. But nothing that had occurred to her thus far seemed foolproof.

If only Josephine would come back home from wherever she'd gone and then return her belongings to her unharmed. But Emily now knew Josephine Bradley was not at all the *honorable* woman she'd once thought her to be. Now knowing Josephine for what she really was, Emily feared that Mr. Peterson would eventually have to obtain some sort of a court order in order to get her possessions returned. That meant even more precious time would be lost before she could finally prove to her aunt and her grandmother that she really was the person she claimed to be.

Lost to such melancholy thoughts, Emily sat with her feet tucked under her in a richly upholstered rococo chair, staring absently into a blackened fireplace. She was so lost in her sad thoughts, she did not hear the back door clatter shut, nor did she notice the heavy footsteps in the hallway until they were almost upon her. When the sound finally did penetrate her dark thoughts and she realized they were too heavy to be Bernice's, she turned toward the door, expecting to see Nora enter the room.

Her heart slammed hard against her chest when, instead, Randall's broad shoulders filled the doorway. Her breath lodged in the base of her throat while she watched his expression go from that of happy expectation to startled surprise to outright anger—all within seconds.

"What are you doing back so soon?" she asked, her words tumbling out in a rush. Her hand flew protectively to her throat where her pulse pounded at an astonishing rate. "Your grandmother didn't say anything about you coming back today."

"That's because she didn't know," he said in carefully monitored tones. His dark eyebrows pulled low over narrowed blue eyes when he then entered the room. "And just what the hell are *you* still doing here? Where's Grandmother?"

"She and Nora have gone to the wharves to purchase fresh seafood for supper. Your grandmother wants Nora to make a large platter of shrimp creole for tonight. I understand that is one of your favorites."

Her gaze darted to the clock while she tried to think of something else she might say to keep his temper down to a minimum. She felt a sickening leap of fear when she noticed that not quite an hour had passed since Bernice and Nora had left and Bernice had warned they might be gone as long as two, possibly three hours.

If that turned out to be the case, Randall had well over an hour in which to toss her out into the street. "But they should not be gone much longer," she added quickly, although she knew that was not exactly true. "They had no other errands." But they had considered taking a drive along the bay. How she hoped those plans would fall through.

"That still does not answer my first question," he pointed out. His jaw muscles pumped furiously while he came ever closer to where she sat staring up at him with wide-eyed horror.

Suddenly Emily's lungs felt devoid of air. Her heart thudded hard against her chest while she slowly pushed herself out of the chair, wanting to be prepared to take flight if necessary. When she spoke again, her voice came out barely above a squeak, which she knew let him know he had the advantage.

"Which question was that?" she asked.

In a failing effort to keep his anger in check, Randall paused to take two short breaths before answering, his teeth clenched so hard his jaw ached. "I asked why you are still here." His facial muscles pumped harder while he studied the pink glow of her cheeks. "You look healthy enough to me." He tried not to be taken in by her beauty while he studied her more closely.

Emily stood before him, frozen while his penetrating gaze moved to the side of her head where she had arranged her hair to cover the small wound that no longer required a bandage. Suddenly, she wished she had asked the doctor to leave the bandage on. "That's true. I am healthy enough to leave, but your grandmother has insisted I stay."

"She what?" he thundered. Any desire to display an outward calm left him. He was being defied by not one, but two women, one his own grandmother. Or was he? Why should he believe anything this tart had to say?

Emily swallowed to break the constriction that gripped the base of her throat. He looked angry enough to actually hit her. She studied the powerful width of his hands, which were already curled into massive fists. "She, ah, asked me to stay."

"Why on earth would she do something like that? Why didn't she send you back to Josephine's like I told her to?" When he stepped toward her then, his arms stiffened and his fists grew so hard his knuckles turned white. "What did you do to make her say such a thing?"

"I didn't do anything. She simply does not want any further harm to come to me," Emily stated, taking a tentative step backward. She felt the space directly behind her with outstretched fingers, searching for any obstacles that blocked her way, too afraid to turn her head and simply look.

"I guess she did not anticipate what harm that might cause upon my return," he said, taking another determined step in her direction. His blue eyes glittered with intent. "Didn't she know how angry I'd be to come back and find that you were still staying here?"

"Randall, please," she said, countering each of his forward movements with a backward step of her own. She had never seen such anger in a man. She was terrified of what he might do to her. "Let me explain."

"What's to explain?" he asked, taking another lithe step forward. His jaw muscles continued to pump in and out while he glared down at her.

"Why I am still here." she answered and took another trembling step backward, aware he was closing the distance between them at a rapid rate. He was now only about six feet away from her.

"You already told me why." His voice seethed with rage. His icy gaze never left hers. "According to you, Gran asked you to stay. But now I am asking you to leave. No, I am *ordering* you to leave."

"Okay. I'll go." Her eyes widened when her next backward movement brought her firmly against a wall. She now had nowhere else to go but forward.

And he was barely three feet away. She was trapped. "Just, please, don't hurt me."

Randall stopped suddenly in his panther-like pursuit and blinked, confused by her words. "Hurt you?" Blinking again, in an effort to understand why she would think such a thing, he glanced down at his hands and noticed they were curled into solid fists. It was not like him to display his anger so openly. He immediately relaxed them both. His voice softened considerably, yet still remained firm. "I don't intend to hurt you. I just want you out of here, now—before any of Gran's friends discover she's been allowing someone like you to stay here."

"Why? What have I done?" she asked, then realized what he meant. He was referring to the way she'd let him kiss her that night on his ship. He thought her a wanton woman. Unable to continue meeting his gaze straight on, she lowered her head to look first at the floor, then she glanced about the room. She hoped to discover a ready means of escape so she would no longer have to endure his condemning gaze, but found none. The only door stood on the other side of him.

"What haven't you done?" he muttered, then shook his head tiredly. He had enough problems at the moment, he didn't need another. "Look, it's not like you don't have someplace to go."

"But I don't," she said, hoping to make him understand her situation yet.

"Don't give me that. You may have been able to convince my grandmother of such tripe," he said, arching his eyebrows with clear warning. If there was anything he refused to tolerate, it was being openly lied to—*by anyone.* "But you and I both know that's simply not the truth. You do have someplace else to go and we both know where."

"But that's just it. I don't." For a brief moment

she forgot her earlier apprehension. She wanted somehow to convince him of the truth. When she returned her gaze to meet his, she saw his facial muscles harden. His anger had returned. In force.

"I'll have no more of your lies," he thundered. "Get out of my house! Get out before I throw you out!"

His hands curled into fists again while he took another menacing step in her direction.

Chapter Nine

Randall's eyes glinted with renewed anger while he closed the last of the distance that had separated them.

"Okay, I'm going. I'm going," Emily offered, then waited for him to step aside so she could do just that.

But he didn't.

He continued to move straight toward her, inches at a time.

Emily's heart hammered painfully against her chest and her pulse pounded with alarming force.

Slowly, he took the final step that brought him to within inches of touching her. His gaze raked across her upturned face, stinging her with contempt while he slowly pressed the flat of one hand against the wall, barely an inch from her right ear. The lean muscles in his cheeks remained rock hard while his eyebrows lowered with intent.

Still holding her chin high, Emily closed her eyes and prepared for the worst. Her stomach knotted with icy tendrils of fear while she waited for the blow that would send her crashing to the floor. When it did not come immediately, she swallowed hard then spoke in a firm voice. "If you'd be kind enough to step out of my way, I'd leave immediately."

Yet, unable to force her eyes open, she listened carefully for any indication that he had fulfilled her request. The only sound she heard above the rush of her own pulse beat was his deep, rapid breath. It was the tingling warmth of those quick, forced breaths against her cheek that finally caused her to reopen her eyes and face his wrath.

Her knees felt like jelly on a hot roll. Randall's face loomed just inches above her own, close enough to detect the silvery flecks that highlighted his pale blue eyes. She stood motionless before him. The clarity of his anger stunned her, but the helpless feeling lasted only a few seconds. Her instinct for survival prevailed.

Quickly she glanced away, not wanting him to see her fear, but then she realized he might view that as fear in itself and returned her gaze to his. She tossed her shoulders back with false bravado. "Well? Are you planning to get out of my way or not?"

Randall studied the high color of her cheeks and the determined thrust of her chin for a long moment before he finally answered. "I think not." He placed his other hand against the wall, near her left shoulder, trapping her within the circle of his arms.

Though their bodies did not actually touch, Emily felt the penetrating heat of his body against hers. She also felt the faint touch of his breath brush past her cheek. He was far too close. She had to put distance between them. She had to get away.

"If you don't move out of my way, how can I possibly do what you want? How can I leave with you standing in my way?" she asked. She forced the words past a painful lump that had formed in the hollow of her throat, then wondered why he failed to comply. If he truly wanted her out of his house, why did he continue blocking her way? Why was he so intent on trapping her against the wall? What did he intend to do to her? Punish her for having so blatantly disobeyed his orders? Waves of apprehension cascaded over her like a harsh, wintery waterfall, causing her skin to prickle into gooseflesh while she waited for his response to her questions.

But Randall had not heard the questions. Being that close to her was having a strange effect on him. Suddenly he did not feel quite so adamant about forcing her to leave, at least not right away. Well remembering the heady sensations her kiss had stirred to life within him that night aboard ship, and knowing the reputation Josie's girls had for pleasing a man in every way, he was willing to compromise to a certain extent. He might be willing to let her stay a few more hours; and if, in that time, she proved to be half the woman he thought her to be, he'd damned sure make it worth her while. He'd gladly pay her top dollar.

The longer he peered into the shimmering depths of her huge brown eyes, the more he realized he desired her. Emily Felcher was without a doubt the most beautiful women he'd ever known. He'd be a fool not to take a moment and enjoy some of the more pleasurable benefits of her trade. It had been months since he'd been with a woman, although until now that had not really mattered. He'd been too busy with work to worry much about his love life.

But suddenly he was in dire need of a woman—*this* woman. No other would do. Slowly, he brought his gaze down to her parted lips and watched, fascinated, while the tip of her pink tongue darted across the surface in preparation for his kiss. The implication was too tempting to resist. He had to have her.

But not here. Not when his grandmother could return at any moment and find them. He would never risk exposing his grandmother's fragile sensibilities to something like that. It would have to be somewhere else.

Taking a deep breath, in an attempt to gain temporary control over his rampaging desire, he pulled his head erect again, but did not reduce the distance between their bodies. He remained scant inches from her. Close enough so that he could still breathe the sweet scent of her hair and feel the warmth that radiated from her sumptuous body.

When he spoke again, the harsh lines were gone from his expression. His voice sounded far less demanding. "Get your things. I'll take you back to Josie's myself."

Though his tone had been soft, bordering on seductive, his words had struck Emily with painful force. He meant to take her back to that evil place.

"Oh no you won't!" she cried, then tried to shove him away only to discover he'd become rooted to the spot.

Not expecting such an adverse reaction, Randall became as angry as he was confused. Why was she so adamant that *he* not be the one to take her back to Josie's? Surely, she understood the reason he wanted to do so. Did he repulse her in some way? Or was she *that* angry at him for not agreeing to let her stay here? Was this her way of punishing him for having decided she should leave? Just who did she think she was?

His anger weighted his voice until it was little more than a low, menacing growl, barely heard above his hard breathing. "Look, sweetie, my money happens to be as good as any—," he started to explain, only to have his angry retort cut short from behind.

"Randall Sanford Gipson!" came Bernice's sharp reprimand from across the room. "Just what do you think you are doing?"

Randall spun about instantly, his blue eyes stretched to their limit, his back ramrod straight. He had not heard her enter. Suddenly he felt like a small child who had been caught with his finger in the pie—something only his grandmother could make him feel. "I—I was just asking Emily if she would like for me to escort her back to her friend's house."

"You mean to return her to that whorehouse?" Bernice asked, glowering with dismay.

Randall's mouth dropped open, momentarily stunned. He had never heard such *colorful* language from his own sweet grandmother—although she did have a way of saying the unexpected at times. "Then you *do* know."

"Yes, she's told me everything," Bernice admitted with an annoyed shake of her silvery head. After having paused in the doorway, she stepped further into the room. Without glancing down, she tugged at her white cotton gloves, removing them a finger at a time. "And I think it's a crying shame. That's why I've decided to help her. Which is also why she is still here. She needed someplace to stay until she can get her life in better order."

Randall thought it just like his grandmother to want to convert this poor, fallen angel—but he also knew it was in the dear woman's own best interest to be rid of Emily as quickly as possible.

When he spoke again, it was with a soft, persuasive voice. "That very well may be true, but I really don't think it was a wise decision to allow her to stay here. And, what's more, I don't think it is in any way wise to let her continue to stay here."

Though the words had been pretty much what

Emily had expected, she watched the scene before her with growing disbelief, amazed by the undeniable influence Bernice Gipson had over her oldest grandson. Suddenly, she foresaw the perfect way to retaliate for his earlier behavior. "I'm afraid he's already ordered me out of his house. I have no choice but to leave."

"Uh, *his* house?" Bernice repeated, turning a cocked eyebrow to him. "So that's the way you plan to be about this. I guess it doesn't matter to you one whit that I want her here."

"Gran, it is better that she leave—for *everyone's* sake."

"And just where do you propose she go? She certainly can't go back to that vile house of corruption."

Randall knew immediately that his grandmother was deathly serious about saving Emily from her wayward life. Still, he could not allow such a woman to live in his house. Too many tongues would wag. Even though the thought of having Emily for a live-in mistress was not altogether displeasing, he had his grandmother's reputation to consider. And consider it he would.

"Okay, I won't send her back to Josie's," he finally conceded, hoping for a compromise. "But she can't stay here either. I'll have to find someplace else for her to live."

"Why?"

Irritated that his grandmother would not simply accept what he had to say, he threw up his hands with disgust. "Because she can't live *here.* And that's all there is to it."

Bernice leveled her gaze at him, making it clear that that was *not* all there was to it. "And just where do you plan to send her?"

"I don't know yet," he admitted, then glanced

back at Emily with an annoyed scowl. "But I'll find somewhere."

"Well, until you do, she stays right here with us," Bernice retorted with a determined toss of her head. She studied his reaction with mounting interest. "I'll not have her out on the streets with no place to go."

"Then I'll find her a place by nightfall," he growled, then shot Emily a determined glare seconds before spinning about and marching angrily from the room.

Two hours passed before Randall returned, his sullen mood unchanged.

"Have Nora help Emily pack her things and carry them down here," he said in a stern voice just moments after he'd entered the front parlor where his grandmother sat in her favorite rocker busily at work on her embroidery. "I've located a place for her to stay."

Quietly Bernice set her needlework to one side and gave Randall her full attention. "Where?"

Randall tapped his boot impatiently against the polished hardwood floor. He didn't have time to answer a lot of questions. He was ready to be on his way—ready to put this annoying situation behind him so he could concentrate on more important matters. "In a small rooming house across town. Call Nora."

"Which rooming house?" Bernice watched the irritated expression on her grandson's face deepen and wondered what it was about Emily that bothered him so. Was he upset because of something the girl had done? Or was he disturbed because she was so beautiful, beautiful enough to tempt his emotions if he allowed her to stay? Bernice was thrilled by the thought. Was it possible someone had finally interested her grandson? She bit her lip to keep from crying aloud the joy such a prospect brought her.

Unaware of the thoughts racing through his grandmother's keen mind, Randall shook his head, as if little concerned. "I don't remember the actual name of the place, but the lady who runs it is named Roberts. What I do remember is that she promised to have a room ready for occupation within the hour. Emily can move in immediately."

"Certainly that can wait until tomorrow," Bernice said, glancing at the clock, relieved to see how late it had become. She'd love to see what happened if Emily and Randall were forced to stay the night under the same roof. "Why, it is almost five o'clock. By the time you load everything into the carriage and drive across town, it will be past supper time. No sense you both going hungry."

"Emily won't have to," he responded. "Mrs. Roberts explained that because so many of her boarders work down around the dock area, which is a good half hour walk from her house, she doesn't put supper on the table until around six-thirty or seven and she leaves the food out until nearly nine. If we hurry, Emily will be there in plenty of time to eat with the others."

"But what about you? When and where do you plan to eat? Nora will have put everything away by the time you return," she said, though she knew Nora could be told to keep a plate warm.

"I'll find something somewhere. Besides, I'm not that hungry. Right now, all I want to do is to see Emily to her new home. Where is she now?"

"Upstairs packing what few belongings she has," Bernice said, hoping to play on Randall's sympathy.

"Good. I'll send Andrew up to get them," he said, then left the room as abruptly as he had entered.

He would not allow Emily to continue taking advantage of his grandmother's kindly nature a moment longer.

Within ten minutes the Gipson's driver had tossed Emily's single valise into the back of the Cabriolet, and the three of them were immediately on their way.

Because Andrew was such a large, muscular man, taking up more than a fair share of the front seat, and the Cabriolet was such a small carriage, Randall had little choice but to allow her to sit in the back with him. Having had plenty of time to overcome the sudden rush of desire he'd felt earlier, and having had plenty of time to put any other feelings into better perspective, Randall was not at all pleased with the idea of having to ride on the carriage seat beside her.

His concern had nothing to do with the very real prospect of being observed while escorting a known prostitute in his own private vehicle. After all, he'd certainly been spotted in their company before. No, what bothered him most about Emily had nothing to do with her occupation whatever. It was more the fact that she had turned out to be as conniving as she was beautiful—and he hated conniving women. Always had.

Frowning with disgust while he settled into the seat beside her, he wondered how she had managed to trick his grandmother into letting her stay after her injuries had healed. How had she then convinced the dear woman that there was any real possibility that she might be willing to change her sinful way of life when, in truth, most prostitutes enjoyed their lifestyles and wouldn't change for anything.

Why should they?

There was no other occupation open to women that compensated quite so generously, especially if they were connected to a reputable house—like Josie's. He wondered then why Emily didn't just order him to turn the carriage around and take her back to Josie's, where she'd be able to earn a lot more money than she could ever hope to make working alone, and be better protected against pregnancy and customers with violent tendencies. Was she perhaps hoping to start her own house? Suddenly, it occurred to him that he was supporting her in her quest to branch off and go it alone. His friends would certainly get a chuckle or two out of that if it were ever to get out.

"I want it fully understood that the only reason I'm doing any of this is because of Gran. If it weren't for her, you'd be out on the streets right now making ends meet the best way you can," he said in a stern voice. He wanted to make his position perfectly clear. She needed to understand right from the beginning that his sudden show of generosity would not be repeated. "I've already paid your landlady the first month's rent, which was ten dollars. That will supply you with both an ample-sized room and three meals a day. But after the month has run out, you will once again be on your own. It'll be up to you to pay your next month's rent—not me."

Emily felt a deep, nagging ache in the pit of her stomach as she listened to what he'd had to say. His resentment was evident, yet she did not fully understand why he disliked her to such an extreme. True, she had stayed at his house, knowing he didn't want her there; and true, she had shown poor judgement the night she'd allowed him to kiss her with such passion, but those were not sufficient reasons to treat the way he was. "And I want it understood that I do plan to pay the money back."

"I haven't asked for the money back. All I want

out of this is your promise to stay away from my grandmother." He refused to look at her. He stared out at the street instead.

"But how will I ever get my trunks back?" Emily asked, her voice full of concern.

"What trunks?" He then cut his gaze at her as if suspecting a trick of some sort.

"The trunks I was forced to leave behind at Josephine's."

"Why were you forced to do that?"

"It was either leave them behind or risk my very life by returning for them."

"And just how would returning for your trunks be risking your life?" he asked, still skeptical. He shook his head at such a ridiculous notion.

Emily frowned while she thought about that. At the time it had certainly seemed as if she would be risking her life were she to return, but now she wasn't so sure. Why *was* she so afraid of going back and demanding her trunks? After all, they were *her* trunks. Then she remembered what Josephine had tried to do to her. A cold wave of disgust and trepidation washed over her.

"I asked you a question," Randall commented, annoyed by her refusal to answer. "Haven't you thought of an answer yet?"

"Why are you so angry with me?" she finally asked. "Is it because I agreed to stay at your house a little longer than you seem to think was necessary?"

"A *little* longer?" he asked, finding that a major understatement. "You should have been out of my house over a week ago."

"I know and I'm sorry. It's just that I had nowhere else to go. What little money I have left and all my other personal belongings are still at Josephine's, and I really was too afraid to go back there and ask to have them back."

"Why? What did you do?"

"Why do you assume I did anything?" she asked, provoked by his judgmental attitude.

"Why else would you be afraid to go back? And just what has my grandmother to do with you getting any of your things back? That's not her responsibility."

"She wanted to help in some way, so she asked her attorney to try to get my belongings back for me. We both realized it might take a little longer to handle the matter through a lawyer, but at the time we thought it would be far wiser than attempting to get my things back ourselves."

Randall's eyes widened with sudden comprehension. So that was how she had worked it. She'd convinced his grandmother to let her stay on until her things could be legally recovered by Edward, and in the meantime she'd probably sent word to Josie not to give up anything until she absolutely had to. But why was it so important for Emily to live in his house? What had she hoped to accomplish? She had to be after something.

"And what is wrong with simply knocking on the Josie's door and asking for your things back?"

"Mr. Peterson has tried that, but no one will give them to him."

No doubt, Randall thought, still believing she'd instructed Josephine to stall as long as possible. He only wished he knew why.

"And until I do get my things back, I have no money to live on. No clothes to wear. Nothing. That's why I allowed your grandmother to talk me into staying with her." She glanced out at the many houses they passed in a failing effort to keep back the tears that threatened to spill.

As Randall studied her pitiful expression he realized why his grandmother had been so easily taken in by her. She was an amazing actress. If he hadn't known better, he'd be sorely tempted to believe her to be the wretched little thing she now pretended to be.

But he *did* know better. "Then what's in the valise?" He glanced back over the seat at the small bag that he suddenly realized had belonged to his grandmother.

Emily wet her lips and gazed down at her folded hands, ashamed that she'd had to accept another person's charity. "Clothes your grandmother bought for me. I couldn't very well go around the house dressed the way I was."

"No, I wouldn't think so," he commented, well remembering the snug-fitting red dress she'd been wearing the night before he left. Though he'd personally rather enjoyed the display of rounded flesh provided by the plunging neckline, it was certainly not the sort of thing his grandmother would allow to be worn in her presence. He then glanced at the simple cut of the mint green dress she now wore and decided it was definitely something his grandmother or Nora had picked out for her. Such a garment was far too demure to have attracted Emily's eye.

"So, until I do finally get everything back from Josephine, I have no choice but to remain in daily contact with your grandmother. She's my only connection to Edward Peterson," she said, not wanting to give up her only real friend in Galveston.

The veins in Randall's neck stood out stark against taut muscles. He was not used to having his requests so blatantly refused. His blue eyes darkened to grey when he shook his head in ready response. "No. I already told you, I want you to leave my grandmother alone. *I* will see to it that you get your blasted trunks back. You can expect them first thing tomorrow morning." He folded his arms across his chest, confident she would then have no further excuse to bother his grandmother. She would just have to forget all about whatever it was she'd been up to.

"Don't be so sure," Emily retorted, remembering that Mr. Peterson had said something very similar to that nearly two weeks earlier and he had yet to produce even her mother's jewelry.

Barely aware that the carriage had pulled to an abrupt halt in front of the rooming house, or that Andrew had turned waiting for his orders, Randall glared at Emily. He wanted her to understand beyond any shadow of a doubt that he had no intention of putting up with any more of her game playing. "I will get your trunks for you. You just stay away from my grandmother like I told you."

Infuriated by his spiteful behavior, Emily returned his angry glower. "Mr. Gipson, I think you should know that I am quite accustomed to seeing *whomever* I please *whenever* I please and I have no intention of changing that. Just what makes you think you have any right to tell me what to do?"

"The fact that I'm paying for your room and board for one thing," he retorted, flicking his hand in the direction of the small frame house centered in a neatly trimmed yard, shaded by several large oaks. His eyes narrowed while he waited for her response to that.

"I already told you, you will get your money back." She, too, narrowed her eyes and met his gaze straight on. She refused to be intimidated by the likes of him. The worse he behaved toward her, the less she felt she deserved it. "It may take a while, but you will definitely be paid back."

"Fine. But until you do pay me back, you are to stay away from my grandmother. Understood?"

Hurt, angry, and confused—seeing no reason to continue this outburst—she thrust her chin forward and hurriedly climbed down from the carriage. "Just see to it that my trunks are forwarded to this address as soon as possible." She refused to look at him and instead brushed the wrinkles from her skirts. "That is if you can possibly remember just where it is you have dumped me."

That was the last straw. It was bad enough the business deal he and Terrence had been working on for months was about to fall through. He was not about to let this little snip of a girl have the last word. "You will indeed have your trunks first thing in the morning. You just remember to do what you've been told. Stay away from my grandmother."

"The only person I plan to stay away from is you, Mr. Gipson. Good day, sir." she said, then snatched the valise from Andrew's waiting hands. Without another word, she turned to face the narrow, planked walkway then stalked angrily toward the front steps, never bothering to look back.

Chapter Ten

If Andrew noticed his boss muttering to himself during the ride home, he had the good sense not to show it. His expression remained stone sober while he kept hazel-green eyes focused on the narrow street ahead.

Randall was furious—as much with himself as with her. He had not thought of one pertinent response to Emily's *im*pertinent behavior, and that was not like him. He was usually quick with a clever response—quick to put a deserving person in his place, but this time his mind had failed him. His thoughts had gone completely blank.

"Impudent wench," he muttered for the sixth time, not caring if Andrew heard him or not.

Why had he let her get away with that anyway? True, he was exhausted, but too exhausted to come back with a clever response? Too tired to tell her exactly what he thought of her sharp tongue?

Obviously, he was.

Sighing heavily, he rested his weary head against the leather seat. When he saw her again, he'd have plenty to say to her. He'd make sure she paid dearly for that last remark. Somehow, some way, he'd make her sorry she'd dared be so tart.

By the time the carriage rattled onto the wide, cobblestone drive that circled in front of the red brick Italian-style villa he'd had built for his grandmother years earlier, Randall had conjured up all manner of reprisal against the impudent little wench—yet none of his ideas seemed quite conniving enough to even the score.

When he entered the house, it was minutes after eight. He was still so lost to conniving thoughts, he did not notice the two large steamer trunks sitting in the middle of the side entry. It was not until he'd nearly stumbled over them that he realized anything blocked his way.

"What the . . ." he muttered, hopping immediately to one side to avoid collision. He blinked with confusion while he fought to keep his balance.

"Those are Emily's trunks," Bernice said, appearing unexpectedly through a nearby doorway. She then headed toward him with tiny, soundless steps. "Edward delivered them while you were gone."

Randal planted his hands on his hips and stared at the two trunks with disbelief. "How'd he ever manage to get them this quickly?" he asked, knowing Josephine couldn't have yet discovered that Emily's plans had fallen through. There hadn't been time for Emily to send a message to her. So why had she suddenly released them? Had she heard about his return from someone else?

"Court order," Bernice explained. "He'd already tried everything else."

So that was it. "But why did he leave them here? Why didn't you have him take them on over to Emily's new residence?"

Bernice crossed her arms, tapping her fingertips against her silk sleeves impatiently. "Because you never did tell me the name of the place. All I know is that a Mrs. Roberts runs the establishment, which is not a lot to go on. But don't worry about these things. Just write down the address and I'll take them to her in the morning. I'm eager to see where she now lives."

"No," Randall said, his tone adamant. "I'll take them to her. There's no need for you to bother yourself."

Bernice studied his determined expression for several moments. She wondered if he planned to use the two trunks as an excuse to see Emily again. "Very well, you may take them to her. But before you do that, you'll need to do something about that broken latch. Edward said the lid kept popping up on the way over here and catching the wind. He's lucky he didn't lose some of her clothing."

Randall bent over to examine the trunk Bernice had indicated a little more closely. "Looks like someone's pried it open. About all I know to do is to tie it closed with a good sturdy rope."

"Then do it. I'd hate for her things to spill out all over the road."

Randall nodded, quick to agree. He knew he would have a hard time explaining some of the outlandish outfits to anyone who might be passing by. "I'll do that right away."

Satisfied that the problem was solved, Bernice returned to the parlor and her embroidery. Meanwhile, Randall could not resist taking a moment to search around inside the open trunk. Lifting the frilly garments out one at a time and holding them high for closer inspection, he was not surprised to discover several of the risqué evening gowns that made Josie's girls so popular.

While he continued his search through the jumbled contents of the broken trunk, he came across several of the sheerest, skimpiest undergarments he'd ever seen. His blood heated when he imagined what she must look like in them. From what he'd noticed, she had just the sort of body that made wearing such frilly undergarments worthwhile.

Suddenly, he wanted more than to imagine her in them. He wanted to *see* her in them, to touch her while she wore them. And why shouldn't he? If he was having to pay for a month's keep, then she might as well do something worthwhile to earn it. Besides, she herself had said she wanted to repay him for the rent. Why not take what she owed him in trade?

Believing he'd struck upon the perfect solution, he tossed her things back into the trunk, eager to take her belongings right over to her. Returning the trunks would give him the perfect excuse to talk with her and make all the necessary arrangements. But, then again, his grandmother would probably question his sudden willingness to be so helpful, and he didn't want to do anything that might shatter her sheltered view of the world.

Morning would have to be soon enough.

Rising early the next day from a sleepless night, Randall dressed hurriedly and went down to breakfast. Having decided to take no more of Emily's impudence, and still believing she may as well repay him with her services as with cash, he quickly wolfed down his food then ordered Andrew to secure the broken trunk with a sturdy hemp rope before loading them both into the back of the springboard.

He could hardly wait to see her stunned expression when he arrived so very early in the day with the promised trunks.

He remembered how skeptical she'd been when he had first told her he would have her things that quickly. Obviously, she had expected him to have more trouble getting a hold of them. What she didn't know was that Edward had already obtained his court order. But that was something Randall didn't plan to tell her—at least not voluntarily. He'd rather let Josephine be the one to tell her the truth. Until then, he'd let her think he'd somehow managed to get hold of the trunks himself.

Just minutes after nine o'clock, Andrew drew the wagon to an abrupt halt directly in front of Mrs. Roberts' boarding house, then slowly secured the reins and climbed down from the high-springed seat.

Eager to strike his bargain, Randall hurried on to the front door, leaving the hapless driver to unload both trunks and bring them inside one at a time.

"Is Miss Emily Felcher here?" Randall asked as soon as a young boy, about twelve, had answered his knock. The boy tilted his head to one side.

"Who?" the child asked, peering cautiously at him through the mesh wire door. He reached up to push his long brown hair out of his eyes.

"Miss Emily Felcher. She's new here. Moved in yesterday." He squinted, trying to see into the house.

"Just a minute, let me go find out," the boy said, then turned and hurried to the back.

Randall frowned, perturbed that the child had not thought to invite him inside. Rocking back and forth from the toes of his boots to the heels, and impatiently swapping his derby from one hand to the other, he waited for the child's return. After several minutes, Gladys Roberts appeared at the door.

"Oh, Mr. Gipson, it's you. Come on in here," she said with a wide smile. She lifted the corner of her apron to dry her wet hands before pushing the door open for him. "Tony said somethin' about you wantin' to see Miss Felcher."

"Yes, ma'am, if it is not too much trouble," he confirmed, already glancing at the stairs, wondering if Emily's room was upstairs or down, and if Mrs. Robert's female tenants were allowed male visitors in their rooms, or if he needed to make arrangements for them to go somewhere else.

"I'm afraid she's not here right now. But if you'd like to leave a message of some kind, I keep a pin board near the door for just such a purpose." She then turned to indicate where he could find paper and pencil.

Randall didn't bother with the board. The message he wanted to leave was not something he should chance letting others read. "Where is she?"

"I don't know for sure. Over on Market Street somewhere. She and another one of my tenants left out of here early this mornin', hopin' to find Emily a job."

"Hoping to find *what?*" he asked, clearly surprised.

"A job. Seems little Katy knew of a job that just opened up down near where she works and offered to go with her to show her exactly where."

"On Market Street?" he asked, still puzzled. There were no brothels on Market Street.

"Yes, at one of the milliners. Even though Emily admitted she had no experience makin' hats, Katy convinced her to at least go by and ask about the job. I guess it was around eight o'clock when they left out of here."

"When do you expect them back?" he asked, as surprised to learn she was out looking for legitimate employment as he was annoyed to know his proposition would have to wait. He'd so been looking forward to getting his due.

"They didn't say when they'd be back. I do know that if the milliner job don't work out, Emily plans to try several other places. She is right eager to find work. And Katy usually has to go on to work herself about ten or ten-thirty, so she won't be able to help her look for very long. That poor little Katy. Sometimes she don't get back home till seven or eight o'clock at night. Pitiful hours for a girl so young."

Randall thought about that. Not exactly the hours of a normal day job, but neither were they the regular working hours of a prostitute. He wondered just what this little Katy did for a living.

By then Andrew had stepped up onto the porch with one of the steamer trunks slung across his shoulder. "Where do you want me to put this?" he asked, when it was apparent no one had paid any attention to him.

Mrs. Roberts stopped her usual rambling when she heard the other male voice.

"Is that one of Emily's trunks?" she wanted to know, stepping forward to examine it.

Randall frowned, having planned to use the trunks as an excuse to see Emily. "Yes. I told her I'd bring them by this morning."

"I know." Mrs. Roberts nodded. "But she really didn't think you'd be able to get hold of them this soon. Oh, please, do bring them both on inside. I'll unlock her room for you. You do have both of the trunks, don't you?"

Randall's frown deepened while he stepped back out of Andrew's way. "Yes. I have them both. Just show my driver where to put them."

When he left several minutes later, it was without having had a chance to speak with Emily. He was both disappointed and somewhat puzzled. He could not understand why Emily would bother going out to look for a regular job. Wouldn't working during the daytime interfere with her nightly activities? Surely she didn't have the stamina for both.

The only thing he could figure: for some reason, she wanted Mrs. Roberts to think she was a respectable tenant. But why would someone like Emily care what her landlady thought? Something was not quite right about the whole situation. Emily was clearly up to something, and he was determined to find out just exactly what.

"Well, did you get the job?" Katy asked the moment Emily emerged from the exclusive hat shop. She had been unable to determine anything from Emily's solemn expression.

Emily stared at her new friend a moment then glanced back at the brightly painted door she'd just come through, still unable to believe it had happened that quickly. Her first job. Her very first job. She wondered what Carole Jeanne would think if she knew she had been forced to find work. Knowing Carole, she'd probably faint dead away. Emily smiled at the thought of what it would take to revive her.

"I start first thing in the morning," she finally answered. "At eight o'clock. Even though tomorrow is Friday and I won't have to work on Saturday, Mrs. Williams wants me to come on in and get started."

"I knowed it!" Katy squealed, her brown curls bouncing about her shoulders as she hopped circles around Emily. "I knowed you'd get the job." She then tossed her arms around Emily's neck and hugged her close. "When I seen how beautiful you stitched closed that jagged tear in my blouse last night, I just knowed you was perfect for this job. What all did you have to do to prove you could do the work?"

Emily shook her head with disbelief. "All she asked me to do was attach a small feather to a hat she was working on, then stitch a tiny satin ribbon around the edge. As soon as I'd handed the work back to her, she looked at it for a second and said

I was hired. I explained that I had no real experience making hats, but she said that didn't matter. I would learn. Then she told me she'd start out paying me five dollars a week plus ten cents extra for each hat I finish. She also told me that if I work very hard and make very few mistakes, I could earn as much as twelve dollars a week. It's been done before."

Katy's green eyes widened at such an amount. "That's nearly twice what I make at the restaurant."

"And twice what I expected to make here," Emily admitted, still unable to believe her good fortune. "And I owe it all to you."

Katy blushed, knowing the praise was largely unwarranted. "No, you owe it all to your own good talent. And to Nicole."

"Who?"

"The girl who had the job before. If she hadn't decided to get married and move off to Wisconsin with her new husband the way she did, then there wouldn't have been no opening here."

"But I wouldn't have even known about the job opening if it hadn't been for you, and the moment I receive my first pay envelope, I plan to buy something special to reward you. What would you like?"

Katy thought about it a moment then nodded toward the display window in front of her. "How about a hat like that one?"

Emily turned and nodded briskly, thinking the black and silver hat quite lovely. "If at all possible, you shall have that very hat. Because of you, I will be able to pay back the money I owe Mr. Gipson within weeks and still have plenty left over for next month's rent. You deserve that hat."

Laughing, Katy nodded agreeably. "I do, don't I? And I also deserve a big piece of Laura Christine's lemon pie." She waved her hand in the direction of the restaurant down the street where she worked. "Come with me. You haven't lived until you've tasted Laura's cooking." She glanced at the clock near the corner of the street. "And we got just enough time to share a fat slice of her pie before I have to start to work. I'll buy."

Linking arms with Katy, who was but a few months older than she, Emily knew she had found a friend she could trust, as much as she ever trusted Carole Jeanne. Smiling broadly, she decided she just might like Galveston after all.

When Emily returned to the boarding house shortly after noon and discovered that Randall had indeed brought her trunks to her, she decided her luck had finally changed. At last, things were going her way. It was not until she searched the trunks for her mother's jewelry and discovered it missing that her mood darkened.

The jewelry, pouch and all, was gone—yet all her money was still in her handbag, as was everything else she carried. Only her jewelry was missing. She thought that awfully strange.

It was when she returned her attention back to the broken latch that she realized what had happened. Randall had forced the trunk open and confiscated her jewelry, probably his way of making certain she did indeed pay him back that ten dollars she owed him.

That one act was all it took to finally break the emotional dam that had been steadily building inside of Emily. She had suffered the devastating loss of her beloved father, coupled with the hurt and confusion she'd felt because of what he had unintentionally allowed to happen to her after his death. Added to those emotions were the anger she felt toward Cynthia for having destroyed her life as she knew it, and the even greater anger she felt for what Josephine Bradley had done. Suddenly, it was too much, she could no longer deny the bitter emotions that burned inside her.

She was furious. Furious for all that had happened to her, but especially furious at Randall Gipson for having taken her jewelry when she needed it to convince her aunt and her grandmother of her identity. He had no right to take anything from her, especially without at least warning her first; and she refused to let him get away with such treachery. She wanted her jewelry back.

At first she considered storming into his house and demanding the jewelry be returned, but after giving it considerable thought she decided that might not do any good. Knowing Randall, he would simply refuse to listen to her complaints and would probably have her physically removed from his house. No, the practical thing would be to somehow come up with the ten dollars she owed him as quickly as possible.

That night, shortly after Katy returned from work, Emily went to her friend's room to ask her if she could possibly borrow the money she needed to repay Randall Gipson in full.

"It's the only way I know to get my jewelry back from him," she explained, trying not to display the anger that consumed her.

"What makes you so sure he's the one who took it? From what you just told me, it could have been this Josephine woman who snatched hold of it."

"No, I don't think so. If Josephine had taken it, she would not have stopped with my jewelry. She would have taken my money, too, what little there was of it. But the money was still there. Only the jewelry pouch was missing. Can you possibly loan me enough to get that jewelry back?"

"That depends. How much money you need?"

"Seven dollars. I only have three dollars left after all the expenses of my trip, and I owe him ten."

"Seven dollars?" Katy hadn't expected it to be that much. "That's more than I make in a week."

"I know, and I'll pay you back just as soon as I've earned my first pay. I promise."

Katy studied Emily's desperate expression for a long moment while carefully considering the request. Emily worried that she might not be willing to part with such a large amount, or that she might not have that much to lend. Finally, Katy shrugged and reached for her bed pillow. "Do I still get the hat?"

Emily sighed with relief as she watched Katy dip her hand deep into her pillow case. "Then you'll loan the money to me?"

"All seven dollars of it," Katy said and quickly counted out the correct amount. "But remember, that only leaves me with a dollar. I sure hope you can pay me back before next month's rent comes due on the first."

"You'll have it long before then," Emily promised and leaned forward to hug her. Tears of gratitude filled her eyes. "I want you to know how very, very much I appreciate this. Without it I could never hope to get my jewelry back, and I do so want to meet my grandmother."

"Now, don't you go getting weepy-eyed on me," Katy warned, wagging her finger at Emily. "I can't stand it when people get weepy-eyed on me."

Sniffing loudly, Emily quickly wiped the tears away with the tips of her fingers. "If there's anything I can ever do for you, no matter what it is, just let me know. I know I owe you a favor—a big favor."

"Well, there is one thing you could do for me," Katy said hesitantly.

"Just name it."

"Let me go with you when you go to claim your jewelry back from this Mr. Gipson. I've always wanted to see the inside of a big house like that."

"Are you sure you want to? I'll have to walk and it is quite a distance from here."

"I'm used to walking," she shrugged. "Just be sure we leave in plenty of time for me to make it on over to work by ten."

"Then we'd better leave right after breakfast on Saturday. I'd go tomorrow, but I don't dare miss my first day of work."

Saturday morning dawned bleak and grey, a dark omen of things to come. Low, overhanging clouds had moved in overnight and threatened to release an early morning downpour. But Emily did not let the dreary weather stop her from treking across town. She was determined to have her jewelry back. And Katy was just as determined to see the inside of the Gipson mansion. They left the house promptly at eight, as planned.

"This is it," Emily said when she pushed open the heavy iron gate and stepped into the spacious, expertly manicured front yard. "This is where the infamous Randall Gipson and his grandmother live."

Katy stared up at the three-story home with its wide overhanging roof and its shaded terraces, awed by the grandeur. "All this house and only two people live here?"

"Well, actually five people live here. The Gipsons have two house servants and a full-time handyman who substitutes as a driver, but the help all live in a large annex at the back."

"The servants have their own annex?" One eye narrowed as if Katy found that a little hard to believe.

"Yes, they have six rooms of their own, including their own kitchen and dining room."

Katy shook her head, again staring at the house in awe. "How disgusting. I can't even imagine what it must be like living in a place this fancy, can you?"

Emily grinned when she thought of the house where she'd spent her childhood because it had been just as large and every bit as grand as this one. But rather than explain what had happened in the past year at that particular moment, she answered, "No, I can't imagine it." She planned to tell Katy all about her past later, when she had more time.

"Some people have all the luck," Katy went on, then lowered her gaze to look at Emily. "Do you think they will really let us in there to see the inside?"

"If Bernice has her way about it, we'll probably be offered tea."

Katy's eyes bulged at the thought. Quickly she brushed any wrinkles from her pale blue cotton skirt and paused to rub the tops of her walking boots against the backs of her dark blue stockings. "And will we accept?"

Emily's expression sobered while she, too, brushed any wrinkles and dust from her own skirts. "That will depend on what sort of mood her grandson is in. He can be very rude when he wants to be."

"Maybe he won't be here," Katy said hopefully, glancing again at the house.

"Don't say that," she admonished as they stepped up onto the shaded veranda that stretched the full width of the house. "If Randall's not here, I can't possibly get my jewelry back from him."

"I forgot," Katy admitted then leaned over to check her reflection in one of the large bay windows near the huge double door. "Well, maybe he'll be in a good mood."

Not after I get through with him, Emily thought, still bitter over the way Randall had behaved toward her Wednesday afternoon. "It doesn't matter to me what sort of mood he's in as long as he gives me back my jewelry so I can finally prove my identity to my aunt and my grandmother."

Several seconds after Emily pulled the cord to the doorbell, the top half of the front door swung open and Nora stepped into view. She looked out at them quizzically. "Miss Emily. What're you doing here?"

"I've come to see Mr. Gipson," she announced with a brisk nod. "I need to speak with him about a very important matter. Is he here?"

"Sure he's here. He's in the dining room finishing up his breakfast. Come on in. I'll tell him you're here." She then swung open the lower half of the door and let them enter. "Who's your friend?"

Katy's eyebrows arched at the servant's familiarity, but if she thought it odd, she didn't say.

"Nora, this is Katy Tisdale. She lives in the same rooming house I do," Emily said as a way of introduction.

"Well, the missus will sure be glad to know you've made yourself some friends already. She wasn't too pleased by Mr. Randall's mule-headed decision to send you away. She's been worried about you ever since."

"She needn't be. The rooming house Randall found is really very nice. I like all the people who live there," Emily assured her.

"That's because we're like one big happy family," Katy quickly put in. "Always willing to help each other." Though she had spoken to Nora, her gaze did not stay with the black woman for very long. She was too busy surveying their elaborate surroundings.

"That's nice. I'm glad to hear it," Nora said, smiling. "Miss Emily needs to have people like that around her."

She waited until Emily had led Katy into the front parlor before crossing the room and disappearing through a sliding door.

Katy blinked, as if questioning what she saw, when Nora suddenly pulled the panel closed behind her. "You can't even tell there's a door there," she breathed, stepping forward to examine the movable section of wall more closely. "If it wasn't for the handle, you'd never know."

Emily smiled despite the turmoil that grew inside her. Katy was clearly impressed by the grandeur. "There are several sliding walls in this house. One even hides a window."

"Why would anyone want to hide a window?"

"Because they wanted an equal number of windows on both sides of the house so it would look right from the outside, yet they didn't actually want a particular window on the inside, therefore they hid it behind a sliding wall."

"Are all rich people that peculiar?" Katy wanted to know.

"No, not all," Emily said, laughing, glad to have a chance to relieve some of the tension that had been building inside her. "Just certain ones come across as peculiar."

"Like this Mr. Gipson?" Katy nodded, as if she understood.

"Yes, like Mr. Gipson," Emily answered, also nodding, while she, too, stared at the false wall.

"*Who* likes Mr. Gipson?" came an unexpected voice from across the room, startling them both.

Gasping aloud, the two women turned to face the hall door where Randall pressed a shoulder indolently against the heavy door frame.

Chapter Eleven

"No one who has any sense at all," Emily retorted, thinking he deserved a quick dressing down for having eavesdropped on their conversation.

Randall's eyebrows arched, but he offered no immediate response while he quietly entered the room. His thoughts were centered on finding some way to be alone with his unexpected guest. He had no idea who the other girl might be, nor could he be sure what her friend knew about Emily's rather risqué lifestyle, therefore he wanted no audience for what he had to say. He preferred to be alone with her when he made his proposition. "Nora said you wanted to talk to me."

"Yes, I do." She met his penetrating gaze straight on, letting him know she would not be intimidated by him—not this time.

"Then follow me to the study," he said, turning to leave. "We can talk there."

Katy, who had not moved so much as to breathe since setting eyes on him, leaned close to Emily's ear just seconds after Randall had turned his back to them.

"Why didn't you warn me what he looks like," she whispered, her words barely loud enough for Emily to hear. "He's absolutely the most handsome man I've ever seen."

"Problem is, he darned well knows it," Emily quipped, also whispering. "Come on, let's go have that word with him. I want my jewelry back."

"Not me," Katy said, raising her voice only a little. Her pale green eyes stretched wide. "Talking to him was your idea. All I wanted to do was see the inside of his house."

Emily frowned. She hadn't really considered having to speak with him alone, but if that's what she had to do to get her jewelry back, then so be it.

"Are you coming?" Randall asked when he noticed she had not followed him to the door.

"Yes, I'm coming," she answered, giving Katy a firm *I'll-talk-to-you-later* look.

Patting her pocket, she checked to be sure the money pouch was still there, hidden safely in the folds of her cinnamon-colored skirt. She headed for the door where he stood waiting, then accompanied him down the hallway and into the study.

While following him along the wide, carpeted corridor that led to the large book-lined room near the back of the house, she mentally reviewed several of the things she intended to say when she finally confronted him. Lost to such angry thoughts, she paid little attention to what went on around her until suddenly she heard the door close behind her. Startled by the noise, she spun immediately around and felt an alarming leap of her senses when she discovered he stood only a few feet away, his gaze roaming over her with shameless abandon.

"And what is it you wanted to talk with me about?" he asked, stepping toward her, finding her presence drew him like a moth to flame. He ran the tip of his tongue across his lips in preparation for that first kiss. Although he did not really plan to take her in his own house, with his grandmother only a few rooms away, he did want at least a sampling of what was to come.

Not having expected such brash behavior, Emily quickly moved away. Her anger turned to instant fear, causing her heart to drum a frantic rhythm against her chest while her gaze darted back and forth between the closed door and his purposeful expression. "And just what is it you think you are doing?"

"What I've wanted to do for days now," he commented. He focused his attention on her parted lips while he slowly lifted his wide, masculine hands to capture her by the rounded curves of her shoulders.

Well remembering the uncanny power of this man, and how utterly helpless she had become while trapped in his arms that night aboard ship, she struggled to free herself. "Unhand me. You have no right to behave like this toward me."

"No right?" he asked, puzzled by such a statement.

"No more right than you had to just up and take my jewelry like you did," she said in an accusing tone. She clutched the seam lines of her dark blue skirt in an effort to keep from strangling him. She had to remain in full control of her senses.

"Your jewelry? What jewelry?" he asked, so confused by her angry words that he temporarily forgot his intention to kiss her. His fingers dug hard into her tender shoulders. "What are you talking about? What jewelry?"

"Don't pretend to be innocent," she warned, then jerked hard to free her shoulders from his painful grasp. Quickly, she moved away from him, putting several feet between them. "You know very well what jewelry. The jewelry you stole from my trunk."

"The jewelry I *what?* Why would I do that?" Although he did not fully understand why she would accuse him of stealing any jewelry, the fact that she had already found him guilty of the act was quite clear.

"Don't bother looking so guiltless, Mr. Gipson. Lying doesn't really become you. Besides, we both know you took my jewelry and we both know why."

"No *we* don't," he quickly interjected. "Why would I want to take your jewelry?"

She shook her head, annoyed that he had not simply admitted his crime and been done with it. "Why? So you could be absolutely sure I'd pay the ten dollars I owe you. Collateral, I guess. Only I never agreed to put up this particular bit of collateral."

Anger turned Randall's blue eyes a dark, dusky gray. "Look, sweets, I don't really know what your scam is, but I didn't take any jewelry and you know it."

"Just like you didn't break the lock on my trunk?" she asked, furious that he continued to deny it.

"That lock was already broken," he informed her. Then suddenly he realized what she was attempting to do and quickly added, "As if you didn't know." He flared his nostrils with obvious disdain. "Might as well give it up. The scheme won't work. Not with me."

"I will not give anything up. I want my jewelry back." She was so angry now her hands shook. "I have brought the ten dollars I owe you." Glaring at him, she reached into her pocket, pulled the pouch out, and thrust it at him. "Now give me my jewelry back. It belonged to both my mother and my grandmother. I want it back."

Randall shifted his weight to one well-muscled leg while he looked first at the money in his hand

and then at her. "And I suppose the next thing you'll want is for me to reimburse you for the loss of this jewelry, which probably never even existed. Sorry. I'm not falling for it. But I do want you to know that I do appreciate getting my money back so soon—just not enough to let you soak me for even more."

"Soak you?" she sputtered. Her thoughts tumbled over themselves while she tried to grasp his reasoning.

"That's right," he said, nodding slowly. "Connive all you want, but there's only one way you'll ever get any more money out of me and that is to *earn* it."

"Soak you?" she repeated, still trying to grasp why he would say something like that. She clenched her hands in frustration. "How dare you say such a thing to me."

"And how dare you try to trick me out of yet more money. It's bad enough that you used my grandmother the way you did—but rest assured, you will not get away with using me like that."

"Using you?" she exclaimed, so angry by that time, she could do little more than repeat his accusations aloud. "*Using* you?"

"My, what an amazing actress you are. Just the right touch of righteous indignation in your voice," he commented, tilting his head as if wanting to view the performance from a different perspective. "You are truly talented. You really should go on the road."

"And you, sir, really should go to hell!" she shouted, stunned by her own angry choice of words.

The lines shaping Randall's face hardened into a grim mask of smoldering rage.

"That's it. I've had enough," he said, narrowing his gaze with dangerous intent while he reached for the door and jerked it open. "Get out of my house. It's bad enough to be called a thief and a liar, but I refuse be told to go to hell in my own home—especially by someone like you."

Emily glowered at him, unable to think of a suitable retort. When she finally did speak, it was with such soul-wrenching fury, her voice trembled. "Not until I get my jewelry back."

"I don't have your jewelry," he shouted then slammed his fist against the open door, causing her to jump. "Will you get that through your thick skull? I don't have your jewelry and I never did. And I damn sure am not about to reimburse you for something I never took. Now get out of my house before I have you thrown out."

Still furious over the hateful way he'd spoken to her, but at the same time willing to admit Josephine very well may have been the one to take the jewelry, she thrust her chin forward and met his wrath with a murderous glare. "Perhaps I have made a mistake. And if that turns out to be true, then I'll apologize for having falsely accused you. But if at some point along the way, I discover you did indeed take my grandmother's jewelry and then decided to keep it from me for some selfish reason, I'll be back. And when I do come back, I'll make you pay a far sight more than the jewelry is worth." Having said that, she spun about and stalked out of the room, her hands balled into fists so tight her knuckles had turned white.

"No, you won't. You'll never get another penny out of me," he shouted after her, not about to let her have the last word yet again. "Not one penny. Do you understand?"

The only response he heard was the loud clatter of the front door as it slammed behind the two women several minutes later.

* * *

"You what?" Katy asked as she hurried to keep up, not at all certain she'd heard Emily correctly.

"I want you to go with me to Josephine's so I can ask for my jewelry back," she repeated with a light shrug, as if it were an everyday occurrence to invite a friend to accompany her on a visit to one of the local brothels. Now that she'd had time to calm down, she believed Randall to be as innocent as he claimed. There was just something about his anger that had convinced her. Therefore, the only other possibility was that Josephine had taken the jewelry. "We've still got time. You don't have to be at the restaurant until ten. That's still nearly an hour away."

Katy's eyes widened at the sheer prospect of such an improbable adventure. "That's true enough. I still got a little over an hour. But what makes you so sure this woman even has your jewelry? Just a few minutes ago, you firmly believed that Randall Gipson had it."

"Well, Mr. Gipson has managed to convince me that he had nothing to do with my jewelry's disappearance. And if he didn't take it, then there's only one other person who could possibly be a suspect."

"But what about one of the other girls who works for her? Couldn't they have taken the jewelry?" she asked, wanting to be sure Emily had thought everything through this time.

"Perhaps, but I don't think they could have gotten away with doing something like that without Josephine at least knowing about it."

"So you plan to just march up to the woman's door and demand your jewelry back?" Katy asked, still not sure Emily had thought the situation through well enough.

"That's the plan, all right." Emily shrugged again, as if it were really a simple matter.

Katy grinned, her eyes sparkling over the thought of doing something so daring. "Okay, I'll go. But if I'm late for work, I want *you* to go in and explain what happened to my boss. I'll want *you* to tell him that the whole reason I'm late is because I had to stop off at a brothel first." She chuckled at the thought.

"Be glad to," Emily said, laughing despite the uneasiness that churned in her stomach. "You just make sure I come away from there in one piece."

"I wonder what my mother would say," Katy muttered, tsking her tongue against her teeth while she hurried to keep up with Emily. "Her beloved little Katherine, off to pay call on one of the most notorious brothels in all of Galveston."

"Better to pay call on one than to work in one," Emily pointed out, then shuddered when she remembered how close she had come to being forced into becoming just another one of Josephine's "girls." She still wondered how she could have been so naive about what was going on around her, and continued to blame her stupidity on the fact she had been unusually tired that night. In fact, she had been so tired that most of what had happened to her during her short stay at Josephine's remained little more than a blur, which was not at all like her. She usually remembered things quite clearly.

By nine-thirty the unseasonably cool wind had picked up, making the dark clouds churn into an angry mass; but no rain had yet fallen. Emily and Katy arrived in front of Josephine's house chilled and windblown, but still determined to see Emily's quest through.

Without pausing to give full consideration to what lay in store for them, for fear she might back out before the deed was done, Emily did not bother repairing her hair or readjusting her rumbled skirts. Instead, she marched straight to the front door and knocked as hard as she could. Katy followed at a much slower pace, her head rotating like a small beacon, as if afraid she might miss something of interest.

"This is some place," Katy commented while waiting for someone to respond to Emily's knock. She stepped back to get a better view of the wide veranda with its elaborate wicker furniture and tropical potted plants. "Hard to believe it's not just another house."

"Well, it's not," Emily retorted, keeping her voice low so she would not be overheard through the open windows. "And you would be wise to keep that fact in mind."

When she heard footsteps within, she turned to face the door. She lifted her chin to a determined angle, hoping that might make her appear more foreboding, then took a deep breath and held it while the right side of the door slowly swung open. She waited to see who would answer.

A petite girl who looked barely sixteen stepped into the doorway. She was dressed in a black and gray uniform and wearing a stark white mop cap over a massive head of dark brown curls. Emily had never seen the girl before, but guessed her to be Sheila, the other of Josephine's two housekeepers and one of the only two people she would expect to be awake at such an early hour.

"May I help you?" The girl asked, reaching up to play with one of the curling tendrils of brown hair that peeked out from beneath her oversized cap.

"Yes, I'm here to see Miss Bradley," Emily announced in her most businesslike voice.

"Oh, but she's not up yet. She doesn't get herself up and moving about until early afternoon."

Emily hadn't considered that. "Well, I have something very important to discuss with her. Could you wake her?"

"Can't it wait?" The girl's gaze darted in the direction of Josephine's room. "She doesn't like to be awakened too early."

"No, I'm afraid this can't wait. It is very important that I speak with her right away."

Noting the serious tone in Emily's voice, the girl took a tentative step toward the east wing, then as if suddenly remembering something, she turned back. "Can I have your name?"

"Emily. Emily Felcher. She'll know who I am."

The girl's face blanched. "You're Emily Felcher? But she told me not to even let you in the house."

Emily's facial muscles tightened. "She what?"

Aware that Emily was rapidly reaching the breaking point, Katy quickly stepped forward. Resting a reassuring hand on her friend's tense shoulder, she shot the young girl a venomous glare, letting her know just how serious the matter could become. "Go wake the woman."

"But—but—," the girl stammered, her brow notching with confusion and fear.

"Now!" Katy snapped, then took another menacing step in the housekeeper's direction. "We don't got all day." She narrowed her eyes with malicious intent.

Taking a step back, Sheila swallowed hard, clearly afraid of what harm Katy had planned for her. "I'll tell her you are here, but I can't promise that she'll see you."

"She'll have to see us because we ain't leaving until she does." Katy crossed her arms to show her adamance. "You might want to tell her that."

Emily stared at Katy with stunned disbelief. Until now she'd always thought of Katy as such a rather quiet, reserved person, but now she was not sure what to think of her. This was a whole different Katy.

"I think that about did it," Katy said with a wry grin, then slowly released the breath she'd held trapped deep in her lungs. "If that don't lure the wench out of her bed, nothing will." Spying a chair nearby, she quickly sat down, heaving another soft, trembling sigh. Emily noticed her face had also turned very pale, letting her know that Katy had just done a very brave thing.

Minutes later, Josephine appeared in the hallway, her eyes puffy from lack of sleep and her expression grim. "Sheila said you wanted to see me."

"Yes, I want to ask you about my jewelry," Emily said, her insides churning from the memory of what this woman had tried to do to her.

"What about it?" Josephine looked from Emily to Katy then back, her eyebrows drew together in a perplexed expression.

"It was not in my trunk when you gave it to Edward Peterson."

"Sure it was. In fact, I know it was," Josephine said, her eyes narrowing as if daring Emily to dispute her word. "After finding the lock sprung, I went through the trunk myself. I wanted to make sure everything was there. I well remember tucking a black jewelry pouch back inside your handbag—along with almost three dollars in cash. I suppose that was missing too."

"No, just the jewelry was gone," Emily admitted, confused by the annoyance in Josephine's voice. She sounded very convincing. "The money was still there."

"Well, if I were you, hon, I'd have a little talk with

Edward Peterson because he was evidently the last person to have your jewelry. And I'd also be a little more careful about whom I go accusing of theft. I may have a few faults, but I'm not a thief."

Emily wet her lips while she tried to decide if Josephine spoke the truth or not. She sounded so sincere in what she'd just told her. Now she didn't know who to suspect: Josephine, Randall, or Edward Peterson. All three seemed so genuinely innocent, but one of them had to have taken the jewelry.

"Come one, Emily," Katy said, aware of the awkward situation. "I have to get on to work or I'll be late. Besides, there's really very little you can do until you've found definite proof of who took your jewelry. If it turns out this woman is the culprit, and you can find some way to prove it, then you can have her arrested by the police. But until then, there's not much either of us can do."

Emily knew Katy was right. Until she had tangible proof, there was nothing she could do to get the jewelry back.

Never had she felt so helpless. Never had she felt such anger.

Yet there was nowhere to direct that anger. Unless she found out who had stolen her jewelry and soon, she feared she would explode with rage.

"You're right," she said. Her jaw clenched against the bitter taste of her words when she spoke to Josephine, "I never should have come here without absolute proof. I'm sorry to have bothered you."

Josephine tossed her head back, looking very smug, which made Katy very angry.

"By the way," Katy said, looking back over her shoulder at the woman as she turned to leave. "If you or one of your *girls* should happen to come across Emily's jewelry somewhere, please contact

Mr. Peterson right away. There's a thousand-dollar reward for whoever turns it in."

Emily glanced at her with an arched eyebrow but said nothing until they were outside, well away from the house. "And what thousand-dollar reward might that be?" she asked, shaking her head at such an absurd notion. "Whatever possessed you to say such a thing?"

Katy lifted her shoulders then dropped them. "I don't know. I just figured that if she was the one who took your jewelry with plans of selling it for a quick dollar, she might be just as willing to give it back if there was a big enough reward. At the same time, I also figured she might be a little reluctant to bring the jewelry back directly to you, especially after having claimed she had actually seen it go out the door with Mr. Peterson, so I decided to say he was the one handling it."

"And what if she does go to Mr. Peterson and asks for the thousand-dollar reward?" Emily asked, not fully comprehending Katy's purpose.

"Then we have her dead to rights," Katy said, shaking her head as if that should have been a foregone conclusion. "I just got one little question I'd like answered about all this."

"And what might that be?"

"Who in the blue-blazes is Mr. Peterson?"

"Emily has only been gone a week, and already I miss her dreadfully," Bernice commented loud enough to distract Randall from his morning newspaper. "It was such a joy to have her here."

Randall glanced up from his reading just long enough to make eye contact with her, warning her that she had broached a sore subject. Ever since his confrontation with Emily last Saturday, he'd tried in every way possible to put her out of his mind and was having a hard enough time putting aside her hauntingly alluring image without all these constant reminders from his grandmother.

Aware something was wrong between Randall and Emily, but not knowing for sure what it might be, Bernice continued, all the while keeping a careful eye on Randall's reaction. "I wonder how she's getting along, all alone in a strange city. How I do wish I'd been told when she had come by here last Saturday. Then maybe I could have talked with her, if only for a moment."

When Randall's only response was to expel a short, primitive grunt, Bernice delved farther into the subject. "Nora told me she left here in an awful rush. No one ever explained why she was in such a hurry to leave or why she didn't stay long enough to say hello to me, too."

"I imagine she had places to go. People to see." He muttered and continued to glare at his newspaper, though he no longer saw the print.

"Yes, as pretty as that girl is, I imagine she has had lots of invitations to go out and do things. Probably has a long line of young men paying call on her by now."

The muscles in Randall's jaw hardened but he refused to be lured into a conversation he wanted to avoid. "I imagine she does. So, it really is foolish for you to worry about her the way you do."

"I can't help it. She was such a sweet girl. It's a real shame about her missing jewelry."

Randall's head snapped up, causing his brown hair to fall forward across his forehead. "What do you know about her jewelry?" He folded the newspaper then pushed his hair back into place. At last he gave Bernice the attention she sought.

"Just what Edward mentioned yesterday while he was by here. He said that although she has her clothes back and most of the rest of her belongings, her jewelry remains missing. Poor girl. The only thing she owned that could in any way prove to her aunt she is exactly who she says she is, and it turns up missing. It's a shame what all that poor girl has had to go through during these past few months."

"Yes, a real pity," Randall muttered, not feeling as generous toward Emily as his grandmother and still not convinced there ever was any jewelry. He also still remembered the ugly accusations she'd flung at him last Saturday in hopes of extorting money from him. And, he remembered how easily she had tricked his grandmother into letting her stay there a lot longer than was necessary. The young woman had to be the most conniving, manipulative woman he'd ever known, and all the beauty in the world could not make up for that.

"I wish I could be sure she's all right." Bernice lowered her head and shook it sadly, all the while keeping a close eye on Randall's hardened expression.

"So, have Peterson check on her."

"I would, but I don't know where to have him check."

"Didn't Emily tell him her new address when she went to see him about the alleged missing jewelry?"

"Evidently not. And you have certainly been very closed-mouthed about where she's living now. If I knew the address, I could go see for myself how she's getting along." She sighed heavily. "I do so worry about her."

"All right. All right. What if I promise to go by there sometime today and check on her? Would that help in any way?"

Bernice brightened immediately "Oh, yes. All I really want is to know that she's getting along all right."

"Then I'll stop by there on my way to the shipping office. How's that?"

Bernice placed her fingers over her mouth so he could not see her revealing grin. "That would make me very happy. Very happy indeed."

"Good. Now may I finish my newspaper?" he asked, annoyed that he'd allowed himself to be manipulated into doing something he had no desire to do. Snapping the paper open, he directed his glower to the latest shipping reports.

"Of course," Bernice responded sweetly. "Anything you want." She then fell dutifully silent while she finished the remainder of her morning tea.

Chapter Twelve

By the time Randall had filled himself with scrambled eggs, ham, biscuits, and honey, and had traveled across the city to Mrs. Robert's small two-story house in a well springed open carriage, the gentle gulf breeze and the soothing warmth of the early morning sun against his skin had lifted his spirits considerably. He loved being outdoors in the morning. He found the hours before the heat of midday came pressing down upon the island to be the most invigorating part of the day—especially during early summer.

After arriving at the rooming house, he descended from the carriage with a light jump and paused to take several deep breaths of sea air before tossing his hat onto the seat. He would much rather feel the warm breeze tug at his hair than at that confounded hat. Besides, he knew as soon as he reached the office he'd toss both his hat and his summer coat over the nearest chair and roll his sleeves past his elbow to get comfortable at last.

The only reason he bothered with a business suit at all was to please his grandmother—because his grandfather had always worn business suits to work. It was also why he had often wished he had remained a ship's captain. At least aboard ship he was allowed to wear what he wanted, and was expected to be outside most of the day, where he could get all the fresh air he wanted. But after his father's death, he had decided it was his duty to come off the ships and take over the management of the Galveston branch of the family business—before that temporary manager the attorney had hired ran the whole thing into the ground.

Pushing those thoughts aside because it did little good to dwell on such matters, Randall glanced toward the small boarding house and remembered his mission. He wondered if Emily would be awake yet, but didn't really care if she was or not. If she was still asleep, he'd simply have her wakened.

Stepping onto the narrow planked walkway that ran along both sides of the street so pedestrians wouldn't have to fight the soft sand when they walked, he ordered Andrew to wait for him in the carriage. He then headed straight for the front steps. It was not until he paused for a moment on the small porch that was barely large enough to accommodate half a dozen chairs and a porch swing, that he realized he had actually started looking forward to another opportunity to see Emily.

Although the girl had caused him only annoyance and aggravation since they first met, for some unfathomable reason he wanted to see her. He actually missed her. Missed her smiling face, missed the teasing sparkle in her pale brown eyes, missed the little innuendos that spilled out of her, and the innocent way she pretended not to have said anything that may have been in the least bit suggestive. If nothing else, she was unpredictable and that made her fun to be with. He looked forward to spending time alone with her.

Feeling that strongly about someone like her

made absolutely no sense to Randall, but then nothing about the different feelings she aroused in him made much sense. If anything, he should loathe her for what she'd tried to do to him and his grandmother—yet more and more, she fascinated him. Even *he* had to admit she was an extremely clever person, just not quite clever enough to outwit him. He was simply not as trusting as his grandmother. And with good reason. He *knew* what sort of woman she was.

"Oh, Mr. Gipson," he heard his name called from within the house, startling him from his reverie. "What are you doin' here?"

He had recognized Mrs. Robert's high-pitched voice even before he saw her shadowy silhouette fall across the front screen. "I've come to see Emily—ah—Miss Felcher. Seems my grandmother has started to worry about her and asked me to stop by and check on her. She wants to be sure she's getting along all right."

"What a shame. You just missed her. Emily caught a ride over to Market Street with Mr. Bebber. He's another one of my boarders. Has his own buggy. Very nice gentleman. Everyone likes him. He's the type that's always offering people rides."

"Market Street? What's she doing there?" he asked, noting that Emily must have recovered from her recent losses awfully quick to already be out on a shopping spree. Why it had only been four days ago that she'd come to him claiming to be dead broke and wanting to extort money from him. He felt his anger return.

"Didn't you know?" Mrs. Robert's asked, pushing the screen door open so they could see each other better. "She's started a workin' for Mrs. Williams. Emily's now a makin' hats. Does very well at it the way I understand."

"She's what?" he asked, surprised. He wondered why she would bother taking on such tedious work when she could make so much more by pursuing her "other" profession.

"She's a makin' hats. Workin' for some French woman named Jacqueline Williams over on Market Street," Mrs. Robert's elaborated, then rattled on in her usual manner. "Didn't you know? She got that job I was a tellin' you about that last time you was here. She started a workin' last Friday."

"Making hats?" That was too farfetched to believe.

"Yes. Ladies hats. And to hear Katy tell it, our Emily is very good at makin' stitches."

Randall didn't doubt that, for she had been a definite stitch in his side from the very beginning. "What time does she usually come home?"

"Not until after six, which really works out just fine because that's about the same time Mr. Bebber gets off. That's the reason she's able to share a ride with him every day. Saves her a havin' to walk."

Randall fell silent while he tried again to figure out why Emily had bothered taking on such a menial daytime job when her nighttime talents could earn her so much more, and with far less effort. The only thing he could figure was that, for some unknown reason, Emily wanted these people to believe she was respectable. But why would she bother? Then he realized the answer: she must be hoping to lure some poor but rich swain into marriage so she would not have to work at all. If she married a man with money, she could live the life she wanted without any effort on her part, and without any worries.

He shook his head, feeling sorry for whoever proved foolish enough to fall prey to her latest scheme, for Emily Felcher was definitely not wifely material and, eventually, no matter how well she tried to hide her past, the truth would come out. When it did, the man would find himself married to a woman who had been intimately known by dozens of men. All the beauty in the world could not make up for the pain and humiliation that revelation would cause.

"Would you like to leave Emily a message?" Mrs. Roberts asked him, cocking her head to one side, as if wondering why he had suddenly become so quiet.

"No, that won't be necessary. I think that just knowing that Emily has found suitable work and has such nice people living around her will be enough to console my grandmother."

"Well, if you're sure."

"Sure enough, thank you." When he turned to leave, he was so lost in thought—from having so accidentally uncovered Emily's latest ploy—he almost missed the steps.

"Are you all right, Mr. Gipson?" Mrs. Roberts asked, clearly worried about his sudden display of bad balance when he tried to keep from falling into one of her flower beds.

"I'm fine," he answered, his facial expression drawn, still deep in concentration. "Just fine. It's the *other* man you have to worry about. Not me."

Mrs. Roberts' eyebrows arched high into her forehead while she watched Randall trudge slowly back to his carriage. She was bewildered by his mention of another man.

Days later, at Katy's insistence, Emily did finally agree to allow an amorous young man by the name of Patrick Freeburg to pay an occasional call on her, but soon regretted the decision.

Although Patrick proved to be every bit as nice as Katy had claimed him to be, and Emily did indeed enjoy his company whenever they were together, she was not at all in love with him. Despite the fact he was unquestionably handsome, and was from a well respected family like her own, his presence simply did not make her pulse race—not the way Randall's had. Nor did she find herself thinking of Patrick when he wasn't with her—not like she did with Randall. Because Randall had so thoroughly ruined her ability to enjoy another man's company, she tried to limit Patrick's visits as best she could, which was not easy, considering his determination to the contrary. Still, she tried to prevent him from developing any true regard for her. She was interested in nothing beyond a casual friendship with him.

She repeatedly reminded Patrick that she held no special feelings for him, yet he continued to find reasons to stop by and see her practically every day. As Mrs. Roberts had so blatantly put it after the second week of constant visits, Patrick Freeburg was rapidly becoming just like another piece of furniture around the place. She teased that she might as well start dusting him.

But between Patrick's constant visits and Emily's long hours at work, she was left with very little time to pursue the matter of her missing jewelry. Only by taking extra long lunch breaks—which she usually had to make up at the end of the day—did she find enough time to travel across town to Edward Peterson's office to find out if any progress had been made.

When it became apparent that she might never get her jewelry back, Emily began to contemplate far more desperate measures. Aware that Edward was making no progress at all, she decided the time had come to take matters in her own hands. She decided to try to contact this stubborn aunt herself. Maybe by describing her mother and explaining what she knew about why her mother had left, she could convince the aunt she was exactly who she said she was, and eventually she might be allowed to see her grandmother.

Wanting to make the very best first impression possible, she bought the most expensive grade of stationary she could find, then spent hours upon hours writing and rewriting her plea, only to be turned down by a hastily scrawled message written on the back of the same envelope in which she'd sent her letter. Her aunt had refused to even read the letter, clearly wanting nothing to do with her.

Soon, after discovering every other avenue that could provide any information already closed to her, Emily began asking questions of everyone who came into Mrs. Williams's hat shop. She wanted to find someone who could tell her *something* about her grandmother, Elmira Townsend.

After a week of further disappointments, and just when she had started to believe the woman who'd given birth to her own mother had never existed, Emily found someone who remembered her—one of Mrs. Williams's older customers.

"Of course I know Elmira," Mrs. Patton told her, while trying to adjust a tiny black satin hat just so atop her massive pile of silvery grey curls. "Or at least I *used* to know her."

Emily felt her stomach tighten with sudden apprehension. "What do you mean you *used* to know her?" She clasped her hands together in her lap to steady them.

"Why, I heard Elmira died over a year ago. If I remember right, she had some sort of dreadful cough. Probably something like the black lung. I know of several people who died from black lung last year."

Devastated, Emily remembered that what little information Edward had managed to uncover about whatever illness had befallen her grandmother had been very, very vague. Had the illness proven fatal? Could her grandmother have died and Edward not yet have discovered that fact? It was possible. After all, he had never actually claimed to have been in contact with her grandmother or even her grandmother's doctor, just with that aunt who refused to believe Emily ever existed.

Heartbroken, Emily took several long, slow breaths to ease the constriction in her throat. "Would you tell me about her?"

Mrs. Patton turned to look at her questioningly. "What would you like to know?"

"Anything. What she was like? How long did you know her?"

Aware that for some reason this meant a lot to the girl, Mrs. Patton set the hat aside and reached for Emily's hands. Her hands felt warm against Emily's cold skin.

"I knew Elmira for quite some time, though I hadn't actually seen her but once since her husband's death. She became very withdrawn after that. Hardly ever ventured into town anymore. But before that tragedy struck her, she was a very cheerful sort of person. Always willing to help when a worthy cause came along. I think her favorite charity was probably the orphanage. She was always so giving of her time and her money. But then she had enough of both to be more than generous. Why do you ask?"

Emily blinked back the moisture that burned at the edges of her brown eyes. She didn't have the heart to go into any lengthy explanation, afraid she would break into tears if she did. "No reason. I was just curious."

Mrs. Patton looked at her a long moment, then

shrugged as if deciding it was really none of her business. "Anyone else you care to know about? I've lived here long enough to know a little something about practically everyone."

For some odd reason, Emily thought of Randall, but was unable to actually say his name aloud for fear the woman might misconstrue her reason for being so curious. "No. I guess not."

Rather than dwell on his handsome image, she immediately turned her attention back to her work, ignoring the way her heart always seemed to flounder helplessly inside her chest whenever she thought of Randall. "So, now that you've actually tried the hat on, do you still want me to add more lace or do you like it pretty much the way it is?"

Although Emily tried her best to concentrate on Mrs. Patton's response, she had a hard time listening to what she had to say about the hat—or anything else. And it wasn't all because of her unwanted thoughts about Randall. She was crestfallen over having learned about her grandmother's death. She had traveled all that way and spent almost all her money, yet would never even have the opportunity to meet her mother's mother. Even so, she could not be denied at least *knowing* about her.

She may never have the chance to actually meet the woman her mother had spoken about with such longing and with such fondness, but she could still try to find out all she could about her. Hearing about her grandmother secondhand might not be the same as having actually met her, but it was better than nothing. And, if she could ever convince her aunt that she really was who she said she was, she might yet be allowed to meet her mother's only sister. That left something to hope for. Everything else may have been taken from her, but no one could strip her of that last shred of hope.

Fighting the sharp pain that had resulted from everything she'd just learned, Emily quickly did what she could to adjust to the grim reality of her grandmother's death. Having decided to turn her energies toward finding out all she could about the woman who had given life to her own mother, she refocused her energies toward that.

The first thing she wanted to know about her dearly departed grandmother was exactly where she was buried. She desperately wanted to see the gravestone and pay her respects. But after having searched most of the cemeteries in the area, and finding no Townsends in any of them, she turned to Edward Peterson to see what he could find out about where her grandmother had been buried.

She was disappointed to learn that the search for her grandmother's grave site might take several days, but at the same time relieved to know Mr. Peterson planned to check into the matter himself and not leave the search to one of his aides. Again, she had little choice but to wait.

Randall was in no mood for a party. He'd had his fill of frivolous conversation and pasted-on smiles the evening before. So why was he headed for yet another of society's biggest events? It made absolutely no sense. Besides it was too hot to stay trussed up in his formal evening attire on such a warm evening.

"Andrew, I've changed my mind." He shouted above the traffic noises. "Don't take me to the Browns' house after all. Take me to Oakley's Tavern instead."

Andrew turned in the seat. A grin stretched wide across his burly face when he noticed that Randall had already come out of his frock coat and was busily loosening his tie. "Yes, sir, Mr. Gipson. Oakley's Tavern it is."

"Make the trip in good time and I'll reward you with a frosty mug of beer," Randall said, also smiling, relieved he had decided to forget the Brown Cotillion. Although he occasionally enjoyed the silliness of some parties and the grandeur of others, tonight he wanted to be away from all that. Tonight he sought simpler pleasures. "Get there within five minutes and I'll treat you to *two* beers.

Andrew snapped the reins high over the horses' heads, sending the carriage forward with a sudden lurch, which also sent Randall's head back with a snap. He laughed out loud when he glanced at his watch. "Okay, it's 9:16. You have until 9:21 to get me there if you want your two drinks."

Racing in and around the slower vehicles, Andrew did his best to beat the five minute limit Randall had set. Even before he had drawn the carriage to a complete halt in front of Randall's favorite tavern, he turned in his seat and looked at him with wide eyed anticipation. "Well, what time is it? Did I make it?"

Randall glanced back at his watch. 9:23. Two minutes too late.

"Of course, you made it. With seconds to spare," he lied, then reached into his pocket to reward him with a dollar, enough to buy six mugs of beer. "I guess you'll be wanting to go into Millie's for awhile," he commented, nodding toward the small saloon directly across the street from Oakley's. He knew how taken Andrew had become with a girl named Stephanie, who was one of Millie's young barmaids. "I'll meet you back here in . . ." he glanced at his watch again before tucking it into his trousers pocket . . . "Let's say, we meet back here in two hours."

Andrew's eyes brightened with delight. Two hours would give him plenty of time. "I'll be here," he vowed, then hopped down from the driver's seat and headed across the street.

Randall wasted little time crossing the wooden walkway and entering the brightly painted tavern. Once inside, he was immediately recognized and greeted by several other men who had obviously made similar decisions about attending the Brown's annual ball. Some had yet to shed their frock coats, but all had lost their neckties and dress gloves somewhere along the way.

"Patrick," he shouted when he noticed his friend sitting at a small table across the room with two other men. As expected, Patrick waved him over.

Randall immediately made his way through the boisterous crowd. "What are you doing here? Why aren't you at the Cotillion?" He pulled out a chair and nodded a greeting to the other two men, whom he immediately recognized as Reggie and John Rourke, both reporters for the *Galveston Daily News.*

"I was just about to ask you the same thing," Patrick said, lifting his whiskey glass to his lips and taking a hearty sip. "Whatever will the poor women do with both of us absent?"

Though Patrick had tried to sound unconcerned about the matter, Randall detected something wrong in his voice.

"Don't tell me you were stood up by some beautiful young belle?" he asked, worried about the unhappy look on Patrick's usually smiling face.

"Not stood up exactly," Patrick explained, not about to lie to his good friend. "She had to work late."

"Work?" Randall repeated, surprised. "You're seeing a working girl?" He looked from Patrick to the other two, his eyes wide with disbelief.

Reggie then nodded, indicating he'd already heard the story. "He's not only seeing a working girl, I'm afraid he's really quite smitten with her. She's all he can talk about."

"*All* he can talk about," John put in, his expression weary.

It was evident these two were ready to discuss something else—anything else—so Randall quickly veered onto another topic. "Oh, well, at least she hasn't thrown you over for another man. Remember last year when Annie Wray abandoned me at the Kilburn's big party because she wanted to go on a late night ride with someone else? That new fellow. Oh, what's his name."

Patrick started laughing immediately. "Do I ever. I guess it wouldn't have been so bad except she took the poor fellow riding in *your* coach, leaving you with no way to get home but walk. I also remember how mortified your driver was when he returned from having shared a few drinks with the other drivers, only to discover the rig gone. He'd thought you'd left him stranded. Walked all the way back to your house in a pair of brand new boots that nearly chewed his toes off."

Randall could laugh about it now. "So, you see, Patrick, you don't have nearly the reason I had to be so glum."

"Glum? Is that what you were when you found out what Anne had done?" Patrick asked, laughing with such force now that tears collected in his eyes. "I, myself, thought you looked mad as hell."

Randall chuckled. He had been rather perturbed. Not about Anne, because she was always doing things like that; but, damnit, he'd just bought that coach. He hadn't even worn the springs in yet.

"I wish I'd caught wind of it," Reggie said, shaking his head and laughing, too. "That would have made a terrific front page story for the paper." He held his hands up as if indicating headlines: LOCAL ROMEO, LEFT IN THE LURCH.

"And no doubt that's exactly where you would've printed it, too," Randall said, cocking an eyebrow as if to show exactly how little he trusted the man, but was too busy laughing to be convincing. "Right in the middle of the front page."

After having spent the past several days worrying about the railroad purchase he and his cousin had been working on for what seemed now like years, it felt good simply to sit with a few friends and laugh about old times. It was just the medicine he needed and it appeared it was also the release Patrick needed.

Reggie drew in several gasping breaths while he wiped the moisture from his eyes with the edge of his knuckle. "No, on second thought, our uncle would probably have refused to let us print it at all. Anne's father is the newspaper's attorney, you know. I guess that's why she gets away with so much. No one dares print anything bad about her."

"No, but the story gets around town just the same," John injected, chuckling along with the rest. "And by the time it does make the rounds, the gossip is usually twice as juicy as any account we might have put in the newspaper. Remember the one about the two of you out on West Beach?" He looked at Randall, shaking his head with disbelief.

"Do I ever," Randall said, nodding enthusiastically. "I thought I was going to have to marry her after that one got rolling."

For the next three hours, the four men continued to talk about every lively event and every mutual friend they could remember—and some they couldn't. As the evening wore on, and the empty glasses piled high, names started to elude them, but the stories were told with as much aplomb as ever.

When Reggie pushed his long blonde hair out of his face for what had to be the hundredth time and peered bleary-eyed at the clock across the room, he noticed what time it had become and sat forward with a start. With a worried frown, he nudged John, who sat slumped low in his chair, his head tilted back against the rim, fighting to stay awake. "Hey, brother, we'd better get on out of here if we plan to help the old man get that paper out by five-thirty."

They had both scraped their chairs back across the wooden floor and were halfway out of their seats before Randall pointed out what he felt to be a somewhat pertinent fact. "What's the hurry? My friends, it happens to be Saturday night." He quickly corrected himself when he, too, glanced at the clock. "Well, no, actually it's Sunday morning."

"That it is," Patrick said, his words now coming out slurred. "It's after midnight so that definitely makes it Sunday morning. Randy, old boy, you really are quite observant."

Randall pressed his teeth into his lower lip to keep from groaning. "What I'm trying to point out to these two fine gentlemen is the fact that the paper doesn't come out again until Monday morning. They still have plenty of time to help get the next edition out."

"Good thing," Patrick muttered, studying the way Reggie and John both held on to the edge of the table in an effort to steady themselves. "I'd hate to read anything those two put out tonight. Why they are literably soused."

"Literably?" Randall repeated, chuckling at the strange word Patrick had just created.

"Soused." Patrick concluded, then closed his

eyes for a long moment. "I think I just might be literably soused, too."

"Maybe it would be best if we all went on home and got some sleep," Randall said, aware that he'd already stayed a lot longer than he'd originally intended. Andrew was probably sitting in the front seat of the carriage waiting haplessly for his return. But, then upon remembering how much money he'd given him for his own drink and revelry, he decided that if Andrew was indeed in the carriage waiting for him, he probably was sound asleep by now.

Finding Randall's suggestion to be a sound one, Reggie and John headed immediately for the door. They showed great skill in their efforts to weave in and around the people who still milled about, as if hoping to avoid stumbling into anyone—but then continued to weave in and out even after they had made their way through the front door. Randall chuckled, knowing it would take them twice as long to get home because they would be covering twice the ground they usually did.

"Time for me to go, too," Randall commented, but when he reached for his glass, wanting to down the last of his beer, Patrick spoke in such a strangely decisive tone it caused him to hesitate with the mug held in midair.

"I'm not ready to go home yet," Patrick announced, finally opening one eye so he could see Randall's face. "I haven't had a chance to tell you about my latest love."

"The working girl?" Randall asked, setting the heavy mug back down.

"Yep. She's a working girl all right," he held up his hands to keep Randall from speaking. "I know. I know. It's not like me to pay call on anyone beneath my social status, but you'd have to see her to understand. She's the most beautiful thing I've ever set my sight on. She has long, *satiny* brown hair and the biggest brown eyes, surrounded by thick, *silky* lashes."

Randall tried to keep from chuckling for she sounded more like a ladies undergarment than anything else. He managed to hold a straight face.

"And she always has such clever things to say," Patrick went on. "She makes me laugh. A lot. And she has the gentlest heart I've ever known a woman to have."

"And does this saint of yours have a name?" Randall asked, reaching again for the handle on the side of his glass.

Closing his eyes, Patrick slumped low in his chair and smiled with sheer contentment while he happily rolled her name off his tongue. "Em-i-ly. Emily Felcher. She's from up North."

Randall's hand tightened around the glass handle, causing his knuckles to turn white. "Who?"

"Emily Felcher," Patrick repeated. Blinking his eyes open, he frowned with obvious confusion. "Do you know her?"

"Yes, I know her. Only too well." he admitted, wondering how much he should tell his friend about his new love. If Patrick weren't so blasted drunk, he'd hit him with the truth—*all* of it. But, in Patrick's present state of drunkeness, he wasn't so sure his good friend could handle it. Knowing what Patrick was like when he'd had a bit much to drink, he figured he would either break down weeping like a small child, or else become extremely angry and take a wild swing at him. He worded his next statement carefully. "And I really don't think she's the girl for you."

Patrick sat forward, frowning deeper. "Why would you say that?" His eyes widened, then narrowed, then widened again while he attempted to focus on Randall's grim face.

Randall waited, still undecided about what he should say before he finally asked, "Just what are your feelings for the girl?"

"I love her. I want to marry her." He smiled a lovesick, off-centered smile. "I want to take her into my bed and make love to her for the rest of my life."

"You said that exact same thing about Nicole," he pointed out, hoping he'd see that what he felt for Emily was not real love. It couldn't be. He hadn't known her long enough to be deeply and everlastingly in love with her.

Patrick thrust his chin forward in a boyish pout. "That was different. Nicole wasn't half the woman Emily is."

"But what if I were to tell you that Emily is not exactly what she seems? What if I told you that she's nothing more than a little conniver, out to get what she can from a man?" He purposely held back the word prostitute, having decided to go easy on his drunken friend.

"Then I'd have to conclude that we are talking about two entirely different women. Either that or call you a liar, dear friend, because the Emily Felcher I'm talking about is none of that," Patrick answered simply. He showed no anger because he truly felt Randall was mistaken. "Besides, if she is really out to pirate all she can from a man, why does she keep pushing me away?"

"What do you mean?"

Patrick looked sick with misery as he plucked idly at the ruffle on his sleeve. "She doesn't like me much. She refuses to even let me kiss her."

Randall set his glass aside again so he could emphasize what he had to say with his hand. "That's probably just part of the game she's playing. By pretending to be so difficult to win, she hopes to make you that much more eager to become her victor. I'm telling you, I know her. That girl is out to get what she can out of you, and she'll continue to string you along until either you decide to marry her or until someone with even more money comes along." It was the whole reason he'd decided to steer clear of her.

"God, I wish she *would* marry me," he said, not really comprehending what Randall was trying so carefully to say.

"What do I have to do to get through to you?" Randall wanted to know, exasperated by Patrick's refusal to understand. "How can I make you see that all it would take to make her forget all about you and all your father's money is for a richer man to come along and show an interest in her?"

"She's not like that," he insisted, again thrusting his chin forward at a determined angle.

"But she is."

"No, she's not. She's the most beautiful, most wonderful, most kindest person I've ever known." He continued to slur his words while making every effort to hold his head erect. "Why she's even kind to children and sick animals."

Randall tossed his hands into the air, aware that Patrick was too blinded by her undeniable beauty to ever see her for what she really was. "I give up. Have it your way. Ruin your life. Just don't say I didn't warn you."

Having said that, he pushed his chair back. "I've got to go. I told Andrew I'd be back at the carriage about 11:30 and it's nearly two hours past that. We'll talk more about this at another time." Preferably when he was sober.

"Yes, at another time," Patrick said, then closed his eyes again, only this time he did not reopen them. Instead, his neck fell slack and his head lolled to one side. When Randall left the tavern a minute later, Patrick was being roused by a burly barkeep who ordered him to go home.

By the time Patrick came to enough to understand what was being said to him, Randall was in the carriage on his way to the house, his brain once again tormented with unwanted thoughts of Emily.

What was it about that woman that refused to let go?

Chapter Thirteen

Randall decided it was his duty to get to know Emily a little better. Somehow he had convinced himself that his motive for pursuing the beautiful wench was nothing short of noble. He would willingly sacrifice himself for the sake of his good friend, Patrick Freeburg.

Unselfishly, Randall vowed to do whatever it took to prove that Emily Felcher was exactly what he had claimed her to be—and thus save poor Patrick from a lifetime of sheer misery.

He knew that this noble undertaking would undoubtedly consume quite a lot of his time; but that was something he'd just have to suffer. Somebody had to do something to save Patrick—and quick. The lovestruck buffoon was far too blinded by the young tart's uncanny beauty and her beguiling ways to ever see what a shrewd little conniver she really was. And Randall knew Patrick never would realize the truth on his own. Not until some caring soul tricked her into revealing her true nature.

Aware it would take something truly drastic to make Patrick finally see the light, Randall had immediately set out to be that caring soul. He felt he was the perfect choice because he had a lot more money than Patrick and lived in a much more impressive house—just the sort of bait to lure the clever fox away from her intended prey.

It was simple logic. He should be gracious enough to save his friend from emotional ruin, no matter what hardships he might incur in the process. At first Patrick would probably be angry with him for having interfered in his personal life like that; but in the end, his friend would appreciate what he'd done. Patrick would see what a sacrifice he'd made for him and be forever grateful for having prevented him from making one of the biggest blunders of his life.

Satisfied that it was in everyone's best interest, Randall formulated his plans to save his friend from ruin. He refused to admit, even privately, that a lot of what Patrick had said about her during their drunken conversation Sunday morning had actually intrigued him. How could anyone be so thoroughly duped by a woman's beauty?

But knowing how clever Emily could be when playing her games, he understood Patrick's gullibility, at least to a certain degree. And because she was so extremely clever, he viewed his quest to expose Emily's true nature as much as a challenge as anything else.

A woman like that would not be readily duped, but the end result would be well worth the effort. He will not only have saved Patrick from her treachery, but at the same time, he would be saving himself from endless hours of plaguing daydreams, because once he'd bedded the beautiful wench, he would finally be able put all thoughts of her aside.

Just knowing what Emily was—or had been until a very few weeks ago—and also knowing how good she must be at her trade to have worked for the infamous Josie Bradley, Randall desperately wanted an ample sampling of her talents. Therefore, through finally bedding her, he would actually accomplish two important goals. One to free Patrick, and one to free himself.

That was why early Monday morning he'd sent her such an elaborate bouquet of red roses along with a gold-embossed card on which he'd expressed his deepest apologies for having behaved so rudely during the past few weeks. Knowing Emily would still be very upset with him for not having fallen for her missing jewelry scam, he felt he would have to proceed very carefully. Therefore, he planned to allow her plenty of time to think about his apology and overcome her anger before making his next move.

He'd wisely decided to be very prudent in his campaign to bed the beautiful seductress—or chance her catching on to what he was trying to do. He waited two days before taking any further action.

He also felt it important that she not discover he knew Patrick and would be very careful not to mention his name. He knew that if she ever linked the two of them as friends, she would immediately suspect his motive, which would alter any chance for success.

When Randall entered the elaborately decorated hat shop late Wednesday morning, dressed in one of his finest three-piece cutaways and a brand new felt derby, he was disappointed to find only two women inside—neither of them Emily.

An elderly woman sat with a ridiculous-looking purple hat plopped down on her silvery head, and a slightly younger woman, who appeared to be somewhere in her mid-forties, stood nearby and wore no covering on her head at all. The younger of the two appeared very surprised to see a man enter the ladies' hat shop—especially one unaccompanied by a woman.

"Hello, I'm Mrs. Williams, owner of this shop. May I help you?" she asked, coming toward him with her hand extended.

"I was hoping to speak with Emily Felcher," he commented then glanced about the room a second time before he reluctantly accepted her hand in greeting. "She does work here, doesn't she?"

"Of course," Mrs. Williams answered, nodding eagerly while she gave him a quick once-over. Her expression remained pleasantly placid and did nothing to reveal whether she approved or disapproved of what she saw.

"But I guess she's not in right now," he said, awkwardly shifting his weight to one leg. The direct manner in which she studied his every move made him feel like he was being judged as a possible prospect for today's lunch. "When do you expect her back?"

"Oh, but she is here," Mrs. Williams assured him, then turned to indicate a door near the back of the room. "She's busy working on Mrs. Turner's new velvetta in the other room. I'll go get her."

"Thank you," Randall responded, then stood quietly near the front while Mrs. Williams disappeared into the back.

Waiting for Emily to appear, he let his gaze wander about the room, noting all the odd creations of feathers, black felt, colorful ribbons, soft velvets, and shiny sequins that had been carefully perched upon satin-covered pedestals. One particularly strange compilation of pink ostrich feathers and black lace caught his eye and he stepped closer to touch it, almost expecting it to shy away from his hand.

When he realized that the elderly woman in the

purple hat was watching him with a most curious expression, he quickly dropped his arms to his sides and nodded an awkward greeting, unaware that Emily had already entered the room.

"Mr. Gipson, what are you doing here?"

Randall spun about, startled, but glad to hear Emily's voice. As always, he was immediately taken by her exquisite beauty and by the graceful way she moved across the room. When he stepped toward her, his smile was genuine. "I just wanted to stop in and make sure you had received the flowers I sent."

Emily's cheeks turned a most beguiling shade of pink. She tried not to focus on the long, curving dimples that had formed along the outer corners of his mouth when she answered, "I did get them. They came early Monday afternoon. And I guess I really should have acknowledged them right away, but I've been so busy lately."

Which was true, she had been very busy; but that had had little to do with why she'd failed to respond to his eloquently penned apology. The fact was, she had found it a little difficult to believe that anyone could experience such a complete and unexpected change of heart. She had wanted time to think more about what he'd written. She couldn't help but suspect the motive behind his having suddenly done something so kind, so considerate.

Just like she suspected his reason for being there now. His smile was far too pleasant, his voice too friendly. He was up to something. He had to be.

"That's perfectly all right," he assured her, aware that she had not been entirely truthful, but not really caring because he did not plan to be entirely truthful himself. "I imagine you've had quite a time of it settling into your new job."

"Yes, but you'd think by now I'd be used to all

the different things I have to do around here. After all, I've been working here for over three weeks now," she explained, then smiled at Mrs. Williams, who had politely returned to her customer but continued to keep a close eye on the proceedings across the room. Ever since her boss had heard the name "Gipson," she had been unable to tear her gaze away from them.

"To tell you the truth," Emily went on to say, returning her gaze to Randall, "three weeks should be plenty of time for me to have adjusted to all the peculiarities of this or any job."

Thinking that such a job must indeed seem very peculiar to someone like Emily, Randall fought the urge to chuckle. He certainly did not want to offend her again, at least not before she had agreed to have lunch with him.

"Well, some things take more time than others," he admitted, then decided he'd had enough small talk. "By any chance, are you allowed to leave here for lunch?"

"Lunch?" Emily swallowed hard at such an unexpected question. Her stomach tightened over the mere prospect of being alone with him again. But was that even the reason why he had mentioned lunch? Did he really plan to invite her out? After all the terrible things they'd said to each other? Surely not. "Why do you ask?"

"Because, if it would not put your job in any jeopardy, I'd like for you to have lunch with me. My coach is right outside. We can eat wherever you like."

He stood before her, so regal in his splendid outfit, Emily immediately wanted to say yes. But caution prevented her from actually doing so.

"But why do you want to have lunch with me?" she wanted to know, aware the invitation simply did not make sense. He did not even like her. Nor she him. Still, the possibility that he had spoken the truth made her blood race and her stomach leap with wild somersaults.

"Because taking you out for a nice lunch would be another way for me to apologize for some of the terrible things I've said to you during the past weeks. I've had a lot of problems to overcome here recently, and, well, I guess I let myself take some of my frustrations out on you," he explained, then glanced at Mrs. Williams, who had not missed a word of their conversation. "What about it, Mrs. Williams? Will you allow Emily a short lunch break?"

"Of course, Mr. Gipson. Take all the time you want," she answered, her head bobbing with what Emily thought was a little too much enthusiasm. "There's no real hurry on Mrs. Turner's hat. Estelle won't even be by here to see how it's coming along until at least four o'clock, maybe not even until tomorrow. Emily should have plenty of time to catch up on her work when she gets back. You two go on and have yourselves a nice time."

"But it's not even noon yet," Emily protested, glancing at the clock and seeing that the lunch hour was still twenty minutes away. Mrs. Williams had never allowed them go to lunch before noon.

"That doesn't matter. You two go on," Mrs. Williams insisted with a brief wave of her hand, then added, "You can finish your work when you get back."

With the decision having been so effectively taken out of her own hands, Emily shrugged in willing defeat. "I guess I accept your invitation," she finally admitted, running her hand over her skirt self-consciously. "I'll just go get my handbag."

Not really knowing why she wanted her handbag,

other than to have an excuse to leave the room long enough to steady the turmoil that had sprung to life inside her, Emily quickly disappeared into the back. Once inside the door, she caught her four coworkers scurrying back to their chairs. Knowing only too well how clearly conversations from the front room carried into the back when the door had been left open, she shrugged then tossed her hands into the air to show her defeat. "What could I say? Mrs. Williams had already given permission for me to go."

The other girls did not respond, they merely grinned at each other while exchanging knowing glances, making Emily want to stamp her foot yet, at the same time, laugh out loud. But rather than give in to either impulse, she tossed her head in an arrogant manner and pursed her lips outward as if she thought herself something special.

"Well, at least I'm being allowed to leave for lunch early. You four will have to wait until the noon hour is announced." Then spotting her handbag among those on the table nearest her own work station, she crossed the room and snatched it up. "I'll see you ladies when I return."

"Must be nice," Stephanie Haught finally said, being the bravest of the lot. She glanced at the girl seated nearest to her, as if planning to hold a private conversation, but spoke loud enough for them all to hear. "First, our dear Emily had Patrick Freeburg, son of the richest banker in all of Galveston, sniffing at her heels. And now, just weeks later, she has Randall Gipson, who is undoubtedly *the* richest as well as *the* most handsome man in all of Galveston, calling for her right here at work. And wanting to take her to lunch no less."

"Yes, it must be right nice," Kim Wilkins quickly agreed, glancing up from her handwork as if she'd just now noticed anyone else was around. "Why, the way I heard it told, that there Gipson family has more money than people like Patrick Freeburg ever thought of havin'."

Stephanie nodded, flattening her mouth into a thin line, as if thoroughly disgusted by the injustice of their situation. "Like I already done told you, it must be awful nice to be so pop-u-lar." She rolled her eyes toward the ceiling to emphasize what she'd said.

"Oh, hush, you two. It's not what you think. He just wants to apologize for something he said to me a few weeks ago. There's nothing more to it than that, and there's certainly no reason for any of you to think otherwise."

"Um-hum," Stephanie said with obvious doubt, at the same time trying to suppress a grin. "And I suppose the reason you just then picked up my handbag instead of your own is 'cause there's nothing at all unusual about a man like Randall Gipson comin' by where you work and askin' you out to lunch like he just done."

"Hush," Emily warned, afraid Stephanie's high-pitched voice might carry into the other room. "He could hear you."

"I wish he would," she answered with a playful toss of her blonde curls, glancing again at the other girls. She set aside the hat she had been pretending to work on and patted her own cheek with the inner curve of her hand. "Then maybe he'd come back here and take a real good look at me. I imagine if he did that, he'd just up and change his mind real quick-like about which one of us he'd rather take to lunch." She batted her eyelids in a very coquettish manner, clearly amused by her own antics. "But then, I'd probably just have to turn him down. I've already got far too many handsome men following me around already."

The other girls moaned at such an outrageous statement.

Emily wished she could stay and hear more of their light-hearted banter, but knew Randall was waiting for her. Taking a deep breath, hoping that might stabilize her rampaging heart and give her the strength she needed to see her through the next hour, she headed toward the door.

"When you get back, we want to hear all about it," Kim said, her voice just loud enough for Emily to hear—but, thankfully, not loud enough to carry into the room beyond.

"Yes," Stephanie agreed. "Make him take you to the fanciest restaurant in town. Ask him to take you to the Gartin Verein. I hear it serves the finest food and hires nothing' but handsome Germans with long, drooping mustaches for waiters who scurry about seein' to your everyest whim. Maybe you could bring one of them back with you. A tall one, with big blue eyes." She smiled wickedly at the thought.

Emily pretended not to hear the giggles that followed when she passed back through the door and again entered the front.

"Ready?" he asked, when he noticed she had finally returned.

Despite what she'd just said to her friends, Emily still felt a little uncertain about his motive for suddenly wanting to take her out. And because she still felt so uncertain, she simply nodded her response then started toward the front door.

"And where would you like to eat?" he asked as he bent forward at the waist to open the door to let her pass.

Emily cast him a decisive smile. "I think I'm in the

mood to have some of that fish on a stick they sell at Oleander Park."

She heard the groans of disappointment filter through from the back and her smile widened. "That is if you don't mind eating on a park bench."

"Whatever you want is fine with me," he responded, glancing curiously from the pleased grin on Emily's face to the tiny door at the back of the shop where he had heard the odd moaning sounds.

Because Oleander Park was only a few blocks from where Emily worked, and because the thought of sharing the close confines of a coach with Randall was far too nerve shattering, Emily suggested they take advantage of the beautiful sunny weather and walk.

Surprised as much by her decision to eat such an inexpensive meal as he was that she had chosen to walk rather than ride, Randall did not argue. He stopped by the coach to remove his hat, jacket, and tie, and told his driver where they were headed.

"Do you want me to follow in case you'll be wanting a ride back?" Andrew asked, peering doubtfully first at the bright, sun-filled sky overhead, then down at the two them, both dressed in long sleeves.

"I don't know," Randall said, then glanced at Emily for a response.

"No reason for him to do that—I enjoy walking. Besides, it's not that far from here." She glanced off in the direction of the park, as if she truly expected to see it from there, when she knew there were far too many buildings blocking the way. "We should be there in no time."

"I guess you might as well wait here for me," Randall said with a shrug, then took just enough time to roll his shirt sleeves to his elbows before stepping back to join Emily. If they were going to have a picnic lunch in this heat, then he planned to be as comfortable as possible.

Emily tried not to notice the way his taut muscles rippled beneath his lightly haired, sun-browned skin when he politely offered his arm to her. She also tried to ignore the fiery sensations that shot through her body like tiny thunderbolts the second she had slipped her arm around his. Suddenly her mouth felt dry and her throat became so constricted near the base that it made swallowing downright painful.

"Lovely day for a stroll," she commented. She tried to sound unaffected while she casually glanced skyward. She hoped, by directing his attention elsewhere, he would not notice the strange impact his touch had had on her.

"Yes, I guess it is," he admitted, but instead of glancing toward the cloudless blue sky like she had hoped, he looked directly at her, noticing how the gulf breeze caught her hair and lifted it gently from her face.

Suddenly he realized why she had been so willing to eat in the park. Obviously, she knew how beautiful she looked with the bright, summer sun splashing down on her hair, causing the auburn highlights to sparkle like glitter. He could barely resist the unexpected urge to bend forward to breathe in its clean fragrance.

"In fact, it is a beautiful day," he agreed, smiling now that he understood at least one of her motives. He decided she was a very clever temptress—clever enough to use *all* her assets to their greatest advantage. His smile widened. He looked again at her shimmering locks of hair and again felt the urge to pull her closer, to feel the softness against his cheek. "Do you often go to Oleander Park for lunch?"

"Oh, yes. I love to feed the seagulls. It seems to relax me."

Somehow he could not picture her enjoying such simple pleasures. "Then why don't you go on down to the beach during your lunch breaks? It's only a few blocks more and there are far more seagulls there."

"Oh, but sometimes I do," she said, turning to glance up at him. As soon as she did, she decided that had been a dreadful mistake, because it reminded her exactly how close they were. She then looked down to where her arm linked through his and became instantly aware of the vast difference in circumferences. He was certainly very muscular for a man who supposedly spent most of his time behind a desk.

Quickly she glanced away so he would not catch her staring at him, but frowned while she tried to figure out how he managed to stay so fit. "Not only do I like to feed the seagulls, I also like to wade along the water's edge, that is when the gulf is calm. The water feels so good when it rushes over my feet and tickles when it draws the sand out from beneath my toes during its return to the sea. It amazes me that the water is so much warmer here than it is back home."

"Oh, that's right, you are from New York. Why did you leave there and come to Galveston of all places?" he asked, thinking a city as large and prosperous as New York would be a prime marketplace for someone of her trade.

"I thought you knew," she said, glancing at him again, this time trying not to be as affected by his nearness. She wondered why Bernice had not told him about her search, but then her heart sank with painful force when she realized the reason: he had never cared enough about her to ask. So, why was he pretending to be interested in her now? This sudden change in attitude still did not make sense. "I came here to find my grandmother. She and my aunt are the only living relatives I have."

"Oh, yes, that's right," he commented, remembering some of the comments she'd made the day she had accused him of stealing her jewelry. Although he did not truly believe that her grandmother was the real reason she had come south, he did not care to start another argument with her and decided to let the matter drop. He fell silent for several minutes before thinking of a safer topic to discuss. "So, how do you like working at the hat shop?"

"I'm getting used to it," she admitted, then lifted her hand to touch her hair, suddenly aware she had forgotten her hat. What must he think of her, being outside without a proper head covering. Only young girls were allowed that freedom. Would Randall now think of her as a young girl?

She hoped not. For some reason, she wanted him to think of her as much older, more mature. "The problem is that there's a lot more to my job than I first realized. Not only do I make hats to the customers' specifications, I also have to wait on the front from time to time, and sometimes, because I am fairly good with numbers, I am asked to tally all the sales at the end of the day. Mrs. Williams hates to do that sort of thing."

"I gather it is the first time you've worked in a place like that," he said, stifling a grin. He wondered how long she could put up with all the petty annoyances.

"It is the first time I've ever worked at all," she told him, wondering why she suddenly felt so willing to discuss herself with him. She was usually such a private person. "I've spent the past five years in a finishing school back East."

Randall nodded, thinking that certainly accounted for her impeccable speech and the manner in which she carried herself. But how could such a common girl pay for five years of finishing school? He drew his eyebrows together when he considered the possibility that she may have been forced to work her trade even at so young an age. For a moment, he felt sorry for her.

Within minutes, the two had reached Oleander park and while Emily sat on one of the benches near a stand of palm trees facing the gentle gulf breeze that was forever present in Galveston, Randall walked across the grass to where the vendor had set up his stand and waited for him to prepare two fish on sticks.

When he returned several minutes later, he found Emily sitting with her back pressed against the bench, her face turned toward the warm rays of the sun, her eyes closed. If ever a woman beckoned to be kissed, it was her; but he refrained from making a public display, vowing to oblige her more than a mere kiss when the time finally came.

"Here you go. Fish on a stick dipped in red sauce and a fresh hot roll," he said as he carefully handed the food to her. When she opened her eyes with such a start, he almost believed she hadn't known he was there. But then it wouldn't do for him to know she was being so coy.

"Thank you," she said and held her hands out to take the fish and the roll. She breathed deeply the delicious aroma, then darted her tongue out to taste the sauce while she set the roll on the napkin she had quickly spread across her lap.

"You are most welcome," he commented, then sat down beside her, careful to place his outer thigh firmly against hers. He was surprised when instead of smiling appreciatively at him the way he'd expected, she quickly moved her leg away, never looking at him while she restraightened her napkin and roll with her free hand.

Frowning at such an unexpected reaction, he continued to watch her while he leaned forward over the grass in order to avoid dripping any on the thick red sauce onto his trousers. He continued to study her embarrassed behavior while he carefully arranged his napkin around the end of the narrow wooden stick that had been used to spear the large piece of filleted redfish. He knew she wanted him to believe she had changed, but even so, enough was enough.

Still, he knew he would have to continue to play the game her way—that is if he still planned to come out the winner.

Wondering just how far she intended to carry this innocent act of hers, he continued to study her nervous expression while he bent forward and took a big bite of fish, immediately aware of the mistake he'd made.

"H-hot," he commented while batting the chunk of scalding meat around his mouth with his tongue. Tears immediately came to his eyes when at last he swallowed.

Emily laughed. She couldn't help it. "Yes, it is hot. I suppose that's why there was all that steam coming out of it. Most people wait for it to cool first." She then indicated her own fish with a simple nod. Although she had licked away some of the sauce, the fish itself was still intact.

Randall tried not to let his embarrassment show and wondered why he'd done such a foolish thing. He had to quit letting his mind wander away from him like that.

"I'll try to keep that in mind," he promised. "Next time we come here, I'll wait until you've taken a bite of yours so I'll know for sure it's not too hot."

Next time? Emily wondered silently when she looked at him. Her heart took an amazing leap skyward when she realized he fully intended to invite her out again. But why? Once was enough for an apology. Just what was he trying to pull?

Finally, she couldn't stand not knowing the truth any longer and decided the best way to find out what she wanted to know was to ask.

"Tell me the truth about something," she said, her eyes narrowing with suspicion. "Why are you suddenly being so nice to me? Why do you even want to be around me? I thought you didn't like me."

"Whatever gave you that idea?" Her directness surprised him.

"I think it might have something to do with the way you ordered me out of your house that last time I was there," she said and lowered her eyebrows to indicate further suspicion. "You do remember that don't you?"

Randall grinned, but continued to eye his lunch carefully, waiting for the fish to cool. "Ah, yes. I believe that all happened shortly after you told me to go to hell."

Emily dropped her gaze, embarrassed by what she had said. Having used language like that could only make him think worse of her. "I guess I got a little carried away that day. It's just that at the time I thought you were keeping my grandmother's jewelry as a way to get back at me for having stayed too long at your house."

"And you now know that I'm not?" he asked. "Then you have located the missing jewelry?"

"No, not yet." She studied his expression carefully, still wondering if he'd had anything to do with its disappearance. "But I will find it eventually—you can count on that." Leaning forward, she took her first bite of fish, then upon discovering it had cooled enough to be eaten comfortably, she took another, but never removed her gaze from Randall's face.

Deciding it was now safe to eat his own fish, Randall also took a large bite then reached immediately to wipe the remaining sauce from his lips with his napkin. He waited until his mouth was clear again before asking, "And what does Josie have to say about this missing jewelry?" He tried to sound only casually interested.

Emily discreetly snatched a droplet of red sauce from the corner of her mouth with her tongue before answering, "She claims she didn't take it either."

Believing he had just tricked her into revealing the truth, that she and Josie had at least discussed the jewelry, he looked at her with a knowing smirk. "And do you believe her?"

"I don't know what I believe. All I know is that my jewelry is missing and there were only a few people who had an opportunity to take it."

"You don't suspect Peterson, do you?" he asked, wondering if she'd tried to extort money from him, too.

"No, not really," she admitted, then frowned. "I don't know who to suspect. You all act so innocent."

"Well, maybe it was one of Josie's other girls who took it," he suggested, though he didn't know why he bothered to offer possible alternatives. He still did not believe there ever had been any jewelry.

"Katy suggested that same thing," she said, not having noticed the casual implication that she was or had ever been a part of Josie's group. "But I don't see how they could get away with something like that without Josephine eventually finding out."

"Well, maybe it will turn up soon," he commented, tired of the direction their conversation had taken. "I hate to see such a disappointed look on a face as pretty as yours."

Emily blinked with surprise. She had not expected a compliment. She didn't know how to respond. "Y-yes, maybe it will."

Randall watched the color rise in her cheek and again marveled at her acting abilities. She was not at all like he'd expected, having given up being overly flirtatious like she had been back when they were on the ship, but she also was not cooly standoffish. She had developed a style all her own, and that both bothered and pleased him. She pretended to be neither worldly, like some of the more sophisticated women did, nor did she pretend to be frail and helpless. She was somewhere in between. Knowledgeable, but not too, and somewhat independent in nature, but again not too. Most of the time he wasn't even sure how he should react to her. She was just too different from anyone he'd ever known.

He finally decided that *brilliant* was the perfect word to describe Emily because she had to be the most brilliant actress he'd ever met. If he had not already learned the truth about her, he would probably believe her to be the true innocent she pretended to be. He'd probably believe that she wanted nothing more from him than she had already received. No wonder Patrick had been taken in so easily.

But he knew, if he was ever to get beyond this young, innocent act of hers, he would have to think of something extremely clever. He also needed to find some way to be alone with her. He certainly couldn't seduce her in a public park in broad daylight, nor did he want to limit the occasion to something as short as a lunch break. No, indeed. When he finally seduced her, he wanted to have all the time in the world.

Finished with his fish long before she finished hers, Randall set the stick and soiled napkin aside and leaned back to a more comfortable position. "This is nice. I enjoy eating outdoors like this. I'm glad you suggested it."

"Yes, it is nice," she agreed, still trying to recover from the unexpected compliment he'd bestowed upon her earlier. For lack of anything else to do with her hands, as soon as Emily finished her fish, she picked up her roll and tore it into tiny pieces, preparing to feed the seagulls. "I always have loved a picnic."

"What a terrific idea." He sat forward and nodded enthusiastically, already knowing the perfect place to take her, a place where they could be uninterrupted for hours.

"What idea?" she asked, confused.

"A picnic. Sunday. I can hardly wait. I'll have Nora prepare some of her fried chicken. It's a little spicier than most, but it is delicious. You'll love it."

"But I didn't say anything about a picnic this Sunday," she protested, panicked by the thought.

"Oh? Then who did?" He looked at her then as if he, too, were confused.

"I think you did."

"Did I?" He placed his hand on his chest as if truly surprised.

"Yes, you did." She nodded with certainty.

"And?"

"And what?"

"What do you think about going on a picnic with me this Sunday?"

"I-I don't know. I have no chaperone," she said, well remembering her body's response to him that last time they had been alone together. She didn't dare risk anything like that again.

Randall lifted an eyebrow as if to question such concern as genuine.

He still believed that most of what she said or did was all a part of her silly act. But still willing to play along as if it meant having what he wanted, he looked thoughtful. "What about that girl who came to the house with you?"

"Katy?"

"Yes, Katy. Why can't she come along as your chaperone?"

"I guess I could ask her," she admitted, still hesitant to agree.

"Then do. We'll have a terrific time. Tell her that I'll come by for the two of you Sunday afternoon about one o'clock. Tell her I know the perfect place for our picnic." Amused by the way Emily seemed to be nervously digesting the idea of their picnic, he wondered what excuse she'd offer him when he arrived on Sunday and discovered Katy was not going with them. He could hardly wait to hear that one. "And you two won't need to bring anything. I'll supply it all. Including a nice *comfortable* quilt for us to lie on." He waited to see what her reaction would be to that, but was not too surprised when she pretended not to have noticed his insinuation at all.

"I can't really promise anything until I've talked with Katy," she stated, wondering what her friend's reaction would be.

"That's fine. I'll send Andrew over this afternoon to find out what your answer is. But, please, Emily, try not to disappoint me. I am so looking forward to this."

He considered reaching out and touching her cheek to give her an idea of what pleasures were to come, but decided against it. He knew that was not the way she wanted to play her little game. She wanted to be courted, nice and proper, and in truth it cost him nothing to pretend courtship—and it might gain him plenty in the end.

"Come on, Emily. Say you'll go."

Emily studied his hopeful expression and decided that her first impression may have been all wrong. She smiled, deciding he wasn't such a bad person after all. "Okay, I'll try to go. I certainly wouldn't want to be the one to disappoint you."

Taking that as a promise of pleasures to come, Randall smiled, contented knowing he would have the beautiful seductress yet.

Chapter Fourteen

Randall was never more dumbfounded than when he arrived at the boarding house early Sunday afternoon and discovered that not only had Emily actually invited Katy to accompany them, Katy had accepted. He had thought Emily would drop all her silly pretenses by then; but evidently he'd misjudged her. She was even more stubborn than he'd imagined.

When he first found out that Katy honestly did intend to spend the afternoon with them, he was furious. He could not understand why Emily continued to bother with such a ridiculous ruse—especially when having Katy along ruined all the plans he'd made to seduce Emily while out by Porterfield's lake. But after he'd had more time to think more about it, he became somewhat intrigued by her cunning. Emily took absolutely no chances, determined to play her part to the hilt. And as long as she continued to pretend to be nothing short of respectable, he felt almost obligated to continue with his role as the smitten gentleman, which meant pretending to court her in a more traditional fashion—that is if he still wanted to be the victor in their little contest of wills.

Because Randall had always appreciated a lively game of wits, he decided to continue playing right along with her, or at least until he could figure out a way to finally outwit her.

He would overcome the challenge and would seduce the beautiful young wench yet. He just hoped his victory wouldn't take too long. Game or no game, he had to have her. He had to get Emily Felcher out of his system once and for all so he could focus on business again.

And soon. Before his constant inability to concentrate caused both him and his cousin to lose that railroad deal. No matter what it entailed, he had to do something to get his wits about him again.

By the time Randall, Emily, and Katy reached the lovely secluded lake Randall had originally selected because of its undeniable romantic atmosphere, Randall's thoughts had become so intent on finding a way around all this proper courting nonsense that he did not immediately hear Katy's exclamation of praise.

"Why this place is beautiful," she said, glancing at Emily to see if she was equally impressed.

Emily nodded appreciatively. The lake was like something in an elaborate painting. It was small and serene, surrounded by a variety of short, sprawling trees. A thick blanket of green grass covered the ground, spattered with a fabulous array of wildflowers. It was hard to imagine a place more beautiful.

"Well, he told me he knew the perfect spot for our Sunday afternoon picnic," Emily commented then breathed deeply the mingled scent of pine and honeysuckle.

While she continued studying the exhilarating beauty that surrounded the shady lakeshore, she was suddenly very relieved and very grateful to Katy for rearranging her plans so she could come along. A place like this could prove very dangerous to a woman alone with someone as handsome and as virile as Randall Gipson. Her insides spun wildly at the mere thought of what could happen if she and Randall ever came to this place alone.

Katy returned her gaze to the beautiful lake that lay just ahead, her expression truly enthralled. "Wouldn't you love to build a house out here and stay forever?"

Again Emily nodded. Although the trees were not quite as tall as those in New York, nor were they as thick or as green, this was the sort of place one could easily learn to love.

Finally, Randall became aware of the conversation between the two and commented, "I agree. This is the perfect place for a house. I have never understood why Raymond didn't build his house here." But the small valley where his friend did eventually build his house was quite beautiful, too.

"Who's Raymond?" Katy wanted to know, leaning forward so she could see Randall's face.

"Raymond Porterfield. A friend of mine. All this land belongs to him, but he lets me come out here whenever I want to do a little fishing or hunting, or if I just feel like being alone for a while. His house is just over that rise." He pointed to a wooded hill in the distance.

Katy's green eyes widened with interest. "Is he unmarried by any chance?"

"He is now. His wife died a couple of years ago during childbirth. He lives out here alone now. But I guess he likes the seclusion. He rarely comes into town anymore. Not like he used to anyway."

"Perhaps you could introduce him to Katy one day," Emily commented, aware that was what Katy had on her mind. In fact, finding the right man was about all Katy ever had on her mind. "How old is he?"

"About my age, I guess," he said, shaking his head at such an oversight. He should have invited Raymond along on their picnic. That would have been one sure way to distract Emily's watchdog friend. If he'd thought to invite Raymond along, he might have managed a little time alone with Emily. But then, he really hadn't expected Katy to join them. He'd honestly thought the chaperone suggestion had been nothing more than a ruse to convince him that she'd at least attempted to be virtuous when she eventually came up with the mundane excuses he'd expected as to why Katy couldn't come. But that had not been her plan after all. Still, he should consider the possibility of inviting Raymond to any future outings.

He smiled when he thought more about it. Raymond was his friend. And because he was such a good friend, he should be willing to divert Katy's attention for an hour or so, especially after he found out that Katy wasn't all that displeasing to the eye. Although her clothing was plain and her hair fashioned in a rather simple style, her facial features were nice enough and she had a very pleasant laugh. Yes, Raymond wouldn't object to spending a little time with someone like Katy, which would give him a better chance to woo the fair Emily.

He chuckled, feeling very good about his own cleverness until he realized that introducing Katy to Raymond had originally been Emily's idea. Obviously she was having second thoughts about all that goodness and propriety, and had already started searching for possible ways for them to be alone—and yet still keep her *respectability* in tact. As always, she amazed him with her cunning. She was playing her role just right.

"Okay, next time we arrange an outing, I'll try to remember to invite Raymond," he assured them. He gave Emily a knowing look. When she responded with a warm smile, his insides flared with renewed expectation. So, she *had* been looking for some logical reason for them to share some time alone. Maybe they could finally get around all this ridiculous game playing—even sooner than he'd hoped.

Shortly after he pulled the buggy into a shaded area near the lake, stopping where the horse could get water and grass, Randall immediately hopped out of the open carriage, eager to help the women down. First, for no other reason than she was seated on the outside, he slipped his hands around Katy's slender waist and lifted her out, then carefully set her down in the tall, pale green grass that surrounded them.

Then, after Emily scooted closer to the outside, he reached for her waist, amazed to find it so much smaller than Katy's had been, though Katy was a proper weight. Why he could almost touch his fingers together on the opposite side of Emily while overlapping the tips of his thumbs in front of her. How could such a full-bodied woman have such a tiny waist? He could hardly wait to see her without all that cumbersome clothing.

When he lifted her out of the carriage and felt the penetrating warmth of her body in his hands, he could not resist bringing those supple curves down against his own hard frame. He smiled with devilish delight when he saw how quickly her brown eyes widened, indicating her own body's pleased reaction. Aware of the intense desire they had for each other, he held her a moment longer than was necessary before he finally released her.

"I'll spread the quilts out," he commented in a

deep voice, leaning so close to her ear that the warmth of his breath spilled across her cheek.

Turning on unsteady legs to watch his agile movements, Emily made no comment while he brought out several quilts from the back of the carriage and quickly layered them across a grassy knoll near the water's edge. But then she couldn't have spoken if she'd wanted. Her mind was in too much turmoil to think of anything pertinent to say—or even anything *impertinent* to say.

The only thing she could think about at that moment was the invigorating effect he had on her whenever they touched. It was as if he held some strange, magical power over her, a power that made her body ache with longing to—to what? Be held in his arms? Be kissed like he'd kissed her that night aboard ship? She blushed when she remembered her wanton behavior that night. Quickly, she pushed such embarrassing thoughts aside and joined Katy in the shade of a nearby tree to watch while Randall returned to the carriage for a large food basket and two stoneware jugs.

Minutes later, he had the quilts spread out in smooth, overlapping layers between two oak trees and had set the food basket near the center. While Emily and Katy started setting out the different containers of food, Randall sat off to one side, his back propped comfortably against a sturdy tree trunk, and watched, mesmerized by Emily's graceful movements. Smiling to himself, he felt that he could sit there and observe her for hours and never be bored with what he saw; but then again, *observing* her was not what interested him the most.

Knowing what he wanted most was to hold her in his arms, he then turned his attention to the voluptuous way she filled out the pretty pink and white summer dress she wore. How he would like to discard that bothersome garment and spend the rest of the day playing with the many treasures that lay beneath.

He had to look away and take several deep breaths when he realized his body had started to react to such tantalizing thoughts. If only Katy had had enough sense not to come. He cursed them both for putting him through such physical torment. His mood darkened. There should be laws protecting men like him from women like them. His mood blackened even more when he realized there *were* such laws—he had simply chosen to ignore them.

"Everything is ready," Emily said as soon as she and Katy had spread everything out. When she glanced at Randall and noticed the dismal expression on his face, she wondered what she'd done to displease him. Only a few seconds ago, he'd been smiling like a contented child.

With confused apprehension, she cleared her throat while she considered the possibilities. Perhaps he was waiting for her to serve him. That was probably it. Men liked for women to wait on them. "Would you like for me to prepare your plate now?"

"Yes, please," he said, glancing down at all the food skattered before them, hoping to concentrate on anything but the hunger he felt for Emily. If he continued to dwell on his growing desires, he would never leave that place with his sanity still intact.

In an effort to lift Randall's mood, although she didn't know why she cared one way or the other how he felt, Emily hurried to fill his plate. She placed several pieces of breaded chicken, a large mound of potato salad, several different kinds of pickles, two rolls, and a fat celery stalk on it. When she had the plate filled to capacity, she singled out a fork and a napkin then carried everything to him. Not about to bend forward in a dress cut as low as the one she wore, for fear of where his gaze might wander, she carefully knelt beside him to hand him his food.

When she did, her skirt folded into his lap, arousing him all the more. Randall looked up at her with a start. Had she done that on purpose? Just what sort of cruel woman was she? If she kept that up, he'd have no choice but to take her right then and there—Katy Watchdog or no Katy Watchdog. There was only so much a man could tolerate. He wet his lips while again trying to regain control of his raging desire. Quickly, he set his plate in his lap.

"What would you like to drink?" she asked, startled by the intense look on his face. "As you know, you have your choice of apple cider or water."

"Water," he commented.

And he really thought he'd like it dashed in his face.

"Then water it is," she answered, trying to sound unconcerned over his strange behavior. Smiling awkwardly, she stood and walked across to the shaded spot near the carriage where Randall had placed the two stoneware jugs. She wondered about the sudden difficulty he seemed to have with his breathing when she bent forward to pull the cork on the water jug then filled one of the glasses she'd found inside the basket to the rim. She was so worried about his odd behavior that when she returned, she forgot all about the low, rounded neckline of her dress when she bent forward to hand him his water.

With all that tempting flesh so aptly revealed to him, and within such close proximity, Randall forced his eyes closed. Moaning softly to himself, he accepted the tall glass of water and quickly drank half its contents. He knew right then, he had to do something to have this woman. And he had to do that something right away. But what could he do to get rid of the ever present Katy?

Suddenly, he had an idea.

"Katy, I've noticed the way you keep gazing out at all the wildflowers," he commented, keeping his tone casual even though he firmly believed he'd finally discovered the perfect solution to his problem.

"Yes, I love flowers," she commented while she set her glass filled with apple cider onto the quilt next to her then positioned her plate beside that. "I always have loved flowers."

"Well then, after you finish eating, perhaps you'd like to pick a nice bouquet to carry home with you." He darted his tongue across his lips while he waited for her response.

"Yes, I think that would be fun," she agreed, looking at Emily to see her reaction. "Why don't we do that?"

Randall frowned, determined that Katy go alone. "Actually, it would only take one of you. The other could stay behind and pack up the leftover food." He then nodded toward the nearest wooded hill, which lay in the opposite direction of Raymond's house. "If my memory serves me right, there should be a pretty patch of wild daisies in a small clearing just the other side of that rise. Do you like daisies?"

"Of course, I do." She glanced in the direction he'd indicated. "How far on the other side?"

"Not far," he assured her. "And I guarantee it'll be well worth the walk." At least it would be for him.

"I'll do that then," she said, nodding her appreciation. "I'll pick enough for all of us. That is if Emily doesn't mind."

"Of course not," Emily said, though in truth she

did mind. She was terrified at the thought of being left behind with Randall, even for a few minutes. She knew from experience what could happen between them if left alone for even a short time.

So did Randall, but he could hardly wait. Thinking his dilemma solved at last, he picked up the fork Emily had handed him and ate voraciously, finishing long before the other two. With his appetite appeased, but not his hunger for Emily, he set his plate aside and waited impatiently for Katy to finally finish her meal. After what seemed like hours, when in fact it was probably more like ten minutes, Katy finished the last of her chicken and lazily put her plate aside, having eaten everything but two small slices of cheese. Smiling with contentment, she leaned back on propped arms and sighed—but made no effort to leave.

"Aren't you going to pick those flowers now?" he asked, ready for her to be on her way. He glanced at Emily's sensuous mouth, more eager than ever to sample her sweetness again.

"I'm too full to move," Katy complained. She closed her green eyes and drew in a long, slow breath as if hoping that might bring her some relief.

"All the more reason to get up and get a little exercise," he commented, believing he might actually strangle the woman if she didn't get off that quilt and disappear into the woods like she was supposed to.

"I guess you're right," she finally admitted. Slowly she pushed herself first to a kneeling position then rose to her feet. "Now, you said those daisies are over that hill right there?" She nodded toward the small rise.

"They were last year about this time," he assured her, though he had no idea what was over that hill. He'd always done his hunting in the woods that ran along the other side of Raymond's house and had never bothered to venture further than the lake in this direction.

"Well, I should be back in a few minutes," she promised, lifting her skirts to avoid snagging them in the blackberry vines or broken twigs hidden in the deep grass while she hurried on her way.

At last, he thought with a smile while he watched Katy go. Like a hungry wolf ready to pounce upon his intended prey, he turned to study Emily's reaction. Finally, they could be alone.

He frowned when he saw no reaction at all, only a wide-eyed look that told him nothing. But then, he should have expected that. Katy had not yet left their sight.

"I guess I'd better start putting away some of this mess," she said, already scraping the remaining food off her plate onto Katy's. She then scraped that entire pile of leftover food onto the ground nearby so the wildlife could nibble at it after they'd left. As soon as she'd done that, she stood and began gathering up the rest of the food, placing the half-empty bowls and empty platters back into the basket.

Aware that she intended to wait until Katy was completely gone before dropping all her silly pretenses, Randall continued to lean comfortably against the tree trunk, dividing his attention between Emily's bewitching movements and Katy's shrinking form. Finally, Katy reached the hill and slowly disappeared from their sight. When she did, his contented smile returned.

"She's gone," he commented after the last blonde curl had disappeared from sight. He expected Emily to put down what she was doing and immediately come over to him. After all, Katy would not be gone forever.

"But she'll be right back," Emily was quick to assure him—perhaps a little too quick. She glanced off in the direction her friend had gone, her stomach churning with sudden apprehension. "You know Katy. She always does everything in a hurry."

"No, I don't know Katy," he commented while he slowly rose to his feet. "And I don't want to know Katy. The only person I want to get to know around here is you."

"Oh?" she responded, disappointed that her voice had come out a mere squeak when she had wanted to sound unaffected by the fact he was headed straight for her with a dark, almost threatening look on his face.

She took a tentative step backward. "And just what is it you want to know about me?"

"For one thing, I would like to be reminded how it feels to hold you in my arms, to feel your body pressed against mine," he said, continuing toward her one lithe step after another, much like a stalking cat. A devilish smile played at his lips, forming long, narrow dimples at the outer corners of his mouth. "I want to kiss you, to discover what womanly passions are hidden away inside you."

"You what?" she asked, even though she really did not want him to actually repeat any of what he'd just said. It was just that she found it hard to believe he had made such outrageous suggestions to her. She took another backward step while trying to find a reason for his sudden brash behavior.

"I said I want to kiss you," he repeated, parting his lips in preparation while he continued to close the distance between them. "You can quit pretending any time now. We both know you know you want me as much as I want you. It's inevitable that we be together."

Confused and panicked, Emily shook her head to indicate he was wrong, yet the actual words of denial refused to pass her lips. Maybe she *did* want him—a little.

Swallowing hard, she allowed her gaze to drift to his parted lips and she felt a strong surge of exhilaration. Perhaps he was right. Perhaps she did want him to kiss her—like he'd kissed her that night aboard ship. But what if that kiss went beyond her control like it had the first time? What if she became just as helpless as she had before? There would be no one to save her from her own passion. No one to save her from making a dreadful mistake.

Then she remembered Katy. Katy would return soon. She could save her should her emotions suddenly leap away from her like they had before.

With any words that might discourage him still frozen on her lips, which were slightly parted, he continued to move ever closer. She watched with an odd sense of fascination while he slowly bent forward and brought his lips to hers.

His kiss was just as potent and just as masterful as she remembered. It aroused more emotion than anything she'd ever experienced in her young life and left her feeling exhilarated and weak, almost as if he'd somehow drugged her by drawing from her own inner passions.

A gathering floodtide of unfamiliar sensations swelled to life inside her, quickly filling every part of her with a tingling heat, leaving her both lightheaded and feeling so unsteady she had to lean against him to stay on her feet.

Randall's reaction was to slip his arms around her to support her and draw her intimately closer. With the hunger of a starved man, he pressed her soft, supple curves hard against his body while he continued to devour her sweetness.

Aware that time was not plentiful, that Katy could return at any moment, he immediately moved one of his hands from the small of her back, where he'd helped her support her weight, to the curve of her breast. When he cupped the voluptuous treasure with his fingers, he was pleased with the soft, sensual moan that slipped past her lips. With his other hand, he worked with the many buttons that held together the back of her dress. Time was of the essence.

Inwardly, Emily knew of the danger that surrounded her. She tried to gather the strength she needed to push him away only to discover his kiss had taken too much of that necessary strength out of her. Trying one last time, she placed her hands against his chest, fully intending to push him away, but discovered she couldn't do it. Instead of pushing, her fingers relaxed against the strong muscles beneath the soft fabric of his shirt and her palms played gently across the smooth surface. She was shocked by how she wished to touch his skin directly.

Never had she desired a man the way she desired Randall. For once, she wondered what it would be like to make love to a man—make love to a man like Randall Gipson.

She knew what they were doing was wrong, but that fact still did nothing to make her stop him, not even when she felt his hand ease beneath the loosened fabric of her dress and move forward.

She trembled with growing expectation while he slowly trailed his fingers across her heated skin. And, instead of gasping with protest when his thumb first came into contact with the sensitive peak he'd sought, she gasped at the shocking pleasure the action had brought. She marveled at the stimulating power this man held in his touch when he gently tugged at the straining nipple.

Suddenly Emily could not find enough air. She

could barely capture enough breath to fill her lungs—but still she did nothing to pull away. She couldn't have if she'd wanted, for he held her well within his magical spell. He had spoken the truth earlier. She did want him as much as he wanted her. Perhaps more, because at that moment she felt ready to give herself to him completely. Give herself as any woman would to the man she loved.

Randall's blood ran hot trails through his body, aware that he'd finally gotten past Emily's stubborn pretenses. He was well on his way to seducing her—at last. Quickly, he tugged on the sleeve of her dress and then at the top of her chemise until he had finally bared one arm and freed one of her breasts.

Glancing off in the direction Katy had gone, he was pleased to see she was not yet on her way back. He tore his mouth from hers and immediately descended on the rigid nipple, suckling it with short draws of his tongue until she moaned aloud with appreciation. Feeling her grow heavy in his arms, which meant she had started to succumb to the intensity of her own needs, he quickly lowered her onto the quilts and frantically began working with the rest of her buttons—all the while continuing to suckle greedily at the breast he'd waited for so long to capture.

Although Emily knew they were rapidly reaching the point of no return, which frightened her enough to send another warning from her brain, the burning heat that had so quickly consumed her had already settled in the very core of her being, fervently urging her not to pull away, but rather finally discover what it was to be a woman. Hot tears of shame pushed past her closed eyelids and scalded her cheeks, but even that did not stop her. She was beyond stopping. She was his, body and soul. Instead of grasping his hands and pushing them away, she writhed helplessly beneath his masterful touch.

"Emily? Randall? Where are you?" Katy called out. Her voice wafted over them from somewhere in the distance, hitting Emily with a cold wave of reality. Suddenly, she was able to drag herself from the sensual haze Randall had created and found the strength she needed to push him away.

"Katy's coming," she gasped. Her eyes flew open with alarm.

Aware it was important to Emily that Katy not find out what she really was, and at the same time not really eager to have an audience when he took the not-so-fair maiden, Randall made a heroic effort to bring his emotions back under control.

He took several ragged breaths through tightly clenched teeth while he quickly tugged first the chemise then the dress back into place then began refastening the buttons. When he had the dress looking the way it had before he'd started, he sat up and straightened his own clothing. His senses still whirled at a frantic pace and his blood still raced with a wild and furious rhythm when Katy slowly came into view.

"You two lazies. No wonder I didn't see you," Katy admonished in a lightly teasing voice when she discovered them both still seated on the quilt. As if unaware she'd interrupted anything of importance, she held out a large bouquet of colorful wildflowers. "Here I have had enough time to gather all these beautiful flowers and you two haven't even finished putting away the food yet."

"You know how it is when two people get to talking," Randall said, meeting neither woman's gaze. "Sometimes they get so carried away with what they are—ah—saying to each other, they lose all sense of—time." He then reached for the nearest pickle jar and tightened the lid. "But it shouldn't take us any time at all to finish putting all this away."

Katy looked first at Emily then at Randall. "I'm sorry. You were obviously discussing something important and I interrupted you. Tell you what, if you'd like a few minutes to finish your little chat, I can always take another little walk."

Emily's eyes widened with alarm. "No, that won't be necessary."

Katy looked at her questioningly, clearly willing to oblige the two.

"She's right," Randall finally agreed, fully aware the moment had passed. He then glanced at Emily, holding her gaze with his own. "We can finish our conversation later—when there's a lot more time."

Emily swallowed audibly but said nothing while Randall bent forward to set the pickle jar inside the basket.

Chapter Fifteen

It was nearly five o'clock before Randall walked with Emily and Katy to their door. Although the trip back from the lake had started out lively and full of conversation, mostly from Katy, Randall had eventually lost interest in everything being said and spent the last part of the trip dwelling on how very close he'd come to successfully seducing Emily.

If only they hadn't been interrupted so soon after he'd finally found his way around those ridiculous pretenses of hers. He recalled how willingly she had surrendered to him, and having finally tasted the fiery passions that burned inside her, he could hardly wait for his next sampling.

Before he left that rooming house, he fully intended to know when and where they could again be alone like that. He had come far too close to finally conquering her to consider quitting now.

But, first, he had to find a way to be alone with Emily so they could arrange their next liaison—this time one that could not be so easily interrupted.

"Katy, I want you to know that I have enjoyed your fine company, but I really do wish you'd go on inside and give us a few minutes alone," he said in a most gentlemanly fashion after it became apparent that Katy did not plan to leave them of her own accord. "I promise you, Emily is safe with me. All I want is a chance to speak with her alone again."

Katy smiled knowingly. "So you can finish that conversation you two started while I was off gathering these flowers?" She glanced down at the large bouquet of brightly colored field flowers she held so tenderly in her hands.

"In a way, yes." He nodded then gave Emily a conspiring look. "I think you could definitely say it has something to do with that."

"Fine with me," Katy said agreeably while she reached for the screen door. "Besides, I really do need to get on in there and put these flowers into some water before they start to wilt. This damp cloth you wrapped the stems with won't keep them fresh forever." She paused just inside the door to smile at him again. "Thank you for including me. I had such a nice time."

"You're quite welcome," he said, watching impatiently while she slowly ambled down the hallway toward the kitchen. He wanted to be sure she was no longer near enough to overhear anything they had to say before he spoke with Emily. When he did finally glance away from the house, he was surprised to see such pale coloring in Emily's face. He immediately reached for her hand and became further concerned when he found it icy cold to the touch. "Are you feeling ill?"

"Sort of," she said, although she wasn't really sure what it was she felt.

If she searched her heart for the absolute truth, she supposed what she felt was a dismal combination of shame and misery. How could she have allowed herself to fall such easy prey to her passions —*again?* What was there about the man that made her lose sight of even her most basic values? She refused to meet his gaze, knowing what he must think of her, knowing she had ruined all chance of any future relationship with Randall.

The really pitiful part about it was that it had happened right after she had started to understand that what she felt for him was more than a simple attraction. Far more.

How could she do something so foolish and so utterly destructive? She'd never understand her own brash actions if she lived to be a hundred.

But Emily couldn't admit any of that to Randall. "I—I guess I ate something that doesn't quite agree with me."

He released her hand then lifted his palms to caress her cheeks, his eyes filled with such concern and such tenderness it brought tears to her eyes. How could he care about her after what she'd done? Surely, he must loathe her for having displayed such shameful behavior. She certainly loathed herself.

"Then I'll be brief," he promised.

Although he lowered his hands back to his sides, she could still feel his gentle touch against her skin. He continued to study her pale features while he spoke.

"I just wanted to ask you to have lunch with me again tomorrow. I thought perhaps we could eat at the same restaurant where Katy works. It's pretty close to the hat shop, which should give us plenty of time to eat. That is, if you're feeling better by then."

Emily's heart soared at the unexpected invitation. It was her chance to redeem herself in his eyes, and at the same time it would be the perfect opportunity to get to know Randall a little better, explore these strange feelings he'd aroused in her. But almost as quickly as her heart had taken flight, it plunged back into the darkness of reality. If she said yes, she chanced being hurt again. And she had barely gotten over the devastating losses of her father and grandmother. Could her heart survive another grave disappointment?

Her first inclination was to save herself from any further emotional trauma by simply declining his invitation; but when it came to actually voicing that decision, she couldn't quite find the words. Despite the emotional harm that accepting his invitation might eventually cause, she truly wanted to be with him. Besides, what real harm could he do while out in public like that? She wouldn't be in danger of losing what little was left of her virtue while dining in a crowded restaurant. And it wasn't as if he'd asked her to marry him or make any other sort of commitments to him. All he'd done was invite her out to lunch again.

Finally she agreed, knowing that if she chose not to see him again, she would be breaking her own heart. "Yes, lunch tomorrow would be nice."

She did not mention the possibility she might still feel a little ill the next day because she had already guessed the source of her pain. She felt fairly certain that as soon as he'd left and she was away from his intimidating presence, she would start to experience an amazing recovery.

"Good," he said. Smiling until long narrow dimples formed in his cheeks, he leaned forward and pressed his lips lightly against her forehead. "I'll stop by for you just before noon. And you might as well warn Katy that I expect to have the best of service," he added and winked playfully, as if nothing shameful or in any way degrading had occurred between them that day.

Emily felt grateful to him for that. Some of the tension drained out of her, easing the heavy feeling in her chest. There was a chance for them yet. Or was there? Only time would tell, which was something he was now offering her.

Still studying her troubled expression, Randall straightened his lightweight summer jacket over his shoulders as if in preparation to leave. But the urge to kiss her again was too great.

He bent forward and, this time, lowered his mouth to hers for a gentle but passionate kiss that was a startling reminder of the uncanny powers he still possessed.

Knowing now what to expect, Emily braced herself for a fresh onslaught of unavoidable passion; but this time, he did not attempt to do more than simply kiss her. He did not try to pull her body hard against his own, nor did he become all too familiar with his hands. Instead, he held his arms loosely at his sides. Only their lips touched.

When he pulled away, his expression had changed. His pale blue eyes had darkened until they glittered dangerous and foreboding. His facial muscles tensed while he looked at her for a long, heart-stopping moment then, finally, he stepped away.

"See you tomorrow then," he told her, his tone revealing none of the turmoil he felt.

It took all his restraint not to steal her away for the night. If only she hadn't fallen ill. If only their circumstances earlier that day could have been different. Oh, how he wanted her—wanted her more than he had ever wanted *any* woman. She had the mysterious ability to set his very soul on fire, and with little more than a simple kiss.

"I won't be late," he promised, then hurried away before he lost all resolve to wait until she felt better—even though he knew waiting would prove to his advantage. Unless the timing was exactly right, he would come out the loser. He would not know the full extent of her passion unless her heart was in it.

Stunned by such a noticeable change in Randall's behavior, Emily stood silently watching while he climbed back into the coach. She did not move again until Andrew had started the coach rolling, headed back toward the main part of town.

True to his word, Randall arrived the next morning on time. At precisely ten minutes before noon, his coach pulled to a slow halt in front of the hat shop. Barely a minute later, he stepped out onto the sidewalk, looking extremely distinguished in his three-piece cutaway.

Emily had spent most of the morning trying to convince everyone in the shop, herself included, that his invitation to have lunch with him did not mean anything special. Even so, she drew in a sharp, gasping breath when she heard her boss formally announce that Randall Gipson had arrived.

"Oh, and you should see the way he's dressed," Mrs. Williams cooed, hurrying away from the window so she would not be seen.

The other girls immediately put aside their handwork and hurried into the front room to get a quick glimpse of him. Emily did not move, but listened carefully for their responses.

"Oh, my. He *is* every bit as handsome as they say he is," Stephanie remarked, tiptoeing so she could see him through the window from where she stood in the center of the room. When she then realized he was almost to the door, she and the rest of the girls scurried back into the other room. Barely seconds after they had all returned to their seats and had quieted the telltale rustle of their skirts, the doorbell jingled.

Leaning forward, toward the other girls, Stephanie whispered in a voice so low Emily almost didn't hear what she said. "Why that man is absolutely gorgeous. And did you see the suit he was wearing? I'll bet that set him back a pretty penny."

"Men aren't gorgeous," Kim quickly admonished, already taking a stitch in the hat she'd retrieved. Yet, seconds after she had spoken, a knowing grin stretched across her face. "But in this case, I'll admit he sure comes close to it."

Although Emily didn't openly volunteer her opinion, she silently agreed with their assessment. If ever a man could be declared gorgeous, it was Randall Gipson. But she decided the word handsome described him far better.

"Em-i-ly," Mrs. Williams called out in a sing-song voice, as if no one in the shop yet knew of his arrival. "You need to come up front. Your guest is here."

Aware that the hour of reckoning had come, Emily slowly laid the narrow ribbons of black velvet she'd been twisting into delicate braids off to one side then lifted her fingers to see if she needed to make any last minute repairs to her hair. When it felt as if every curl was still in place beneath the stylish yellow and white hat she'd chosen to match her summer dress, she slowly rose from her chair. Looking at the other girls, she brushed imaginary wrinkles from her billowing skirts, then immediately gathered up her handbag and walked into the front room to greet him.

"You look beautiful," he said, eyeing her appreciatively. "Glad to see the color back in your cheeks."

Not yet comfortable with the compliments he so often bestowed upon her, Emily blushed prettily and looked away.

"Hungry?" she asked, hoping to redirect their conversation to a topic that would in no way embarrass her.

Randall nodded vigorously and reached for the door. "I'm famished. Let's go eat."

When Emily looked to Mrs. Williams for permission to leave five minutes early, the woman beamed proudly. "I'll see you two in a little while. Enjoy yourselves."

Knowing the woman had as much as given her blessing, Emily stepped through the door then waited on the other side. Tiny shivers of awareness skittered down her spine when she finally gathered the courage to look directly at him. She noticed how truly splendid he looked in his tailor-fitted business suit. Stephanie had not exaggereated. He was as gorgeous as he was handsome. Dangerously so.

She swallowed to clear the constriction tightening around the base of her throat. "Katy told me to be sure that we sit at one of the tables along the east side of the restaurant. That's the area she's usually responsible for," she said, choosing what seemed a safe enough direction for their conversation.

"Good. Let's find one near the back so we can have a better chance to talk," he suggested. He wanted to tell her how taken he'd been with her yesterday—how pleased he'd been with her passion for lovemaking. And, now that she had her color back, he was more eager than ever to get on with his conquest.

"Yes, I think we do need to have a little talk," she agreed, not meeting his gaze, even while she allowed him to help her into his coach. Although it would have been a lovely day for a walk, she did not suggest it—not at all certain her legs could carry her that far without risking a collapse. Just seeing him again made her feel weak as a kitten inside.

"You do?" he asked, surprised at her openness. "And just what is it you think we should talk about?"

Emily considered putting off the conversation until they had reached the restaurant, but decided it would be better if they discussed the matter in private.

"About what happened yesterday," she said, still unable to meet his probing gaze. Instead, she studied the stitching in her traveling gloves. "I really don't know what came over me, and I am truly ashamed of what I did. But I wanted you to know, I have given it a lot of thought and I will never let something like that happen again." She blushed when she remembered just how far they had taken their passions. Her skin still tingled in some of the places he'd touched her. "I'm not usually like that."

Randall studied the high color she'd forced into her cheeks and sighed wearily. So they were back to playing games, were they? Well, he'd managed to get past her playacting once, he could do it again. "I understand. I should have realized it was a whole new experience for you. I never should have allowed myself to get carried away like that. I feel I should apologize for having treated you like that." He tried his best to sound sincere when what he felt mostly was annoyed.

Emily looked at him with such open gratitude that tears filled her eyes.

Remarkable, he thought as he gazed into the shimmering depths of her golden brown eyes, because it was really the only way to describe her. If he didn't know better, he'd honestly believe her to be truly repentant about her past.

"So, am I forgiven?" He reached out to gently stroke her cheek with his palm, thinking that was just the right gesture.

"I—I guess." She then smiled and blinked away the tears, her lower lip still quivering with gratitude.

"Good. Then we won't mention it again."

Glad that was over with, Randall then rested his arm along the back of the seat, just inches above her shoulders—close enough to touch her if he wanted, but without actually doing so. He was clever enough to know that if he ever wanted to reap the amazing rewards she had to offer, he'd have to continue playing right along with her. Besides, even if she did want to pretend to be prim and respectable, who was he to stand in her way? After having sampled a taste of her forbidden pleasures, he already knew she'd be well worth whatever efforts he had to display.

Upon arriving at the restaurant just a few minutes after twelve, they found only two empty tables along the east side of the room. Never having eaten there before, and not knowing if they should seat themselves or wait to be seated, Randall paused near the front door to decide what to do. But after taking a quick look around and noticing the quality of patrons that had crowded into the small room, he decided this was the type of place where customers were expected to seat themselves. Most of the people in the room were huge, burly men who appeared to be either dock workers or warehouse stockers.

Aware that his chances of running into anyone he knew were actually very slim in a place like this, he decided against sitting in the back of the room where cigar smoke usually grew thick and conversations quite boisterous. Instead, he chose the closest of the two tables, carefully remembering to pull out Emily's chair for her.

"I hope the food's good here," he commented, glancing at the other tables while he settled into his own chair.

"I don't know about the rest of the food, but their pie is delicious," Emily told him, remembering the day she and Katy had eaten there. Immediately searching the room for a menu and spotting the day's selections scrawled across a large slate near the front door, she shrugged with momentary indecision, then made her selection. "I guess I'll have the broiled ham."

Randall glanced around to see where she'd gotten that information and, after he too spotted the board, he mulled over the selections then nodded his agreement. "I think I'll have the broiled ham, too." It certainly sounded tastier than potluck stew or pan-broiled chicken gizzards.

Emily then noticed Katy near the back of the room and waved to catch her attention. Minutes later, Katy brought them two large glasses filled with water, two napkins, and two fresh settings of flatware.

Smiling perceptively at the pair, Katy memorized their orders then disappeared into the back. Within minutes, she returned carrying two plates, each ladened with enough food to feed a small family. When she placed the steaming platters on the table in front of them, she grinned. "Eat up. There's plenty more where that came from."

Emily blinked at the contents on her plate, knowing she would never be able to eat all that food, but thanked Katy anyway before she picked up her fork and scooped her first mouthful of peas. Finding them to be delicious, she immediately reached for her knife and cut a small piece of ham.

"This is good," Randall commented after he had swallowed his first bite.

He sounded as surprised as she had been after she'd sunk her teeth into her own first bite of ham because, after having seen the ridiculous amount of food and how haphazardly it had been slopped onto their plates, she'd formed certain doubts.

"It *is* good," she agreed. Quickly she cut another bite and placed it in her mouth.

"That's a good girl," Randall commented while he, too, cut off a second hefty bite. "I want to see you eat everything on your plate."

Emily laughed, knowing that was asking the impossible. Those may be normal portions for longshoremen, but they were outrageous amounts for a common shopworker like herself.

"All right, but only after you've eaten everything on your plate," she teased, aware her laughter had broken the last of the tension still lingering between them.

For the rest of their meal she was finally able to set aside all her earlier misgivings and simply enjoy Randall's company. She refused to dwell on any thoughts that might prove unnerving. She refused to wonder what he might be thinking of her, or even consider the obvious fact she had started to fall in love with him. She wanted simply to enjoy being with him—enjoy nothing more than listening to the sound of his voice and feeling his appreciative gaze upon her cheek.

After eating her fill, she pushed her plate aside and watched while he took his last few bites. There was something physically stimulating in the way his lips caressed the food when he pulled it off his fork and into his mouth. The slow, sensuous way he chewed it drove her to utter distraction. Not only did he look incredibly handsome, he even ate incredibly handsome—a realization that both bothered and pleased her.

When Randall glanced up and caught her staring at him with such open fascination, he smiled, causing her to blush and look away. Thinking it was all still part of her coy little act, he dropped his gaze to his food again and took his last bite. When he finished with that, he also pushed his plate away and reached for his water glass. "I'm so stuffed, I actually hurt."

"But you didn't eat everything on your plate," she pointed out, delighted when he rewarded her comment with deep, rich laughter.

"I did my best," he said. Tilting his head to one side, he stared at her, mesmerized by the attractive dimples that had formed at the outer curves of her mouth. For a moment, he fought conflicting emotions.

Oddly enough, a small part of him had started to wish that Emily truly was the lady she pretended to be—a lady he could be proud to be seen with—a lady who would make a respectable if not somewhat unpredictable wife. But then another part of him was glad she was none of that.

That part of him could hardly wait until their next intimate encounter. If she could set his very soul on fire with just a few passionate kisses, he could imagine how astounding it must be like to actually bed her. His whole body ached with anticipation.

Emily felt awkward at the sudden intensity in his expression and reached for her handbag. "I guess we'd better be getting back. I have a lot of work to finish today."

Randall had not expected to feel so disappointed by her decision to leave, especially when he'd known all along that she would have only enough time for a quick lunch. It wasn't as if she had promised to spend the entire day with him.

"Just let me find out what I owe this place, then we can be on our way."

He waved to catch Katy's attention. After learning that the two meals cost sixty cents total, he singled out a dollar, handed it to her, then told her to keep the change.

Katy beamed with appreciation and quickly tucked the money into her pocket. "I'll do that. Thank you." She then hurried away, as if afraid he might have a change of heart.

Emily waited until Randall had stood and reached for her chair before pushing away from the table. She felt all giddy inside when they then walked together toward the front door and then to the carriage because, rather than offer his arm like he usually did whenever he walked with her, he had rested his palm possessively against the small of her back, creating all manner of turmoil to skitter about inside her. Her thoughts were so focused on the warmth spreading through her that she almost did not hear his next words when he spoke.

"Think you'll possibly be hungry again by supper time?" he asked, his manner casual. He pulled his hand away and allowed her to precede him into the carriage.

Emily bit her lower lip in an effort to contain her excitement. "I'm not sure. I suppose by then I might be."

Was he really planning to invite her out again that soon? Twice in one day? It thrilled her to know that he enjoyed her company that much.

Then she remembered Patrick. She'd promised over a week ago to have dinner with him.

Her heart then sank to the very depths of her soul and she was forced to admit the truth. "But even so, I'm afraid I already have plans for tonight."

Randall scowled, wondering just who and what those plans might include. "Well, what about tomorrow night? I know of a very nice little restaurant that serves extraordinary food. You'd love it."

It was not the food that tempted her, but she made no comment while he continued.

"It's out near the west end of town," he explained, not about to give up until she'd said yes. "Right on the beach. They always have fresh seafood cooked about any way you'd want it, and the place is rarely crowded during the week."

It sounded wonderful and the only reason Emily did not agree immediately was because she couldn't. She was having too hard of a time catching her breath. The thought of dining with Randall in some secluded little beachfront restaurant had sent her senses spinning at a maddening rate.

"Please, say yes," he prompted, afraid she intended to let her stupid game-playing get in the way of his plans.

"Okay, yes," she finally agreed. "I'd love it."

Relieved that she had yet to suggest a chaperone, Randall hurried to finalize their plans. "Good. I'll stop by for you around seven."

"What should I wear?" she wanted to know, having no idea if this place was formal or casual.

Randall grinned, tempted to tell her not to wear anything at all, knowing that would certainly simplify matters for him. But in the end, he kept the comment to himself and assured her that the sort of thing she had on would be appropriate.

Later that night, after a long boring evening with Patrick, Emily went on to bed as soon as she'd returned, but discovered she could not fall asleep. After an evening spent comparing the dull way Patrick made her feel to the lively way Randall made her feel, she was more certain than ever that she'd fallen in love with Randall. For the first time, she wondered what it would be like to be married to him. The thought of one day becoming his wife and bearing his children thrilled her, making her feel more alive than she'd felt in years.

If only she could be sure he felt the same way

about her. Then she would be truly happy. But for now it was enough to know he had put aside all their many differences and actually wanted to spend more time with her.

Chapter Sixteen

With Randall Gipson suddenly taking up so many of her evenings, coupled with the long, tedious hours of her job, Emily found it increasingly harder to pursue information about her grandmother.

Although she'd tried twice more to convince her aunt to talk with her, the woman still refused to open her letters; and as of yet, Edward Paterson had been unable even to locate her grandmother's grave, and really did not seem to be trying too terribly hard. The more she asked him questions about his search, the more vague he seemed.

Still, her Aunt Elizabeth remained the biggest problem. Her refusal to believe that Emily's mother had ever born a child was what finally forced Emily back to asking total strangers to tell her what little they might know about her grandmother. It was by sheer luck that she eventually located a few more kind souls who had actually known her.

Even so, she found very little satisfaction in the vague sort of answers they were able to give her. The few people who had known Elmira personally were always quick to admit that they had not actually seen her for years. Evidently, her grandmother had become a very private person in her later years.

Therefore, what Emily really needed was to ask her questions of someone who had not only known her grandmother personally, but had loved her as family—someone who would have taken the trouble to travel out to her home, several miles out into the mainland, to visit with her during those last few years. What she really needed was to somehow convince her aunt to talk with her. But, as time went on, and her aunt continued to ignore her pleas, Emily realized that would never be. Her aunt honestly believed she was some sleazy shyster out to get her hands on their money, and because of that, her aunt would never accept her as the niece she really was.

The situation bordered on hopeless.

If it had not been for Randall and all the attention he'd bestowed on her over the past few weeks, Emily felt certain she'd have fallen into a deep, dark state of depression, forever lost to her ever growing despair. But as it turned out, his almost daily visits and the ever increasing amount of time they spent together—either at the rooming house or away—kept her from constantly dwelling on her personal problems. Randall had brought a certain light to her otherwise dismal life, and she would be forever grateful for that.

"You're smiling again," Katy pointed out while she slowly pushed against the rough-planked flooring with the tips of her toes, causing the porch swing to dip gracefully backwards. "Want me to guess why?"

Emily quickly reined in her thoughts. "No, I don't want you guessing why."

"That's because you know I'll guess right," Emily said, nudging her playfully with her elbow. "That's because you were thinking about Randall again."

Emily was not going to deny the truth, but she

also wasn't about to admit it aloud and thus give Katy the extreme satisfaction of knowing she was absolutely right—again. Instead, she tilted her head against the back of the swing and watched the sturdy chain that held the wooden seat suspended. "It's really none of your business what I'm thinking."

Katy also rested her head against the top board but her attention was drawn to a small wood spider busy constructing his latest work of art in the far corner of the porch. "Is it also none of my business where he's taking you tonight?"

"For your information, he's not taking me anywhere," she said defiantly, but as soon as she had spoken the words, a sad feeling of melancholy swept over her. Though she'd seen him during lunch, and would see him again tomorrow, she knew she would miss him dreadfully in the hours between. But at least it would give her an opportunity to wash both her clothes and her hair. "He has some sort of business meeting he has to go to tonight."

"Then what about tomorrow? Is he coming by for you tomorrow?"

Emily suppressed a smile when she rolled her head sideways to look at Katy. Just knowing that he did indeed plan to come by tomorrow lifted her spirits considerably. "Yes, tomorrow we're supposed to have an early supper at the Crosswinds, after which we're planning to take a little ride out in the country."

Katy's green eyes widened while an amused grin tugged at one corner of her mouth. "Alone? Just the two of you?"

"Unless you are thinking of inviting yourself again," Emily said, teasing her friend, yet knowing that whenever Katy had gone with them it had always been at her special request. "But then again, as long as his driver is there with us, I don't suppose you could say we will be completely alone, so there's really not a lot to worry about. Besides, I imagine you already have plans of your own for tomorrow night."

Katy laughed, delighted that she did indeed have plans of her own. "Yes, tomorrow is June eighth. Raymond and I are going to that concert at the Tremont tomorrow night. Too bad Randall doesn't like that sort of thing or we could make it a foursome."

Emily returned her gaze to the ceiling and frowned, perplexed by something in what Katy had just said. Thinking back, she remembered that while they were still on the ship, Josephine had told her that Randall actually loved that sort of thing. Josephine had also mentioned that he was always getting his name in the society column for having attended some elegant function or another. She'd said he enjoyed everything from gala balls, to summer concerts, to the opera. Yet, whenever he took her out, it was always to someplace simple.

After a quiet dinner in some out-of-the-way restaurant, they either spent their evenings taking long, leisurely walks along the docks or on some secluded beach, or else they went carriage riding through the countryside. He'd never once suggested they go to a public concert or a play, or even to the circus that had been in town earlier that week. Nor had he ever bothered to introduce her to any of his friends, other than Raymond Porterfield, and that was merely because Katy had wanted to meet him.

Suddenly, Emily wondered if the real reason he avoided crowds whenever he was with her was because he was ashamed of her.

Or worse.

It occurred to her then that he just might have

another lady friend, one a little more special to him than she was—one who would not take too kindly to the fact he was seeing her on the sly. Emily's stomach knotted at such a painful thought. What if he was already engaged to someone else? What if he was merely leading her on? But why would he do that? Why would he put such an important relationship as an engagement in jeopardy like that? It just didn't make sense.

Aware of Emily's sudden change in mood, Katy sat forward, bringing the swing to an immediate halt. She cocked her head to one side while she studied Emily's troubled expression. "What's wrong? Did I say something to offend you?"

"No," Emily assured her, trying to sound more cheerful than she actually felt. Her mind continued to be plagued with all the reasons Randall might want to keep his relationship with her a secret. "It's just that I suddenly realized I wouldn't have an appropriate dress to wear to a concert even if he did ask me."

She fell silent again. Maybe that was part of the problem. Perhaps he was afraid she'd embarrass him by wearing something inappropriate.

That prospect angered her. Just because she wasn't as wealthy as the rest of his friends didn't mean she could not afford at least one nice ball gown. After all, she wasn't destitute. She did earn respectable wages and she had had enough sense to save a goodly portion of those wages.

"I know what you mean," Katy agreed with a slow nod. "I spent all the money I had in this world on the dress I'm planning to wear tomorrow night. It's hard for me to imagine that some women spend that sort of money on their clothing every day."

Well, it wasn't all that hard for Emily to imagine because before her father had died and left her practically penniless, she'd shopped in the most exclusive boutiques in New York and dined in the most expensive restaurants. But those days were gone. Now she had to be more practical.

Still, she could afford one such gown and wondered how she should go about letting Randall know that without sounding too forward.

Randall sat on the edge of his bed, staring grimly into the darkness that surrounded him. He hated to admit it, but he was gradually becoming increasingly obsessed with Emily. She had already affected his work. It had become impossible for him to concentrate on anything or anyone else for very long—and earlier tonight she'd been the sole reason he could not enjoy the concert.

Although Annie had looked stunning in her burnished red gown with her dark hair swept up with impressive strands of cracked pearls, his thoughts were on Emily. It had bothered him that while he was stuck there at that concert, she could be out on the town with someone else. Perhaps Patrick. Or perhaps a stranger. Or had she actually stayed home and washed her hair like she'd said she would?

Questions like those concerning Emily and her whereabouts had plagued him the entire evening. And as if that wasn't enough to drive a sane man totally mad, now she was not only affecting his waking hours, she was also disturbing his sleep. After having been held at bay for almost three weeks now, he felt very close to losing his mind.

What remained the hardest for him to understand was why she kept putting him off the way she did. He had made every effort to play the game her way by courting her ever so properly and complimenting her every chance he had. So why did she continue to pull away whenever he tried to make advances toward her? What exactly was she waiting for? Was there a logical explanation for her wanting to delay the inevitable like that?

Well, if there was a logical reason, he certainly couldn't figure it out. The harder he tried, the more confused and totally frustrated he became. The simple fact of it was that the more time he spent with her, the more he wanted her; a fact of which she was obviously very aware because several times during the past few weeks she had allowed him to kiss her and hold her close; yet whenever he tried to turn the kiss into something a little more intimate, she immediately pulled away.

Randall was rapidly reaching the end of his rope. He wanted to know when she intended to give up this absurd act of hers and finally reveal her true, passionate nature. Just what did she hope to gain by keeping up such a ridiculous performance? Did her reluctance to give in have something to do with him? Had he done something wrong, something that had displeased her in some way? Or maybe she was hoping to gain something that still lay just beyond his comprehension.

At first, all her pretenses had not really bothered him, but that was when he still believed it was only a matter of time until he finally seduced her. Now he had to wonder how much time she thought she needed.

Aware he had already reached the very limit of his endurance, he threw up his hands and made a personal vow to force her to give in—the very next time they were together.

No more games. Just plain old, up front, everyday seduction.

He'd conduct the evening very carefully, making sure everything went just right. First, they'd have that private little supper at the Crosswinds he'd promised her, then he would take her on that cozy little ride out into the country. Only this time he would not allow her to push him away. This time, Emily Felcher would be his.

With that vow planted firmly in his heart, Randall lowered himself back into bed and was finally able to get some sleep.

"Randall?" Emily broke into his thoughts, although she had fully intended to wait until he had finished eating. She was just too eager to find out the truth to put it off any longer.

"Hmm?" he responded, his mouth full of spaghetti. His blue eyes reflected the candlelight in a most beguiling way when he glanced up at her.

"Do you mind if I ask you a personal question?" she asked, trying not to be distracted by how handsome the soft lighting made him look.

"Uhh-um," he answered and shook his head to indicate that he did not. He reached for his water glass while waiting to hear what her question might be.

"I was just wondering why it is that you never take me to any of the fancier restaurants uptown. Why do we always eat in some small, out-of-the-way place like this one?"

The question took Randall by surprise. The answer to that seemed pretty obvious. Why did she think?

"Because I hate crowds," he answered immediately, pleased with himself for having thought so quickly. "But mainly because I don't want to have to share you with anyone else."

Emily hadn't considered that. "But what makes you think you'd have to share me?"

"I know my friends. The minute they met you, they'd swarm all around you, wanting you for themselves, and I really don't think I could stand very much of that. Maybe I'm selfish, but that just happens to be the way I feel."

Emily smiled, pleased by his answer. "Then it's not because you are ashamed of me?"

"Ashamed of you? Why would I be ashamed of you?" He was honestly puzzled. Although she was not the sort of woman one took home to meet the family, she was extremely beautiful and carried herself very well. If he ever had to be seen out in public while in the company of a woman of her reputation, he would prefer it to be her.

"I don't know," Emily answered, unaware of his thoughts. "I figured maybe you were ashamed because I'm not wealthy like your other friends."

"What has that got to do with anything?" he asked, confused by such a statement. What was she after now? Another compliment of some kind? "What you lack in wealth, my dear, you more than make up for with beauty."

Emily stared down at her hands. Did he really think her beautiful? She certainly hoped so. Still, she found that hard to believe for she had seen several truly beautiful women in Galveston and did not think she in any way compared. "Well, if you ever do decide you'd like to go to something like a concert or a play, don't worry about my finances. I can easily afford a new ball gown."

Randall wondered where she'd come across that kind of money, then remembered she'd had "other plans" more than once during the past few weeks. That angered him. "Why do you think you'd have to buy a new gown for something like that? What's wrong with the ones you have?"

Realizing he was referring to the horrible outfits Josephine had bought for her, Emily blushed with embarrassment. "I really don't think they are very appropriate for a social evening in Galveston."

That depended largely on her definition of social. "Tell you what, if it means that much to you, I'll take you to a concert or a play sometime in the very near future. I'll even buy a special dress for you to wear." That is if she proved herself worthy of a fancy new dress later once they'd reached the highlight of their moonlit ride. He smiled, looking forward to the pleasurable events that still lay ahead.

"I couldn't let you do that," she protested, upset that he would even suggest such a thing. "I just wanted you to understand that if you ever wanted to do something like that, it would be fine with me."

Randall shook his head, still confused by the reasoning behind such a strange conversation. If she had not wanted a new dress, then why did she bring up the subject at all? "All right, I'll be sure to keep that in mind. But for now, all I want to do is pay for our meal and take that special drive I promised you. I thought it would be nice to ride out and take a look at the lighthouse."

"But I thought the lighthouse was in Bolivar, on the mainland."

"It is, but you can see it from across the bay. It really is a spectacular sight." Having said that, he pushed his chair back and dropped his napkin onto his plate. He took just enough time to pitch several coins onto the table, then quickly helped her with her chair. "Let's go."

The ride out to the bay that overlooked the lighthouse took only fifteen minutes. Being not quite nine o'clock, it had been dark for less than an hour when he pulled the carriage off the main road. He stopped within a few yards of the gently lapping shore and motioned toward the spectacular view with a wave of his hand. "Now isn't this everything I promised it would be?"

Emily nodded that is was indeed and tried to concentrate on the phantom-like glow across the water, but her attention remained focused on Randall and the fact that they were out there all alone. Of all nights for Andrew to become ill. Already her heart hammered wildly with concern because it had always been Andrew's presence that had kept their passions from getting out of hand. But tonight she'd have to find another source of self-discipline. But what? She'd already proven that she was helpless to stop herself without something to help restrain her emotions. Her best plan of action would be to make certain he never had a real opportunity to try anything.

"Doesn't that view send chills down your spine?" he asked, breaking her thoughts while he leaned closer.

It wasn't the view that sent the massive array of chills cascading down her spine. And when she felt him move even closer, she scooted as far away from him as she could.

"Aren't you glad I decided to share this with you?" he wanted to know, seemingly unperturbed by her retreat as he continued to move slowly toward her.

"Yes, of course," she said, her mind frantic with the need to put a safer distance between them—before he tried something extremely dangerous like kissing her. Her heart slammed hard against her breastbone when she glanced at him then and saw the dark glaze of open desire in his eyes. "In fact, this place is so beautiful I'd like to get out and walk closer to the shore so I can get a better look."

Perfect, he thought, wetting his lips with eager anticipation while he watched her climb down.

"That's a good idea. I'll just grab a few of the quilts I brought with me and lay them across the ground so we can be comfortable while we watch the ships ease their way through."

Emily swallowed hard when she turned to look at him again. She had not realized he'd brought quilts. "That really won't be necessary."

Necessary or not, he reached into the back of the carriage and pulled out two thick patchwork quilts then jumped agilely to the ground. "I think that patch of grass over there would be perfect, don't you?" He indicated a small, grassy knoll near the water's edge.

"I guess," she said, watching apprehensively while he set one quilt aside and quickly shook the folds out of the other. Her dark eyes widened with instant alarm after he finished with the first quilt, then lowered the second quilt directly on top of it, rather than place them side by side, like she'd hoped.

"Go on," he encouraged, nodding toward the cozy pallet. "Sit down and make yourself comfortable while I start a fire."

"A fire? On a night like this?" she asked, thinking that was a bit much. It had to be seventy-five degrees outside.

"If I don't set a little camphor on to boil, the mosquitoes will eat us alive out here," he explained, already gathering large pieces of driftwood and tossing them into a pile several yards from where he'd spread the quilts. Eager for this night to be perfect, he then surrounded the wood with rocks and shells so the flames couldn't spread into the grass. "Don't worry it won't take long to get this thing going."

Emily was afraid of that and within minutes he had a nice fire blazing and had gently placed a small iron pot in the very center of the flames. Soon the ocean breeze carried the pungent smell of camphor.

"There, that should keep the mosquitos and gnats from bothering us." He rubbed his hands together in anticipation when he returned to Emily's side then quickly made himself comfortable on the quilt beside her.

"Isn't this nice?" he asked in a low, silky voice just seconds before he moved closer to her.

"Yes, it is," she admitted, though her racing heartbeat cautioned the utmost of danger. "It is very lovely out here." Sitting with her feet at her side, she tucked them closer to her then self-consciously arranged the hem of her skirt over her slippers.

"But not nearly as lovely as you are," he said, rolling over on one well-muscled thigh so he could be closer still. "The moonlight does exceptional things to your hair."

Emily reached up to touch the brim of her tiny hat, wondering if she'd forgotten to put it on. "Why do you say that? You can't even see most of my hair."

"Something I plan to remedy right now," he murmured, then rolled to his knees and gently removed the hat and its accompanying ribbons.

Emily sat mesmerized by his movements while he then pulled all the pins from her hair and combed the silken mass with careful fingers until it fell softly across her shoulders. His delicate but deliberate movements caused tiny bumps to form beneath her skin.

"There, that's better," he said and gazed longingly into her eyes while he slipped his hands from her hair then cupped her chin with his strong fingers. "I guess you know I'm going to kiss you."

Emily nodded, having seen that particular look

several times before. She shuddered with expectation.

"And this time, you are not going to pull away," he cautioned, his voice soft and coaxing but his expression determined. With no further comment, he bent forward and brought his lips to hers in what started out as a maddeningly sweet kiss but immediately flared into something more.

Emily was so overwhelmed by the wondrous sensations overtaking her body, her eyes drifted closed so she could enjoy them all the more.

While his lips continued to hold hers imprisoned with their magic, his arms came around her shoulders and pressed her closer, leaving her feeling both weak and exhilarated. She leaned her weight against him as much to feel his strength as to keep her bearings.

Randall moaned when he felt her body pressing against his, indicating she was as eager as he. Slowly, he leaned back, bringing her down on top of him. When he did, her hair fell forward, spilling down around his face and neck, and her full, young breasts flattened against his chest, arousing him all the more.

With the passion of a man who had been denied for far too long, he brought his head up off the quilt in an effort to devour as much of her as he could, plunging his tongue into the sweet recesses of her mouth again and again. Unsatisfied with the pleasure that brought him, he rolled until he was the one on top, his body pressing down on hers.

Emily's eyes flew open with surprise at such a quick, unexpected change in their positions, but before she could react with any indication of protest, her eyelids slowly grew heavy again. A now familiar throng of delightful sensations moved slowly through her body, leaving her captive to the warm, languid feeling of contentment so overpowering it quelled all her earlier sense of panic. For the moment, her mind was unable to focus on anything but the sheer wonder of his mouth and how intimately he'd pressed his body against hers.

Even after he slipped his hand between her and the quilt and undid the many stays and buttons along the back of her dress, she did not offer a protest—though deep down she knew she should. She knew only too well that what they were doing was wrong.

But she was too caught up in the spinning vortex of pleasure that Randall had created to do anything but give of herself willingly. She was unable to overcome the sheer intensity of the emotions that had so suddenly sprung to life—unable to cope with their volatile strength. Instead of protesting or trying to free herself, she followed her heart's bidding. She lifted her arms to encircle his strong neck and slipped her fingers into the soft thickness of his curling brown hair.

A strange sort of fire raged uncontrollably inside her. The heat from it was as frightening as it was thrilling—so frightening that she again sensed the danger that surrounded her, but she still could not find the strength necessary to push him away. He held some sort of mystic power over her, a power that made her body refuse her own commands. She felt utterly helpless, yet at the same time wondrously alive, but soon those two feelings blended into one, and all she felt was the desire to know more of this madness.

Certain now that Emily had no intention of pulling away, Randall devoured her kisses all the more while he worked the stubborn buttons one at a time. When he had the last button undone and the opening pulled apart, he wasted little time slipping his hand into the garment. Slowly he worked his hand forward until he was able to cup one of her heaving breasts through the thin fabric of her chemise.

It was then, while his mouth continued its sensual assault on hers and his hands tugged frantically at the satin ties of her undergarment, that the growing sense of the danger finally overpowered the new awakenings of Emily's passion. With what strength she had left, she pushed hard against his shoulders—but he did not fall away as she'd intended.

"Randall, don't." She pleaded, but her words came out muffled, lost in the warmth depths of his mouth. Then when he managed to tug the front of her dress down over her shoulder, in his effort to get the bothersome garment out of his way, she pushed harder. "Randall, no!"

It was as if he couldn't hear the panic in her voice. He never lessened the hungry pressure against her mouth while he continued to pull frantically on her clothes.

Chapter Seventeen

Panic filled Emily. Randall had no intention of stopping. She had to do something to free herself, but what? He had her pinned beneath his weight. Therefore, it had to be something she could accomplish with her hands. Suddenly, she thought of his hair. While he continued his onslaught of kisses and his eager attempt to undress her, she reached around to the back of his head and grasped a thick handful of his dark, wavy hair and gave it a sharp yank.

When he brought his head up with a perplexed jerk, she took advantage of the distraction and shoved him away. She immediately curled herself into a sitting position, holding the front of her dress in place with both arms.

Having believed he'd finally won, Randall was furious. His blue eyes glinted like cold steel in the silvery moonlight. "Why did you do that?" he demanded to know. The muscles at the back of his jaw pumped in and out with repressed anger. "Why, when we both know that you want me as much as I want you."

"Because it is wrong." She bent her head and sobbed with shame, knowing that what he'd said was true. She did want him every bit as much as he wanted her, but that still did not make it right. "Because that's the sort of thing you just don't do until after you are married."

Randall stared at her, dumbstruck. *Married?* So that was it. She actually believed that by continuing to lead him on the way she had, she could somehow trick him into marrying her, even though he knew about her past. She must truly have thought he'd prove just as gullible as Patrick had been, which as he recalled was why she'd decided to give up such a lucrative profession to begin with.

Having finally realized the true extent of the games she'd been playing, he became even more overwhelmed by his anger. Did she really think he was so fop-headed that he'd marry a known whore just to finally know her pleasures?

Glaring at her, because evidently that was exactly what she had thought, he then noticed the oh-so-pitiful way she bent her head and his anger burst into a cold rage. She really did believe he was foolish enough to be tricked into marrying her. Well, if that was her ploy, he'd have no part of it. But then, again, if he didn't continue to play her game, he'd also have no part of her. Therefore, he had no choice but to continue playing along, that is if he wanted her full and eager participation when he finally did figure out a way to outwit her on this.

And that was exactly what he did want, her fullest and most eager participation when the time finally came. It was the only thing that had made all that silly game-playing worthwhile. Otherwise, he could have taken her weeks ago, back when he'd first started to grow tired of her ridiculous pretenses. Or he could have simply broken down and paid her for her services; yet if he did that, he could never prove to Patrick how very shallow her affections really were—so shallow that they could be had even when no money was involved.

So, for the time being, he would continue to play her games, but with one major difference. This time, they'd be playing by *his* rules. And, *this time,* he'd show absolutely no mercy. No matter what it took, no matter what sort of lies he had to tell, he would make damn sure he came out the winner.

With that vengeful vow planted firmly in his heart, he took several deep, steadying breaths while he quickly worked to formulate a plan. When the first glimmer of an idea presented itself, he finally spoke.

"You're right," he said, amazed at the calmness in his own voice when he was still so consumed with anger. Thinking it just the right gesture of sincerity, he then gently reached forward to caress her down-turned face with the inner curve of his fingers. "I should have known better. It's just that you are so desirable. I guess I just lost my head. Please forgive me."

His next words tasted bittersweet as they rolled out of his mouth for he felt it was time she had a good strong dose of her own deceit. "And after you've finally found it in your heart to forgive me, promise that you'll marry me. Right away."

"What?" Emily's head came up with surprise.

"Marry me. Without delay. I can't bear the thought of having to wait for a formal church wedding. That could take months to prepare and I really don't think I can wait months to finally have you. In fact, I'd like for us to be married this very coming weekend. Please. It doesn't have to be anything fancy, does it? Just say that you'll marry me."

His words came out so unexpectedly and in such a rush that Emily only heard about half of what he'd said—but half was enough to let her know he was serious. "But what about your grandmother? Didn't you tell me that she's gone off to visit her sister in Jefferson for a few weeks? Don't you think we should wait at least until she returns?"

"Then your answer is yes?" he asked, pleased at how easily she'd become entangled in her own web of lies. "Does that mean you'll marry me?"

Emily blushed, knowing she'd be a fool not to marry the only man she had ever truly loved. Still, it all seemed to be happening too quickly. "Why is it you've suddenly decided you want to get married?"

"I'd think the answer to that would be obvious. Because I love you," he said, surprised when those words did not stick in his craw the way he'd thought they would. He then decided that his revenge tasted far too sweet for such lies to really bother him. "I have loved you since the very first day I saw you."

"You have?"

When she searched his eyes for the truth, he turned away, but not before she glimpsed the sincerity in his proposal. He desperately wanted her to say yes. Her heart soared with joy. The man she loved wanted to marry her. How lucky could one woman be? "All right, yes, I will marry you; but only if you will agree to wait until your grandmother has returned."

"But that could be weeks," he protested, knowing it would be better for what he had in mind if he could carry his ploy through before his grandmother returned. "I can't possibly wait that long. Please say you'll marry me this coming weekend." He reached out and caressed her neck with his hand, hoping that would help lure her into his trap.

"I appreciate your eagerness. I really do. But it just wouldn't be right to exclude your grandmother from something like this," she said, knowing how hurt Bernice would be if they didn't include her.

Aware that Emily was adamant about waiting until his grandmother had returned, and well knowing how headstrong she could be about such matters, he quickly revised the plans that had been formulating in the back of his mind. "Again, you are right. We really should wait until she's come back. And I'll agree to waiting for her, if you'll agree to something in the meantime."

"What?" She asked, knowing as she gazed into his glimmering blue eyes that she would agree to just about anything.

"Agree to marry me just as soon as she returns, and also agree to let me throw a small dinner party at my house next weekend so I can officially announce our engagement to some of my closer friends. It won't be anything big, just a few couples I'd like to have meet you. We can also invite Katy and Raymond if you'd like."

Emily was thrilled to know he finally wanted her to meet some of his friends. "That would be fun. What do you want me to do?"

"I don't want you to do anything but come and look beautiful. Besides, there won't be that much to do. I don't plan for it to be anything elaborate. And since Nora has asked to have the weekend off so she can go visit her family, I'll probably just have the whole thing catered." He then pulled Emily into his arms and embraced her. "I think you should know, you are about to make me the happiest man on the face of this earth."

Emily blinked back her tears of joy. "I'm so glad. I really do want you to be happy."

He smiled, pleased with how easily she'd fallen prey to her own wicked little scheme. "And I will be. Happier than you can ever imagine. Just you wait and see."

Emily's mind was still in a daze the next morning when she awoke just minutes after the sun had turned the night sky a dusky blue. Staring out her bedroom window while the first golden rays of morning peaked through a distant cloud, she still found it hard to believe that Randall had actually proposed to her. But the joy that surrounded her heart in a plush cushion of splendor let her know that it was absolutely true. She had not dreamed any of it. Randall Gipson had indeed asked her to marry him.

Overwhelmed with a need to share her glorious news with someone, even though Randall had asked her to keep their plans a secret until the engagement party, Emily hurriedly bathed and dressed then went to Katy's room to see if she was awake yet.

When all she received in return for her knock was a mumbled response to go away, Emily tried the knob, found it unlocked, and went on inside.

"What do you want?" Katy asked, pulling her pillow up over her head to show how unhappy she was with such an early interruption. "Is there some sort of problem I should know about? Don't you know that this is Sunday? We don't have to be at work today. And church services don't start until ten-thirty. Therefore, why are you in here at the crack of dawn trying so rudely to wake me?"

"It's not exactly the crack of dawn," Emily said, glancing at the clock to double-check the time. "Why, lazybones, I'll have you know it's well after eight o'clock."

"Oh, wonderful. I could have slept at least another hour. Just what in the blue blazes is so important that it couldn't have waited one more hour?" Her mouth, which was all that Emily could see of her beneath the pillow, flattened with annoyance. Clearly Katy was not the type who always awoke in a cheerful mood.

Emily shook her head and grinned, wondering how Katy would respond to a direct approach. "It's nothing really important, I guess. I just thought I'd mention that Randall proposed to me last night."

Katy came out from under her pillow with a start, sitting straight up, her green eyes suddenly wide. "And just what did he propose?"

"Marriage, silly," Emily said, cocking her head to one side at the implication. "What did you think he proposed?"

"Well, considering Raymond once told me that Randall was the type who would never get married, I didn't know what he might have proposed," she said, still looking at Emily with a raised eyebrow. "Are you sure it was marriage he proposed?"

"Yes, I'm sure it was marriage. In fact, if he had his way, we'd be married as soon as possible. He doesn't even want to wait the few months it would take to put together a big formal wedding." Which was a little sad because she really would have liked for Carole Jeanne to be there, too. But she knew New Orleans was too far away to expect her to come on such short notice. Carole would just have to make do with a formal wedding announcement afterward.

Katy studied Emily's joyful expression a few moments longer, then slowly the look of doubt eased from her face. "You're telling me the truth aren't you?" she asked. Her voice filled with excitement. "When are you planning to get married?"

"Just as soon as his grandmother returns from visiting her sister in Jefferson, which could be as early as next week because he's decided to send her a telegram telling her our good news. I guess it really all depends on how sick his aunt was to begin with. The whole reason Bernice went up there was to help nurse her back to health."

Katy sank back against her pillows, her mouth agape, clearly finding it as hard to believe as Emily had. "Wait until I tell Raymond. He'll never accept it."

"No, you can't. I promised Randall I would not tell anyone. He wants to surprise everyone at the engagement dinner he's planning for next weekend, and you and Raymond are to be invited to that."

"Then why did you tell me?"

"Because I thought you should have time to prepare. I want you to be my maid of honor."

"Me? Your maid of honor?"

"Of course, you. You just happen to be the best friend I have."

Katy shook her head, as if she had her doubts about that. "Well, if I'm the best you can do in the way of a friend, then I guess it's my duty to accept."

Emily laughed and was just about to embrace her friend when a sharp knock sounded at the door, breaking the moment.

"Katy? Is Emily in there with you?" It was Mrs. Roberts.

"Yes, she's here," Katy responded and quickly flung back the covers, padded barefoot across the room, and opened the door.

"Good. I've been looking for her. She has a fancy package waiting' for her downstairs," she said, then looked directly at Emily. "It's from Sanford's Dress Shop down on Market Street. Special delivered."

"On a Sunday?" Katy asked, truly impressed,

then turned to look at Emily, her eyes sparkling with excitement. "Should I dare guess who it's from?"

While Emily shot Katy an amused grin, Mrs. Roberts tapped her fingertips together, as if debating whether or not to inform them of something more.

"I sort of accidentally read the note that was pinned to the side. It says that the package is from Mr. Gipson. It also says Emily is to expect the owner herself to come by sometime this afternoon to check the fit for any necessary alterations."

"Then it *must* be a dress," Katy concluded, watching while Emily hurried from the room.

"As big as that box is, it could be two dresses," Mrs. Roberts commented, then followed Katy out the door and toward the stairs.

By the time they had reached the top step, Emily was already on her way back up, with the bulky box clutched in her arms. "Come on, Katy. Let's go to my room so I can find out what's inside."

Katy didn't have to be asked twice. She immediately spun on her heel and followed Emily toward her room.

"I hope you two plan to show me whatever it is later," Mrs. Roberts called out, knowing the girls deserved their privacy. "I'll be downstairs waitin' to see." She chuckled while she slowly headed back down the stairs.

Emily waited until Katy had closed the door before she started tugging on the bright red ribbon that held the box together. Finally, the ribbon gave way and Emily was able to see what was inside.

"Look at that," she commented, in instant awe of the beautiful garment inside. Her brown eyes widened with disbelief when she slowly pulled the black sequined gown out so Katy could see it, too. "It's beautiful."

"And there's a card," Katy pointed out, when an

ivory colored envelope fell to the floor at their feet. She knelt and picked it up, handing it immediately to Emily. "What does it say?"

Emily set the gown aside, spreading it carefully across the end of her bed, then accepted the envelope. Wetting her lips with anticipation, she pulled the flap open and slipped the folded card from inside.

"It's from Randall, all right," she said, glancing up at Katy after quickly scanning the message. "He says he wants me to wear this dress to the dinner party next weekend. He says its an engagement present."

"Some engagement present," Katy said, eyeing the dress with open fascination. "I'll bet that cost him a small fortune. It's absolutely beautiful." She bent forward to touch the elegance.

"Then you think it would be all right to accept it?" Emily wanted to know.

Katy looked at her as if she were two parts missing. "You'd be an idiot to refuse something so beautiful. Go try it on. I want to see how it looks on you."

Emily hurried behind her dressing screen and quickly pulled off the simple cotton dress she'd been wearing and replaced it with the magnificent creation of black silk and sequins. When she stepped out to let Katy see, she felt very much like the princess in a fairy story.

"It fits perfectly," Katy said, surprised at just how well it did fit. "I doubt the seamstress will have to make any alterations on this dress."

And she didn't. When Shelly Sanford arrived shortly after two o'clock supplied with a wristband full of pins, she shrugged her shoulders and admitted there was nothing for her to do. The dress was perfect as it was. All she could do was stand back and admire her handiwork.

Shortly after the dressmaker left, another messenger came to the rooming house, this one with a letter for Emily. It, too, was from Randall. But rather than read the letter with everyone watching, Emily politely tipped the messenger a penny then carried the letter to her room so she could read it in private.

His first words thrilled her to tears for they stated how very pleased he was that she had agreed to marry him. But his following words immediately darkened her mood. He would be unable to stop by that evening like he'd planned. He was too busy getting everything arranged for the engagement party. He would not be able to see her again until sometime late Monday evening, at which time they could finalize their plans.

When he did stop by just before bedtime on Monday evening, Emily was so pleased to see him that she did not question why he was so late. But knowing she had probably expected him hours earlier, he explained that he'd spent most of the evening extending personal invitations to his friends for Friday night's dinner party and was pleased to announce that all four of the couples he'd invited had agreed to attend. Couples he'd chosen specifically because they were known for their keen sense of prudence.

Wanting her at his house before the first of their guests arrived at eight, he promised to send a carriage for her shortly after seven, adding that he would personally see her back to the rooming house after all their guests had left. He was so preoccupied with his plans for Friday night he almost forgot to kiss her when he left.

* * *

Randall waited until everyone had finished eating before he rose from his seat and stood next to his chair, near the head of the table. Smiling proudly, he held out his hand to Emily and waited until she stood at his side before tapping his sugar spoon against his water glass to quiet his friends and get their attention.

"I have an announcement to make," he said after everyone had turned to see what he wanted. "And I think it is something that will probably surprise the lot of you."

Katy smiled, watching him expectantly, but the rest of Randall's guests exchanged questioning glances before returning their attention to him.

"I guess the best way to go about this is just to be out with it," he said, already reaching for his wine glass. "And the simple truth of it is that Emily Felcher has agreed to marry me."

A low murmur swept the room while heads turned in every direction, each wanting to see the others' reactions.

"Now I'm sure this comes as quite a surprise to most of you, and to tell you the truth, I have actually surprised myself with this one," he said, smiling at Emily, hoping she did not catch the double meaning behind his words. "But I want you to know that I understand what I'm doing, and I'm dead serious about seeing this thing through."

He bent forward to place a kiss on her cheek, then turned back to face his friends with a pleased smile. "Now I want to know which of you plans to offer the first toast to my happiness?"

Raymond was the first to his feet. Quickly, he filled his empty glass with wine from one of the many decanters on the table. "I will. I'll gladly toast your happiness." He waited until every glass had been refilled and everyone waited expectantly. "I must admit I find this all very hard to believe. But if this is what Randall wants, then I say all the happiness to him."

Everyone echoed with agreement and the glasses were quickly drained, including Emily's. Within seconds the glasses were refilled, and a second toast was made. Then a third.

Soon, Emily began to feel a little tipsy and had to press her fingertips against the table to steady herself, but she wasn't sure if the dizzy feeling was from all the wine she'd drunk or from the excitement of having heard her engagement to Randall spoken aloud. That made it seem more official somehow. She was soon to marry the man she loved. Just knowing that made her feel all warm and liquidy inside.

After several rounds of toasts had been made, and after most of the wine decanters at the table had been emptied, the guests finally set their glasses aside and came forward to personally congratulate them both. Emily could not remember ever being so happy. Even after everyone had left, and she was all alone with Randall, the warm feeling stayed with her. For once, she was not afraid to be alone with him. Instead, she looked forward to the opportunity to tell him just how she felt.

"Randall, I truly liked your friends," she said, smiling with contentment while he filled their wine glasses yet again with what had remained in one of the decanters at the far end of the table. Although she really did not think she should have anything else to drink for fear her legs would no longer hold her, she would not refuse him a private toast if he wanted one. "Do you think they liked me, too?"

"How could they not? You are the most beautiful, most beguiling woman they've ever met," he said as he held her glass out to her. He smiled at her because that had been the truth. She was exquisite.

Emily blushed at such complimentary words, but did not look away from him like she would have in the past. This time she allowed his gaze to hold her in its sensual embrace. "Do you really think I am beguiling?" She liked the sound of that.

"You are the most beguiling, most alluring woman I know," he said, his voice low, his words slow and sultry. "I can hardly believe that you have agreed to be my wife. I must be the luckiest man on earth."

Emily's heart took wing because that was just the sort of thing she wanted to hear. "And I can hardly believe you are soon to be my husband. That one day, very soon, we can share our love in the way men and women are meant to share it."

Randall warmed at that thought, his blood churning with renewed desire. Swallowing hard, he took her into his arms. He knew he had to play this very carefully. "I just wish I didn't have to wait that long to know what it is like to make love to you," he said, nuzzling her hair and smiling at her shivery response. "I want you so much it actually hurts."

"And I want you," she admitted, staring up into his silvery blue eyes with longing. "I want you just as much as you want me."

That was what he'd hoped she'd say. "Then let me make love to you. Don't make me wait another minute. Not when we are practically already married anyway."

"But—," she started to protest, only to have her words taken from her by a startlingly passionate kiss.

"Please, Emily," he murmured, after pulling away so that his breath fell softly against her lips. "What real harm can it do? In our hearts we are already husband and wife. If it weren't for my grandmother being away, we'd already be married. You know that."

Emily closed her eyes against the warm, tingling sensations flowing through her, aware he'd spoken the truth. He'd stated repeatedly that he didn't want to wait for his grandmother's eventual return. The decision to put the wedding off until Bernice could be there with them had been hers, and hers alone. Why should she punish him for that? Why should she punish herself? He was right, in her heart she was already his wife. Why shouldn't she show him just how very much she loved him?

When she then opened her arms to him, she felt none of the guilt or shame she had in the past. All she felt at that moment was the overwhelming desire to make her future husband happy.

Chapter Eighteen

Randall quickly downed the last of his wine, tossed his glass haphazardly onto the table, then went immediately into Emily's embrace, his hour of triumph finally at hand.

When he first closed his arms around her, he suffered a short twinge of guilt, recalling all the lies he been forced to tell in order to finally taste this moment of victory. But he quickly pushed the uneasy feelings aside by reminding himself that what he'd done was justified. Emily had yielded only a small measure of the deceit she had been so willing to bestow upon him. He had no legitimate reason to feel even the slightest amount of guilt; she fully deserved to fall prey to someone else's schemes for a change. Still, it was not easy to brush the unexpected pangs of guilt aside.

But Emily was too much in love to feel anything but the overpowering desire to show her future husband how very much she needed and wanted him. She felt no shame, nor even any of the initial shyness she'd known before, not even when his lips came down to claim hers in another of his fiery, passionate kisses.

His mouth continued to devour hers hungrily

while he slipped the now empty stemmed glass from her hand and placed it on the table beside them. Never did their lips part.

The knowledge that her hands were now free to explore—free to touch her future husband in much the same way he touched her—intensified her emotions and she pressed her mouth harder against his while she gave her hands free rein. She wanted him to know how strong her desire had become. With an eagerness born from a woman's passion, her tongue sought his with sensual frolic while her fingers pressed into the taut muscles of his back.

Randall wasted little time on the amenities. Having waited too long for this moment, he immediately bent at the knees just low enough to scoop her into his arms. His lips never halted their greedy assault, not even as he carried her out of the dining room and raced up the stairs. Certain that satisfaction was soon to be his, he took the steps in long, hurried strides, two at a time. He knew she would not pull away this time. At long last, he would come away the victor.

His eagerness grew to unbearable proportions when he neared his bedroom door, which he'd purposely left open. When he carried her inside the dark room, he halted barely long enough to kick the door closed behind them.

The same moonlight that had entertained them during many of their rides out into the country streamed into the open window, spilling a soft island of silvery light across the awaiting bed and giving him just enough light to make his way safely across the room.

"Emily, I have longed for this moment for what seems like forever," he said, his voice ragged with the desire that raged inside him when he gently lowered her into the center of that delicate glow. The words he'd spoken were the truth, for he had become virtually obsessed with his desire for her, and now, at long last, he was about to have her.

Knowing his moment of triumph was upon him, he stared down at her for only a moment, watching the way she gazed back at him with heavily lidded eyes. Soon, he would experience those special talents of hers firsthand—yet, suddenly, he had a strong need to draw out the long-awaited event. He wanted to make his moment of victory last for as long as he possibly could. Slowly, but methodically, he reached for his own buttons and started to undress.

Emily did not turn away with shame or embarrassment, even when he peeled away the last of his undergarments and then stood proudly before her in the faded moonlight. Instead of diverting her gaze, she looked at him with open fascination. She had never seen a man's body before. He looked magnificent. She felt her blood stir at such an invigorating sight.

When Randall returned to her side, he was completely and gloriously naked. The heat of his body penetrated Emily's clothing, making her long to be naked, too. She trembled with expectation when his hands then moved to her buttons and slowly worked with them until the material of her fitted bodice became slack against her skin.

Kneeling beside her, he gently tugged at the volumes of black silk until he finally had the garment removed. He then tossed the gown haphazardly over his shoulder, where it sank to the floor in a black, rustling heap. Her undergarments soon followed, as did her slippers and stockings, until he finally had her just as naked as he. Smiling contentedly, he then lowered himself to the bed beside her and she shivered with renewed anticipation.

"You are exquisite," he said with honest admiration when he glanced down to appraise her firm, young body in the glimmering moonlight.

Emily responded to his thrilling words with a soft moan, turning eagerly into his arms again. When she again felt the warmth of his embrace and her body pressed so intimately against his, she had no lingering doubts, no feelings of impending danger. She was exactly where she wanted to be, where she belonged, in the arms of her own future husband. A smile curved at the corners of her mouth when his head dipped to kiss her again. She angled her head just enough to accommodate another of his fiery kisses. While her heart opened to the resulting rush of madness, it seemed unbelievable that a man this wonderful wanted to be her husband. She would know such joyful pleasure the rest of her life.

The warmth of her newly awakened love spread quickly through her body and forced her deeper into the languid feeling of euphoria that he had created for her. Once again their mouths explored each other—first sampling, then devouring.

Soon the languid warmth turned into a molten storm tide of desire. She gasped at first with protest then with pleasure when Randall's lips left hers to begin a teasing trail of tiny, hot kisses down her throat, toward her collarbone, then dipped downward again until he reached her straining breast. Emily cried out while she savored the shattering sensation that exploded inside of her the moment his mouth glided over the hardened tip. A swelling blaze of uncompromising need burned uncontrolled inside her when he slowly pulled at the sensitive tip with his mouth, drawing it rigid with desire.

She clutched helplessly at his back, letting him know the level of her urgency; but instead of moving to fulfill the need that so completely consumed her, he repeated the same sensual act on the other breast, bringing her more splendid pleasure.

Writhing beneath him, Emily was desperate to find some measure of relief from the exquisite torture he'd brought upon her. She lifted her head forward to kiss the top of his head, hoping to lure his mouth back to hers and somehow slow the powerful torrent that had risen inside her.

But instead of appeasing her, Randall proceeded to drive her into further ecstasy. While his mouth continued to arouse the one breast with tiny suckles and nips, his thumb gently teased the other. Hot shafts of pure rapture shot through her, until Emily was sure she could bear the onslaught no longer. She dug her fingers deep into his back. "Now, Randall, please, now."

Though she was not entirely sure what could be done to quell the desire burning inside her, she did know enough to realize only Randall had the power to stop it. "Please, Randall. Now."

Randall knew the time had finally come to claim his prize. After kissing each thrusting breast one last time, he rose higher above her, then down again to fulfill their needs. When she showed the forethought to cry out with discomfort upon his initial entry, he had to smile with admiration. She was a very thorough actress indeed. But, rather than break the spell with any unproductive accusations, he chose to play right along with the pretense.

"It won't hurt for long," he promised, his voice soft and assuring while he moved slowly inside her. "Trust me, Emily. It won't hurt for long."

Although the pain had been unexpected and still burned to some extent, Emily did trust Randall and forced herself to relax in his arms. Within a very few seconds she began to respond again and the lingering pain gave way to deep, throbbing waves of longing that lifted her ever higher, until she finally crested the top, taking him along with her.

When it was over and she had settled beneath the covers in the warm, protective crook of his arm, she was astonished by what had happened. Finally, she understood what it meant to be a woman.

Even Randall had found their lovemaking to be nothing short of astounding. So astounding, he could not possibly let her go after having known her pleasures only once. Something that remarkable deserved at least one more sampling. He decided he could wait to have that final moment of justice.

"How about some more wine?" he suggested, knowing it would take him a little while to recover from something so earth-shattering. "And perhaps you'd like something sweet to nibble on."

Thinking nothing could be sweeter than his kisses, she shook her head and smiled. "No, I'm not hungry."

Afraid if he didn't find something to fill their time she might suggest leaving, he leaned forward to lightly nip at her ear, wanting to keep her appeased until the time came to take her again. To his own amazement, he found himself becoming immediately aroused again, and decided there was no longer a reason to wait. He took immediate advantage of her uncanny ability to arouse him.

"Are you sure you aren't hungry?" he asked, his tone suggestive, then eased the covers back and dipped his head to tug at her breast with his teeth and his tongue.

Her desire for him flared again instantly, only this time she knew what was to come and she gave of herself even more eagerly. While their kisses quickly regained their earlier momentum, she allowed her hands the same pleasures he allowed his. She explored every curve and contour of his body, pleased with his shuddering response. Again, their desire to have each other spiraled ever higher, allowing them to soar to their passion's limits—and beyond.

When Randall rolled away from her the second time, his hunger again abated, he did not linger beside her nor did he offer her the warmth of his arm like he had before. Instead, he tossed back the tangled covers and climbed immediately out of bed.

Emily watched while he quickly tugged on his trousers, thinking he was probably headed downstairs for more wine or for that something sweet he'd mentioned before. She didn't realize anything was amiss until he suddenly spun around and glared at her with such a pleased smirk on his face that it sent sickening chills through her.

"What's wrong?" she asked, confused. Her eyebrows knitted into a perplexed frown while her stomach crawled into the very pit of her soul.

Randall frowned, too, while he crossed his arms in front of him and studied her surprised reaction. "You know, Emily, originally I'd planned to send you from my bed with nothing more than the knowledge that you'd been outsmarted, but after that amazing performance, I wouldn't feel quite right in doing that." He stepped over to a nearby chair and pulled his wallet out of his dinner coat then tossed it at her. "There's over a hundred dollars in there. Take it. You were worth every cent."

Horrified by the hard expression on his face, Emily pulled herself into a seated position, clutching the covers to her breasts. Her world felt as if it had crumbled into a hundred tiny pieces. "I don't understand. Why would you give me money?"

"Because you were well worth it, my sweet. In fact, you were so darned good that I almost wish that I *could* marry you—*almost.*"

"Wh-what do you mean?" Her lower lip trembled while she waited for his answer, not really wanting to hear it, but knowing she had to. She had to understand what had made him change so suddenly.

"What I mean is that turnabout is fair play. Haven't you ever heard that old saying?"

She nodded that she had, but had yet to make sense of what he was babbling about. "But what has that to do with me?"

"You've been bested, my dear. That's all there is to it." He shrugged to indicate it was as simple as that.

Tears filled Emily's eyes, making it impossible to see. "You mean you don't love me?"

Randall looked at her with disgust, tired of her silly games. "Don't look so pitiful. You got exactly what you deserve. Now get out."

It felt like pure acid had been poured into Emily's bloodstream and was burning a painful path right through her heart. "But why? Why are you doing this? I still don't understand."

"Oh, you understand all right," he said, his angry gaze boring into hers. "Now get on out of here. You can take the money with you, but leave the wallet. My grandmother gave that wallet to me. It once belonged to my grandfather. I treasure it much like you claim to treasure that jewelry your grandmother was supposed to have given you."

"Supposed to?" she repeated, wondering what he'd meant by that.

He shook his head with ready contempt. "Do you really think I believed that poor little orphan in search for her long-lost grandmother story?"

"But it's true." She may not have thought to word it exactly like that for she hadn't really thought of herself as an orphan, but it was absolutely true.

"Of course it's true," he muttered, then bent over

to collect his boots. "I'm going downstairs to have another drink. I want you out of here by the time I get finished." Then without offering another word, he stalked out of the room with his boots tucked up under his arm, leaving Emily to stare after him, confused and devastated.

After putting her rumpled "engagement" dress back on, Emily fled the house in shame, unable to believe anyone could be so cruel. Although she saw a carriage waiting for her near the front door, she ran off in the opposite direction into the darkness, not caring what dangers awaited there.

When she arrived at the rooming house over an hour later, she was relieved to see all the windows dark. She did not want to face anyone with her shame, at least not yet. But soon, she realized she would have to admit to everyone that she and Katy had told that her engagement had been a farce, especially considering there would never be a wedding. She just hoped they would never have to know why.

With tears still streaming down her face, she hurried through the back door, which Mrs. Roberts had left unlocked for her. She had just enough presence of mind to lock it as she'd been asked, then took the back stairs up to her room and quickly closed the door behind her. Without bothering with a lamp, for the darkness helped to hide her shame, she flung herself onto her bed and cried bitterly for hours.

The sky was already stained a pale shade of pink before she was able to sit up and think rationally about what had happened. When she did finally begin to sort through all he'd said and done, her confusion remained but her anguish slowly turned into justifiable anger. He'd had no right to treat her like that. Though he'd seemed to be trying to push the blame off on her, she'd done absolutely nothing to deserve such cruelty. It was then, when she realized she'd done nothing wrong, that he'd done such an evil thing to her for no real reason other than to shame her, all the love she'd felt for him turned to hate. Stripping away the black sequinned gown and wadding it into a heap, she vowed to get even with Randall Gipson for the horrible thing he'd done to her. Although she didn't know how, or even when, she knew that one day she'd find a way to get her revenge.

Oddly, Randall did not feel as pleased with himself as he had expected. Though he fully believed that Emily had deserved a good, strong dose of her own vile medicine, he was not happy with having been forced to stoop to deceit.

Aware he needed something stronger than wine to appease the gnawing doubts he was suddenly having, he waited until he'd heard the front door clatter shut, then carried an entire whiskey bottle into his study and closed the door so he wouldn't be disturbed until he was finally ready to be disturbed. That was one good thing about his employees, they understood that a closed door meant stay out. He would be able to drink himself into oblivion without anyone being any the wiser.

By the time he had drunk half the contents of the bottle and decided it might be wise to return to bed and get at least a few hours sleep, he was staggering drunk. Far too drunk to notice the bloodstains on his bedspread or that his wallet lay in the wadded covers untouched.

It was late the following morning, after he'd forced himself out of bed and had already gotten fully dressed, that he first looked around for his wallet and spotted the dark brown stain.

The sickening realization that she *had* been a virgin hit him like a hard fist in the gut. The pain she'd indicated when he'd first taken her had not been an act after all. And if that had been true, he had to wonder how much else about her was also true?

His hands trembled when he reached out to touch the dried stains. Emily *had* come to him a virgin. Damn to hell, she *had* been a virgin! He curled his hands into fists and pressed them against his pounding skull at the sudden realization that everything she and his grandmother had told him had probably been the truth. But how could it be? He'd seen the way she'd dressed aboard his ship. He'd seen the way she tantalized the men. But then, a woman that beautiful could tantalize any man she wanted without really trying. He had assumed her guilty simply because of the company she'd kept.

The horror she must have suffered. His shame was overwhelming, making his stomach lurch with disgust. He hurried to the basin to relieve himself of the previous night's stale whiskey.

While he wiped his face with a cool, damp cloth, he considered what he should do to rectify the situation, if indeed it could ever be truly rectified.

The first thing he should do seemed pretty clear. He had to apologize to her. That is if she would let him. The thought of what she must think of him after what he'd done made him physically ill and he knew that the only possible cure would be to finally talk to her, explain why he'd done what he'd done—that is, if he could somehow come to understand that part of it himself.

But even more important than making her understand that he'd had a reason for what he'd done, or so he thought, he wanted to ask her to marry him—

really marry him. Just knowing that she was not the tainted woman he'd thought her to be, that she was actually the sweet little innocent she'd always pretended to be, made his heart leap with excitement. Now there was no reason not to marry her—except perhaps for the understandable fact that she probably hated him with a passion. But that was something he felt certain he could overcome. It was something he'd *have* to overcome, because suddenly it was very clear to him that the powerful feelings he'd felt for her were far more than a man's simple desire for a woman. Amazing as it seemed, the feelings he had for Emily Felcher were clearly and undeniably love—only he'd been too blind to see it.

"I'm sorry, Mr. Gipson, but she just plain refuses to see you," Mrs. Roberts said, shrugging her shoulders as she stepped down from the bottom stair. "I'm not really sure what you did to make her quite that angry with you, but she says she's not comin' out of her room for no reason, and she meant it."

"Then may I have your permission to go up and talk to her in her room?" he asked, his blue eyes pleading that she understand how important it was to him. He had to talk to Emily. He had to try to explain why he had done the terrible thing he'd done, but more important than that, he wanted a chance to apologize—and if necessary, beg her to marry him. He felt marriage would be the perfect solution to everything. Not only would it make an honest woman of Emily, it would allow him to spend the rest of his life trying to undo some of the things he'd done to her.

More than anything, he wanted to erase that last memory of her, huddled in his bed like a frightened child, tears spilling down her cheeks. What he yearned to see was her smile again, just as he yearned to be her reason for smiling. But first he had to find some way to talk with her. "Please?"

"I'm sorry," Mrs. Roberts said, shaking her head. "I simply can't allow nothin' like that. I run a respectable rooming house and there are certain rules I got to follow, as much for my own sake as the tenants. You'll just have to come back another time—after she's had a while to cool off a bit more. That's really the only choice you got because until that girl is willin' to come down those stairs and talk to you, there's not much you can do. If she don't want to see you, that's all there is to it. I have to respect what she wants."

Driven to desperate measures, Randall reached for his wallet, the same wallet Emily had refused to touch the night before. He closed his eyes briefly against the sharp pain that bitter memory had created, then forced his eyes back open to look at Mrs. Roberts again. "What if I were to offer you a little something special as a reward for helping me out," he suggested, only to be cut off before he could state exactly how much of a little something he had in mind.

"Mr. Gipson!" she exclaimed, slamming her fists down on her ample hips. "I suggest you get yourself on out of here right now, before I up and decide to take a broom to you." She wagged her head belligerently. "If and when that girl decides to come down those stairs and talk to you, then you can see her all you have a mind to. But until then, you are just not goin' to see her."

"I'll be back," he warned, aware her mind was already set against him. He wondered how much Emily had told her.

"I don't doubt that. But unless she changes her mind before then, it really won't do you a whole lot of good. And I warn you, that girl is real upset with you about something. I could tell that she's been cryin', even though the door."

Those words sliced into Randall like a knife. He hadn't meant to hurt her like that. But then, giving that thought a second consideration, it wasn't entirely true. He *had* meant to hurt her, but that was when he still thought she was a conniving little tramp out to trick either him or Patrick into marrying her. Yet now that he knew the truth, he desperately wanted to take that pain away. But how could he if her landlady refused to let him see her?

Disappointed, yet still undaunted, Randall stormed out of the house in an angry huff, more determined than ever to find some way to speak with Emily. He would make amends for what he'd done and start over fresh.

Suddenly, she was the only thing in his life worth fighting for.

Dauntless, Randall tried twice more that day to speak with Emily and again on Sunday, but each time was promptly and efficiently turned away by a woman he soon came to think of as "Warden Roberts." And, in addition to having to face her each time he came to the door, there was always at least one more person sitting out on the porch watching his every move, until finally there were six of them lined across the front.

Aware he was not about to get past "Warden Roberts" or the ever watchful rocking-chair-brigade that had gathered on the front porch to defend the premises, Randall decided the safest and probably the most effective action he could take at that point was to wait and catch her on her way to work.

Monday morning, he awoke before dawn and quickly dressed. He wanted to be waiting out in front of the hat shop when Emily arrived. He didn't want to put off talking to her until lunchtime, nor did he want the entire shop alerted to the unforgivable thing he'd done, as much for Emily's sake as his own. He knew that in most cases, no matter who was actually at fault, it was the woman who suffered the blame.

By seven-forty, he sat directly across the street from the hat shop, partially hidden in the shadows of his parked coach, flowers in hand, watching the front door like a hawk. To make absolutely certain Emily did not slip by him, he sent Andrew into the back ally to keep an eye on the back door. One way or another, he planned to have that talk with her, and he planned to have it before she stepped inside the building.

At five minutes before eight, Mrs. Williams and a tall, blonde girl who looked to be about Emily's age arrived in front of the shop from different directions at precisely the same time. They chatted a few moments, then Mrs. Williams unlocked the door and they went inside, leaving the door open to allow a fresh morning breeze inside. By the time the many windows along the side of the building had been opened as well as four across the front, two more girls had entered the shop, but neither had been Emily. Though he had not glimpsed their faces, neither had walked with the same grace nor had styled their hair with the same flair.

At precisely eight o'clock, Mrs. Williams returned to the front door, turned over the sign that announced they were open, then stepped outside to glance down the street. She looked at her watch and frowned, then noticed the coach across the street and stared at it for a moment.

Randall did not bother to duck out of sight, though he'd felt an odd inclination to do just that.

Instead, he sat steadfast in his seat and continued his vigil for Emily, who was now obviously late for work. Even so, he intended to have his say before she went inside. He'd see later what he could do to make up any lost time to the shop owner after they had finished talking so Emily would not lose her job as a result of the time she'd spent with him—although he doubted she would still want to work there after hearing what he had to say. After she married him she would no longer have any reason to. She could then devote her time to whatever made her happiest.

When ten more minutes passed and the sidewalks slowly filled with pedestrians Randall became increasingly impatient and shifted restlessly in his seat. Leaning forward to be able to watch more of the street, he patted the heel of his boot against the wooden floor of the coach with a rapid rhythm. Where was she? What was keeping her?

Soon the street was filled to capacity with a variety of buggies, coaches, horses, and wagons, passing by in opposite directions at a hurried pace. But none of them ever stopped—until twenty minutes after eight, when finally a small carriage with a dented side pulled to a halt beside the narrow boardwalk out front.

Randall glanced inside, hoping to find Emily, but the only person in the dilapidated carriage was the driver, a man dressed in ill-repaired but clean clothes. Judging by his wide shoulders and incredible height, Randall guessed him to be a delivery man of some sort. With nothing else to bide his time, he watched while the man quickly looped the tether strap around one of the posts in front of the hat shop then walked inside.

When he later came out empty-handed, Randall realized he had not come by to pick up a delivery and wondered what sort of business a man like that could have in one of Galveston's most exclusive hat shops. Surely, he couldn't be one of Mrs. William's customers. Why, most of the hats in her shop cost over half of what that man probably made in a week.

But Randall didn't have long to dwell on why a man like that would have gone inside such a fancy hat shop. He had to keep his attention focused on the door. He wanted to be sure Emily did not slip in unnoticed. Yet, after another thirty minutes passed and there was no Emily, he decided she must have done just that.

Climbing out of the coach, finding it a relief to stretch his long legs at last, he hurried down the narrow alley that ran along one side the shop and emptied into a much larger alley in the back. There he found Andrew sitting on top of a huge packing crate, his arms folded, his hat brim pulled low, and his chin buried deep in his chest—sound asleep.

"Andrew!" he called out in a strident whisper as he neared the sleeping driver.

"Huh? What?" Andrew came awake with a start. Blinking profusely, he shoved his hat to the back of his head and hopped off the crate. He tried his best to look busy, though it was obvious he had no idea just what it was he was supposed to be busy doing. "What happened? What do you want?"

"How long have you been asleep like that?"

Andrew blinked again, then looked at the crate accusingly. "Was I asleep?"

Randall shook his head, exasperated but kept his voice low so they would not be heard inside. "Either that or there was some sort of wild animal loose back here because I heard incredible snoring noises when I first walked up."

Knowing he was noted for snoring at levels that could shake treetops, Andrew looked sheepishly at the ground. "I'm sorry, Mr. Gipson. I didn't mean to doze off like that and I really don't know how long I was asleep."

Randall studied his apologetic expression, then shrugged, aware it would do no good to rail at him. "Well, at least now I know why I never saw her enter the shop. She must have slipped by you while you were sleeping and gone in the back way."

"So what are you going to do now?"

"Go in and ask to speak with her," he said, as if that should have been a rather obvious answer. He certainly was not going to wait until lunch.

"Alone?" Andrew asked, doubtful.

"Yes, alone," he answered, glancing at Andrew, puzzled.

"But what if Miss Emily tells that boss of hers that she still don't want to see you?"

"What if she does? It's not like I can't find my way into the back room where she works and talk to her anyway."

"But what if that boss of hers tries to stop you?"

Randall looked at his tall, hulking driver with a questioning lift of his eyebrow. "Think about that for a moment. I'm six-foot-two and Mrs. William's barely over five feet tall."

"And?" Andrew asked, as if waiting for more of an explanation than that.

Randall dropped his shoulders, wondering just how sleep-addled the poor man really was. "How in this world is such a tiny little woman going to stop a man as big and as determined as I am from doing exactly what I want to do?"

Andrew scratched his head and thought a minute. "With a gun, maybe?"

Now it was Randall's turn to blink. He hadn't thought of that.

"Maybe you'd better come with me."

Chapter Nineteen

"What do you mean she isn't here?" Randall asked, glancing at the door to the back room. His gripped tightened around the flowers he'd brought, crushing the stems into a crumpled heap. His eyes narrowed with immediate distrust. "She has to be here. It's Monday."

Mrs. Williams thrust her chin out and met his gaze straight on, indicating she would not be intimidated by him. "I mean just what I say. She isn't here and she is not going to be here. Fact is, she isn't coming in to work at all today. She's ill."

"How do you know?"

"A friend of hers, a Mr. Parks Bebber, stopped by less than an hour ago and told me not to expect her, that she was too ill to even come down from her room and eat. He said I really should not expect her for days."

Randall raked his hand through his hair, his frustration bordering on anger. All he wanted to do was talk to Emily. To apologize for the terrible thing he'd done. Was that really such an unreasonable request? "And did Mr. Bebber happen to mention just what this illness of hers might be?"

"No, and it really is none of my business. I just

hope she gets better soon because she happens to be one of my best workers." Her chin lifted higher.

The muscles at the back of Randall's jaw pumped rapidly when he spun around to look at Andrew. "Now what do I do?"

Andrew shrugged. He also took a precautionary step backward.

Mrs. Williams offered a suggestion. "You might stop by the rooming house and leave those pretty flowers for her there. I realize she can't be accepting visitors because she's so ill, but those flowers are sure to make her feel better."

Randall's shoulders sagged with disappointment. Although what he really wanted was to talk with Emily, leaving the flowers at the rooming house was the only real means of contact he had at that particular moment. "Can I at least ask one favor of you, Mrs. Williams?"

"Why, yes, of course." The thought of doing a favor seemed to unruffle her feathers a might and she finally relaxed her chin.

Randall reached inside his coat and pulled out a business card. "If and when Emily Felcher ever returns to work again, would you have a messenger sent to this address to let me know? I'll gladly pay whatever the cost."

Mrs. Williams smiled, glad that his favor had been such a simple one. "Of course. I'll dispatch a messenger right away."

With that settled, he returned his attention to Andrew. "Come on. We've got some flowers to deliver."

As expected, when he arrived at the rooming house, Gladys Roberts refused to let him past the foyer, but did agree to take both the flowers and a quickly penned note upstairs to Emily's room. He hoped the note would prove the next best thing to talking with her. If they couldn't actually speak in person, at least he could still let her know how truly sorry he was for everything he'd done.

He waited at the foot of the stairs with his next breath lodged somewhere near the base of his throat while Gladys carried the flowers upstairs. He refused to leave until she had returned and told him exactly what Emily's reaction had been. With any luck, Emily would change her mind and come downstairs after all.

"Well, what did she say?" he asked as soon as the portly landlady had started back down the stairs—alone.

"Nothin'," she said, her gaze distant with thought while she continued down the steps.

"She didn't say *anything?* Anything at *all?*" he asked, believing that highly uncharacteristic of Emily, who always seemed to have some opinion about everything.

"No, not really. She just took the flowers when I handed them to her then tossed them right into the trash. She did thank me for my trouble, though."

"She didn't even bother to read the note?" He was crestfallen.

"I don't think she even saw the note."

"Well, would you please go back up there and tell her there was a note?"

"I don't think that would be doin' you much good. Emily just ain't interested in anything you have to say, at least not right yet."

Randall ran his hand over his face, temporarily distorting his features. He wondered what he should do now. "Tell me, how did she look?"

"Terrible. There ain't a bit of color in her whole face except for the dark circles right under her eyes.

She looks like she hadn't slept in a week. That sure must have been some fight you two had."

When Randall nodded that it had been, his face contorted from the resulting pain and self-loathing. Tears of more than simple frustration glimmered in his eyes, forcing him to look away. "Thank you for trying. I appreciate your trouble."

Then with drawn shoulders, he turned and walked slowly out of the house, only vaguely aware that Andrew followed. He tried to figure out some other practical way of letting her know that he was truly sorry for what he'd done. There had to be a way to get a message to her. He just had to think harder.

Or possibly he was thinking too hard. So hard, he had missed the obvious. Maybe what he needed the most was to give his mind a rest. Think of something else for a while.

Although he knew he would never be able to get much work done in his present state of mind, Randall had Andrew drive him on to his office. He hoped, by surrounding himself with a lot of activity, he could get his thoughts off the sheer hopelessness of his situation, at least for a little while.

It was while he sat at his desk, surrounded by various letters and documents, all in need of his attention, his mind finally took a new direction. And when it did, he suddenly realized the perfect way to prove to Emily that he was dearly sorry for what he'd done. He'd find her grandmother's grave for her. If what she'd told him was true, and he now had every reason to believe that it was, Peterson had not yet located the woman's final resting place. By stepping in and taking over the search, he could prove not only that he cared, but that he now believed her. It was the perfect solution.

Having made up his mind to do everything he

could to help, he headed straight out the door and practically ran the two blocks to Peterson's office. He needed a few practical details before he started his part of the search. He also needed to make sure Edward had still not located the grave.

"Yes, that's right," Edward said, nodding while he set aside the papers he'd been reading so he could give Randall his full attention. "I am supposed to be trying to locate Elmira Townsend's gravesite, but I'm afraid I've become extremely busy with other important matters during these past few weeks. Ever since that explosion aboard the *Harbor Vixen* I've been busy as I can be negotiating lawsuits. I really haven't had time for anything else."

"Then tell me what you know about the woman and I'll see if I can find out where she was buried."

Edward sighed, then looked about the cluttered room. "Let me think. Where is that file?"

After a few minutes' search, he came up with it. "Here, everything I've managed to find out about the woman is in here. Take it with you."

Randall accepted the file gladly. "Do you think she's more likely to be entombed on the island or buried on the mainland?"

"I really have no idea. Read the information and decide for yourself. All I do know is that she hasn't been buried in either the city cemetery or that one out by the medical center; but there are enough private cemeteries around here to keep a person busy searching for weeks. All I can do is wish you luck."

"Thanks, I'll probably need it," Randall said, tucking the file under his arm. "I'll let you know whatever I find out."

"Just let Emily know. That poor girl won't rest easy until she can finally pay her last respects. Find that grave and I imagine she'll be deeply and forever grateful."

That was what Randall was counting on—or at least grateful enough to finally listen to what he had to say.

Randall read through Edward's notes later that same afternoon but, the more he read, the more confused he became. It seemed odd that the only real verification of Elmira Townsend's death was nothing more than the word of some stranger Emily had talked with in the shop where she worked. Edward hadn't even noted the woman's name, which probably meant that he had not bothered to question the woman himself. He'd just accepted the information Emily had given him as fact. It didn't appear that Edward had even tried to locate Elmira's official death certificate. The most he'd done was ask for a listing of those buried in the city cemetery near town and the state-owned cemetery over by the college.

It also seemed strange that Elmira's youngest daughter, a woman by the name of Elizabeth Davis, was still alive—yet so dead set against talking with anyone about her mother. That simply didn't make a whole lot of sense, not if the mother was really deceased. Why would anyone go to such trouble to protect the dead? No, something about the whole situation just didn't seem right.

Randall tilted back in his chair to consider everything more fully, but the more he thought about the situation, the more he believed that Elmira Townsend was still alive, which was why it had become so difficult to locate her grave. The poor woman probably didn't even have her grave site picked out yet.

Believing that to be the case, he immediately

began his search, but not for a grave site—for the woman herself. By noon, three days later, he had discovered that the woman indeed was still alive, though living as a recluse out on the family plantation.

Because he'd come by that information so easily, simply by asking around until he'd located Elmira's personal doctor, he wondered just how slipshod a search Edward had conducted to begin with. If the man was treating his other clients with as little consideration as he'd shown Emily, Randall wondered if he should be looking for a new lawyer himself. Obviously, Edward had far more business than he could handle properly, which meant everyone suffered.

By two o'clock the same day he'd talked with Elmira's doctor, a Spanish-looking man by the name of Reyes, Randall had decided just how he planned to use the information he'd been given. Taking pen in hand, he wrote Elmira an eloquent letter then sent it to her by personal messenger, asking for permission to bring Emily out to meet her.

When he received a written response later that same day, he was confused by what he read. The letter was filled with what appeared to be the disjointed ramblings of a madwoman. In the letter, she claimed to have already paid the hundred thousand for what she wanted and even if she was one of the wealthiest women in all of Texas, she refused to give him a penny more. She then demanded to see Emily immediately and told him that if he didn't send her the proper address right away, she'd go to the authorities and have him arrested for what he'd done.

Randall had immediate doubts about his decision to bring the two together, worried that it might hurt Emily further to discover the woman was not altogether sane. But then, there were many among the elderly who had lost at least a partial grip on reality. He really had no right to keep them apart. His next thought was to go right on over to the rooming house and tell Emily all that he'd discovered, but he knew he'd never get past the "Warden Roberts" and the "porch chair gang," so he chose an entirely different approach.

Quickly he wrote another letter to Elmira Townsend, this time giving Emily's address like he'd been requested. He ended the letter with a special request of his own. He asked that whether the woman decided to contact Emily in person or by letter, that she please tell her granddaughter that he'd been the one to bring them together, and that he desperately wanted to talk with her.

He hoped that message, coming from her very own grandmother, would finally convince Emily to listen to him.

Digging out another two-dollar gold piece, he handed the second letter to the messenger who had been waiting for over two hours for the response. Laying the coin on top of the letter, he asked that it be delivered right away. He also asked the man to wait around at least long enough to find out if there would be a response to be brought back either to him or to someone else in the city.

"If there is a response, and you go to the trouble to deliver it tonight instead of in the morning during your regular hours, I'll pay you triple your usual fee."

"Yes-sir," the young man said, tucking the letter into his shirt pocket. "If there's a message to be brought back, I'll sure wait on it." He was already pulling on his black leather riding gloves when he headed for the door. "You can definitely count on me."

* * *

Emily stared off into the darkness, still too despondent to bother with the lamp, though it was only a few feet from where she sat. It had been days now since she'd left her room, and until that afternoon, when she'd finally decided to try some of the stew Mrs. Roberts had brought up to her, it had been days since she'd eaten. Now the food lay in her stomach like lead and she waited to see if she could keep it down, though she really didn't care if she did.

Somehow, during the past few days, she'd found her way past the initial pain, and had even gotten over the initial anger, until she finally reached the point where all she felt was a hollow numbness inside. It was as if she'd reached inside her heart and turned off all her more painful emotions, and that was good because for the first time in days, she didn't hurt. She felt absolutely nothing inside—except perhaps a little sick to her stomach. And tired.

For days, she hadn't slept more than a couple of hours at a time.

And now she didn't dare even lie down, because whenever she did finally doze, she relived that horrible night in her dreams, and the pain returned as strong as ever. It was just easier to stay awake and continue not to feel anything than chance having that happen, so she sat upright in her chair, staring out into the darkness, not thinking about anything but the heavy feeling in her stomach. She even refused to pay any attention to the light knock at her door.

"Emily?"

In the back of her mind, she knew she'd heard Mrs. Robert's voice calling out to her, but she was too afraid the woman would say Randall's name again to respond. Emily preferred to stay enveloped in her emotionally indifferent state.

"Emily? I know it's late, but there's someone here to see you."

Emily pressed her eyes shut, she did not want to hear his name again. She didn't want to be reminded again. All she wanted was to be left alone.

"Emily? Are you in there?"

"Tell him to go away," she finally called out. The words broke through the numbness that had shielded her heart and wrought renewed pain. Tears filled her eyes, but she thrust her chin forward and dashed them away with the backs of her hands. She refused to cry over him anymore.

After noticing a soft rustling noise in the hallway, she heard Mrs. Robert's muffled voice through the closed door. She sounded angry. "You are not supposed to be up here. I asked you to wait downstairs!"

Emily's heart filled with panic. Randall was just outside her door hoping somehow to trick her into his bed again. Shame flooded her.

But the responding voice was not his. It was not even that of a man.

"I'm not about to wait downstairs. This is too important!"

The next sound was of something solid being tapped against the door. "If you are really in there, Emily Felcher, you come out this very instant."

Emily looked at the tiny glimmers of light filtering through the cracks above and below the door and wondered just who that may have been. More out of curiosity than because she'd been commanded to do so, she pushed herself out of her chair and went to the door.

"Who's out there?" she asked. Her hand rested

on the door bolt while she pressed her ear against the wooden surface.

"Don't you ask who's out here. You just open this door like you were told."

Still curious to know who was so very angry with her and why, Emily did open the door, but only a few inches. When she peered out into the lighted hallway, she did not recognize the woman standing beside Mrs. Roberts. She was an older woman, dressed all in black and she looked very small and very frail. She also leaned heavily on a shiny black cane and swayed slightly from side to side, her expression dazed. Emily's first assessment was that the woman had imbibed a few too many spirits. She tried not to recall what that tipsy sort of feeling was like because it reminded her of *that* night. She had to wonder if things would have been any different had she been fully sober. Desperately, she pushed that thought aside.

"Yes? What do you want with me?" Emily glanced then at Gladys Roberts and noticed the apologetic expression on her face. She nodded, indicating she understood this woman was the one at fault, not her.

"What do I want with you?" the old woman repeated. She narrowed her pale brown eyes then produced something shiny from her pocket. "Why I want to find out what you know about this."

Emily looked down to see what it was and was surprised to find her missing ring. In a purely reflexive action, she reached out into the hall and snatched it out of the woman's glove.

"That's my ring. What are you doing with it?" she asked, her tone more accusing than she'd really meant for it be.

The woman's expression turned cautious while she slowly stepped forward. "Open that door so I can see you." She continued to sway from side to side, but always catching herself before she quite lost her balance.

Just as cautious, Emily opened the door only a few more inches. She'd never had to deal with a drunk woman before. But perhaps she wasn't really a drunk—just so old, she teetered a little more than she tottered. But whichever reason, her inability to stand steady made Emily nervous.

"You still haven't told me how you came to have my ring."

The old woman reached up and gripped Emily's jaw with her fingers, turning her face toward the nearest hall light. She squinted when she leaned forward to carefully study Emily's face. "You do look like her. Can it really be?"

Emily and Gladys exchanged questioning glances, but Emily did not pull away. She let the woman continue her close examination. "Please, ma'am, tell me how you came to have possession of my ring. I'd really like to know."

"It was sent to me about two and a half months ago," she answered, as if that was not important. "On April 8, if that was on a Monday. Along with a note demanding ransom." She then met Emily's astonished gaze. "Did you send me that note?"

"No, of course not," she said, horrified the woman could think such a thing, but not yet realizing why anyone would have sent this woman a ransom note in the first place.

"I thought not. Someone who'd just been handed a hundred thousand easy dollars would not be living in a wretched little place like this."

"Well, I never," Mrs. Roberts complained, her chest puffing out like a protective hen. "I'll have you know—."

But whatever it was she would have the woman

know, was not to be told because the old woman interrupted her immediately.

"Oh, hush up. I wasn't talking to you. I was talking to Emily." She reached up to dab her forehead with a small lace handkerchief she'd produced from her pocket. "My, but it's hot in here. This house could use more windows."

Aware the woman was leaning more heavily against her cane and growing paler by the moment, Emily finally thought to invite her inside. "Maybe you should come in and sit down for a few minutes."

She stepped back and hurried to light the lamp she'd neglected earlier.

"Thank you. I am feeling a little light-headed," the woman said after she'd entered the room and settled into the only chair. She continued to dab at the dampness that clung to her pale forehead and along the sides of her face.

Feeling awkward to be looming over the small sagging form seated before her, Emily stepped back and sat on the edge of the bed. She bit her lower lip while she tried to decide what to do next.

"Would you like for me to stay?" Mrs. Roberts asked from the doorway, clearly still upset about the woman's earlier jibe.

Emily realized it might be better if she left them because Mrs. Roberts had a tendency to say some pretty rude things whenever she was riled, and judging by her narrowed eyes and her stretched nostrils, she was definitely riled. "I guess not. I think I can handle things from here."

"Then do you want me to close the door?"

"No, just leave it open," she decided wisely, still not knowing what to expect from her strange visitor.

"I'll be downstairs if you need me." Mrs. Roberts

gave the woman one last angry glower, then tossed her head to a pretentious angle and walked off.

Emily returned her attention to her visitor. Some of the color had returned to her leathery cheeks, but she still looked awfully pale, as if she hadn't seen the out-of-doors in years. "Who are you? You haven't told me your name."

"And you haven't told me what you know about that ring. How do you know it's yours?"

They both then glanced down at the ruby and diamond circlet Emily had been absently twirling in her hand.

"Because it belonged to my grandmother," Emily said, her voice reverent. "It was especially designed for her."

"For your grandmother? And just how did you come to have it?"

"She gave it to my mother on her sixteenth birthday and then my father gave it to me on mine. But I lost it a few months back. In fact, I lost them both."

"Both?"

"Yes, there was a matching necklace. I lost that, too." But the more Emily thought about it, the more the word 'lost' just didn't sound appropriate. "Or rather they were taken from me."

Tears filled the old woman's eyes and she began to tremble so violently that Emily feared she was having a tremor and would soon lose consciousness.

"Come to me, Emily."

When Emily looked at her then, she suddenly knew who her visitor was, for when she gazed into the old woman's eyes, she saw her own mother's eyes. "Grandmother?"

The old woman nodded, so overcome by emotion she could no longer speak. Using her cane for leverage, she stood then opened her arms.

Emily flew into Elmira Townsend's embrace and together they sobbed aloud with joy. It was several minutes before either of them said anything.

"My dear, sweet Emily. It really is you. At long, long last, my prayers have been answered."

Emily pulled away enough to see into her eyes. "Then you know about me?"

"Oh, yes. I've known about you since right after you were born. Your mother wrote to me often." She looked hurt from having had to make that declaration.

"But I didn't think you answered her letters."

Elmira looked away, tears of regret shimmering in her eyes. "I didn't. I couldn't. But I wanted to." She then looked at Emily again, her expression pleading. "You have to believe me. I wanted to."

"But I don't understand any of this. I thought you were supposed to be dead."

"Believe me, until tonight, I thought I was supposed to be dead, too. But, suddenly, I feel very much alive," she said then reached up to dab away the tears still clinging to her eyes with the corner of her handkerchief. "And I owe it all to you. Hurry and pack you things. You're coming to live with me. It's where you belong."

Chapter Twenty

Quickly, Emily tossed everything she owned into her two trunks, a valise, and two large pillow cases. The only thing she left behind was the black engagement dress Randall had given her, which she snatched up off the floor and folded neatly then placed on the bed with a note pinned to the sleeve stating that Katy should have it. With a few alterations, Katy could have a beautiful gown perfect for the opera or attending the theater with Raymond.

She smiled when she thought of her friend, so happy now that she'd found the perfect man at long last. If only Randall had possessed more of Raymond's fine qualities. But he hadn't. Randall was a rogue in the worst sense of the word.

She just hoped that by leaving Galveston Island, she could finally find a way to put him completely out of her mind. Although she could never hope to forget what he'd done to her, for with that one incident he had ruined her life forever, she desperately needed to put aside the feelings she had for him.

While she stuffed the last of her clothing into a bulging pillow case, she vowed to do just that. With new surroundings, and new family to become acquainted with, eventually, she should be able to forget Randall altogether.

Shortly after eleven o'clock, Emily looked around her bedroom one last time. A large black man with greying hair dressed in a bulky black and grey driver's uniform was summoned upstairs and told to carry all her baggage outside. Within minutes, they were seated in an elegant coach and were soon on their way.

Minutes after they'd taken off down the dark, almost empty streets of Galveston, Elmira bent forward and dug frantically through the contents of a small bag tucked away inside a small compartment beneath the floor of the coach. When she found the bottle she wanted, she quickly opened it and poured a measured dose into a small glass, then downed it, explaining that she was supposed to take her medicine regularly but had forgotten to do so before she arrived.

During most of the two-hour ride to the plantation, Emily's grandmother dozed restlessly at her side, muttering in her sleep about things that did not always make sense. Feeling instant compassion for the woman, despite all the heartache she'd caused her mother, Emily slipped an arm around her to comfort her, and bravely faced whatever changes that were about to occur in her future. No matter what life on her grandmother's plantation turned out to be like, it had to be better than what she'd experienced in Galveston thus far.

On her very first night she'd been drugged by someone she'd thoroughly trusted, then assaulted by someone else she'd thought trustworthy, and finally robbed of her grandmother's jewelry. She'd then been given refuge in Randall's house only to be tossed back out onto the streets again the moment she'd started to feel the least bit safe. But the very worst had not happened until Randall had pretended to love her—pretended to want to marry her. She shuddered at the bitter memory and tried to refocus her attention on whatever still lay ahead for her.

She knew that one of the first things she should do after she'd settled into her new home was send word to Mrs. Williams explaining that she might not return to work for quite some time, if ever.

For some reason, that realization made Emily a little sad, because, despite the long hours and tedious work, she knew she'd miss the friendships she'd formed there.

Also, she would want to write a long letter to Katy, inviting her to come out and visit the first chance she had. She would also want to explain why she had left so suddenly like she had, in the dead of the night.

Although she had told Mrs. Roberts some of the reason she had decided to leave, and knew the dear woman would relay her regrets on to the others, Emily felt Katy deserved to know the whole truth. But Katy would be the only one ever to be told about the terrible thing Randall had done. Of all her friends, only Katy could be trusted to know the reason she had come away from her own engagement party so broken-hearted and so full of shame that she could no longer face the world.

Even so, it would be a while before Emily could bring herself to write such a letter. Until then, she hoped Katy would be satisfied with the explanation she'd given Mrs. Roberts. She had not known her grandmother was coming for her and, therefore, had not had enough time to stop by her room to tell her good-bye. Once her decision to accept her grandmother's invitation had been made, she'd had little choice but to hurry.

She just hoped that everyone at the rooming house would abide by her wishes and not tell Randall where she'd gone. She would never get over her pain or her humiliation as long as he continued to pursue her.

When Randall did not hear from Emily's grandmother by four o'clock the following afternoon, he decided another short visit to the boarding house was in order. He wanted to find out what Elmira Townsend had decided to do after receiving Emily's address.

On the way home from the shipping office, he had Andrew stop by the rooming house so he could ask if Emily had had any unusual visitors that morning, or if she'd received any long overdue messages.

"I appreciate your concern, but I—ah—I'm really not at liberty to say anything," Mrs. Roberts answered him, but failed to look him squarely in the eye. Instead, her attention seemed focused on the activity on the street outside her door.

"Why?" Randall wanted to know, stepping over so that he came within her line of sight. "What harm can it do to tell me if she's had a visitor or if she's received a note of some sort?"

Forced to meet his gaze, Mrs. Roberts' expression hardened with determination. "Emily has asked me not to discuss her private life with you in any way."

Randall clenched his hands into tight fists at his sides, but refrained from letting his anger get the better of him. He tried to keep in mind that this woman was just doing what she'd been asked to do. "And you aren't willing to tell me if she's had a visitor or even a simple letter?"

"No, sir, I'm not." She crossed her arms, further proof she meant what she said. "If you're really wantin' that sort of information, you'll just have to be gettin' it from her yourself—but then again, she's *still* not speakin' to you."

"Fine," he said, his expression rock hard. "Then you can just tell that stubborn woman something for me." He paused to suck in a long, measured breath. "You can tell her that I'm damned tired of her constant refusals to hear me out. All I want to do is apologize to her. But if she's too mule-headed to let me do even that, then so be it." He waved his hands for emphasis. "And you can also tell her it's quite safe for her to come out of her room now, or even go back to work if she feels the need, because I don't plan to bother her again."

Though he truly impressed her with his sincerity, he knew that everything he'd said was a blatant lie. Still, he hoped that by pretending such righteous indignation, she'd feel safer about coming out of that blasted room of hers.

"Anything else?" Mrs. Roberts asked, jutting her chin forward, as if personally insulted by his anger.

"No, that should pretty well do it," he said, then spun about and marched angrily out of the house. He'd give Emily one week to come to her senses. If she wasn't back at work by then, he'd come right back there and take that house by storm if he had to. Meanwhile, he'd try to find out what her grandmother's reaction had been to his second letter himself.

Emily came downstairs the following morning and discovered the table in the main dining room set for only one. Thinking that odd, she went on into the kitchen and asked the two servants she found sitting on either side of a small worktable if they had yet been told about her.

"Oh, yes, ma'am," the younger of the two said,

quickly rising to her feet. "We were told you'd be down for breakfast sometime this morning. Are you ready to eat now?"

The other girl reached for a small basket filled with fresh eggs. "How would you like your eggs, ma'am?"

Emily frowned, then looked around for a clock, wondering what time it was. Had she slept so late that she'd missed dining with her grandmother? "When I was just in the dining room I noticed only one place was set. Has my grandmother already eaten?"

The two shook their heads in unison.

"No, ma'am, we don't expect her down today," the younger one explained. "That trip into the city last night took a lot out of her. She doesn't get out of the house that often. But she did tell Chrisaundra to see to it that you had a nice breakfast and were made to feel right at home. She explained that you are her granddaughter and will be living here for awhile and told us to see to your every whim."

"And who is Chrisaundra?"

"I am," the older girl said, then curtsied prettily. "I'm Chrisaundra, and she's Lahoma. We work here."

Emily looked at the two Indian girls, who both appeared to be close to her own age and wondered what information they might be willing to tell her about her grandmother.

She tried to appear only casually interested when she stepped forward to pluck a grape from a freshly washed mound left in the center of the table. "How long have you two worked here?"

"I have worked here for nearly six years, since I sixteen," Chrisaundra said, smiling proudly. "Lahoma has worked here only four."

"Five, in September," the younger one quickly corrected.

"And who else works here?" Emily decided she might as well become acquainted with the people she'd be living with for awhile.

"There is Samuel, of course," Chrisaundra supplied willingly. "He has worked for the Townsends the longest, for nearly forty years. He started out a slave, but right after the war he was given freedom papers. Although most slaves took off after that, Samuel decided to stay and was soon made a butler. Then after Mr. Townsend died, Samuel also was made the missus's personal driver, though she hardly go anywhere. I imagine you met Samuel last night. He was the one who drove into city."

"Why do you claim she hardly ever goes anywhere?"

"Because, she goes very little. She's gotten feeble in the past few years," Lahoma put in, clearly eager to talk. "Except when she went to the doctor the few times that he couldn't make the trip out here, she hasn't bothered to leave this house in probably ten years. Not since she found out her oldest daughter had died, which I understand happened right after her husband had died. I guess she couldn't handle the two deaths coming so close together. She's been like a hermit ever since. She rarely leaves her room and lives on little more than her doctor's black tonic."

"But who oversees the plantation?" Earlier, Emily had glanced out her bedroom window and noticed acres upon acres of cultivated fields.

"Her other daughter, Miss Elizabeth." Lahoma's expression turned sour, as if she held a personal grudge against this other daughter. "Although Miss Elizabeth lives on Galveston Island, she comes out here at least twice a month to make sure Thomas keeps everything running smooth. Thomas is her overseer. She hired him personally." Lahoma's black, expressive eyes widened with concern, as if she suddenly realized she'd said too much. "Please don't think I don't like Miss Elizabeth, because that's not altogether true. At least the woman has taken it upon herself to see that this place doesn't get run down and she sees to it that her mother never runs out of her tonic. If it wasn't for Miss Elizabeth and Dr. Reyes, the missus wouldn't never have any company at all."

Emily's forehead drew into a troubled frown. "What sort of tonic does she take?"

"I don't know. Miss Elizabeth claims it's some sort of vitamin tonic that the missus has to take in order to keep her health up since she doesn't hardly ever eat, and when she does, it's never enough to keep even a church mouse alive. But if you ask me, it has more than a few vitamins in it."

"Why do you say that?"

"Because if she goes too long without it, she turns downright mad."

Emily's eyes widened with alarm. It certainly did sound as if there was something more than a few vitamins in her grandmother's tonic and that worried her.

"But please don't tell no one we told you about her tonic. We could get into a lot of trouble," Lahoma put in quickly. "I really don't know why I mentioned it at all, except maybe that we're both worried about her. When she's in her right mind, she really is a nice old woman. She only gets mean when Miss Elizabeth causes trouble or she hasn't had her tonic."

Later, Emily mulled over all she'd learned while she ate breakfast and continued to dwell on it when she went upstairs to visit with her grandmother. But when she entered Elmira's bedroom, she found her sleeping too soundly to be wakened.

Since a bottle of what Lahoma had referred to as her grandmother's tonic stood on the table beside the bed, she picked it up, opened it, then put it to her nose and sniffed of it. It smelled harmless enough, like licorice candy; but when she touched her finger to the rim then put a droplet in her mouth, her face wrinkled from the bitter taste.

It certainly didn't taste like licorice. In fact, it had the same bitter aftertaste as the spiced tea Josephine had had sent up to her that night she'd later become so disoriented. Evidently, the same drug Josephine had used on her was also in her grandmother's tonic.

Although she could not be sure, she suspected the bitter ingredient to be some form of opium. It accounted for her grandmother's growing dependence upon it.

Setting the bottle back down, and again gazing at her grandmother's pale, withered face, Emily realized the tonic was slowly draining her grandmother's life away and that frightened her. She did not want to lose her so soon after having finally found her. She had to do something to save the poor woman from herself, yet understood enough about the nature of the drug to realize she couldn't just take the tonic away. What she'd have to do was slowly wean her somehow.

She decided to begin this campaign to free her grandmother of the terrible, debilitating drug by diluting the tonic with a few tablespoons of water. She would also do what she could to keep her constantly occupied so she wouldn't have time to think about any discomforts the diluted tonic might cause, aware that those resulting discomforts would make her want more.

For the next two weeks, Emily continued to dilute the tonic, each time adding a little more water than before and pouring off the excess liquid. Although her grandmother soon became very cranky between her doses of medicine, Emily did not stop. She was determined to free the woman of her addiction.

It was during one particularly cranky spell, while Elmira sat in a rocking chair rocking hard and sweating profusely, that Emily knew she'd better start a conversation to divert her attention or risk the woman taking another dose of medicine too soon.

She decided the time had come to find out why her grandmother had never answered any of her mother's letters. She had originally planned to wait until the woman was in better spirits, but now that the tonic had been cut nearly in half, Elmira was not often in a pleasant mood.

"Grandmother, I know it is not something you want to talk about, but I really would like to know why you never answered any of my mother's letters. I know she wrote to you often, each time hoping you'd find it in your heart to finally forgive her."

"Because I couldn't," she answered, flexing her mouth from side to side with short, restless movements. "Don't you see? I *couldn't.*"

"No, I don't see. Why couldn't you answer at least one of her letters?"

"Because my husband wouldn't allow it. Eleanor had hurt him by what she'd done. Hurt him badly."

Elmira then looked at Emily as if she was about to impart some untold secret. Her mouth continued to twitch spasmodically, but her words were clear. "Your mother ran away and got married without her father's blessing. Fact is, Douglas forbade her to go. Pleaded with her not to. Yet she went anyway. That hurt him. He'd planned for her to marry Joseph Wilcox. But she refused. She'd told Douglas she would, then suddenly refused. All because of your father. That not only disappointed him, it shamed him."

Tears filled the old woman's eyes, but she did not bother to wipe them away. "After that, Douglas declared that if Eleanor actually did choose to run off and marry that nobody from up North, she would no longer be a daughter of his. If she was willing to go against his wishes like that, she was never to set foot in his house again. After she ran away, Eleanor no longer existed for him. He was that hurt."

Emily fought her own onslaught of tears, unaware that there had been that much pain on both sides. "But if those were his feelings, and not yours, why couldn't you have at least responded to one of my mother's letters? She was hurting, too."

Elmira leaned her head against the back of her chair and stared off at the ceiling while she continued to rock, though more slowly now. "I knew she was hurting. But I couldn't go against my own husband like that. Not when she'd been warned beforehand what to expect. Eleanor understood what she'd be doing, but she married him anyway."

She looked at Emily again, her eyes pleading with her to understand. "But I did try to find her right after Douglas died. Although I didn't feel it would be right for her to come back here, into this very house. I did want to see her. I was willing to go to her, meet her anywhere on the face of this earth in an effort to finally make amends." She then dropped her gaze to her hands, which were clasped together and pulsating. "But it was too late. Your mother was already gone. You can't know the pain I suffered then—finding out my oldest daughter was dead so shortly after my own Douglas had died. I hurt so much, I hid myself away in my room and refused to come out even to eat. My grief became so overwhelming, Elizabeth had her doctor come out. He prescribed a tonic that eventually gave me back some of my strength and calmed my nerves just enough to allow me to sleep."

"Is that what you're still taking?" she asked, nodding toward the tall, black bottle that was never far from her grandmother's side.

"Yes, it's got the vitamins I need to keep up my strength."

"But wouldn't it be better to get your vitamins directly from your food?"

"Yes, but sometimes I can't keep all my food down and I have to rely on my tonic."

"But you seem to be keeping your food down pretty well these days," Emily pointed out.

"That's because you are so good for me." She smiled and reached out to pat Emily's hand. "Since you've been here, my appetite has nearly doubled. I enjoy sharing my meals with you. You're good company."

"And you are also good company," she quickly assured her, though that was not always true. Sometimes she was extremely cantankerous. But that was because of the opium. Or rather because she was no longer getting as much of it as she had in the past. "I can't remember when I've enjoyed anyone's company more."

"Oh, that reminds me, your gentleman friend has written to find out how you are getting along," Elmira commented, patting her skirt pocket with her hand. "I guess I should take the time to write him again. He seems eager to know if you are doing well."

Emily's heart froze. "What gentleman friend?"

"Why, your Mr. Gipson, of course."

The name cut through Emily's protective shell

like the cold blade of a dagger, causing her instant pain. "Randall knows I'm here?"

She wondered who she could blame for that. Surely not Katy or Mrs. Roberts. They would never tell. Or would they?

"Of course, he knows you're here. He's the one who sent your address to me in the first place. Didn't you know that?" She blinked as if trying to remember. "Didn't I tell you, your Mr. Gipson was the one who located me then sent me your address?"

"No, you didn't," Emily said, confused about why Randall would do something so nice; but then decided his ulterior motive was to trick her back into his bed somehow. Tears of shame filled her eyes when all the anguish she'd fought so hard to forget came rushing back. "I thought you'd found me because you'd somehow managed to trace that ring back to me. But it really doesn't matter who helped bring us together, just as long as we stay together."

"My sentiments exactly," Elmira said, glancing at the medicine bottle and wetting her lips. "What time is it? Is it time for my medicine yet?"

"No, not for another hour," Emily quickly assured her, then for no other reason than to keep her grandmother's mind occupied with something besides her growing discomfort, she asked about Randall's letter. "How often does Mr. Gipson write to you?"

"He's written to me twice since that night I went into town to get you. Once just a few days afterward, to find out if I'd ever managed to find you. Then, after I finally remembered to answer that one, he wrote again to tell me how happy he was that I'd invited you out here to live for awhile—and, of course, he wanted to find out how you are getting along. I got that second letter just this morning, but

I plan to answer this one right away, probably this afternoon after I've had my nap. He sounds truly concerned about you. Is he your special beau?" Her eyes lit with excitement.

"No, of course not," Emily said, a bit too adamantly, still wondering why Randall had bothered to search for her grandmother. Why, he hadn't even believed there *was* a grandmother. She stared down at her hands, puzzled by the whole thing. "He's just a friend, and barely that."

"Oh? And I was thinking about inviting him out here for a short visit." She bent forward to watch Emily's reaction. "Is that perhaps something I shouldn't do?"

"No," she said, then frowned when she looked back up, frustrated by her own answer. "I mean yes. That is most definitely something you should not do. I don't want to see him."

"Not even after what he did?"

"Especially not after what he did," she answered, thinking of that night at his house and not of the fact he'd somehow been instrumental in bringing them together.

"Well, then, it's a good thing we had this talk," Elmira said, nodding while she studied Emily's determined expression. "I'd have made a terrible mistake."

Elmira then fell disturbingly silent, making Emily try to find something else to talk about. Anything else. "When I was in the kitchen earlier, Lahoma told me that my aunt Elizabeth is past due for a visit. I wonder what is keeping her away. I'm anxious to meet her."

"Well, don't expect too much from that one," Elmira warned her.

"Why?" she asked, thinking that an odd thing for a mother to say about her younger daughter.

"I guess I should warn you. Elizabeth has pretty well inherited her father's anger when it comes to any mention of your mother. It will probably take her a while to finally take a liking to you."

"Because I'm my mother's daughter," she concluded and finally understood why her aunt had been so adamant they never meet.

"Exactly. So during those first few times you two meet, try not to let her bother you. Eventually, she'll come around."

Elmira's words formed the only comforting thought Emily had to fall back on when the time finally did come to meet her mother's only sister. Like Elmira had warned her, Elizabeth's initial greeting was not one of warmth nor acceptance. Far from it, for although Elizabeth claimed to be very delighted that Emily had found her way home, her eyes revealed something entirely different.

It was an eerie feeling to stare into a face that looked so much like her mother's and see such open hatred. Despite her grandmother's later reassurances, Emily truly doubted that she and her aunt Elizabeth would ever be close.

Chapter Twenty-one

Later, on the same day that Elizabeth had come out to check on the plantation, another woman by the name of Laura Goodsworth stopped by to see how Elmira was getting along. Although Mrs. Goodsworth visited only a few times a year and stayed but a few minutes each time she came, she remained there long enough to meet Emily and learn about her connection to the family.

By the end of the week, news of Elmira's beautiful long-lost granddaughter had spread like wildfire. Soon, letters arrived by personal messenger, all asking when it would be convenient to pay a personal visit.

Elmira thought it amusing that until they'd learned about Emily, many of her friends had not been concerned enough to write as much as a short note asking about her welfare. "But now they are curious as they can be about you," she said with a cackle. "That's why everyone is so eager to meet you." She indicated the stack of letters on the table beside her. "Problem is, if I say yes to every one of these, you'll be deluged with a constant stream of visitors."

"That sounds nice," Emily said, thinking it would

help Elmira keep her mind off her tonic. Although her grandmother had not shown as much interest since she'd cut the strength down till it was barely a third as effective as it had been, the bottle was always nearby. Even so, Emily was confident that one day very soon she could admit to her grandmother what she'd done, and should then be able to convince her to give up the vile liquid entirely.

"Well, it may sound nice to you to have so many visitors, but believe me, it would be much more trouble than it's worth. We wouldn't have any time for each other. But, then, I do hate to turn them down." She sat and thought about it for a moment, then her eyes lit with an idea. "I know. I'll have a special party. That way I can introduce you to everyone at the same time." She grinned, forming pleasant wrinkles at the outer corners of her mouth. "Now won't that shock their stockings off. After ten years of me hardly ever showing my nose, I'll have one of the grandest parties ever to be held in South Texas."

"That's not necessary," Emily quickly said, thinking it might be a bit much for her grandmother to handle. Although Elmira seemed a lot stronger, she still had her physical limits.

"It might not be necessary, but it sure will be fun," she said, a bright pink rising to her cheeks. "And I think it'll be just the thing to put a smile back on that pretty face of yours. Let's see, when would be the best time to have it?"

While she twisted her face with thought, Emily wondered about the comment concerning her smile. Was she really as transparent as all that?

Despite the fact it had been over a month since her shameful encounter with Randall, which should have been plenty of time to get over the bitterness she still felt whenever she thought of him, she still dwelled on the terrible thing he'd done. There seemed to be no getting past the hurt or the anger he'd caused. The pain gripping her heart was just as strong as it had ever been. She had tried to keep the sadness from actually showing, but evidently she had failed. Even her grandmother had sensed her sorrow.

"I guess I really need to look at a calendar," Elmira went on to say, unaware of Emily's melancholy thoughts. "If I get the invitations out right away, we could have our party as early as the first Saturday in August. That would mean being able to introduce you before the summer season was over, and it would still give me over two weeks to prepare. Actually, that would be perfect because most of the people who leave the island every year to avoid the worst of the typhoid months will have returned by then. I'll be able to invite all my old friends and their families."

Agreeing that a party might indeed be just the thing to put a smile back on her face—and on her grandmother's face as well—Emily immediately began to help planning it.

By the end of the afternoon, the two had reached several decisions. They knew exactly what sort of refreshments they wanted to serve and what sort of entertainment they would hire. All they really needed to get the whole process underway was to travel into town and have the invitations printed. Elmira was so excited by their new plans she had Samuel take them to Galveston that very next morning so they could get the invitations made and also buy Emily several new dresses and a very special gown for the upcoming festivities.

To Emily's delight, her grandmother suggested they stop at the restaurant where Katy worked to tell her about their plans and to share a fat piece of lemon pie. At first, it amazed her that her grandmother would be so willing to forgo the fancier restaurants for such a common place, but then decided it was just like her to be so considerate. It was while they were seated inside that Emily promised Katy she'd write and tell her everything that had happened since last they'd talked.

Just days after they returned from the city and the first invitations had gone out, Emily started to receive early callers. Young men she'd never met suddenly appeared at her grandmother's door, presenting their calling cards and asking to meet Elmira's granddaughter.

Elmira was thoroughly delighted, but Emily was annoyed by their unwanted attention. She did everything she could to discourage them, knowing only too well that she was a "fallen" woman. Because of Randall's cruel prank and her own gullibility, she had been robbed of what a woman holds most sacred. She was no longer marriageable and that was obviously the sort of relationship her callers were interested in. They wanted a marriageable young woman with possible connections to lots of money.

The Tuesday before the party, Emily had yet another male visitor. But because she never recognized the names anyway, she did not bother to ask who was paying call. She simply retouched her hair and went downstairs to greet him, hoping whoever he was, he would not stay long.

When she entered the main parlor just a few minutes later, she was not prepared to find Randall standing in the center of the room, his hands linked behind his back, patiently waiting for her.

"What are you doing here?" she asked. Her hand flew protectively to the throbbing pulse at the base of her throat. Just seeing him again send a whirlpool of painful emotions splashing through her.

If only he weren't so handsome, with his thick brown hair and his incredibly blue eyes.

If only she didn't still care about him.

She blinked back her tears and set her jaw at a mutinous angle. She'd not fall prey to her own treacherous emotions again.

"I've come to pay call on Galveston's latest belle." His gaze swept over her with deep longing when he stepped forward to greet her. Although what he wanted most was to take her into his arms and hold her close, he held only the one hand out and smiled. "My dear, I'm afraid you have suddenly become the talk of the town."

"And just what do they say about me?" she asked, ignoring his gesture of friendship. Tensing against the onslaught of tattered emotions still raging through her, she turned a shoulder to him and stared out the window. What was it about him that tore her heart into such tiny little pieces?

"Just that you are the most beautiful, beguiling woman ever to grace this entire state," he told her, frowning at the bitterness in her expression. "But then, I already knew that."

Emily's legs trembled from the sheer weight of the emotions she'd fought so hard to forget. She leaned heavily against the back of a nearby chair when she turned to face him again. Her voice was cold and her expression so full of hatred that it sounded foreign even to her. "What is it you want with me?"

"I just want a chance to apologize. That's all I ask." He held his hands spread palms out as if to promise her he wouldn't even touch her if that's what she wanted. "Let me have just a few minutes of your time."

"After what you did to me?" When she looked at

him then her brown eyes bore the full force of her anger. "Why should I?"

"That's a good question. And I wish I had a good answer for it, but I don't. There really is no reason you should hear me out."

"Then please leave," she said and pointed to the door, appalled by the obvious way her hands shook.

"Not until I've had my say. Whether I deserve to be heard out or not, I am not leaving here until I've at least had a chance to apologize."

"Then apologize, so I can finally be rid of you." She stared at him with fury-darkened features, wondering how much more she could possibly endure before she burst into shameful tears.

At that moment, Samuel appeared in the doorway. Never had Emily been so glad to see anyone. She turned to him expectantly.

"Miss Emily? The missus wants you to bring her some fresh flowers so she can fill the vase in the dining room."

Emily thought that rather odd, since it was usually Chrisaundra who brought in the daily supply of cut flowers, but did not question an opportunity to leave the room. Smiling triumphantly, she turned back to her unwanted visitor. "I'm sorry, but I'll have to go now. I must see to my grandmother's wishes."

Then, without giving him the opportunity to voice a protest, she snatched open a drawer and came out with a pair of small scissors then spun about and left the room. She didn't as much as breathe again until she was halfway down the hall that led to the back door.

Just when she believed she was rid of him and could finally relax, she heard his heavy footsteps in the hallway behind her. Heaving a long, impatient sigh, she turned back to face him. "May I ask where you think you are headed?"

"Wherever it is you're headed. You haven't heard my apology yet."

Emily pursed her lips for a moment, then turned her back and proceeded out the back door, careful to slam the door between them. When she heard the door open again and realized he really did intend to follow her into the garden, she became so annoyed, her fingernails dug deep trenches into her palms. Yet, at the same time, she felt oddly pleased that he seemed so determined.

She waited until she was in main area of the garden and had knelt beside a small flowering rose bush before bothering to speak again. "And just what do you hope to accomplish with this apology of yours?"

"I'm hoping to be forgiven so we can start over." He knelt beside her.

The return of Emily's anger was immediate. She stood again and brandished the two blooms she'd just cut as if they were weapons. "You expect me to forgive you for what you did to me? Just like that. Forgive you for ruining my entire future? For ruining *me?*"

Randall felt the very life drain out of him. His face contorted with the pain her words had wrought as he forced himself back to his feet. "I'd hoped you'd somehow find it in your heart to forgive me for that, yes."

"But why should I?" She was so angry now she wanted to slap him, to bring him some degree of the same physical pain she suffered.

Thinking those very actions justified, she stepped forward to do just that, but Randall caught her arm before she could complete the blow.

"The only answer I have is to tell you how very

much I still love you," he stated simply, all the while holding her by her wrist. "Because I do still love you and I still want to marry you."

"As if I hadn't already fallen for that one," she muttered, gritting her teeth while she tried to wrench herself free of his painful grasp. "I can't believe you think I'm foolish enough to fall for that same gambit twice."

"But it's true. I've come here to ask again that you marry me."

Believing it a ruse to ease his guilty conscience, if indeed he had one, she wanted no part of it. "I'd rather you wallow in the knowledge of the terrible thing you did. Marriage happens to be something that is supposed to be based on love and mutual respect—not guilt."

Randall realized he would never convince her with mere words. His only hope was to show her. Pulling her hard by the arm, he spun her toward him and captured her in his embrace. Pressing her body firmly against his, he then dipped his head to take her mouth in a kiss so passionate, it weakened even him.

When he eventually pulled away, she was outraged—not at all the response he'd wanted.

"How dare you!" she spat vehemently, still trying to wriggle free of his grasp. "How dare you come here and—."

The last of her angry sentence was lost to yet another long, hungry kiss; only this time, when he broke away for much needed air, she did not seem quite as angry as she had before. If anything, she seemed almost afraid of him, and he felt that was an encouraging sign. If nothing else, she had stopped struggling.

"Randall, you have no right—."

Again he stole her words by bringing his mouth

down on hers, and again she came away from the experience appearing a little less angry.

When she looked into his determined expression then, she felt almost like smiling—*almost.* She wondered if everything she tried to say to him would lead to another kiss. It was certainly a concept worth testing.

"How can you—." Sure enough, he dipped down to take yet another kiss, but this time she felt her body respond. Despite all he'd done to her, she still loved him and he still had the power to make her swoon. It may not make sense, but it was true. When he lifted his head again, she had to swallow before she could speak.

"—possibly stand there and—."

Another tantalizing kiss.

As his mouth continued to work its magic, a familiar hunger overtook her, and despite her firm resolve not to let her heart lead her astray ever again, she felt herself leaning against him, accepting his embrace. Although it had been nearly seven weeks since she'd last seen him, it felt as though she'd been in his arms only yesterday. There was just something about him that set her very soul on fire.

"Emily, please believe me when I tell you that I love you," he murmured, pulling away just enough to speak the words. His heart soared when he realized the anger was gone from her eyes. "I know I've hurt you, and I also know I don't deserve your forgiveness, because what I did was nothing short of despicable, but I do so want you to forgive me. I was a fool, but I've had a lot of time to come to my senses. All I want is a second chance."

The words fell soft and sweet against her cheek, causing her to close her eyes and moan in response. She desperately wanted to believe him.

Although she had yet to speak any actual words

of forgiveness, Randall knew he'd found the response in her he wanted. He pressed her soft body intimately against his then dipped his head for yet another passionate kiss, relieved when he was met with no resistance. It was not until he brought his hand around to cup the underside of her breast that she suddenly pulled away, her anger returned.

"How dare you! That's all you want, isn't it? To seduce me again. I'm not good enough to marry, but I'm good enough to keep your bed warm. Is that it?"

"No, not at all. All I want—." This time it was his turn to have his words cut short.

"I don't care what you want, but I'll tell you what I want. I want you to take your sugary sweet words and your handsome smile and get out of here. I don't ever want to see or speak to you again," she shouted, so angry and so hurt, she did not care who heard her. "Go find someone else to seduce. I've had enough!"

With that, she flung the two crumpled flowers into his face and ran out of the garden, leaving him too stunned to follow.

Randall had never seen anyone so angry. He watched her hurry across the yard to the back veranda and waited until he'd heard the back door clatter shut before finally turning to leave. Rather than return to the house, certain he'd be refused entry even if he tried, he bent to her wishes. He chose not to run after her or try one last time to talk to her. Instead, he followed the narrow path that led around to the side of the house and curved toward the front, where he'd left his carriage.

When he passed by the front veranda, he was surprised to hear his name whispered with such urgency. He glanced up, hoping that Emily had had second thoughts, but saw no one. It wasn't until his name was repeated that he realized the voice was unfamiliar and that whoever was calling to him had done so from inside.

"Mr. Gipson. Please wait there. I'll be right out."

Within seconds, the front door opened and out stepped Elmira Townsend. He recognized her from the huge painting that hung in the front parlor where he'd been asked to wait.

"I'd like a word with you, if I may," she said, keeping her voice low. She glanced back toward the house as if checking to see if any shadows lingered about the open windows.

"What do you want to talk about?" he asked, thinking it odd that the woman seemed so adamant to speak with him privately.

"About my party."

He blinked. "What party?" He'd been too wrapped up in his misery to keep up with the latest social happenings.

Elmira hurried over to the edge of the porch then gazed down at him, clearly pleased with what she saw. Her pale brown eyes sparkled when she spoke. "I'm having a party this weekend in Emily's honor and I'd like for you to come."

"I don't think Emily would want me there," he said, knowing that was an understatement. "I think she'd be very angry with both of us if I showed up."

"You let me worry about that. Just say that you'll come."

Randall studied the hopeful expression lifting the old woman's face. "Why?"

"At first, I thought you might have been the one who sent me that ring I'd given Emily's mother years ago and demanded so much ransom. But I quickly realized that was ludicrous. What would a man of your means want with a measley hundred thousand. You are already worth millions."

Randall's forehead wrinkled at the mention of the ring. He'd forgotten all about Emily's initial claim that her grandmother's jewelry had been stolen from her, but obviously it had been the truth. But then why shouldn't it have been? Everything else that she'd told him had been true, too. "You paid a hundred thousand to get back that ring?"

"Yes, because I was informed that I'd be told exactly where I could find her if I left the money at a specific spot. And then I never heard another word. But that's neither here nor there. Although I would like to know what became of the necklace, it's not really all that important. What is important is that I like you. And after seeing that kiss in the garden, I could tell that Emily really likes you, too. She just doesn't seem to realize it yet." She frowned as if wondering about her granddaughter's stupidity. "Or maybe she does realize her feelings, but is afraid of them for some reason."

Randall could well imagine why and shook his head with regret. "If you saw what happened when I kissed her, then surely you also saw what happened *after* I kissed her. I really don't think she would want me at your party."

"Don't you want to come?" Elmira looked hurt.

"Well, yes, but . . ."

"Then come," her expression immediately lifted. "The party is this Saturday night and starts at eight o'clock." She then started to walk away as if everything had been decided, but paused just a few feet from the door with an afterthought. "Come fashionably late and be sure to wear something that will really dazzle her."

Randall watched her disappear through the same door she'd appeared from, wondering if he'd heard their conversation right. Although he still had grave doubts about coming to the party, he was smiling when he returned to the carriage. "Andy, old boy, I'll want to stop by Smith Brothers and have myself fitted for a new suit." He glanced back at the house and laughed. "I want something really dazzling to wear Saturday night."

Andrew looked at him with a raised brow, as if suddenly he doubted his boss's choice of words, but nodded his agreement when he started the carriage back toward town.

The day of the party, when Emily first climbed out of bed, she felt a little ill, but quickly convinced herself that her churning stomach and the accompanying dizziness was the result of a bad case of nerves. Rather than disappoint her grandmother, she forced down a warm biscuit with jelly and eventually felt better. By the time she had to start getting dressed, she was back to her old self—dismal though that was.

Because the party was scheduled to begin at eight o'clock, Elmira had asked Emily to be ready by seven-thirty so they could both be downstairs to greet any of the early arrivals.

Although she really didn't feel up to an entire evening of forced conversation and frivolous laughter, she hurried to be ready on time.

At precisely seven-thirty, her grandmother appeared at her door wanting to be sure she was almost ready and that she didn't need anything.

"Does the dress still fit?" Elmira wanted to know, studying the emerald gown carefully.

"Yes, Grandmother, it still fits. And why wouldn't it? You bought it only two weeks ago."

"I know, but I saw you wear it only the one time, and that was before everything was completed. I was worried that the seamstress may not have spent enough time with all the alterations."

"Well, as you can easily see, it fits just fine." She spun about to let her grandmother view the back as well as the front of the emerald silk gown with its tiny white pearls and its delicate lace trim. "I don't think the seamstress could have done better."

"I agree," she said, blinking with pride. "You are just as lovely as your mother. You will really turn the heads tonight."

"I'm not so sure I want to turn any heads tonight," Emily informed her, wishing her grandmother would put aside any matchmaking notions she still had.

"You'll change your mind after you see some of the handsome men I've invited to this thing," Elmira said with a decisive nod and a twinkle in her eye. "By the way, if someone by the name of Shawn Lindsay introduces himself to you and asks you to dance, say no. He's a handsome devil, but he's also a notorious womanizer. You'll want to have nothing to do with him. But as for the rest of the young men that have been invited, dance to your heart's content."

Emily really didn't feel like dancing, but she did want to make her grandmother happy. That was the whole reason for agreeing to the party in the first place. "I promise. I'll dance as much as my poor feet will let me."

"Good. Glad to hear it," she responded, her smile broadening. "I'd better go downstairs. The first of the guests will start arriving any minute. Come just as soon as you finish getting ready."

"But I am finished," Emily said, giving herself one last appraising look in the mirror. Her dress hung in perfect folds from a well-fitted waist and her hair was a masterpiece of dark, swirling curls, each held perfectly in place. She even wore the beautiful double strand of white pearls her grandmother had insisted she wear. "Why? What have I forgotten?"

"Your radiant smile. I don't know where you left it, but you'd sure better find it before the guests arrive." She then winked playfully. "You'd think you were headed for a hanging instead of a special party being held in your honor."

Aware just how much her grandmother cared for her, Emily did smile and was able to hold on to that smile for the next hour and a half while she stood beside her and her Aunt Elizabeth near the front door, greeting the guests one at a time. It was not until she had glanced up and noticed Randall's expectant gaze coming toward her that her smile suddenly faltered. Tiny bumps of apprehension sprang to life beneath her skin.

"What are you doing here?" she asked when he stepped forward, his hand outstretched in formal greeting like everyone else. Rather than cause an angry scene in front of her grandmother's friends, she allowed him to take her hand and squeeze it lightly. A wild scattering of sensations shot through her arm, making her jerk her grasp free again.

"Is that the only question you know?" he asked, keeping his voice low so only she could hear. Smiling, he admired first the fit of her gown, then her face. Though it seemed impossible, she became more beautiful with each day that passed. "Well, my sweet Emily, if you really must know. Your grandmother invited me."

"Why would she do that?" She stared at him with disbelief then at her grandmother who looked quickly away. Suddenly she felt betrayed by the very woman she thought loved her.

"Perhaps it is her way of thanking me," he suggested, shrugging that the reason she'd invited him really didn't matter. It was the fact that she *had* invited him that was important.

"Why would she be thanking you?"

"For helping bring the two of you together."

Emily thought about that. "And she's right. You do deserve to be rewarded for that."

Randall's eyes widened with surprise. He'd expected another argument, not an unconditional agreement. "So, am I to take that as a personal thank you?"

"Take it in any way you please." Although she was grateful to him for having found her grandmother, she was not grateful enough to forgive the terrible thing he'd done.

Aware he'd taken up enough of her time for now, and to linger any longer might cause needless speculation, he simply nodded then stepped back. "There are others wanting to meet you. I'll have to wait and talk with you again a little later."

Emily didn't know whether to take that as his reason to leave, or some sort of personal threat. Although the unexpected sight of him had made her long to find happiness in his arms again, she refused to give rein to those feelings. She didn't need any more pain in her life, especially the kind he caused. Therefore, her best choice of action was to avoid his company whenever possible. And whenever it was *not* possible to avoid him, she could still remain cold and distant.

"Don't count on it, Mr. Gipson," she said with a haughty lift of her chin.

"I count on nothing else," he said, then saluted her by touching his finger to his forehead before he turned and casually sauntered toward the crowded ballroom.

Aware that several people may have overheard at least parts of their unusual exchange, she tried to appear unaffected after she turned to greet the next person, who had waited patiently several feet away.

When the music started at nine o'clock, Emily was immediately swept onto the dance floor and kept there by a steady stream of eligible young men. Each hoped to be the one to capture her attention. But, despite their constant efforts, the only person to hold her attention for any real length of time, was Randall.

She hated the way most of the younger women in the room had flocked around him like a gaggle of silly geese. She also hated the easy way he tossed his head back and laughed at so much of what they had to say. He certainly seemed to enjoy the attention they gave him. And who could blame them? He looked incredibly handsome dressed in his well-fitted black frock coat and grey trousers. She wondered why he never bothered asking any of them to dance, then decided he probably didn't want to chance breaking the set.

Bitterly, she realized that was one of the biggest differences between them.

Unlike him, she did not enjoy the vast amount of the attention the many young men in the room had bestowed upon her. She dearly wished Katy would come so she would have someone to help her take her mind off of Randall.

She stood on tiptoe and gazed about the room to see if Katy had yet arrived and frowned with further disappointment when she did not find her friend. Katy had told her they'd be late, but how late? It was already ten-thirty—past time for her to be there.

"Lose somebody?" a male voice asked from directly behind her.

Startled, Emily spun about, halfway expecting to find Randall but surprised to see an unfamiliar man standing only inches away. "Not really. The person I'm looking for hasn't arrived yet. I can't imagine what is keeping her. She should be here by now."

"She?" he asked, then leaned forward until his face was almost on top of hers and smiled. His pale green eyes glittered with delight. "Good. At first I was afraid that the person you were looking for might be a special man." Without warning he reached for her hand. "Hello, beautiful lady, my name is Shawn Lindsay. I was a little late getting here so I haven't yet had the opportunity to meet you."

Emily recognized the name right away as the one person her grandmother had warned her against, and with obvious reason. Although he allowed her to withdraw her hand, he continued to hover over her like a hungry hawk ready to strike. True, he was an incredibly handsome man, but something about him made her shudder and take a precautionary step backward.

"And I'm Emily Felcher, Elmira Townsend's granddaughter." It did little good to move away. He immediately closed the distance.

"I had a feeling that's who you were," he said, then glanced at the dance floor where several couples were enjoying a light waltz. "Why isn't a woman as beautiful as you out there dancing to her heart's content? Don't tell me that these other men haven't found the courage to ask you. Because, if that's so, I fear we are surrounded by a room filled with idiots."

"No, they've asked. And I have danced. A lot. Too much, in fact. After that last polka, I became tired and decided to get a breath of fresh air," she said, giving him the same excuse she'd given the others.

"Good. I'll go with you." His eyes sparkled with

expectation as he placed his hand near the small of her back.

"No, that won't be necessary," she said, but realized he would not be as easily deterred as the others had been.

"Oh, but it will give us the chance to become better acquainted."

Not wanting to hurt his feelings, and not wanting to admit she'd lied just to have a few selfish minutes to herself, Emily finally offered a friendly smile and nodded her agreement. "All right. But I doubt I'll be out there very long."

He motioned for her to go ahead. "I don't know, it could be that once we're out there, you'll discover you prefer the solitude and darkness to the bright lights and confusion in here."

Just before passing through the double French doors that led out onto a small veranda overlooking a portion of Elmira's plush gardens, Emily glanced back to get one last look at Randall and was surprised to find him watching her. She shuddered at the grim expression on his face, expecting him to follow and make some sort of trouble.

While leaning against the ornate bannister that encircled the veranda, and retaining a careful distance from Shawn, which was not easily accomplished, Emily kept her eyes trained on the door. But Randall never came.

Several minutes later, when they returned to the main ballroom, she discovered Randall had left. For some reason, she did not feel as relieved about that as she had expected. Sadly, she wondered if he'd left alone.

"Would you like to dance?" Shawn asked, nodding toward the dance floor, still hovering over her like a vulture.

"No, I'm not feeling too well. I think I'd better

go upstairs and lie down for a little while," she said. Fighting the tears that had sprung to her eyes, she turned and hurried away.

It angered her to know that Randall still had the ability to hurt her—even when he wasn't there.

Chapter Twenty-two

The following morning, Emily awoke feeling worse than she had the day of the party. Although she had barely eaten anything the evening before, she felt extremely nauseated and when she first stood up out of bed and reached for her clothes to get dressed, she became so light-headed she had to sit down to keep from passing out.

Her grandmother came into her bedroom just a few minutes later to announce that breakfast was almost ready and noticed how deathly pale Emily looked. She immediately ordered her back into bed then sent Samuel into Galveston to get the doctor.

By the time Dr. Reyes arrived a little after noon, Emily already felt much better, but Elmira insisted the doctor examine her anyway.

"According to Lahoma this is the second day Emily's been like this. I'm worried that she might be coming down with something serious," Elmira explained, wringing her hands with concern. "And I certainly don't want that to happen. This child means too much to me."

Dr. Reyes nodded, "I agree, if she's had these same symptoms for two days now, then I think it would be a good idea to examine her." He immediately tugged on the hem of his sleeve to remove his coat. "You say she has a stomach disorder and feels clammy and faint whenever she first tries to get out of bed?"

Not certain to which of them he'd directed his question, Elmira and Emily both nodded, but Emily was the one to speak.

"But then after I've been up awhile, I slowly start to feel better," Emily explained, then shrugged. "I think it's probably just a bad case of nerves. I have had a lot on my mind lately."

"Well, whatever it is, it is stealing part of your blood supply from your brain. But any number of ailments could cause that, including severe anxiety," he said, not ruling out anything, then turned to Elmira. "This won't take but a minute."

Aware he wanted Emily to have her privacy, Elmira started immediately for the door. "I'll be right outside in the hall if you need me."

As soon as she'd closed the door, Dr. Reyes reached for his medical valise. "While I'm finding the instruments I'll need, why don't you slip out of that wrapper. You may stay in your nightgown, if you'd like. It's loose enough for me to work around."

Spreading the items he needed across the bedside table, he proceeded with his examination. After only a few minutes, he smiled and started putting his things away, half of them unused.

"You may tell your grandmother to come back in now. I think I know what is causing your stomach problem and your dizzy spells."

Emily hurried to open the door, then returned to the bed and quickly slipped her wrapper back on. Rather than climb back beneath the covers, she simply sat on the edge of her mattress, beside her grandmother, and waited for the doctor to finish organizing his satchel. After a few minutes more, she finally had to know what he'd discovered, "What is it? What do I have?"

"Oh, I'd say about seven and a half months," he said, then glanced up at her with a pleasant smile, his black eyes sparkling. "Don't look so unhappy, I don't mean to imply that you have seven and a half months to live or anything like that." He tilted his head to one side. "Actually, I think your husband should be here for the good news. Is he around?"

Emily's eyes widened with concern. "I don't have a husband."

The doctor's smile fell into a thin, flat line. "You aren't married? Oh, my, that certainly puts a whole new light on the situation. I'm not so sure you will think this such good news after all." Grasping her gently by the shoulders, he bent forward to meet her gaze straight on. "My dear, I'm afraid that you are going to have a baby. I can't be absolutely sure until I've run a few simple tests, but I am almost certain that you are with child."

"No, I can't be," she said then looked at her grandmother to see what her reaction had been. Tears filled Emily's eyes when she saw the shocked look that had turned her grandmother's face so pale. Her hands started to shake uncontrollably when she looked back at the doctor. "Please, no. I can't be."

"I'm sorry, but I honestly believe you are," Dr. Reyes repeated, his expression deeply sympathetic. "Do you happen to know who the father is? Perhaps he would be willing to marry you before you get too far along. I know it won't stop the gossip altogether, but it will look a lot better to those who do eventually realize your indiscretion. And it will also be better for the child to have his father's name."

"No!" she gasped, her face turning as pale as her grandmother's when she looked pleadingly at him.

"No, you don't know who he is?" Suddenly, the doctor's expression went from gentle concern to stern disapproval.

"Yes, I know who it is," she said. "But he would never marry me."

Elmira reached over and placed her hand over Emily's. Her voice remained calm and reassuring. "You can't know that until you've talked with him."

"Yes, I can. He's already told me that he'd never marry me. You see at first he pretended he wanted me to become his wife, but that was just something he'd said to—to—to seduce me."

"Oh, my," Elmira said, then bent forward and put her arms around Emily's trembling shoulders. "My poor child."

"Well, I'd at least give it a try," Dr. Reyes suggested, tucking the last of his instruments away then closing his bag. "Although I haven't yet run any tests, I feel certain that you are almost two months pregnant, maybe more. If there is any chance he will marry you, if for no other reason than to give this child a legitimate name, it should be done, and soon."

Emily bent her head with shame. "No. I don't even want him to know that I am having his child. I don't see that it would do the baby any good to have a father who resented both him and his mother." She didn't know why, but she felt certain the child would be a boy.

"The decision is up to you. But for now all I can suggest for you to do to lessen these morning miseries that you've been having is to eat a few crackers or a dry biscuit or two before you get up. If you can have your complete breakfast in bed, all the better.

Just keep it light. And don't try to get up too soon afterward."

He hurried to put his coat back on. "Also, I suggest you ease out of that bed in the morning, no quick movements. But that's about all you can really do to prevent these morning complaints. If none of that helps, then you'll just have to stay in bed until any queasy feelings pass." He adjusted his lapels just so. "Good thing about the morning complaints, they usually last only a few weeks."

"Thank you, doctor," Elmira said when she realized he was about to leave. "And I know I can count on you to be discreet about this matter."

"Of course." He nodded as if that had been understood. "And before I go, I'd like to know how you have been feeling. To look at you, I'd say you feel better than you have in years."

"I am better, much better," she admitted. "And, thanks to Emily, I'm not taking my tonic anymore."

"You're not," he asked, truly surprised. His forehead knitted into a perplexed expression. "But I don't understand."

Elmira glanced back at Emily and smiled proudly. "Then I'll try to explain it to you on the way out. About all it really amounts to is that Emily started watering down my medicine," she said as she linked arms with the doctor and headed for the door.

"You knew about that?" Emily called out, then blinked with surprise.

"Oh, yes, I realized it almost from the day you started."

"And you weren't upset with me?" She had dreaded the day her grandmother found out for fear she wouldn't understand it had been for her own good.

"Upset? Heaven's no. I was pleased as punch that you cared enough to do something like that. That's why I fought right along with you. I could have slipped an extra dose of tonic at any time, but I didn't." She shook her head proudly. "And, eventually, I was able to quit taking the tonic altogether."

"And there were no complications?" he wanted to know, his expression still full of concern.

"Oh, don't misunderstand me. It wasn't easy. At first, I ached all over and I sweated a lot, especially at night. But because I knew quitting was what Emily wanted me to do, and that it was what I really needed, I stayed with it. And now that I've been off of it for over a week, I've never felt better." She pranced about to prove just how good she did feel. "So, Dr. Reyes, the next time Elizabeth stops by for another bottle, you can tell her I won't be needing it."

The doctor looked at her thoughtfully for a long moment, then glanced back at Emily. "I'll be sure and do that." He continued to appear lost in thought when he then followed Elmira out of the room.

Emily sat there, stunned, as much by her grandmother's unexpected revelation as by the fact she was going to have a child. What would she ever do with a baby? Glancing down, she tried to envision the tiny life growing inside of her. She also tried to envision herself holding that life in her arms. Slowly, she smiled. Although it would mark her as a fallen woman for the rest of her life, and would mean added hardships for everyone, including the child, she would no longer have to spend the rest of her life alone. She'd have a child to share her love. The thought of that pleased her immensely.

By the time Elmira returned from seeing the doctor downstairs, Emily had already come to terms with her condition. Although there would be problems, and she would never be fully accepted by society again, she would have someone to love. After her grandmother was gone, she would have her child to help see her through the lonely years ahead.

"I have only one question," Elmira said after reentering the room. She paused just long enough to close the door before crossing over to the bed and sitting down beside Emily again. "And you don't have to answer it if you really don't want to. I am aware you have a right to your privacy."

"What is the question?" She looked down at her folded hands, having already guessed the nature of the question.

"Is Randall Gipson the father?" she asked, then quickly added, "Because if he is, I really do think you should tell him."

When she did not respond right away, Elmira put her arm around Emily and offered her a supportive squeeze. "Darling, no matter who the father is, I really do think he has a right to know."

"No, he doesn't," she said, her voice filled with desperation. "Randall has already refused to marry me once. He has no rights at all. He's never to know."

"In a few months, after the baby has started to grow, don't you think he'll figure it out?"

"I'll just have to make sure he doesn't see me then."

"And how are you going to accomplish that? He knows where you are. What's to keep him from stopping by here for a visit?"

"Me. I'll write him a letter demanding that he never come out here again." Her face lit with hope. "I'll tell him that if he does come, I'll refuse to see him."

Elmira frowned. "I still think he has a right to know. The child will be his too."

Emily thrust her chin forward and tried to steady

her trembling lip. "No, this will be my child and mine alone. Randall is never to know he exists." She then turned and looked at her grandmother. "Please, promise me that you'll never tell him. Please."

"He'll never hear it from my lips," Elmira vowed then shook her head. "The way I see it, telling him is your responsibility, not mine. I just hope you'll change your mind."

"I won't," she said, then stood. "I'll start the letter right away. Samuel can deliver it this afternoon."

Elizabeth did not appear too pleased when she first learned that her mother had stopped taking her tonic. When she confronted Elmira with what the doctor had told her, she was very angry.

"I don't understand. You need that tonic. It has all the vitamins and minerals you have to have to stay healthy," she said, waving her arms about as if that might help encourage Elmira to start taking her tonic again.

"It also had something in it that was keeping my mind bogged down in a haze. I couldn't think clearly while I was taking that tonic. Now I can. The doctor even agrees that quitting was a good thing."

"I still don't understand. Why did the doctor come out here, if not to resupply you with your tonic? You certainly don't look sick to me."

Elmira glanced at Emily, who sat in the corner quietly listening to the exchange. When Emily shrugged that it didn't matter, she then turned to look at Elizabeth with a pleased grin. "He came out here because I'm going to be a great-grandmother. Only I didn't know it at the time."

Elizabeth looked puzzled for a minute, then her eyes widened with understanding. She then looked at Emily, who offered a weak smile, not yet knowing what sort of reaction to expect from her aunt.

"She's going to have a baby?"

"Yes, isn't it wonderful?" Elmira said, her eyes twinkling with expectation. "We're going to have a baby in this house again."

"Why, yes, of course. It is wonderful news," she said, though her expression did not equal her words. She looked horrified. "When is the baby due?"

"The best the doctor can guess, somewhere around the end of March," she said and grinned at the possibilities. "That's a good time for a child to be born. Just when the cold weather eases up and mild weather begins."

"Yes, perfect timing, I should think," Elizabeth said, staring at Emily as if she'd suddenly broken out with some dreaded disease. Then, as if the matter was not all that important, she quickly changed the subject. "But, back to our earlier discussion, don't you think you should start taking that tonic again?"

"No, the doctor says as long as I eat at least two good meals a day, I shouldn't need any liquid vitamins."

"But what about your sleep? Surely you can't be sleeping well without it."

"Oh, but I am. I'm sleeping quite well. True, I don't sleep as many hours as I used to, but it hasn't effected my health. Dr. Reyes says that's because older people don't always need as much sleep as the younger ones do. So, you see, I don't need the opium anymore."

Elizabeth's eyes widened, and she pressed her hand to the base of her throat. "You mean there was opium in that tonic?"

Emily decided she didn't sound quite surprised

enough, and wondered why her aunt would want her grandmother to stay addicted to such a powerful, thought-reducing drug, then realized that Elizabeth had liked having no input from her mother when it came to running the plantation. For the first time since Elizabeth's unexpected arrival, she stood and spoke. "Yes, it had opium. And it was literally destroying Grandmother's will to live."

"Oh, my, I had no idea," Elizabeth said, stretching her eyes a little too wide. "Well, then, of course you shouldn't take any more of that vile medicine. How lucky you are to have stopped taking it at all."

"Wasn't luck that helped me stop, it was Emily," Elmira announced proudly. "She's brought nothing but changes with her since her arrival."

"That's for certain," Elizabeth commented, then forced a polite smile. "We should certainly be grateful that she finally found us."

"And we have Randall Gipson to thank for that," Elmira said, then looked at Emily, gaging her reaction. "He was the one who finally located me."

Emily's heart ached just from hearing his name. She crossed her arms over her middle in a protective gesture.

"Randall Gipson?" Elizabeth repeated. Obviously, she had recognized the name. "Randall Gipson of Southwind Shipping?"

"One and the same."

Emily took a deep breath to still the quivering sensations that plagued her. "Excuse me, I'm not feeling too well. I think I'd better go lie down for a few minutes. Call me when lunch is ready." Then, before they could possibly say his name again, she hurried out of the room.

It was nearly half an hour before Elizabeth appeared at her door.

"May I come in?" she asked. Having opened the door several inches, she peered inside.

Emily really was in no mood to put up with her aunt at the moment, but knew she had to try to get along with her for her grandmother's sake. Slowly, she sat up and indicated she should come in. "Yes, of course."

"Thank you," Elizabeth said, her tone unusually agreeable, then stepped inside and quickly closed the door. "I was hoping I'd have a chance to talk with you before I left."

"You aren't staying for lunch?" Emily asked, surprised. Before, whenever Elizabeth came to check on the plantation, she'd always had lunch with them.

"No, I have too many things to do this afternoon. I need to get back. But I did want to speak with you before I left." She then sat on the bed beside Emily. Her eyebrows knitted as if what she planned to discuss was not going to be easy—for either of them.

"About what?" Emily felt a cold, uneasy knotting in her stomach.

"About the baby," Elizabeth said, then reached forward and took Emily's hands in hers.

Finding the friendly gesture a little disconcerting coming from her aunt, Emily stared at her, dumbfounded. "What about the baby."

"Surely you know what an embarrassment this is for Mother."

"Is it?"

"Of course it is. And—well—I'd like for you to consider going somewhere else to have this child. Perhaps back to New York. Perhaps to some friend's house."

"I have no friends in New York."

Elizabeth's eyes narrowed for only a second. "Surely you have friends somewhere."

Emily thought of Carole Jeanne, but wasn't sure what her friend would think of her present predicament, then realized Carole would pass no judgments. "Of course, I have friends somewhere. I have a very close friend in New Orleans."

"Is she a close enough friend to be willing to take you in until the baby is born? Of course, I'd be willing to help with any expenses you incur. It really would be best for you to have that child somewhere else."

Emily didn't answer right away, she couldn't. Her throat was too constricted. The thought of having to leave her grandmother was too painful.

"I realize Mother has not said anything to you about leaving to have this child. And to tell you the truth, she probably never would. She is pretending to be very brave about this situation. But deep down inside, I can see that she is hurting. She is afraid of what her friends will think, and you really can't blame her for that. It is a shameful situation."

Emily felt a strong impulse to look away, but continued to meet Elizabeth's condemning gaze. "I wouldn't do anything to hurt Grandmother. You know that."

"That is why I'm suggesting you go away. Not forever. Just long enough to have this child. When you come back, you can pretend that you married some fine young man while you were away and that the baby simply came early. Lots of babies are born early. And if you waited at least six more months before coming back, then no one could be sure of the child's exact age, and no one would ever have to be the wiser."

Including Randall, Emily realized. "And you are sure this is what Grandmother wants?"

"Positive." Elizabeth rubbed Emily's cold hands gently, bringing them a touch of warmth. "I realize we have never been very close, but that's because I was never very close to your mother. We always had our differences. But that's no reason for me not to help you with your present situation. Send word to your friend telling her you are coming and I'll arrange passage. I will also send enough money with you to help take care of both your room, food, and medical expenses. While you are away, you will want for nothing. I'll make sure of that."

Emily thought about it. Although she preferred to stay right were she was, she knew Elizabeth was right. The situation would be terribly difficult on her grandmother and it wasn't right that her grandmother have to suffer. Elmira had shown her nothing but kindness since her arrival. It was time to return some of that kindness. "All right, I'll go."

"Good. I'll stay long enough for you to write that letter to your friend in New Orleans. That way I can take it with me and see that it is mailed right away," she said, then asked. "You don't foresee any complications arising with this friend, do you?"

"No. If for some reason Carole's family doesn't want me to live in their home, I know she'll help me find a nice place to stay until the baby is born. There should be no problem with that."

"Good. Then I'll arrange passage. I'll send word when I know the exact time you'll be leaving, but expect it to be as early as next week. The sooner you leave, the sooner you can be settled in your new home. And the less likely the complications the trip will cause to your health."

Although Emily was filled with regrets, she knew she had made the right decision. "That's true. I'll be ready to leave whenever you say."

Chapter Twenty-three

Although Elmira tried to convince Emily to stay, Emily's mind was made up. Believing it was best for everyone concerned, she packed her things and prepared for the trip to New Orleans. Elizabeth had sent word on Monday that her ship was to leave Thursday morning at ten and that she was to have a cabin all to herself so she could be comfortable.

Because of all the kindness that Elizabeth had shown her in the past few days, Emily had been forced to reassess her earliest appraisals of her aunt. Perhaps, the initial coldness Elizabeth had displayed had been the result of the harsh feelings her aunt still felt for her mother. Elizabeth's reluctance to accept her had obviously had nothing to do with her. That was comforting, as was the fact that Elmira seemed more than willing to let her stay right there to have the baby.

Still, Emily knew it was best she leave. Although she didn't particularly care what the gossips had to say about her, she did not want her grandmother hurt, nor did she want her newborn child scorned. She especially did not want Randall becoming any the wiser.

"Are you absolutely sure I can't convince you to

stay?" Elmira asked, her eyes filled with tears as she drew her shawl closer around her trembling shoulders. It was still dark outside and the early morning wind was a little stronger and a lot cooler than usual, making Emily's departure all the worse. "You really aren't up to taking such a long trip. After all, yesterday was the first morning you haven't woken up feeling deathly sick."

"I know, but my mind is made up," Emily said firmly, then lightened her tone. "Don't look so sad. You'll see me in about a year."

"I'd better. It's sad enough I lost my daughter. I shan't lose you, too." Her face grew even more pensive. "By the time I see you again, the baby will be five or six months old." Her lower lip protruding much like a small child's.

"It's for the best," Emily said, then bent forward to kiss her grandmother's cheek. She smiled when she reached up to tuck away an errant curl that the brisk wind had kicked up out of her grandmother's soft white hair. "Just remember that I love you and I will write often."

"Be sure you do," she said, wagging her finger with warning while she continued to blink away the tears. "And you be sure you take good care of yourself."

"I will," Emily promised, then swallowed back the pain and climbed into the awaiting carriage.

Knowing how hard their parting would be on her grandmother, she and Emily had both decided they should say their farewells right there. It would be too much of a strain for her grandmother to have to face traveling all the way back home after such a tearful parting.

"And you take good care of yourself too." She leaned forward in her seat so her grandmother could still see her.

"I'll have the baby's room all ready for you," Elmira called out just as the carriage started to move, taking the soft island of light with it.

"And don't forget, you promised a cradle that rocks," she shouted, waving frantically through the window, though she wasn't sure if her grandmother could still see her. She strained to catch one last glimpse of the woman she'd come to love so dearly, but could not make her out in the surrounding darkness. Because she had asked that Katy meet her at the docks at seven, she had been forced to leave long before daylight.

When she finally did arrive at the docks, it was several minutes past seven. Katy was already there, waiting for her. The wind had picked up considerably and it tugged at Katy's wide skirts, making her use both hands to keep them from billowing up above her ankles.

"Oh, Emily, don't go," Katy pleaded, rushing forward to greet her friend with a tearful embrace. She had to speak loudly to be heard over the loud splattering sounds of the water splashing against the docks. "You're making a big mistake."

Emily hugged her friend close, then pulled away, placing one hand on her hat to keep it from blowing away. "I thought I explained the situation thoroughly in my letter."

"You did, but I still think you are making a big mistake." Tears glimmered in Katy's green eyes, showing just how concerned she really was. "You should swallow your pride and tell Randall everything."

"What good would that do?" Emily asked, wishing her friend would understand. She hadn't asked Katy to come early so they could argue. She'd simply wanted a chance to tell her good-bye. "At the most, it might force him to do what he'd consider the right thing and marry me. But that's not what I want. I don't want him marrying me because he has to."

"But what about the child?" Katy asked, reaching up to pull a strand of hair out of her eyes so she could see Emily better. "That child has a right to know its father."

Emily placed her hand over her abdomen reverently and spoke in a voice so soft Katy almost couldn't hear it above the roar of the wind. "My baby is never to know his father's identity. In fact, I plan to tell my child that his father died in an accident right after he was born. It will be the best."

"For who? For you maybe, but not for the baby. And certainly not for Randall."

"I'm sorry, Katy, but my mind is set. I'm going away to have this baby and when I return, the story I plan to tell everyone is that while I was away I married but lost my husband just days after the baby was born."

"And what about the child's last name? Won't everyone think it odd that his last name and your last name have remained Felcher?"

"There are ways to have your name changed," Emily reminded her. "And that's just what I plan to do, have my name legally changed before the baby is born."

"You are that determined to see this through?"

"I'm as determined as I've ever been about anything." Deciding it would be better to change the subject before they ended up in a heated argument, she nodded toward the passenger office. "Let's get out of this wind. I need to check my baggage in anyway."

Once inside, they were met with sheer bedlam. People rushed about the office area packing papers and whole files into large boxes while others hurried to secure the windows. The man at the ticket window was frantically counting out a large amount of money then handed it to a man who stood with his hand out, waiting.

"And how may I help you?" the harried man asked when Emily stepped up to the window.

Emily looked around at all the confusion then spoke hesitantly. "I'm Miss Emily Felcher. I believe my Aunt Elizabeth Davis has booked passage for me on the *Virginia Sue* to New Orleans. I was told the ship was to leave—," she began, only to be interrupted.

"There'll be no ships leaving out of here until after the storm has passed."

"The storm?"

"Sure, haven't you heard? We've got us a hurricane headed this way. Could hit just about anywhere."

Katy and Emily gasped in unison. "A hurricane?"

"Sure thing? Where you two been? The news is all over the docks. That's why everyone's out there battening down their ships. If that hurricane should come up this way, she could do a lot of damage before she's done."

"How do you know there's a hurricane out there?" Katy wanted to know, bending low so she could look out one of the two windows that had yet to be boarded.

"Because Captain Hicks says there is," he told them. "He managed to stay just ahead of it all the way in to port last night. Said if it does come on up this way, it could be here as soon as nine o'clock. Look, I don't have time for all this chatter," he said, looking at Emily again. "You've got one of two choices, miss. You can either wait somewhere until the storm passes and go then, which probably won't be until sometime tomorrow—if then. Or you can ask for your money back. But you sure need to hurry and decide. There's no time to be wasting. It's already seven-thirty. So, do you want your money back or not?"

"Not. I prefer to wait," she decided quickly. "When should I check back here?"

The man looked annoyed. " 'Pears to me, after the storm has passed would be a good time. Now, if you don't mind, I've got things to do. Good day, ladies."

With that, he turned his back to her and helped another man take everything out of one of the filing cabinets and put it into a heavy wooden crate.

Emily turned to Samuel, who had waited by the door with the first of her trunks. She bit her lip with indecision. If she went back to her grandmother's to wait out the storm, it would mean another tearful parting and, too, she might not be able to get back in time for when the ship finally did leave.

Eventually, Katy solved her dilemma. "Why don't we go back to the rooming house to wait? That way, after the storm has passed, you won't be too far away. You can easily check back here later this afternoon to see when the ship plans to leave."

Emily nodded that would be the best. "Samuel, take my trunk back to the carriage. Looks like I won't be leaving Galveston for a while yet."

After Samuel delivered Emily, Katy, and Emily's baggage to the rooming house, he left, eager to get back home before the storm hit.

Because Mrs. Roberts had already heard the news, she and the tenants who had returned to help were busily boarding up windows and tying her prized rose bushes into place with sturdy rope. As soon as Emily was sure her things were out of the way, she and Katy went outside to lend a hand.

By the time they had all the windows and doors

secured and as many of the plants as possible tied to something sturdy, it began to rain hard. The wind whipped the huge droplets against the house with such force it sounded like bullets. Despite the heavy boards that had been nailed directly over the shutters, the wind rattled the windows and made the entire house feel as if it were about to collapse. Within an hour, they could see through the tiny cracks in the shutters that the water in the yard stood almost a foot deep and was continuing to rise.

Emily had never witnessed a storm so severe and at one point was certain they would blow away, but the house stood its own. Although one shutter finally gave way and was ripped from its foundation, causing the glass beneath it to shatter, the rest of the house remained steadfast. Then, shortly after one o'clock, the wind suddenly died down and the rain became nothing more than a light, summer shower.

When she and Katy went to the broken window and looked out, they were alarmed by what they saw. Large pieces of houses, barns, ships, and even parts of animals and dead fish floated in the several inches of water still standing in the yard.

The storm had been a bad one.

Aware the storm was over, Parks Bebber hurried to the front door and ripped away the boards he'd nailed in place earlier. Seconds later, he stepped out onto the front veranda and moaned.

Emily and Katy soon joined him, further appalled by all the twisted wreckage that lay strewn across the yard. A peculiar stench filled the air like nothing Emily had ever smelled before. She covered her nose with her sleeve until she'd had more of a chance to get used to it.

Even though all the houses around them still stood, the fact that a part of a roof and someone's front door had lodged themselves against the front of Mrs. Robert's house let them know that in other parts of the city the homes had not fared so well.

"Appears we had a pretty bad storm tide wash over us," Parks commented, rubbing his chin thoughtfully while he studied the debris further "By the looks of things, the water did as much damage on its return to the gulf as it did on its initial rush over the island."

Emily shuttered at the matter-of-fact way in which he spoke. Were storms like these a natural order of things in Galveston?

He turned when Mrs. Roberts joined them outside. "Good thing you thought to draw up a tubful of fresh water. It'll be weeks before the salt settles this time."

"I wonder how much damage the docks took," Mrs. Roberts said, shaking her head dismally at all the destruction.

Emily did, too. Suddenly she was very concerned about the ship that was to take her to New Orleans. Then, despite herself, she wondered if Randall's shipping company had sustained serious damages.

The rain had stopped, leaving a dreary grey cloud hovering overhead. "Shouldn't be long before the streets are passable. I'll take a quick ride down to the docks and see what I can find out, though I imagine the worst of it was along the eastern part of the island." He shook his head. "After I've checked on that, I'd better head right on over to where I work and see if they need any help clearing away from the storm."

"Will you send word back here?" Emily asked. "I really would like to know when my ship might be leaving."

Parks nodded that he would. "But I think it's a pretty sure bet that you'll be spending the night here. Judging by all this wreckage, we had us one heck of a storm. Nothing will be sailing out of here today." He then followed Mrs. Roberts back into the house.

Katy saw the disappointment on Emily's face and placed a supportive arm around her. "Maybe this was some sort of sign from God, trying to convince you not to go."

Emily looked at Katy with a raised brow. "Do you honestly expect me to believe that God ravished an entire city just to keep me from going to New Orleans?"

"He's done stranger things," she pointed out, her expression hopeful.

"Ka-ty," she said, with plenty of warning in her voice.

"So, I don't want you to go," she admitted with a shrug, then glanced back at the house to be sure they were alone. "I still think you should stay right here in Galveston and face Randall with the truth."

"I can't," is all Emily was willing to say on the matter, then quickly changed the subject. "Look at all that rubble. I suppose we'd better change into some old clothes. Looks like there'll be a lot of work to do around here. Might as well pitch in."

"In your condition?" Katy asked, clearly disapproving.

"Just because I'm going to have a baby doesn't mean I'm helpless. I feel fine. Besides, the sooner we get her yard cleaned up, the sooner we can hope this stench will go away."

When Parks returned an hour later, he found Katy, Emily, Mrs. Roberts, and two other tenants in the yard, piling the debris into large stacks. He stayed just long enough to change his boots and tell Emily that there would be no ships leaving the docks for days. There had been considerable damage to the harbor and most of the ships.

"You should see all the damage," he went on to say, his eyes wide with concern. "Both Tarpley and Southwind Shipping were virtually destroyed, and Henderson Freight Lines fared no better. Fact is all the way to Market Street the town's a shambles."

Emily's heart lodged in her throat. She wondered if Randall had been in his office when the storm struck. If so, had he been injured? She had to know. "Were there many people hurt?"

"Lots of them. So far the death count is at twenty-six, but it'll go much higher than that before they're through." He then looked at Katy. "That restaurant where you work is in a real bad way. Although your boss wasn't hurt too bad, I imagine he could use your help with the cleanup. If you want, I could drop you off there on my way back to the warehouse where I work. I only came back to get some sturdier boots and a few more tools. The whole side of that place was blown away and will have to be built back so the looters can't get in."

"I'll get my cloak," Katy said, hurrying to do just that. Though it was still August, the storm had been followed by unseasonably cool weather.

Emily wanted to go, too, but knew she'd just be in the way at the restaurant when she could be of considerable help right where she was. She followed Katy inside. "See if you can find out if Randall was hurt," she said, her face filled with concern.

"I thought you didn't love him anymore."

Emily lifted her chin. "I don't, but I would like to know if he was hurt or not."

"Then I'll try to find out," Katy said, patting her arm reassuringly. "Just don't you do anything to strain yourself while I'm gone. I imagine that hospital is already filled to capacity as it is."

It was several hours after dark before Katy and Parks returned, both so tired they could hardly stand. Emily waited until Katy had eaten, and bathed away some of the grime she'd collected with a wet sponge before slipping into her bedroom to ask about Randall.

"The way I heard it, he's hurt all right, but his injuries must not be too bad because I also heard that he was working at the docks along with the rest of his men, trying to salvage what he can from the storm."

Emily was both relieved and alarmed. "How much damage did his business suffer?"

"I never did go down there and take a look for myself, but the people I talked to told me that two of his buildings had completely washed away and that the other four were barely standing. I also heard that every ship he had in port took on some sort of major damage. Fact is, only a very few ships were left seaworthy—and that one you were going to take to New Orleans is not one of them. I hear it could be weeks before it takes off again. I guess it depends on who gets to the shipbuilders first."

Emily's shoulders sagged. "Well then, I guess I'd better go on back to my grandmother's. There's no reason for me to stay around here that long."

"I don't think you have that option," Katy told her. "The bridge has a big section missing and the ferry was also damaged. Looks like you're stuck here for the time being. Unless of course you'd rather go over to your Aunt Elizabeth's house and stay there." She spoke as if she truly didn't expect that to be the case.

Emily looked at her for a long moment while the realization struck. She'd forgotten all about her aunt. "I don't even know that she came through the storm," she admitted, suddenly awash with shame.

"I guess I'd better go over there first thing in the morning to see how she is."

Because Elizabeth's house was near the north side of town in the area where the land rose highest above sea level, her lavish home had received very little damage. When Emily arrived the following morning, she was surprised by how little destruction there had been. The only real indication there'd been a storm at all was the fact that several large plants had snapped in two, leaving bare spots in her garden.

When Emily went to the door, Elizabeth greeted her warmly, and after hearing that it could be days or possibly weeks before the ship set sail, she immediately invited Emily to stay there.

"I'll send a messenger down to the docks daily to get a report on the workers' progress so you won't have to miss that ship," she promised. "I'll also send word to Mother that we both came through the storm in one piece. She'll be glad to hear that you are planning to stay here until your ship is repaired."

Emily was grateful for a place to stay. Although she knew Mrs. Roberts would never turn her away at a time like that, she knew she'd feel awkward staying there, sharing a room with Katy. Immediately, she returned with Elizabeth's driver to get her things and left Katy a note explaining where she'd be.

Although she had expected a visit sooner, it was several days before Katy appeared at her aunt's door. At first, Elizabeth tried to send her away, but Katy was too determined to speak with Emily to be bullied.

"Are you sure you're a friend of hers?" Elizabeth asked, when the girl refused to leave. She looked at Katy with a peculiar expression.

"Yes. I happen to be her very best friend," Katy said, clearly annoyed. "Just ask her, she'll tell you." She then waved a small white envelope in front of her. "And I have a letter here for her. A letter she's going to want to see."

"Very well." She sighed, stepping back just enough to let Katy enter. "I guess it will be all right for you to come inside. I'll go upstairs and tell Emily that you are here."

Moments later, Emily rushed down the stairs alone, eager to see her friend and hear whatever news she had. "Any word on when my ship might be ready to sail?"

"Any day," she said, twisting her mouth with disappointment. "The shipbuilders are working day and night."

Though that had clearly been bad news for Katy, it was just what she'd wanted to hear. "And have you heard anymore about Randall?"

Katy's expression suddenly went blank. "As a matter of fact, I have a letter here for you—from him."

"How'd you get it?" she asked, her forehead drawing into a perplexed frown.

"He brought it to me himself. Somehow he discovered that you were here in Galveston and asked me if I'd be willing to take this letter to you. And since I'd already planned to stop by here to see how you were getting along anyway, I agreed to be his messenger."

Emily looked at the envelope in Katy's hands with sudden apprehension. "That's a letter from Randall?"

"Yes. It's a little rumpled because I've had it stuffed in my handbag all day, but it is definitely a letter, and it's definitely from Randall."

Emily swallowed hard when Katy then thrust it at

her. Slowly, she pulled the flap open and slipped the letter out. Her breath lodged in her throat while she carefully unfolded it then read the contents.

"He wants to see me. He wants to be sure I'm all right," she said, trying to ignore the wild stirring of her heart.

"See? He must still care about you to want to know if you are all right," Katy pointed out, hoping to convince her. "Obviously he is thinking about you.

Emily refolded the paper and tucked it back inside the envelope. "If he's thinking about me at all, it is because he can't find anyone else to warm his bed," she said, her voice strained with bitterness, her heart breaking into a thousand pieces.

"You can't believe that," Katy said. "As handsome as he is, Randall Gipson could have his pick of women. Most of the ones I know would give their eye teeth to have him try to seduce them."

"Maybe so, but this woman would rather keep her eye teeth—*and* her dignity. Tell him that I refuse to see him."

"Tell him yourself," Katy complained. "I've got too much to do these days to go traipsing all over the city looking for Randall Gipson."

Emily nodded, indicating she understood. "That's all right. I'll send a letter by personal messenger."

Katy moaned, then held out her hand. "I'll take it to him. Just don't say anything too hateful. I may still be around when he reads it."

Emily hurried to write her return message in which she explained that she was leaving Galveston just as soon as the ship she'd booked passage on was repaired. She also told him not to try to locate her beforehand because she did not want to talk with him.

For Katy's sake, she tried not to sound too spiteful. She had experienced Randall's temper firsthand, and knew it would be better if Katy didn't have to deal with him in that state, especially when Katy was still seeing his good friend, Raymond.

Before Katy left she agreed to take the letter to him early the next morning. She also promised to stop back by Elizabeth's for another visit before the time came for Emily to leave.

"Since the ship is almost repaired, I guess it won't be long before you have to go. That is, unless you've finally come to your senses and changed your mind about leaving."

Emily looked at her with an arched eyebrow. "You never do give up do you?"

"Not when I think I'm right," Katy admitted, then grinned. "And in this case I know I'm right."

"Even so, I'm going," Emily stated in no uncertain terms. "And there's nothing anyone can do to stop me."

Katy tilted her head to one side and studied Emily's determined expression for a long moment, then shrugged. "Whatever you say." Then she turned and walked lightly out the door.

Chapter Twenty-four

Emily was outside sitting on the front veranda watching the gardener repair some of the damage that had been done to Elizabeth's yard when she first glanced up and noticed Katy climbing down from a carriage. She thought it strange that Katy had rented a cab when her friend was usually so frugal with her money. Then, when she noticed the seriousness in her friend's expression when she headed toward the house, she knew something was wrong—terribly wrong. Katy looked very close to tears.

Grasping her skirts with both hands, Emily hurried down the steps to meet her halfway.

"What's wrong?" she wanted to know, her heart hammering while her mind raced, wild with speculation.

"It's Randall," Katy said, bending slightly while she tried to catch her breath. "He's been hurt."

Emily couldn't believe the pain. "Randall? How badly?"

Katy swallowed hard, took two more deep breaths, then looked away as if unable to bear seeing Emily's reaction. "I-I think he's dying."

The breath was sucked right out of Emily. *Dying?*

Katy pressed her eyes shut before finding the courage to continue. "One of the buildings he and his men were trying to save suddenly broke apart and collapsed. Evidently Randall was inside and was crushed by a heavy beam. Although he's not been fully conscious since, he has been calling out your name. That's why Raymond rushed right over to the restaurant to tell me. He knew I'd know where to find you."

It was then Emily realized the driver of the carriage was not a cabbie, as she'd first thought. It was Raymond. Her hand pressed against her mouth to keep the scream swelling in her throat from bursting forth when she saw his grim expression. He sat on the carriage seat with his back ramrod straight, his eyes trained straight ahead, and his hands holding the reins in a death grip.

"Emily, I know you said you never wanted to see him again, but you have to come. The man is *dying.*"

Although Emily had imagined doing great bodily harm to Randall many times over the past few weeks, she was terrified by the thought he might actually die. All the pain and degradation he'd caused her meant nothing now. She had to go to him. "Let me tell Elizabeth where I'll be." She paused. "Where will I be? At the hospital?"

Katy shook her head sadly. "No, the hospital was still too full with storm victims to take him. He's at his house. The doctor can only come and go twice a day, but Nora is there to take care of him the rest of the time. She rarely leaves his side."

That sounded just like Nora, Emily thought as she ran quickly into the house to tell Elizabeth what had happened and where she'd be. Even though Elizabeth had never been told about Randall's involvement in Emily's life, she was aware that Randall was some sort of friend. When Emily turned to hurry back outside, she called out to her, telling her to send word if there was anything she could do to help.

Emily called back that she would, but if he was dying, there really wouldn't be much anyone could do. With that realization pressing painfully against her heart, she hurried to the carriage where Raymond and Katy waited, and climbed inside. The carriage lurched into motion even before she was settled onto the seat beside Katy.

No one spoke during the race across Galveston. No one had the courage to.

When they arrived in front of the house, Raymond hopped down to tether the horse while Katy and Emily leaped to the ground and ran immediately toward the front door.

"Hurry, Emily, hurry," Katy encouraged between pants for air while they lifted their skirts higher to take the front steps two at a time.

Tears burned the backs of Emily's eyes when she was then directed upstairs, to the very same bedroom where she and Randall had made love. When they entered the dimly lit room and discovered Randall's lifeless form lying in the bed with a single sheet pulled taut to the middle of his bare chest, Emily thought she could not bear the pain.

"Oh, Randall, *no,*" she sobbed then rushed forward, tears blinding her every step. By the time she reached his bedside, her heart ached with such unbelievable force, she could no longer remain standing. She sank to her knees beside him and grasped his hand in hers, pressing it hard against her cheek. Her breath came in short bursts when she felt no life in his hand. Devastated, she sobbed all the louder. "Randall, please don't die. Please, open your eyes and talk to me. Tell me you will be all right, that you are not going to die. Please."

When there came no response, she bent her head forward and wept openly. It was then that she heard the door clatter shut behind her, followed immediately by a sharp, metallic click.

Still kneeling, she turned to look at the door, wondering if she'd just been locked in for some reason and why. Before she could turn back to look at Randall again, she felt his grip tighten around her hand and she gasped at the unexpected pressure.

By the time she had spun back around to face him, he'd already tossed back the covers with his free hand. She watched, astonished and confused while he sat up and swung his legs over the edge of the bed to face her. Although his chest was bare, he wore a pair of dark blue trousers and still had on his boots.

"Okay, your wishes are granted. I'm not going to die, my eyes are now wide open, and I'm definitely ready to talk," he said, then reached his free hand down under her elbow and lifted her up onto the bed beside him. "So what do you suggest we talk about? The weather perhaps? I understand we've had a pretty severe storm here lately."

Angered by his trickery, she yanked herself free and ran for the door, only to discover it was indeed locked—from the outside. When she spun around to face him again, there was so much anger in her eyes, he felt compelled to comment. "And I think we may have a whole new storm brewing right now."

"You lied to me," she accused, still trying to grasp the fact he was not injured. Glancing down at the strong virile body before her, her hands curled into fists at her sides. "There's not a scratch on you. You lied to me. Just so you could get me to come over here."

"No, I didn't lie to you," he corrected, lifting a

finger as if indicating a valid point. "Katy did. But I was certainly in on it. So was Raymond. Pretty clever, don't you think?"

He looked so proud of himself that Emily wanted to bring him all the bodily harm he'd pretended earlier and then some. "*Clever?* Why you—you—you're nothing more than a wretched, low-down, sorry, despicable, lying, cold-blooded snake."

Randall blinked then nodded agreeably. "Well, I'd like to think I had a few other attributes worth mentioning, but so far, most of what you've had to say is true." He eased out of bed then took several small steps in her direction, as if testing the safety of such a move. "I did lie, I certainly can't deny that. But it was the only way I knew to get you here. I'd already tried everything else."

"So you were willing to use Katy and Raymond just to get what you wanted," she pointed out, her eyes narrowing, dark with fury while she began to back away from him.

Aware he was making no progress, he stopped advancing toward her. "That's true too."

"Oh, so you admit it."

He nodded then shrugged his shoulders, bringing her attention back to the fact that he wore no shirt and that he now stood only a few yards away. She swallowed hard in response, then railed at him with yet more of her anger.

"You blackheart! First, you lied to me to get me into your bed, and now you are lying to me again just so you can . . ." she paused while she thought about that. "Just what *do* you hope to gain with all this foolishness?"

"A wife," he said, crossing his arms with determination. "And my child."

Emily's stomach knotted with such fear she suddenly felt ill. "And how do you know about that?

Did Katy tell you?" How could her friend betray her like that?

"No, Katy didn't tell me. I received a letter from your grandmother this morning and she told me all about it. Although the letter had been written to reach me just before ten o'clock the Thursday you were supposed to leave, the bridge into the city had already been blown down and the ferry was damaged enough that no one from the mainland could get into Galveston until one of the two was repaired. The ferry went back into service yesterday, but the letter didn't reach me until today."

"I don't believe you. Grandmother promised me that she would never . . ." she started to say then remembered exactly what her grandmother had promised: he would never hear about the baby from her *lips.* By *writing* about it in a letter, she had managed to keep her promise yet still let Randall know. Emily fought a sudden impulse to grin. She'd never realized how very crafty her grandmother could be.

Unaware of the direction Emily's thoughts had taken, Randall offered to show her the letter. "If you'd like to see what she wrote for yourself, I'll gladly show it to you. It seems your grandmother thinks I have a right to know about my child."

"And how do you know that what she said in that letter is true? How do you know that my grandmother isn't a two-faced, blackhearted liar like you?"

Randall grimaced at the intended barb, but answered the question honestly. "Because I confronted Katy with the letter and she admitted it was true, all of it. By the way, it might interest you to know that Katy also believes I have every right to know about my own child. What I want to know is why you think you had the right to keep that information from me."

"Because I don't owe you anything—except maybe my contempt," she said, narrowing her eyes to show that she meant what she said. "Not after what you did."

He stared at her with a hardened expression for several seconds, until Emily feared that he was planning some form of retribution for what she'd done. Taking a deep breath, she prepared for the worst and was stunned when instead of exploding with pent-up rage, he ran his hand through his hair and looked away, his expression suddenly full of regret.

"Maybe you're right. Maybe I didn't deserve to know about our child. But the fact is I found out. And I am not turning my back on either this child or you."

"I think it's a little late for that," she said, looking at him bitterly. "You turned your back on me months ago. Remember? That night you tricked me into your bed then laughed in my face. You do remember that, don't you? You claimed I actually deserved to be treated like that."

Randall's face became distorted with pain. "Yes, I remember. I also remember that, at that particular time, I thought you did deserve it. That's because I still believed you were a . . ." He didn't know how exactly to word his statement to where she wouldn't become angrier still. "To tell you the truth, Emily, when I first met you, I thought you were just another one of Josie's—*girls.* When I set out to seduce you, I thought I was seducing a 'practiced' woman."

"You thought you were *what?*" she shrieked, her voice climbing to octaves she'd never before knew existed. Her breath came in short, wild bursts.

Knowing he'd predicted right, that his confession had indeed made her angrier, he hurried to explain. "It was the circumstances. The way you were dressed. The flirtatious way you behaved when you were on the ship. And the fact that you and Josie seemed so friendly."

"So, simply because I was with a known madam, you assumed I was exactly like her," she said, wanting his meaning verified. She then remembered that Edward Peterson had reached a similar conclusion, and somewhere in the back of her mind her mother's voice rang out. 'You are only as good or as bad as the company you keep.' Still, it was not fair to judge a person because of someone else's actions.

She stared at him angrily while she tried to quickly sort through all the emotions that had become tangled inside her. "But if what you say is true, why didn't you just offer to pay me for my favors instead of tricking me into your bed with a lot of lies about marriage."

Randall grimaced, knowing that with each new fact he divulged, he risked making her all the angrier. "Because, at first, I thought we were playing a game of some sort, a game in which you pretended to be a respectable woman and I pretended to court you accordingly. But then, when I did everything I thought I was supposed to do and you still didn't let me into your bed, and then you started mentioning marriage, I decided you were trying to trick me into marrying you. If I'd only known then that you'd been telling me the truth all along."

"And just when did you finally realize that I was being honest?"

Randall took a few more steps in her direction; but when she lifted her foot to take another step back, he stopped. His eyes met hers while he tried to think of some way to convince her that what he was about to say was the truth. "I am ashamed to admit it, but I didn't realize that you were telling the truth until I saw the bloodstains on my bed. That's when I realized you'd never been with anyone else. And that's also why I *know* that the child you are carrying is mine."

"You're wrong," she said, lifting her chin proudly. "This child is *mine.*"

"Emily, no woman can produce a child alone," he pointed out, then eased a tiny step forward. This time she did not back away. "That baby is just as much mine as it is yours."

"Oh, so now that you know I'm carrying your child, you suddenly want to marry me," she said, so filled with hurt she wanted to burst out in tears, but her pride prevented that from happening.

"That's not true and you know it," he said and took another tiny step in her direction. Slowly, he closed the distance between them.

"*How?* How do I know that?"

When she looked at him then, there was so much painful confusion in her eyes that he felt a hard, throbbing ache fill his chest. "Because I came out to your grandmother's house to ask you to forgive me long before I knew about the baby." He took another slow step toward her, bringing himself within touching distance. "As you probably recall, that was weeks ago. Yet I'd already realized how very much I love you."

She looked at him a long moment while she thought back to that day in her grandmother's garden. It was true. He had said that he loved her, and he had even mentioned wanting to marry her. But she had thought that was just another attempt to get her back into his bed. "But how do I know I can believe that? After all you've done, how do I know that I can trust you?"

"Look into my eyes, Emily."

She could do nothing else. She had become mesmerized by the intensity of the emotions she saw there.

Randall slowly moved his arms forward and pulled her into a gentle embrace. "I do love you, Emily. And not just because you are carrying my child, although I do find that a wonderful bonus. I love you because you are you, and I can't bear the thought of spending another day of my life without you. Please, say that you will marry me. Please give me the chance to spend the rest of my life trying to make you happy."

Emily's mind was in such a whirl, she could not keep a straight thought. All that she knew for certain was that she was in his arms again and it felt so right to be there.

"Oh, wait a minute," he said, his eyes widening from something he'd just remembered. He then pulled away so abruptly, he left Emily momentarily disoriented.

"I've got something here for you," he explained as he hurried over to his dresser and pulled open the top drawer. Turning his back to her so she could not see what he did, he lifted something from inside, then slowly pushed the drawer closed again.

"What is it?" she asked, leaning to one side in an effort to see around him. As usual, her curiosity had the better of her.

"An engagement present," he announced, turning to face her again, yet keeping whatever it was behind him so she could not see it.

It was far to small to be another dress. "Well, what is it?"

"First, you have to agree to marry me."

Emily's eyebrow shot up with suspicion. "You mean to tell me you're willing to resort to sheer bribery?"

He nodded that he was. "Anything that might make you finally promise to spend the rest of your life with me. You have to understand that I don't want you just for today, or even just for tomorrow—I want you forever. Please, Emily, promise me that we will be together *forever.*"

"And if I don't say yes, then I don't get the present."

Randall couldn't stand it. He had to see her reaction.

"Actually, it is already yours," he admitted then produced the beautiful ruby and diamond necklace her grandmother had given her mother so many years ago.

"My necklace," she gasped, her eyes filling with instant tears. "How did you ever get it?"

"Seems that Josephine's place was hit pretty hard by the storm. In fact, it was so badly destroyed, it will have to be torn down," he said as he gently turned Emily's back to him. He brought the necklace over her head and down in front of her, his arms circling her neck.

"But I don't understand, what has that got to do with my necklace."

"Because Josie suddenly needed a new place to live, and a new place to house her business, she had to find a way to get her hands on some quick money. So she decided to try to sell the necklace among other things." He bent forward in his effort to work the tiny clasp.

"Then she *did* take it," Emily tried to turn her head to where she could see his face, but couldn't.

"Sure she did. She's also the one who sent that ransom note to your grandmother," he told her, smiling when he finally fastened the necklace into place. "And it might please you to know that she's sitting in jail right now because of her crime." He tested the necklace, to make sure it would not come apart, then turned her by her shoulders to face him.

"But I don't understand. If she's in jail, why don't the police have the necklace?"

"Because the chief is a close friend of mine and after I explained the situation to him, he agreed to let me be the one to return it to you," he answered simply. "Considering I was the one who brought her and the necklace into the station in the first place, I guess he figured I was not going to pocket it."

Emily gazed up at him, touched by what he'd done. "How'd you ever catch her?"

"She made the mistake of trying to sell it to Patrick Freeburg, who in turned mentioned it to me. Well, when I heard a description of the necklace, I knew it was yours. So, I had Andrew take me over to the hotel where she was staying and I offered to buy it myself," he said, grinning. "And the rest—as they say—is history."

When he then slipped his arms back around her in a loose embrace, his eyes glowed with such warmth, she knew immediately that what she saw was love.

"Thank you," she said, her voice emotionally strained. She blinked to clear her vision, aware that for the first time in weeks the tears that filled her eyes were joyous. "Thank you so much."

"But I didn't trick you over here because I want your gratitude," he said, bending closer, until his lips were but a scant inch from hers. "What I want is for you to say you'll marry me."

He leaned forward and tugged his lower lip across hers, sending a wild array of delightful shivers through her.

"So, what do you say? Will you marry me?"

When she did not respond right away, he darted his tongue out and teased her upper lip. "Please,

Emily? Marry me? Make me the happiest man on earth?"

Already knowing that she would say yes, Emily fought to keep a serious expression on her face. "Only under one condition will I ever agree to marry you."

Randall looked at her for a long moment, worried about what that condition might be. Clearly he didn't trust her.

"What sort of condition?"

"That this time, *I* be the one to plan the engagement party," she said, laughing at last. "I don't particularly like the way yours turn out."

Laughing right along with her, he dipped forward and kissed the corner of her mouth.

"Anything you want, sweetheart. Anything you want," he said, his eyes sparkling with happiness.

"Oh? Are you implying that I'm to be the boss in our family?"

"Only until the *real* boss gets old enough to take over," he said, then patted her abdomen playfully before he bent forward and shared with his future wife a wildly passionate kiss—a kiss that promised they would be together *forever.*

SUMMER LOVE WITH SYLVIE SOMMERFIELD

FIRES OF SURRENDER (3034, $4.95

Kathryn Mcleod's beloved Scotland had just succumbed to th despised James IV. The auburn-haired beauty braced herself fo the worst as the conquering forces rode in her town, but *nothin* could have prepared her for Donovan McAdam. The handsom knight triumphed over her city and her heart as well! She vowe to resist him forever, but her traitorous heart and flesh had othe ideas.

AUTUMN DOVE (2547, $3.95

Tara Montgomery had no choice but to reunite with her soldie brother after their parents died. The independent beauty neve dreamed of the journey's perils, or the handsome halfbreed wa gonmaster Zach Windwalker. He despised women who travele alone; she found him rude and arrogant. They should have hate each other forever, yet their hunger was too strong to deny. Wit only the hills and vast plains as witnesses, Zach and Tara discove a love hotter than the summer sun.

PASSION'S RAGING STORM (2754, $4.50

Flame-haired Gillian Kendricks was known to the Undergroun Railroad only as "the Guardian Angel." In reality she was a youn Philadelphia beauty with useful connections which she doesn' hesitate to use to further her secret cause. But when she tries t take advantage of her acquaintance with the very handsome Lt Shane Greyson who carries vital papers to Washington, her pla backfires. For the dark-haired lieutenant doesn't miss much. An the price of deceit is passion!

Available wherever paperbacks are sold, or order direct from th Publisher. Send cover price plus 50¢ per copy for mailing an handling to Zebra Books, Dept. 3412, 475 Park Avenue South, New York, N.Y. 10016. Residents of New York, New Jersey an Pennsylvania must include sales tax. DO NOT SEND CASH.

HEART SOARING ROMANCE BY LA REE BRYANT

FORBIDDEN PARADISE (2744-3, $3.75/$4.95)

Jordan St. Clair had come to South America to find her fiance and break her engagement, but the handsome and arrogant guide refused to a woman through the steamy and dangerous jungles. Finally, he relented, on one condition: She would do exactly as he said. Beautiful Jordan had never been ruled in her life, yet there was something about Patrick Castle that set her heart on fire. Patrick ached to possess the body and soul of the tempting vixen, to lead her from the lush, tropical jungle into a FORBIDDEN PARADISE of their very own.

ARIZONA VIXEN (2642-0, $3.75/$4.95)

As soon as their eyes met, Sabra Powers knew she had to have the handsome stranger she saw in the park. But Sterling Hawkins was a tormented man caught between two worlds: As a halfbreed, he was a successful businessman with a seething Indian's soul which could not rest until he had revenge for his parents' death. Sabra was willing to risk anything to experience this loner's fiery embrace and seering kiss. Sterling vowed to capture this ARIZONA VIXEN and make her his own . . . if only for one night!

TEXAS GLORY (2222-1, $3.75/$4.95)

When enchanting Glory Westbrook was banished to a two-year finishing school for dallying with Yankee Slade Hunter, she thought she'd die of a broken heart; when father announced she would marry his business associate who smothered her with insolent stares, she thought she'd die of horror and shock.

For two years devastatingly handsome Slade Hunter had been denied the embrace of the only woman he had ever loved. He thought this was the best thing for Glory, yet when he saw her again after two years, all resolve melted away with one passionate kiss. She *had* to be his, surrendering her heart and mind to his powerful arms and strong embrace.

Available wherever paperbacks are sold, or order direct from the Publisher. Send cover price plus 50¢ per copy for mailing and handling to Zebra Books, Dept. 3412, 475 Park Avenue South, New York, N.Y. 10016. Residents of New York, New Jersey and Pennsylvania must include sales tax. DO NOT SEND CASH.